ARIANRHOD

The Pirates' Web – Book One

SANDI CAYLESS

Sunskerry Press
www.sunskerrypress.com

ARIANRHOD
The Pirates' Web – Book One

Copyright © 2021 by Sandi Cayless

First published 2016 as The Pirates' Web: Arianrhod

ISBN 978-1-9993259-2-3

Sunskerry Press
Scotland
www.sunskerrypress.com

www.sunskerrypress.com

CONTENTS

1: SHIPPING IN

The *Half Moon in a Puddle* was a busy place at the best of times. When there were several ships on stopover in the relatively safe haven of Merkat Three's commercial space dock, it was busier still. Most of the time the locals paid scant attention to the comings and goings of the regular and irregular clientèle, apart from a rapid visual appraisal to see if they looked as if credit could be extorted from them, but when Captain Cinnabar Ahxenta and her first mate Tallica Apnis stepped through the light-veils of the holo-door one evening, a great many eyes swivelled over. Most stayed there.

Captain Ahxenta was a tall woman, her first mate scarcely less so. They had to be: in their line of trade it paid to look intimidating unless you were very well versed in self-defence or packed an arsenal that would make a small battalion run for the nearest hills. As it was, the two women covered both additional bases. In their business, self-preservation and advanced military capability were almost requisite.

"The *Arianrhod* must be in then," one toper at the bar whispered to his companion as he took a sip from the mug he was nursing. "I heard a rumour that she was due – damage from some clash with the Coalition out near the Dryssicon Minor asteroid mining station."

"That's bollocks," his friend said firmly but quietly, lest the newcomers overhear. "She's not the only PSS in: the *Tallulah* and the *Green Comet* both hauled in yesterday, for refit so they say. For an overhaul of their armouries more like. Something's up, I bet."

"As long as it's nowhere near here, Jurry my lad, that's all I can say," the first replied.

The two withdrew their eyes from the pair when they realised that their stares were being returned with an intensity that bored through to their very souls. It was unwise to upset the captain and first mate of a private starship, especially one as well-known as the *Arianrhod*.

The private starship *Arianrhod* was a regular sight in the Web, as Merkat Three's huge orbital space dock facility was familiarly known, she being a sizeable craft and Merkat Three being a free port which any ship could use without let or hindrance, questions rarely being asked as long as docking fees were paid up front and a cursory glance over ship's manifest indicated nothing illegal, dangerous or politically unwise. The *Arianrhod* was an independent trading vessel owned and commanded by her captain and as a Private, she was run by a crew of merchant spacers who obtained cheaply and distributed at pecuniary advantage various cargoes across several galactic zones and sectors. The *Arianrhod* and her sister ships were known informally throughout the local and distant star systems of the charted galaxy as Pirates, the common flag of the Trades Alliance, under which they flew, being a discrete skull and crossbones in a delicate shade of shell-pink that was widely and facetiously referred to as the *Jolly Rowena*, for reasons that had been swallowed up in the mists of time.

Captain Ahxenta strode to the *Half Moon's* sturdy bar and ordered a couple of pots of ale for herself and her first mate. The proprietor lost no time in fulfilling the requisition: these were old customers and he knew their reputations. Not so the burly stranger who considered himself first in the queue.

"Hey, who are you to be pushing in here? We're waiting!"

"So I see," the captain responded dryly. "Put it on a tab, Ally," she added to the owner cum bartender.

"Aye, aye, Captain," he responded, adroitly moving a couple of empty glasses out of range.

"Let's find a table over yonder," Jurry whispered to his buddy. "I still have the bruises from the last one."

The two gathered their drinks and scuttled over to a handy booth where they could watch any fun that ensued in relative safety.

"I said we were here first, lady!" pursued the annoyed customer, indicating himself and the two behind him, who were nodding.

"No you didn't; you said you were waiting," Ahxenta contradicted, eyeing the three of them with faint derision as she picked up one of the mugs of fizzing brew that had been placed before her on the counter. "Thanks," she added to Ally.

"You're welcome, Captain."

"Just a sodden minute!" the brawny stranger interrupted, poking the captain on the arm. "What kind of joint is this that you can waltz up and shove people out of the way and this bozo here lets you?"

"You hadn't ordered," Ally pointed out.

"I was about to when this bitch pitched in. Hey, you!" he called to Ahxenta's back view as she ignored him and stalked off.

The captain stopped in her tracks and handed her mug to her first mate with the instruction to find them a table. She turned.

"You and your friends got some sort of problem, mister?" she enquired genially.

"You're the one with the problem, lady. We were here first!"

"So what do you want me to do about it? Put a plaster on your hurt pride for you?"

"You'll pay for our drinks," he told her, stepping forward and prodding her arm again with a large forefinger.

"Or you'll pay," added one of his friends with a leer.

"Sorry about the mess, Ally," Ahxenta called over as she slid her hand shields into place and drew back her left arm.

At the first punch, the brawny man's head snapped back. His momentary lack of balance was enough to topple him when the captain's leg caught the back of his knee. She ducked as the other two waded in. In moments the space before the bar was a mêlée of legs, arms and unbreakable crockery as gleeful locals joined the fray. The weighty man had regained his footing and, eyes aflame, searched out Ahxenta. With a snarl he grabbed the nearest stool with the intention of braining her. It was a grave error. As he made a futile grab for the seat, she gave him such a kick in one kidney that he collapsed in a heap. He had made the classic mistake of assuming the furniture was mobile. It was not. In fact it was securely attached to the floor: the *Half Moon in a Puddle* had seen this sort of action before and was quite prepared for it.

"Break it up, break it up!"

The roar of the *Half Moon's* security team could be heard from every amplifier in the place as they pushed their way in. Ten minutes later and peace was restored, clothing reordered and sweat and blood wiped away. A few strays were rounded up and hauled off. The hefty individual who had begun it all had levered himself into a sitting position against the bar, supported by one of his mates.

"You'll pay for this!" he snarled up at Ahxenta, who was calmly dusting herself down.

"I already have: look at the state of my uniform. You're lucky I don't send you the cleaning bill."

The friend of the injured man made a pull for something in his chest pocket. Before he could even abstract the weapon he felt a cold jab at his right ear and looked fractionally around to see the business end of a very large phase rifle just millimetres from his eye.

"I wouldn't, if I were you," Tallica Apnis advised him gently.

The man moved his hand slowly out from his body, palm open, but with his left hand he flicked out something from his belt. There was a flash and he crumpled to the floor, his small sidearm skittering off across the boards to be gathered up and removed by a quick hand among the crowd.

"They never learn," Apnis said coolly to the captain. "Come and get your drink before it warms up."

She sheathed her weapon and strolled through the milling throng, the onlookers making way without a murmur.

The man who had started the brawl sat stunned, stroking the prone form of his friend.

"Don't worry," Ally the barman soothed. "He'll wake up in a few hours with a headache but that's all – Commander Apnis never sets more than level three when she's out relaxing."

He called over two circulating acolytes and ordered one to collect the scattered glasses and mugs. Reaching beneath his counter, he then hauled out a bundle of packets. "Hand round the ship's biscuits; they're fresh in today from the bakehouse," he told the other. "And tell Captain Ahxenta they're on her tab. I'm not made of credit."

"Tell her yourself," the young man retorted. "I want to go home later with both my arms."

"You'll go home without a job to come back to if you don't do as you're told," his boss threatened. "Get on with it."

The waiter carried out his manager's injunction some trepidation, keeping a safe distance. To his relief the captain replied with only a sardonically raised eyebrow and carried on drinking, whilst keeping a weather eye on her surroundings.

"A few troublemakers in tonight," the erstwhile barfly said to his mate from the safety of their small booth.

"Always the same when the pirates heave-to in force, Malty, and given there's three at least in the Web, we can expect more. Don't know who stupid-shorts is, though. Never been here before, that's for sure. Nobody around this place would tangle with the captain of the *Arianrhod*. Somebody should tell him."

"It won't be me. Drink up, Jurry boy, and I'll order us another: I made a pocketful of credits out of a bunch of tipsy trippers from a luxury cruise liner on stopover from Mellifly to the Cygilla Prime Resort-Dorm," Malty bragged.

"What line did you use? Buy these trashy souvenirs or my kids will starve? I'm an ex-officer of the twenty-third injured in action and trying to make a living to top up my pitiful pension?"

"No, I told the truth," said Malty smugly. "I'm an ex-spacer of the mercantile that lost my job after a freebooter vessel took out the cargo drones of three company ships and our business went under."

"Bet you didn't tell them that you were one of the crew of the freebooter and the company that lost the cargo drones sent the marines in after you to put a stop to your mercantile activity."

"Course I didn't, what do think I am, stupid? But look you, Jurry, that's Captain Fleetskup of the *Tallulah* and he's on his own: what's he want?"

"From what I hear of Murmur Fleetskup, he wants an eyeful of Tallica Apnis," snorted Jurry. "He's not the only one, she's a looker. But it seems he's expected as he's not been given his marching orders. Something's in the wind."

"Aye, they've set the privacy shield," Malty noted with a hiccup, sliding his eyes sideways to view the other table, where a diffuse glow had begun to permeate the locality. "But keep your eyes on your ale, mate, or you'll find them spooned out and served to you on a plate."

The captain of the *PSS Tallulah* had indeed more on his mind than the charms of Commander Tallica Apnis and he sat down quickly, giving a cursory glance round that took in most of the surrounding tables and their occupants, the majority of whom were trying to look the other way. He turned back to his two fellow officers, his mouth pursed up like a shut knife, and nodded.

"Well, Captain, let's hear it," Captain Ahxenta demanded, a little less than politely. "We haven't got all night. Sarie Jikelleli won't be in: the *Comet* needs urgent hull breach repairs and she doesn't trust the Dockers' Guild crews to handle it without a senior officer standing over them with a whip."

"She's got a first mate," Fleetskup responded sourly.

"He's laid up in *Green Comet's* medbay having his leg sown back on. Raiders, Jikelleli reckons, though raider attacks are getting too numerous to be believable, given the number of recent reports that are coming in about an upsurge in attacks against various shipping lines. If you ask me, the Coalition is at back of a lot of the trouble out in the Belts. And elsewhere – I noticed the docking fees were upped again when I was in the harbour office, and they wouldn't take no way in hell as an answer to the bill they tried to push on me," Ahxenta grunted. "And the Port Authority was no help either. Extra security, the reps there told me when I linked over to shout at them."

"Extra pay-offs more like," Apnis interrupted.

Merkat Three prided itself on the level and quality of its security services. They were in place to keep the peace, more or less, and a portion of the funding for their operation was paid out of docking fees. The vast web of interlocking structures that formed the mighty space docks and ancillary trading, marketing and domestic facilities of Merkat Three took a deal of patrolling was the argument, and much specialised equipment and many officers were perforce needed.

"That's as maybe," Captain Murmur Fleetskup rumbled. "I leave my personal exec to do the tallying-up, that's what he's paid for. But he comes across a few things here and there and he's heard from an old mate that came in on one of the process-runners from out the Dryssicon Major mining station that there's been a recent spate of attacks on the larger ore-carriers…"

"That's nothing new," Apnis broke in. "The ore-carriers are often targeted on return from drop-off: their main payload bays are empty but their coffers tend to be full of stuff that's mighty expensive to purchase on the open market – so the rumour goes, at least."

"Let me finish, Commander Apnis," Fleetskup continued self-righteously, raising a reproving finger. "You're right about the empty payload bays on return, but several cargoes of *raw ore* have been blasted off more than a few of the carriers on the way out to their processing stations. It's reckoned by my exec's buddy that it has to be an inside job because the blast points are far too precise for any fast-manoeuvring raider fighters. The docking grapples for the payload pods are targeted so that the pods can be released in one piece and scooped up by the raider mothership's tractors. The carriers are left minimally damaged, so…"

"So they can be easily repaired and a new set of payload pods attached for the next run," finished Ahxenta. "But where's the point in stealing unprocessed ore? Unless you've got a large and very well-hidden processing plant, you'd be better off lifting processed stuff."

"More security attached to processed goods and the processing stations are nearer to densely populated and hence well-patrolled areas," Tallica Apnis suggested. "So who are the raiders' customers? They're sure as hell not using the stuff themselves."

The three looked at one another, their minds whirring as they digested the information. After a moment, Ahxenta gave a nod.

"Raiders don't usually leave ships intact, it's not their style; destroy any evidence and get out is their normal practice. It sounds like one of the Co-Scutters out to make some credit on the side," she said in a low voice, stroking her chin with a thoughtful hand.

"You think, Cap?" Apnis asked, raising an eyebrow.

The Coalition of Systems Currently Under Treaty, or Co-SCUT as the confederation was now and then termed, was a tight union of a substantial number of planetary systems bound by trade and trade-related non-aggression treaties to assist one another and to present a unified front against threats to regional stability from both inside and outside the galactic zones, sectors and areas in which the Coalition operated. Many non-Coalition members were of the opinion that one of the main tenets of the inner circle of the organisation was the mandate to make life difficult for any system outside its sphere of influence or that of its main rival treaty organisation, the Interstellar Systems Protectorate. As a result, a number of systems independent of both found themselves obliged by conditions to form their own more open union, the Non-Treaty Alliance, to guard against undue interference from the Coalition.

"That brace of Friskianx frigates that tried to demand our cargo with menaces not so long ago was certainly guided by other minds: two Friskianx ships on their own wouldn't dare fire on a PSS without at least a fleet of back-ups," Ahxenta declared.

"Maybe they had back-ups but they didn't show," Apnis shrugged, grinning. "They made one hell of a mess of our aft shielding even so and seriously bent our hull plates, not to mention trying to surgically remove *our* cargo pods. We should sue them for damages."

"So you *did* have a clash with the Coalition," Fleetskup put in. "I'd heard the rumour. But good luck trying to sue a Coalition member, especially the Friskianx; you'll not likely win."

The captain and first mate of the *Arianrhod* exchanged glances and wry smiles. Murmur Fleetskup had no more a sense of irony than a plastic shuttle.

"So that's your news?" Ahxenta went on, trying to summon up a dreg of interest as she lifted her mug of ale. "A rash of attacks on big ore-carriers heading into Dryssicon Major that look to be inside jobs but they're carried out by raiders and backed by what might be one or more Coalition member worlds?"

"I don't know if the Coalition *is* at back of it," Fleetskup frowned, wrinkling his brow. "That was your idea. But a lot of ore is being redirected somewhere that's not the Dryssicon processing stations. What the Interstellar Trading Consortium will have to say is anyone's guess. They're the biggest customers for processed ore and they're Coalition, thought the Dryssicon stations are independent."

"Maybe whoever lifted the raw stuff will process it themselves and sell it to the ITC at a better rate than they'll get from the Dryssicon Ore Exchange," Apnis suggested. "But why are we interested? We don't deal in ore; it takes up too much space for too little profit for a start and it sure as hell would mess up our cargo holds."

"We *are* interested in what the raiders are up to," her captain reminded her. "Especially if they're linked to the Coalition. And if they have insiders at Dryssicon Major that give them a heads-up, where else have they got insiders? This new attack wave we're hearing about is said to be hitting trade lines, though the *Comet's* the only PSS that's been targeted, as far as I'm aware. Always assuming *your* news is accurate," she said to Fleetskup.

"That's what my exec found out. But Buntle's no fool: he's been my exec for years and I trust him implicitly. So if he reckons that this friend of his is on the up-and-up and his word can be trusted, then I believe him. And that's not all..." The captain of the *Tallulah* pursed his lips and gave a furtive glance over his shoulder as he leaned closer to the other two. "I *have* heard, from another source, that the recent trouble out in the Belts *is* Coalition-managed, that they're turning a blind eye to the increase in raider traffic and may even be supplying the raiders with ship-parts and information."

"What's your other source?" Ahxenta enquired sharply.

"That I can't say," the other responded. "But this I will say..."

"Please don't," Apnis murmured under her breath, but was swept aside as Fleetskup raised a finger conspiratorially.

"There are Coalition agents not a light-year from here with their ears to the ground and their noses pressed up against every porthole they can find. I'll tell you more at the talks in two days' time that the Trades Alliance and the Merkat Advisory Council have called. I have to go; my first mate's holding the bridge and I'm needed aboard."

"As if Melly Goodsocks can't look after the bridge without him on her back," Apnis commented to the retreating form as the privacy shield reformed round their table. "And if these Coalition agents have their ears to the ground and their noses pressed up to various portholes, they're not going to be bothering us, are they? They'll be too busy cleaning their ears and wiping snot from their noses."

Captain Ahxenta was examining her wrist communit, where a holo was pouring out across her hand. "It's Sarie Jikelleli: the *Comet's* hull repairs will take all week and then some, so we won't see her tonight. She'll see us tomorrow in the *Subspace* as she's got things she wants to discuss but not in front of the Advisory Council and its hangers-on. But her first mate's out for at least a month and her crew is jumpier than a spot of spit on a hotplate. So what do you think to Tallulah Tommy's information?"

"Maybe Tommy Buntle's mate is a raider insider and he's passing on rubbish to stir up trouble among Coalition and Trades Alliance members, not to mention the Interstellar Systems Protectorate, the Non-Treaty Alliance systems and all the independents out there."

"Buntle's a lot savvier than Murmur Fleetskup," Ahxenta pointed out. "And as captain's personal exec aboard the *Tallulah* he'll be privy to a lot of information. And he gets out a lot – Fleetskup's a lazy article at the best of times; he delegates his admin officer to delegate the jobs he should be doing. So Buntle's in a position to find things out and he has a lot of contacts."

"So why would Buntle pass rumour on to Fleetskup?"

"Because he thinks there's more than a grain of truth in it and forewarned is forearmed: I must check around my contacts and see what I can dredge up. But as Fleetskup owns the ship, everyone on board depends on him for their livelihood, including Tommy Buntle – though why Fleetskup thinks he needs an exec officer, I don't know. But I suspect Buntle's been feathering his own nest for years at the *Tallulah's* expense – why else would he stay on as an exec to a bumbling ass like Murmur Fleetskup?"

"Because he has a criminal record and nobody else would employ him?" Apnis postulated. "Or it's an easy number, as Fleetskup isn't exactly a shining light in the world of commerce. And let's be honest, Cap, anyone who's served aboard a PSS isn't likely to be first in line for any job that comes up in a regular mercantile fleet are they?"

"You have a point, Tallica. But drink up, the locals are getting rowdy and Ally's sent for reinforcements. And I for one am not up for another bout of fisticuffs this evening."

2: BASEWORK

The following morning at oh eight hundred brought a grim-faced Captain Jikelleli of the *PSS Green Comet* to the *Sunlight Subspace Diner*, a small eatery that took up a handy spot adjacent to the Web's main marketing suite. The latter took up a prime section of Merkat Three docking facility's green level four of inner belt two and was the place where the chief business of the huge trading ships that used the Web was transacted. Jikelleli nodded briefly to a handful of acquaintances and slid into a chair next to Ahxenta and Apnis. They had already commandeered a corner table and were awaiting the delivery of their meals via the serving hatch.

Without speaking, Jikelleli invoked the privacy shield and spread her fingers over the menu pad, conning down the length of the list as it sped past. She tabbed the toggle, placed her order and sat back to eye her fellow officers.

"Hard night?" Apnis enquired sympathetically.

"My first mate won't be fit even with a month in Merkat medbay," she responded sourly. "I had him transferred there on the advice of my chief medic. And yes, hard night: I've had a stiff session with a senior rep of the Dockers' Guild over the extra levies they've added because of the damage to my ship and the extra facilities they say they have to provide for repair and refit. The breach was worse than they first thought, allegedly. Given that they were the ones that checked it over and told me what it would cost to fix, they've no right upping the price tag at the last minute when they know I've no damn option but to cough up if I want an intact ship."

"How bad was it?" Ahxenta asked as she pulled her breakfast from the slot at the server hatch.

"Bad enough. As well as the loss of my cargo pods I had a couple of near-hull cargo bays knocked out, half my sensor arrays are offline and I've no shields or phase cannon operational on my port side. I've run over her a couple of times with my chief engineer and he reckons at least a week and a half, even with the repair crews running flat out and my boot up their collective backsides. But the repair crews are all part of the Guild and they're calling the tune."

"How many casualties apart from Ace Periwinkle?"

"Too many. He was the worst but I've a couple of others with broken bones and at least a dozen with lacerations, ice-burn, you name it. My medbay's on overtime and I can't afford to put more in Merkat's facilities. At least I could offload most of my residual cargo here, though some of it was damaged beyond repair. That's what took the rest of the night: I wasn't going to let any dock-rats loose aboard the *Comet* without both my eyes on them. And I've had the local security reps on my back as well, worried about the Incident, as they're calling it. Scared that the raiders are getting closer to the Web and they'll have to pull their socks up."

"Was it really raiders that attacked your ship?" Ahxenta asked her fellow captain shrewdly.

Sarie Jikelleli was a woman of average build, average looks and average charisma but way above average intelligence. She narrowed her sharp grey-blue eyes and compressed her lips tightly as she took in the two opposite.

"Raiders my arse," she responded shortly. "I analysed every one of the flight paths of the fighters that my tactical stations recorded and I made sure we picked up every scrap of debris from any of them that we did manage to take down. Not that there was much to pick up: they had a couple of sweepers that kept out of the line of fire but made damn sure there was little evidence left. I don't think they expected us to make quite the fight of it we did and they didn't want any of their own traces to remain when and if the cold dead hulk of the *Comet* was eventually salvaged. Our main cargo was recorded as agricultural implements for the agro colonies of Vreskota Two over by the Outer Reaches Archipelago."

"But it wasn't," Apnis guessed.

"Oh but it was," Jikelleli informed her. "Only the implements were pre-armed fusion-powered rock pulverisers for blowing out solid-cored asteroids to utilise as agro-cells. And they were in my outer hull cargo bay pods, which are of course eminently detachable. The raiders got a bit more than they bargained for when I loosed the pods using extra thrust and ordered my gunnery crews to target the fuel cells of the pulverisers, once they'd got far enough from the *Comet* to cause us minimal damage."

"So your attackers didn't know precisely what you were carrying and took the chance on grabbing your cargo before they tried to take you out, or they did know that your payload was agro-implements but not their nature and attacked you to get them and everything else they could. But how do you figure they weren't bona fide raiders, apart from their fighter flight paths?" Ahxenta demanded.

The captain of the *Green Comet* might have been tired but she had not lost her recall facility. "Their hulls for one: the signature elements of the hull fragments we brought in are definitely based on the usual meta-jurillium alloy that's used in the hull plating of most high-spec ships and it's the material of choice for thin-skinned fighters as well as bigger guns. You can only feasibly get the stuff by mining and the two main places we know you can dig it out cost-effectively are Beta Zegonia 68c and its New Zegonia colony, though there are minor sources on Jurgall Three in zone Beta and on Kirtish in Mu, and probably in a few other places as well. The Zegonias are independent though both are in Coalition-controlled space. They're said to supply anyone with a big enough pocket but no way will the Ore Exchange of 68c supply meta-jurillium to anyone bar the Coalition, as there's a current dearth of the processed stuff. And we know from stray bits of raider hulls that *have* been netted in the past that they don't major in Beta Zegonian jurillium – it's usually been traced to smaller suppliers. But the metallic traces we got definitely point to fairly recent extraction from a Beta Zegonia 68c ore-body; so they're new or relatively new ships with hulls based on 68c meta-jurillium – and that means Coalition meta-jurillium. So these were not the nasty scumbags that we're used to dealing with."

"Or they're exploiting the remains of ships they've taken out and salvaged," interrupted Apnis. "Wherever they hide, they must have a damn good line in shipbuilding or a set of dockyards under their regime. And then there are the cargoes of plating they thieve."

"But that's not all," Jikelleli continued. "My tactical ops have had a good hard look over the battle holos and they've concluded that the fighter designs, though close to known raider blueprints, are *not* the same; but somebody's made a damn good job of matching them up."

"You mean they were deliberately designed to resemble your average raider fighter?" Ahxenta questioned.

"That's precisely what I mean, Cinnabar. I've got one of my team trying to source a speck of genuine Beta Zegonian meta-jurillium alloy now, so that we can definitively match the specimens we picked up. But my best guess is that somebody somewhere is sending out imitation raider fighters from what's probably a damn good imitation raider mothership to harass the shipping lanes. I'm not sure if they're targeting the big carriers in particular or just any cargo ships. But they meant business and I bet they weren't taking hostages for ransom.

They were just damn unlucky that I could jettison my cargo pods with enough force that I could use them as torpedoes. But here's my breakfast and I'm famished. Arguing 'til you're blue in the face with a bunch of greedy dockers is tiring work."

"But you got back in one piece and were able to tell the tale," Apnis ruminated, tapping a rapid finger on the table. "You don't think they meant you to get back, badly damaged, sure, but back alive so you could verify the rumours of increases in raider attacks? Just how accurate were the shots to the *Comet?*"

"Accurate enough to severely disable my comms and a lot of my weaponry. But you've got a point, Tallica, though they obviously sustained losses as well," Jikelleli said. "The mothership recalled her fighters when it was evident that they were getting the worst of it. She didn't wade in herself but then raiders never endanger their base ships if they can help it, they're too rare and precious. We'll need to assess data from other assaults we come across and analyse attack patterns, areas, types of target, ship materials and so on."

"We'll be hard put to get information out of ships that are not part of the Trades Alliance," Ahxenta told her. "Or even out of other Privates: some of our fellow-captains are a tad tight-lipped when it comes to where they've been and what they've been up to. But there may be a few heading in, given that the TA sent out an all-points bulletin. Word must be filtering in of an upsurge in attacks against ships and shipping lines, including ones that fly under the TA flag; the TA's upper ranks are evidently worried. But has any ship been taken out completely in what seems to be this new wave of violence, I wonder? Those are the raiders' favourite tactics after all: steal what they can, destroy their target to silence any witnesses and remove as much of their own traces as they can."

"If they left the crews intact they'd be able to spread the news and possibly give evidence as to size of attack fleet, weaponry, tactics and so on, and they might be able to provide directional information that could well be traced back."

"I doubt it. The charted galaxy's a big place," Ahxenta pointed out. "And no raiding party worth its space salt is going to take a direct line to a point of attack anyway. They'd switch compass points a dozen times and criss-cross their own trails to foil any bloodhounds that are liable to be on their tracks."

Captain Jikelleli pondered for a few moments as she made her way through her morning rations. The other two waited, cogitating on events likewise.

"You may be right about the shots to the *Comet*, now I think about it," Jikelleli said eventually. "Ace Periwinkle was in a direct line of fire as he'd gone down to the inner bays to lend a hand in sealing the breaches there as he's an engineer to trade; and we had a lot of other casualties but no deaths, thank hell. But the raiders or whoever they were *must* have sustained fatalities, as we took out a number of their fighters; though that's normal in a raider attack and they pulled back when the second cargo pod exploded in their faces. Their sweepers were in mighty quick as well. I've studied raider attack patterns in the past as I've lost family to them, and sweepers are usually at the back and out of the firing line. But what would have happened if we were carrying a normal cargo and they got the upper hand? I doubt they'd just leave us full of gaping holes and sail off into the starlight."

"Unless someone that was part of the set-up did know what your cargo was and could work out what was likely to happen if you were attacked," Ahxenta stated baldly. "They'd probably not tell the fighter pilots, but they *would* recall them when things started to go belly up."

"So you're suggesting that we were meant to get back to base and this would be the base we'd get back to…" Jikelleli paused.

"There *are* a lot of Privates and other independents that fly out of the Web, or use it regularly," Apnis put in shrewdly. "And the Trades and the Advisory Council *have* called a meeting here for tomorrow."

"A lot of good eggs in one basket," Ahxenta observed dryly.

"Some would argue over the good bit," Jikelleli told her. "But I don't like the pattern that's emerging."

"No way is the Coalition liable to take out part of a facility like Merkat Three, even if it has had a hand in whatever this new raider threat is," Tallica Apnis stated. "Coalition ships are as numerous here as Protectorate or Non-Treaty. It strikes me that all this is a way of stirring up strife and making life troublesome for the ISP or the NTA or any other allied bodies in order to persuade non-aligned systems that the Coalition is a better bet for planetary security than anybody else, so join up and pay your levies or else."

"Cynic," her captain laughed. "But it may not be the Coalition behind your Incident, Sarie, despite the meta-jurillium signature."

"If it's not the Coalition or their hangers-on, then who else?" the captain of the *Green Comet* demanded. "Somebody that's got access to mines or stores that belong to Beta Zegonia 68c, obviously."

"Remember what Fleetskup said," Apnis reminded Ahxenta. "He reckons that the recent trouble out in the Belts is Coalition-managed in that the Coalition's closing its eyes to a build-up of raider traffic, supplying ship-parts and information to raiders and so on. But then there's the business of Coalition-managed cargoes of raw ore blasted off ore-carriers on the way to the processing stations on Dryssicon. Mind you, most of the information's come out of Tommy Buntle, or at least a buddy of his, who reckons that there has to be an insider on Dryssicon passing information on to whoever's hitting the ore-ships because the blast points on the targets are far too accurate to be the hit-and-run shots of average raider fighters," she told Jikelleli. "And now it seems we've got bogus raiders that might be linked to one or more Coalition systems or are using Coalition meta-jurillium alloy? This is getting more like a mind-puzzle by the minute."

"Somebody with a big stick is trying to muddy the waters maybe," Ahxenta posited. "I did a little checking last night but I didn't find out much. Coalition ore from the Belts is being lifted for processing somewhere other than Dryssicon by unknowns, the Coalition Central Council is ignoring raider attacks but is carrying out its own intrigues and we have raiders that are not what they seem. New kids on the block maybe, that want to set up as the neighbourhood bullies and the usual Coalition mischief-makers are getting too caught up with them to pay the usual attention to their own ploys? I'd be grateful if you could send your findings on a tight and secure beam to my senior science officer, Sarie," she requested. "We'll pass you the results of our own analyses on our little skirmish and see if there are common elements. It seems as if the Coalition and its allies, or rivals perhaps, are getting a bit out of hand. Fighting an action on one or two fronts is bad enough – fighting with anyone and anything that moves is just pure idiocy, unless you've got a lot of help from somewhere."

"Will do. And I don't like the notion of the lot of help: people that give you *that* kind of help always expect a return and it's often a price you wouldn't want to pay."

"That's for sure," agreed Apnis. "The Coalition may end up having to watch its own back and various other parts of its anatomy."

The *Arianrhod* sat almost motionless, the great docking struts of her berth holding her secure in their tight embrace. She was an enormous vessel by Merkat standards, not pretty in her lines as she resembled little more than a great flattened, smooth-edged box, but she was space-pink in colour and glowed jewel-like against the dark of star-spangled space, despite the red-lit restraining cross-pieces of her present harbourage. The damage sustained in her recent firefight was obvious in the disparate areas of scoring on her hull, but an army of repair bots was busy, crawling like ants over the hull plates, assessing, reporting and repairing with industrious efficiency. The scaffolding that supported the various rebuild equipment was conspicuous across a fair proportion of hull and looked like a piece of netting thrown awkwardly but efficiently over a rather angular beached whale.

As Ahxenta and Apnis hove to in their shuttle and made into the small aft bay prepared for them, the doors to space closed behind. A few moments later and, pressures equalised, the inner airlock panel slid across and their craft taxied forward into fully pressurised space. Chief Engineer Crizz Cottontail had been waiting their arrival on a small viewing platform above the bay. The two in the shuttle spied her as they eased their cramped limbs from the confined flight seats of the craft and, stretching to restore suppleness, they headed over. The chief slid down the rail to meet them.

"Repair crews busy I see," the captain greeted her.

"If busy you call it," was the grim response. Cottontail had been a ship's engineer for over thirty years and had slim patience with repair crews. "If those bots went any slower they'd be going backwards. But we're getting there. We have a few days before she'll be spaceworthy but the bills are coming in – I've already had Dockers' Guild finance office reps on the comm about when they're getting paid for the work that's been done so far."

"What did you tell them?"

"When I've checked their repair work and passed it as fit, then I'll inform you and you'll deal with it. It'll do, though: they know better than to cross any of *Arianrhod's* crew."

That notion seemed to give Cottontail some small satisfaction, for she grinned to herself and invited the two returned officers up to her office in main engineering to skim over operational readouts. On the way the three discussed the talks that the captain and first mate had had with both Fleetskup and Jikelleli, weighing up the evidence and applying it to their own situation. The upshot was a trip to *Arianrhod's* science facilities, where Dr Azular, the Berzic senior science officer, tended to hole up in a small office when he was not on the bridge or in his laboratory. He had already collected together as much on the *Arianrhod's* own Incident as he could lay his long-fingered hands on and had an array of holos to show the command officers. With the readings that Ahxenta had asked Jikelleli to send over and the chief engineer's data on the hurt that their own ship had sustained, the four officers began to piece together a pattern that was becoming more and more suspect by the minute.

The targeted areas of both ships had taken very precise hits and of sufficient force to cause substantial but not irreparable damage. It appeared that the shots were carefully calculated to detach cargo pods and disable those parts of the ship that were liable to take retaliatory action or to call for help. The main habitable areas were not targeted specifically and neither were the bridge areas, although external arrays that informed tactical and other ship's stations had also been attacked with a degree of precision that spoke careful malice aforethought.

"We'll be taking a lot to this meeting tomorrow," Ahxenta stated. "There's supposedly a high-ranking rep from the Trades Alliance to be there, but I'm a bit reluctant to discuss our full position: who knows how much the TA and its associates have been compromised? Merkat's Advisory Council will have ears in on it as well as it's the co-organiser of the doings and the Dockers' Guild is sending reps. We'll have a pre-meet with the PSS captains that have managed to make it in – looks like there'll be very few of us but I can send out a message on the Ultraviolet III. The *Hexameter's* on her way I know, but I've nothing on the others as yet. This place *might* end up being a target if systems domination is part of the equation, but it would be a stupid move in anybody's book, given its size, its strategic positioning and its vast advantages in terms of supplies and facilities."

"But how will our damage, these delays and the damn bills affect our trade?" asked Cottontail. "We've quotas to meet, haven't we?"

"We'll make them, never fear. You haven't let me down yet, have you, Chief?"

"We've never been as bad hurt as this, except when we ran up against those Treskk pirates a couple of years ago, and we paid *them* back in triplicate, as I recall."

"We did. But keep me updated, hourly if you don't mind, Chief. And if anything new in your department comes to light, Azular, link it in immediately. I'd best do the rounds. Tallica, you take the conn. I'll be along when I can. I want to stop in and see our guys in medbay and get the doc's lowdown on the situation at her end. If we're short on personnel, we'll all have to fill in on longer shifts. I don't want any slackness, even if we are in port. Hop to it, people."

"Aye, ma'am," came the concerted response as the four parted for their separate duties.

The medbay of the *Arianrhod* was busy; several of the crew were walking wounded and were assisting their less fortunate colleagues in order to relieve some of the pressure on the medical staff. The chief medic, Axellina Flintlock, was cheerfully sanguine that most would be back to some form of light duty within a week or two as she directed the captain's eyes to the readings on the monitors above the nearest medi-couches. Ahxenta was less optimistic and ordered her into the medbay office for a chat.

"The truth," the captain demanded once the door had smartly sealed and she faced the doctor.

Flintlock's smile did not waver a fraction. "It's not looking overly positive for a couple of our people at the minute," she admitted. "But you never tell a patient that they're going to be in rehab for a month. Psychology has a lot to do with healing: you know, mind over matter. If I tell them they're doing fine and will be out of here sooner rather than later, they tend to believe me. And if their subconscious believes me, I've won the first battle of the war. You remember *that* in a tight spot. You tell the opposition they're toast and sound like you mean it and you'll have the advantage. The upper echelon might not believe you, but any underlings listening in just might, and lapses on their part as a result might give you an edge."

"Thanks for the lecture, Doc, appreciate it," Ahxenta informed her somewhat sarcastically. "What's the real picture, capacity-wise?"

"We're coping, but barely. I've indented the stores at Merkat for a couple more intensive care cradles: you'll find the bill on your comm. But my people are stretched and we're one down – you know Zaik Oak took a hit; not serious but he'll be out of action for a while. And we have a large crew, Cinnabar; just one more experienced medic would make a difference."

"If you know where to get one that'll pass muster and that means not from Merkat. What are Fleetskup's like? Any worth borrowing?"

"I'll check it out and let you know," Flintlock told her.

"Do that. I'll be on the bridge."

"And Cap?"

"Yes, Doc?"

"Smile as you go out, dammit. You're the representative of the Great Maker around here and they all look up to you."

The bridge was sparsely manned as the ship was in port and Ahxenta spent a little time checking in with her tired officers. Apnis had been chivvying a gang of Merkat dock-rats engaged in cargo offload and had decided to get down to the aft cargo bays and wield her tongue personally, lest they tamper with any part of the *Arianrhod's* remaining payload meant for delivery to Xerophyte IV in a couple of weeks' time. Chief Crizz Cottontail took the trouble to come up from her lair below decks and take over at the engineering station to relieve her second, Lieutenant Gem Ferry, who was wilting visibly.

"At this rate, you'll need to get the doc to deal us all out a tonic," Cottontail observed morosely to the captain as she wearily ran yet another diagnostic on the main reactor core.

"Double scotch would fit the bill a good deal better," was the response. "At least our armoury is more or less intact and once we've resupplied that's one more job marked off the list. Our little wrangle with that pair of Friskianx frigates that tried to excise our cargo and incinerate our hides has left us with more than a few battle scars. But I hope Azular's been able to pin down a link between the Friskianx boats and the ships that attacked the *Comet*: that would be something to take to this damned meeting tomorrow."

As if in answer, the senior science officer called in to report the results of his recent analyses. The fragments of Friskianx hardware that had collided with and stuck to the *Arianrhod* as she faced her opponents and blew parts of them to smithereens, he informed her, not only contained elements that were a close match to the meta-jurillium alloy samples that Captain Jikelleli's team had identified and had confirmed as originating from Beta Zegonia 68c, but they were of relatively recent extraction, given the ore-body signature inherent in the molecular make-up of the material. Ahxenta instructed Azular to send a copy of his report to the *Green Comet's* captain and then leaned back in her chair to reflect.

Ships that were masquerading as raiders; a Coalition member world's fancy frigates that were obviously recently built, possibly by the same outfit? And these same ships appeared to be attacking TA-linked Privates and goodness knows how many more vessels? And the calculated attacks on larger ore-carriers out of Dryssicon Major, seemingly by raiders that appeared to have both an element of insider assistance and backing by someone or people with Coalition links? And Fleetskup's belief, sparse as the evidence was, that the Coalition was ignoring the rise in raider activity and provisioning raider ships; *and* managing other conflicts such as the reported incidents out in the Belts… Either the Coalition was getting up itself or there had to be another unknown factor at work, some puppet-master somewhere yanking quite a few strings at once, several of which must belong to Coalition members.

Cinnabar Ahxenta and Tallica Apnis found themselves the first of the PSS representatives in the assigned meeting room. The early pre-meet session Ahxenta had asked for with those of her fellow PSS captains and senior officers whose ships had made it into the Web was to update them on her findings and suspicions and to glean any relevant details that she could from them. With agents from various bodies scheduled to attend the main muster, she not happy to discuss certain aspects of recent events in their presence, given the possibility, albeit remote, that the Trades Alliance may have been compromised.

Murmur Fleetskup was close behind the two from the *Arianrhod*, flanked by his first mate Melly Goodsocks and his ubiquitous exec, Lieutenant Tommy Buntle. Captain Fleetskup was preening himself a little that he had helped out his fellow spacers by lending them one of his senior medics, Dr Puzzle Greenwing. With a pair of skilful hands and a lifetime of expertise, he would be an asset to the medbay team. Ahxenta was reluctant to tell him that Greenwing, an old comrade of Axellina Flintlock, was doing so well that she was inclined to poach him: the *Arianrhod* could do with another experienced med officer and he would fit the bill nicely.

"I expect you heard that the *Hexameter* and the *Equinox* both made it in?" she asked him.

"Only just, in *Hexameter's* case," was his response. "But I expect Bee Lyvy Coxen will put in an appearance?"

"She and her first mate will be here," Ahxenta confirmed. "Jury Djassi called a short time ago and he's on his way in too. We'll have to link to any others in the vicinity but certainly not for this meeting. You never know who can intercept a comm link even on the tightest of closed channels and I sure as hell am not going to trust connecting my own systems from here. The main meet can go out, but our little session here will have to be completely closed."

As she spoke, the door panel slid aside and Captain Bee Lyvy Coxen of the *PSS Hexameter* and her first mate Commander Rosee Charellis strode in, accompanied by Sarie Jikelleli of the *Green Comet*. Greetings were exchanged, hot drinks were commandeered from the facilities at the wall and the seven command officers, with Buntle of the *Tallulah*, arranged themselves around the central table to await the appearance of the final two members of the small PSS group. It was as Ahxenta was checking out the availability of linkages to PSS ships in the local area that the door opened once more.

The captain of the *PSS Equinox*, Jury Djassi, and his first mate, Gallisty Tynissel, arrived breathless and apologising for their lateness.

"Got tied up with two trade reps from Zidexall Primary who were being sticky over coughing up for the desalination rig they ordered.

Took us a lot of sourcing, so they can damn well pay full price for it," Captain Djassi announced. "Either that or it stays in my hold: there are plenty other water worlds out there that would have a use for it, as I told them."

Ahxenta cut in before Fleetskup could air his ponderous opinion on the obdurate nature of the miserly natives of Zidexall Primary.

"The *Obsidian Sky* and the *Quarkstorm* are both in range but there are no other TA-linked Privates close enough in to take part. They understand it'll be the main event only," she informed the assembled officers. "Grab your drinks and bites, we'd better get to it before the desk-bound big guys and the Dockers' Guild reps roll up."

As those present hastened to comply, Ahxenta began on the spate of attacks on the Dryssicon ore-carriers: one of her own contacts had verified that the situation was giving rise to concern, although he had no information on the rumour that the attacks were aided by insiders, as Captain Fleetskup had put forward. That comment gave the latter the occasion to call upon his trusty aide Buntle who had, it appeared, more details on the number and location of the most recent assaults. The governing council of the Dryssicon stations had put out a call for extra military cover from their bordering systems on the premise that they were likely to be next affected if the bandits widened their scope in local sectors. The existence of an inside mole no-one was prepared to speculate upon.

Ahxenta then turned to Fleetskup's news of trouble in the Belts and reminded the *Tallulah's* captain that he had promised to reveal further facts at the current meeting. The look on Fleetskup's face told the group that he had little more to tell as he fumbled for words and cleared his throat, but he reiterated his earlier opinion that Coalition agents were all over the place and that he suspected them to have infiltrated Merkat Three and hence the Web itself.

"Given that this *is* a free port, the Coalition and its members have as much right to use it as we have," Jury Djassi cut in. "In fact, there are two ships only a couple of bays over from the *Equinox* that are as Coalition as a broken promise."

"Friskianx League loaders," Gallisty Tynissel shot impudently at Ahxenta. "No doubt looking for a berth as far from the *Arianrhod* as may be, though they're in repair bays. But what kind of agents are we talking about? Rumour-mongers? Spies? Assassins?"

"You'd be high on the list if they were assassins, Cinnabar," Apnis informed her captain.

"Hah! I'd like to see them try!" was the reply. "But has anyone else heard any more about this trouble out in the Belts?"

None of the others had more news other than that much of the reported disruption appeared to involve blockage to Belt shipping lanes in the form of damaged or destroyed ore drones, long chains of which were used to ferry ores abstracted from the smaller asteroids of the Belts to the larger ore-hoppers and thence to the ore-carriers, most of which plied their trade between the Belts and the processing stations of Dryssicons Major and Minor.

The more pressing matters of the attacks on the *Arianrhod* and the *Green Comet* were the major concerns of the PSS officers, however, and those not familiar with the whole story were eager to be brought up to speed. Ahxenta, with additions from Jikelleli, outlined the clues: fighter and mothership designs so akin to those of typical raider vessels that the resemblance looked to be deliberately planned; their modern construction as shown by the recently-mined Beta Zegonian meta-jurillium alloy used in their hull plating; and the precise hits on both ships that caused considerable but not lethal damage. Holos of the samples the *Green Comet* had collected were brought into play, matched against those collected by the *Arianrhod* after her run-in with the Friskianx.

"Just like the ore-carriers out of Dryssicon that I told you about!" Fleetskup called out, gratified. "Very precise, looked like there had been charges set at the locking points before the ships even set out that could be triggered to loose the cargo pods!"

"That wasn't the case with *my* ship," Ahxenta informed him icily. "Friskianx targeting systems have certainly improved since last we made their acquaintance out in the lanes. No way would they have been able to hit us so precisely before."

"I figured that as well," Jikelleli agreed, nodding. "There's been an upgrade in the usual technology of whoever hit us to get that degree of precision and damage. No way could the raiders we know and hate so well have carried that out, even just a few months back. So either the scumbags that hit us weren't genuine raiders or they were and they've upped their game and their technology. The question being, if the latter *is* the case, where did the tech come from and who paid for it? And what's more, why?"

The group around the table looked at one another for a while in silence as each digested the information and the implications of it.

"So we have somebody or some group trying to convince us we're being subject to increasing raider attacks and using their own forces to do it, or somebody's kitting out a taskforce of raiders and possibly providing the targets," Ahxenta surmised. "We need to know who else has been the subject of raider attacks recently and to what extent. It can't just be ore-carriers and TA-linked Privates. But these Friskie frigates with the same hull signature as the raiders: they interest me big time. I can't see Coalition Central outfitting its member worlds as well as a replica raider fleet if it's at bottom of it. The Friskianx are lesser fry in the Coalition net in any case and there are bigger and more prosperous Coalition members out there that would be first in line for new and advanced tech."

"Were these recently-built upmarket frigates really Friskianx?" queried Jikelleli. "Or were they very clever fakes as well?"

"Sarie my friend, you have a very good point," Ahxenta admitted. "And that hadn't occurred to me until now. But all our tactical data point to the conclusion that they were real. We must reanalyse their ion trails and our bits of debris if we can, and go over our tactical yet again. But meanwhile…" Her lips curved into a wicked grin. "There *is* one thing that I would like to have done on the QT."

"Do tell," Apnis invited.

"You mentioned two loaders belonging to the Friskianx League not a shuttle's throw from your berth," Ahxenta said to Jury Djassi.

"I can see where this is going, Cap," Apnis laughed. "You want a sample of their hulls."

"I sure as hell do. How about it, Jury? One of your guys up for it? I could give you Tallica; you just have to get her close enough."

"I've got a better idea," Apnis said slowly. "Just let me think it through and I'll get back to you and let you know. We have time on hand in the Web, after all," she added ingenuously to Ahxenta.

The captain nodded in agreement, narrowing her eyes: she had read the subliminal message. "Cook it your way," she told her. "But — well-planned and executed assaults on Dryssicon ore-carriers by non-raiders that are either purely Coalition or backed by it? I wonder who's funding *that*, if it *is* the case. And conflict in the Belts that's said to be Coalition-managed? It strikes me that big and powerful as the Coalition is, it has no way got the credit or the time, or let's face it the structure and resources, to organise this sort of set-up. I reckon that we may have another agent at work here. Possibly some group that have been fermenting their strategies for some while and have decided that now's the time to begin to show their hands?"

"Pure speculation!" scoffed Fleetskup.

Bee Lyvy Coxen of the *Hexameter* was not so sure. "You know, Cinnabar, you're not the first that's raised that. I've heard here and there that some of the hard-to-reach systems on the outer edges of sector sixteen of galactic zone Beta have been ordering in resources such as comms crystal arrays and sending out carriers to intercept the delivery ships to collect the cargoes. Payment is made up front, which is unusual as it is. We haven't had much contact with those systems over the years as they're as far out as can be reached using the normal hyperspace highways and they're not well-patrolled, even though most of the habited worlds are nominally Non-Treaty Alliance and the NTA should be keeping its eyes on them. They keep themselves to themselves and don't seem to stir up trouble, though there's been an increase in sightings and exchanges recently: enough of an increase to warrant attention. It *has* been said in the past that one or more of those systems were the source of the raiders but that was quashed as the attacks we've heard of have all been in sectors well away from them and the few ships that have visited these systems not only came back safe, they came back with the news that they were given free range to see anything they liked. Which naturally they took advantage of, in case there was anything worth trading for, or stealing in some cases. Which there wasn't, apparently."

Coxen's first mate Charellis raised a cautionary hand. "If they have the tech that seems to be at bottom of the recent attacking ships' successes, they would have the tech and the nous to hide it from any nosey-parkers that tried to probe too deeply."

"And we would only hear from the ships that had visited and got back," Ahxenta put in. "There may have been clandestine visits to the sector sixteen edge systems by people that didn't want others to know their business. And if their business out there, especially if it was less than legal, went belly-up, they wouldn't be bawling about it to the NTA, the ISP or anybody else and asking for aid, would they?"

The Interstellar Systems Protectorate, or ISP as the body was usually known, was a close association of a large number of planetary systems in the more populous sectors of the galaxy outwith Coalition and Non-Treaty Alliance boundary areas. These systems and their outpost settlements and colony worlds were bound by various pacts and trade contracts, the chief of which was the financing, supply and running of shared emergency, military and law enforcement services. Each member was obligated to contribute an agreed number of vessels and personnel to the whole and most member systems kept a standing force of ISP ships and stations within their jurisdictions. The main problem in galvanising the ISP to action was its vast size and spread, as agreement from the ISP Council was required before any joint task could be undertaken. Individual systems had authority to mobilise their own parts of the various fleets, but it was noticeable that some were more reticent than others to commit to action.

"Got a point there, Cinnabar," Jury Djassi agreed. "I suggest we keep this speculation to ourselves for the present and stick to the recent attacks for this meeting. There'll be Dockers' Guild reps as well as Advisory Council and TA agents, won't there? As the Guild members are responsible for station and ship repair as well as cargo handling and whatever else, they'll want to be up to scratch on anything that's liable to jeopardise that."

"That's right," Ahxenta agreed. "And we have Captains Bluejohn and Peakfrost on the *Obsidian Sky* and *Quarkstorm* in comms range for link-up as well. As it's near time for the official meet, we'll close up now. Anyone want to add anything before I break the privacy seal?"

Only Fleetskup had a few meandering nothings to put in, but he was largely ignored as the others availed themselves of the several minutes left to take comfort breaks and refuel their drinking cups.

"Here's the first delegation," Apnis warned them as she pointed to the external viewscreen. "Bloody hell!"

"What is it?" a number of voices demanded.

"Look at those badges! I'm damned if it's not the Coalition and it's come mob-handed…"

3: DISCLOSURES

That agents from Merkat's Advisory Council, the Trades Alliance and the Dockers' Guild were to attend the meeting was known to the PSS officers; the presence of a party representing the Coalition of Systems Currently Under Treaty was a bolt from the blue for all of them.

"Dammit!" Ahxenta exclaimed. "I want this recorded from every fizzing angle! Tallica, set your sensors to scan for anything remotely resembling bugs, weapons, aliens, unknown tech or bad body odour," she instructed. "Are you getting this Grey? You, Adhara?" she added to the two holos that had materialised over the projector port of the link-up system.

The captains of the *Obsidian Sky* and the *Quarkstorm* were quick to respond and grimly acknowledged, agreeing to keep close eyes and ears on everything pertaining to the proceedings and on all they could scan for in the vicinity on their way into the Web. Both were on the bridges of their respective ships.

"Here to disclaim any knowledge of or links to the happenings out at the Dryssicon stations and the Belts or anywhere else in between that these raiders are supposed to have hit recently, I'll be bound," Murmur Fleetskup muttered between ground teeth.

"Probably," Tommy Buntle agreed. "I'll make our own records as we go," he added snidely, setting up a small device that caused Apnis to look at him suspiciously.

Commander Melly Goodsocks caught the look and winked over at her opposite number from the *Arianrhod*, shaking her head slightly and raising her eyes to the ceiling. Like most of the PSS cohort, she considered the redoubtable Tallulah Tommy superfluous.

They waited. The door panel hissed aside and four people wearing the insignia of the Coalition in garish colour on their chests strode in purposefully. The air could be cut with a knife as, intensely aware of the tension they had created, the front-runner of the party spoke.

"I'm Spendle Doosbak, senior executive Central Council member of the Coalition of Systems Currently Under Treaty. This is my aide Grendle Treeshanks and this is Council member Redson Wells. And this here is Bick Micklemouse, a free trader of the Friskianx planetary system; he's here as an independent observer."

Doosbak spoke hurriedly, as if desperately trying to get all of the unpleasantness out of the way. He was unsuccessful: as he mentioned the designation of the small man bringing up the rear, there was an audible hiss. He looked around sharply for the source but the stony silence that greeted him hid the culprit. He waited for a response.

"Once the other reps arrive we'll continue the introductions, since the TA and the Merkat Advisory Council *did* call the meeting in the first place," Ahxenta informed him levelly. "Although we were *not* informed that Coalition representatives would be a part of it."

"No, I don't expect you were," Spendle Doosbak replied. "It was a last minute decision," he parried. "We requested a meeting with the Trades Alliance as soon as possible and with representatives of their major trading associates, which would include you. Once we realised there was to be a meeting here today, we asked to be part of it."

"And just who informed you that there would be a meeting here today?" Sarie Jikelleli enquired in a dangerous voice.

There was a fractional pause as Doosbak shuffled and evaded her gimlet eyes. "We have envoys here frequently; this is a free port after all. There *is* a lot of traffic and a lot of information circulating."

"So there is," she agreed equably. "And you haven't answered my question. Let me repeat it, in case you misheard me the first time. Who informed you there would be a meeting here today?"

He was spared a reply as the door slid across once more and three agents from the Trades Alliance, two from Merkat Three's Advisory Council and two from the Dockers' Guild arrived in a body.

"Any more come in here and it'll look like a suits' picnic," Tallica Apnis muttered to Ahxenta amid a flurry of greetings, introductions and invitations to avail themselves of the drinks and other facilities.

Once everyone had found a seat around the table, the most senior of the three TA agents began the proceedings with a quick headcount and a nod to the officers from the *Obsidian Sky* and the *Quarkstorm* on the holo system.

Jikelleli, however, was not so easily put off track and demanded again how the Coalition quartet had found out about the meeting. She was loudly seconded by Murmur Fleetskup, intent on showing he was a voice to be reckoned with.

"The Coalition members, *however* they got to know of the meeting, asked to be included as they have urgent communications to make as regards the spate of attacks from which we have all suffered; targets *have* included Coalition interests," the senior rep from the Advisory

Council, Krendak Maelstrum, interrupted a trifle severely.

The looks of complete contempt and mistrust that decorated the faces of most of the others present deterred him for only a second.

"Despite what some of you may have heard," he went on, with a stern look at Fleetskup, "The Coalition has suffered damage to ships and goods on a par with that inflicted on targets allied to the Trades Alliance and various other systems and organisations."

"How convenient," Sarie Jikelleli cut in as the trio of TA reps interjected with a staccato series of critical comments.

"It's been bad!" Doosbak put in angrily and began an account of what he claimed were serious breaches of Coalition-managed systems and installations.

Ahxenta could see out of the corner of her eye that Bluejohn of the *Obsidian Sky* had ordered a check from one of his bridge stations and moments later the results were evidently flowing across his status board. She caught an imperceptible nod from his holo-projection and raised an eyebrow: so there was substance to the Coalition's story.

As Doosbak carried on with the tale of the complete destruction of a long string of ore-drones off Selliden, Bluejohn's reaction was a fractional shake of the head: that one was false.

"I think you'd best stick to the facts," Ahxenta curtly informed the Coalition agent.

"What?"

"Captain Bluejohn?" she invited, gesticulating at the holo-figure.

"Your total destruction of a string of ore-drones, according to *my* information, was a run-in with a rogue asteroid because your drone-pilot had gone off course on the way through the Selliden system," the captain of the *Obsidian Sky* said equably.

"Who told you that?" Doosbak demanded as the Trades Alliance reps expressed their disgust with several muttered oaths.

"Your own reporting system," Bluejohn replied. "You, or at least your member, filed a damages claim, which was naturally rejected."

The man spluttered. "How did you get access to secure Coalition reporting systems? How could you?"

"The same way you managed to find out that we had a meeting here today, I expect, and then stuck your oar in," Bluejohn told him. "As Captain Ahxenta says, perhaps you'd best stick to the facts. You'll have trouble convincing us you're on the level otherwise."

Seething with anger and mortification, Doosbak checked his note-holo and then reeled off other damaging incidents that he claimed had been done upon Coalition members, with minor additions by his

Council colleagues, who appeared chastened by the recent exchanges. The free trader Micklemouse was markedly silent.

"That's why I would like to make a suggestion – and it's only a suggestion," Doosbak added hurriedly, looking at his TA counterpart and fearing serious disputation or worse. "I would like to suggest…"

"Get on with it, we haven't got all day," Bee Lyvy Coxen urged irritably.

"I suggest that we put out a joint statement that we deplore the situation and are united in our determination to deal with it."

"Why tell us?" Jikelleli spat out. "We're not the Trades Alliance; we're independents that fly under the TA flag and pay plenty for the privilege. This is politics. You should be having this dialogue with their reps here, or better still with the TA Council and the other joint bodies that run, or think they do, this blasted corner of the mapped galaxy. Why bring this up here and now?"

"Because the situation is immediate, given the upsurge in crimes against both our trades' bodies, and others I suspect, and the matter should be immediately circulated and dealt with. It affects us all," he announced pompously.

"You wanted to hear how badly we'd been hit and what we know and you're using this political hogwash as the excuse to gate-crash this meeting," Ahxenta inferred astutely. "We're telling you nothing. I suggest you pack your traps and quit whilst you're ahead."

"Please!" Maelstrum of the Advisory Council cut in. "This gets us nowhere. Mr Doosbak has brought us up to date with how things are sitting within the Coalition. Do the representatives of the Dockers' Guild have anything to add at this point?"

"Who appointed you chairman?" Fleetskup muttered as the chief of the two Guild delegates, who had been sitting enjoying the flying arguments, merely stated that, as usual, her members would be the ones left to patch up the damage and she would hope that, in the case of extra work, she would be provided with the wherewithal to draft in additional gear and dock-workers.

"That's a matter for Merkat's Budget Disbursement Committee."

"It'll be a matter for all of you if we don't get more dock-rats and updated equipment," she responded. "Don't expect us to pick up the pieces of your fleets and sew them back together. We're stretched to breaking point as it is, as no doubt Captain Jikelleli could confirm."

"If you mean you're taking your time to repair my ship and I'm paying over the odds for what you *are* doing, that's certainly the case," Jikelleli snapped in reply.

"We're short of manpower and short of equipment, and the gear we have is hardly adequate to what it's expected to do," was the curt response. "You have an argument with that, you take it up with Port Control and marketing."

"I will," Jikelleli informed her as the voice of the head of the Merkat deputation interrupted in an effort to defuse the situation.

"There's another major issue to discuss," Maelstrum continued. "I would like to bring you up to date with something that has only just come to our attention." He paused portentously.

After a rapid recap of the troubles that were causing concern, he came to his point: the governing council of the Dryssicon stations had asked for additional fleet support from the systems bordering their own, the argument being that those systems were expected to be the next targets if the raiders expanded their activities in what seemed to be their current sphere of operations locally.

"We know," Ahxenta enunciated icily. "We heard about it before you came in, from Mr Buntle there. Any other major matters?"

Maelstrum started up, a half-finished query on his lips, but electing to ignore her interruption and interjections from Captain Fleetskup, he added that the Dryssicon bases had also appealed for more general aid to the Interstellar Systems Protectorate.

Doosbak was trying to appear visibly shocked by the update, but it was obvious to most of those present that the news was not news to him. He nonetheless made suitable noises of surprise, revulsion and sympathy and then looked at the three Trades Alliance reps to see how they would take his next point.

"In view of that situation, I have a suggestion to make. I suggest that one of our number here," he gesticulated in the general direction of his associates, his finger coming to rest on the small figure of Bick Micklemouse, who shrank back. "I suggest that our independent rep, Mr Micklemouse here, takes passage aboard a Trades Alliance vessel heading for Dryssicon, to meet with the Council there in order to assure *them*, and to show whatever or whoever is pulling a fast one, that we stand united in any response to the situation, particularly in providing aid to the Dryssicon stations."

"Does the phrase 'no way in hell' ring a bell?" Ahxenta retorted before any member of the TA delegation could take offence.

"It's not our business to provide aid; the stations haven't asked us for a start," Bluejohn put in from the *Obsidian*. "And what would be the point of shipping one of you lot to Dryssicon for a chat to the locals? You want to go, you can use your own damn transport."

"Who is this *we* anyway?" Jikelleli demanded, slapping her hand on the table. "The PSS fleet may fly under the TA flag but we're not handfast to it, no matter what you may think."

"I was not referring specifically to a private starship, or necessarily to those few of you here," Doosbak put in hurriedly and untruthfully. "My suggestion was directed to the Trades Alliance representatives." He looked expressively at them.

"We'll all consider the matter and get back to you," the Merkat Three head rep put in diplomatically. "Is that agreeable to all those present?" Maelstrum added, looking around for sounds of assent.

The response was less than enthusiastic but it sufficed and in the absence of further business, he closed the meeting. All but the PSS officers were quick to escape the meeting room, bidding speedy goodbyes. The TA reps were seething and no doubt off to report on the double to their governing body.

"Get the privacy seal back up pronto and make sure your recorder and detectors are active, Tallica," Ahxenta said abruptly. "Captains Bluejohn and Peakfrost, you'd best both stay on line and set your channels to the highest privacy setting you have. And I need another drink," she added, stepping to the dispenser to collect a strong one.

Steaming beaker in hand, the captain of the *Arianrhod* surveyed her colleagues gravely. "So what do you make of that?" she queried.

"Somebody else muscling in on the Coalition's area of operations and they don't like it," Captain Jury Djassi opined. "It's our party and we want to run it our way. If there's anyone going to bully the smaller systems then it's going to be us."

"You could be right, Captain," agreed the *Hexameter's* Commander Charellis. "But how do you prove it? And what's this hogwash about having a Coalition snitch on a TA-affiliated ship, which means one of ours whatever Doosbak says?" she asked the group in general. "The TA reps were up in arms over the very idea."

"Their problem not ours," Apnis told her.

"Not if one of us is approached to ferry the little pipsqueak to Dryssicon. Figure they're after cheap transport and think we'll be taken in by this diplomacy lark?" Charellis asked ironically.

"They're up to something. I figure they want a mole in one of our ships and think he'll fit the bill," Apnis replied. "I wouldn't give him houseroom in an outside latrine."

"I've had enough," Ahxenta told her colleagues. "There's some game being played and we're being pulled into it whether we want to play ball or not. Grey and Adhara, as soon as your ships get into the

Web, let me know your schedules and we can set up a meet. Tallica, we have other business in marketing so we'd better get to it. Anybody got anything else to add at this stage? Fleetskup? Bee? Sarie? Jury?"

Everyone caught the unspoken message that although the privacy seal and their anti-bug equipment and other protective devices were top notch, Captain Ahxenta was taking no chances that somebody somewhere and somehow had even half an eye or part of one ear close enough to eavesdrop. She trusted nothing and no-one. Calling a halt on her own behalf, she hitched her phase rifle over one shoulder and set off through the door, her first mate on her tail.

"Marketing?" Apnis queried softly as they trod the quiet corridor.

"*Half Moon*," the captain replied briefly. "I need my lunch and I have a hunch we'll get more sense out of the hangers-on in there than we will out of the entire assembly of Merkat Three, Web-side or planetside, and that includes the TA sub-office."

"Suits me. You paying?"

"No. You are."

"Aye, aye, Captain."

The *Half Moon in a Puddle* was as busy a place as ever when the two officers of the *Arianrhod* strolled in as if they had all the time in the galaxy. Ally was on hand and filled two beakers to the brim with ale before the two could speak.

"On me," he informed them. "You look like you need 'em. Had a hard time with the Coalition, the Trades and the Dockers as well as Merkat's usual brace of bootlickers?"

"How in blazes did you get to know who was there?" Apnis wanted to know.

"A freebooter calling himself Bick Micklemouse rode in here last night looking like the weight of the system was on his shoulders and a couple of my regulars took it upon themselves to try and lighten his load by abstracting some of his trouser credit," Ally replied in a low voice as he wiped the bar with a dirty towel. "They got nowhere very fast – I guess this Micklemouse is as wily as they are when he's sober, being a free trader, apparently. So he said anyway. And his ship's a ramshackle old bus-run special out of the Mellifly system and it's shot to pieces, apparently. He was on stopover here to get it fixed and to attend a meeting, so he said."

"There's an awful lot of apparently and so he said, Ally," Ahxenta noted. "If I didn't know better, I'd think you didn't believe him."

"All I *am* saying is," Ally went on, lowering his voice further and leaning forward over the counter, although there were very few close enough to overhear, "A guy who wears a platinum jewelled chrono and quality traps and has a credit slip with a Primus Twelve Gold Standard logo on it, and talks and acts like Micklemouse, is either a brilliant con-artist or a mediocre fish in somebody's fancy pond. And given he almost got the better of Jurry and Malty, he has a few brain cells to rub together. But he wasn't so savvy that he could keep his mouth shut after a few mugs of ale slid down his throat. He let out that he had high-flying friends in the Coalition here on business and he was part of it. There was a meeting being rigged with the Privates, the Dockers, the Trades and Merkat's great and good."

"And was there any mention of what this meeting was about?" Ahxenta queried.

"Oh, the attacks on Dryssicon ore-carriers and other suchlike hits. There've been a few; and a few that are not known about, according to Mr Micklemouse. But people are beginning to run scared, Captain; it seems word's getting out about trouble out there. But Micklemouse bravely defended the Coalition and sort of let slip that these Coalition pals of his were mighty put out that the Coalition bozos were getting blamed for a lot that wasn't their doing – apparently."

"Was this before or after he'd had a few jars?" enquired Apnis.

"After. But your name was mentioned, Captain – in an effort to get information out of me, actually. He wanted to know how long you'd been in, the state of your ship, what had happened to it, where next you were headed. Naturally, I know nothing. I'm just a guy that runs a bar and tries to make a living. I don't get involved in doings beyond the limits of the Merkat system and the Web. You drink in my place occasionally and pay your bills up front is all I know."

"When you're not trying to feed me free beer to try to worm out of me the answers to some of those questions you seem to have been asked," Ahxenta remarked dryly.

"Please, Captain! I know better than that!"

"Probably just as well. So what's this about a ramshackle bus-run special that Mr Micklemouse is apparently the commander of, when he isn't asking around bars about me?"

"I didn't really follow it up…"

"I bet you did. Out with it."

One look at *Arianrhod's* captain and Ally realised that he had better respond with all he knew. "It's a small one-man prospector cum freighter: an old Comet Six workhorse with added protected storage sections and external latching for attaching carrier pods."

"Many's the unusual load that's been carried in one of those," Apnis interrupted sardonically.

"It looks like it's been through the wars but my partner works in the repair bays in the middle belts and she reckons there's nothing structurally wrong. The repair crews don't have full access, naturally, but the ship's sections are sealed tighter than a Zidexallian's wallet on a wet washday, spy cams are all over, and there's shielding in all the operational sections so they can't get into the engines. Micklemouse says they don't need stripping and energising so he doesn't want the expense. All that the repair crews are tasked with is smoothing out the bumps on the hull, applying a new skin of rad-repelling coating and providing a bit of internal beautification, but given the ship's as shiny as a new-minted cadet's ranking insignia inside, apparently, there's not much work – and hence not much profit."

"Apparently?" repeated Ahxenta. "There's that word again."

"It struck my partner that the outside of the ship didn't match the inside, is all," Ally assured her. "And one-man operated trader rigs don't tend to be as clean and tidy as Mr Micklemouse's rig. She's seen them all and his was peculiar in that respect."

"Out of Mellifly you said?" Apnis queried tartly. "Not much good has ever come out of Mellifly: too busy turning other people's assets into their own pocket linings, most of them. Handy stopover for the edge of civilisation tourist trade routes and a fair few mercantile holdings that can't find berths elsewhere."

"His ship's out of Mellifly, he mentioned, so I guess that's where he berths when he isn't travelling. But he's not a native," Ally said.

"Really?" Ahxenta returned silkily.

The barman shifted uneasily. "I expect that you're aware that he came originally from the Friskianx system?"

The captain nodded in acquiescence, her eyes narrowing. "He told you that?"

"No, my partner did; they have to go through the ship's log to verify various details and that's where the ship was originally bought by its present owner – Micklemouse. But most of his last few sorties into port were at Mellifly and that's his contact station."

"What are his ship's armaments like?" Ahxenta shot at him.

"No idea. I'll try to find out if you like."

"Don't bother. And we three have not had this conversation, of course. We're here for lunch is all. What's on your specials board?"

"Just getting them up, here they are," Ally replied, punching up the relevant instructions on a handy console.

In response, a series of images came to life, projected into the ether from the various holo-grids that dangled from his rather grimy ceiling. Ahxenta and Apnis studied the offerings briefly, ordered their choices and chose a private booth over at the side, well away from the bar but with a good view of both the main door in and out of the place and the rear exit.

"Be back in a tick, I need to get rid of all that coffee I drank earlier," the captain said. "Order us a couple more beers."

"That's the kind of job I like," Apnis called after her.

Once she had slipped back into her seat and the privacy shield was in place, the captain of the *Arianrhod* looked quizzically at her first mate.

"We've got room on board for a ship the size of a freight-carrying Comet Six, even with extra rigging for storage, if we use one of the our bigger outer bays. We can leave one of the big shuttles planetside. As Crizz Cottontail keeps telling me the *Gadfly* has long been in need of a complete overhaul, she can stay."

Apnis was troubled. "You're not seriously considering picking up a hitchhiker like Bick Micklemouse? Even from a distance he smells like a barrel of rotten fish."

"What better way to get a good look at his ship without half the Web raising their eyebrows over our interest in it?"

"So you're interested?"

"He's a Friskianx freebooter that rolls in here and pretends to be what he's not, he has such strong links to one of the Coalition's chief minions that he can gate-crash a top-level meeting and he flaunts a Primus Twelve Gold Standard credit slip. He's got a ship that even the seasoned petty larcenists of the Dockers' Guild can't get into and he makes enquiries about me behind my back. Yes, I'm interested."

"And he reckons that there've been attacks outside the ones we know about in Dryssicon space and in other places that have escaped general notice? So why if he's such an elite subversive with the degree of access to knowledge that he seems to have does he spill the beans to Ally and a couple of the barflies that hang off the flypaper in the *Half Moon*?" asked Apnis.

"That, Tallica, is a question I'd like an answer to," the captain replied as their meals emerged at their elbows, courtesy of the serving hatch. "If he's such an easy target for exploitation when he's half-seas over, who in their right mind would entrust him with anything important?"

The two pondered the question as they ate their way through the large portions that the chef of the *Half Moon* seemed to think they needed. Apnis waved her fork over her plate and looked up.

"You know what I think?"

"I can guess, but you'd better tell me."

"Either he's a lot smarter than he looks and is playing the game his way, or he's being used to spread misinformation or rumour by someone or ones that are keeping a tight grip on his strings."

"That's two of the possibilities I'm considering," the captain told her. "But let's take the second: with someone who's on the face of it such a bad risk, who would take the chance that he wouldn't land them in the dung along with himself? Unless they can actually operate his mouth for him at a distance, or unless he doesn't know who he's working for and thus can't incriminate them, the game wouldn't be worth it. And given that he *is* linked to the Coalition…"

The first mate nodded. "So that leaves us with the notion that he's an actor of phenomenal skill – which of course he isn't."

Ahxenta agreed with a wry smile. "Allowing Merkat Three's dock-rats full and free rein to your ship without leaving someone aboard to watch their every move is just plain stupid unless you've got every nook and cranny sewn up tighter than a miser's purse strings."

"Which he appears to have," the first mate pointed out.

"And bedizened with so much surveillance gear that a fly can't fart without it being recorded for posterity. So is he the only one aboard his ship or does he have something or someone hidden in the hold that he wants to keep so secret he won't risk anyone seeing it or anything detecting it?"

"He's being used to transport prohibited goods or persons from A to Z?" hazarded Apnis. "But why if that's the case would he be part of a Coalition delegation that worms its way into a meeting called by the TA and Merkat's Advisory Council to discuss the hullabaloo over attacks on shipping and ore-processing stations like Dryssicon?"

"To make sure his cargo gets to Dryssicon safely?"

"But why a rodent like Micklemouse, pardon the pun? He's not exactly the kind of guardian you would want to entrust something – or someone – precious to, is he?"

"If you've got something secret or very pricy to shift on the sly, you don't hire the fanciest rig in the sector do you? That's asking for serious interference. There are enough freebooters out there, not to mention raiders, that'll not only get wind of it, they'll be baying at each other for the honour of taking it down. But a one-man trading rig out of Mellifly is hardly something they'd go out of their way to intercept. It wouldn't be worth the fuel for a start, not to mention the cred factor when they boast about their derring-do among their own kind in the bar later."

Apnis thought for a moment. "Even if that's not the case, it's an idea. A boat out of a half-bit place like Mellifly — a one-man at that — that ships into Merkat for overhaul and sits about in the Web's repair docks with its only crewman in a meeting where we, not to mention the great and the good from the Trades Alliance, the Coalition, the Dockers' Guild *and* Merkat's Advisory Council can certainly verify his presence... Good scam. Maybe he *is* a criminal mastermind, only he's so good at it that it only shows up in the dark."

"Very funny and no he isn't," Ahxenta said firmly. "He's an idiot that's being used. But by whom and for what is the issue. Friskianx! He's got nerve, I'll give him that."

"Not much though," her first mate chuckled. "When he realised that *he* was the one that the Coalition wanted to put aboard a PSS, he looked like a sprinter with nowhere to run. I noticed that he didn't say much in there — too busy looking us over and taking notes."

"But who put the Coalition up to the trick of parking one of their snoops on one of our ships? Doosbak doesn't strike me as the type. I wonder if *his* strings were pulled to do it and make sure Micklemouse was the one, given he was in the meeting anyway."

"I have a suggestion to make. I suggest that one of our reps here takes passage aboard a Trades Alliance vessel heading for Dryssicon." The first mate mimicked the Coalition representative so accurately that the captain laughed. "But if Doosbak's just a link in the chain, Cinnabar, that chain stretches mighty far and it's a complex one."

"And the governing council of the Dryssicon stations is asking for additional military back-up from its nearest systems," remembered Ahxenta. "It looks like they've already been sent some and they didn't think it was enough. Wonder what their neighbours think? If they're next on the agenda for an official visit from the bad guys, the first thing they won't do is speed their best troops and ships off to Dryssicon; they'll keep them in their own backyard, as they're all pretty minor worlds and mostly mining colonies. And the majority are Coalition in name. But if the ISP's been asked for deck-pounders as well, the situation's got a goodly number of people well rattled."

"We'll see. But let's buzz for another beer, talking's thirsty work," Apnis said, raising her mug pointedly.

"Go ahead, you're paying," the captain reminded her. "Doosbak obviously knew about the request for military aid by the Dryssicon stations, though he was pretending he didn't. But I don't think he knows who or what are responsible for these attacks. Whoever they are, if they're not Coalition-backed, then someone's trying pretty hard to make it look as if they are."

The commander evidently had other matters on her mind as they waited for the beers to appear. Once two schooners were fairly settled onto their table and the remains of the other dishes cleared, she looked across at her senior officer.

"On another note, Cap… Friskianx…"

"That pair of Friskie League loaders berthed out near the *Equinox*. No, I hadn't forgotten. You mentioned another plan, no doubt for very good reasons of your own, given that you announced to the place in general that we had time on hand in Merkat, which we don't. Let's hear the grisly details."

4: SAMPLES

The first mate of the *Arianrhod* sat silent for a minute, her thin face pensive in the dim light of the booth. She tapped her fingers on the table top and looked across at her captain and long-time friend, tilting her head slightly sideways with an expression that suggested that she was unsure of the reaction.

"Come *on*, Tallica," urged Ahxenta. "We don't have much time on hand here as you know, so what's the bite? And what's the plan?"

"The bite is I don't trust Tommy Buntle as far as I can kick him, he and his recording contraption, and if he thought we'd be trying to get bits of hull from Friskie ships he might just shoot his mouth off for a wad of extra credits in his trousers; or worse, cause *us* trouble, given that we've caused the Friskianx quite a bit."

"Can't say I agree," Ahxenta said. "He's too fond of his own skin to expose it to potential harm."

"Depends on who's pulling his strings or paying his bills," Apnis contradicted. "He had plenty to say and tell us about the how many and where of the latest assaults out at Dryssicon and elsewhere in the closed meet, but he was as silent as the vault in the extended session. I watched him. He was eyeing us and taking note of everything that was said. Even if he's half as efficient as Fleetskup gives him credit for, he's efficient, and whatever he's got up his sleeve, he won't hang about before putting it into action. So we need to move fast to get samples. But getting bits of hull from a pair of Friskie League loaders won't be easy: a stray bot or a stray anything that floats too close to another vessel without authorisation in triplicate will be blasted, so that's out. But I did do some checking while you were in the powder room to see what the Friskianx ships were in for. They've had a few scratches, apparently; the result of an accident with their loading gear at their last stop, according to their repair logs. So they're here for restoration. But that's odd in itself: two loaders in for repair at the same time and with the same fault? And no way would any Friskie come in knowing that we and a number of our PSS colleagues were here, given *Arianrhod's* less than salubrious reputation with them and our last little sortie amongst them, unless they were desperate."

"How do you know what the repair logs of the Friskies say?"

"I've a buddy that's a Dockers' Guild member: a senior docker in the repair sheds and the security liaison rep. I saved his hide once in a bar brawl in the *Half Moon* and he doesn't forget. I got him to make enquiries: he thought it was odd to have a pair of loaders in for the same fix-up. What I suggest is that I get a casual appointment in one of the Guild repair teams and do the hull scraping myself. I couldn't let my mate do it as it's not exactly safe. But I'm sure he could get me in on a casual ticket with short-term Guild membership – they've always got a backlog of posts and few people to fill them. I'm seeing him after lunch, in fact in a couple of hours from now. Azular could fabricate enough fake idents that I could take my pick and the doc can spare some time for a temporary face job, if she knows the score. And I would like to do the mission before bringing the other captains in on it. That way, nobody can pre-empt me – I hope."

"I see. I don't like it, but I see. And you're on. With one proviso: I'm coming along too."

"No way in hell, Cap! One, it's my idea and if I slip up your hands are clean; two, you're in command, it's your ship and you're needed there; three, we can't both be absent at once or somebody's going to notice. And put two and two together and smell a game plan."

"You win. Let's get the details sorted."

The workload aboard *Arianrhod* was lessening: repairs were going well and the patients in medbay were on the mend. The assistance of Dr Greenwing, Axellina Flintlock admitted, was making a difference. As a very experienced senior with berths ranging from military to planet-based, and on ships more long-ranging than the *Tallulah*, he brought knowledge as well as skill. He was also becoming more and more disillusioned with his present billet, Flintlock hinted heavily. Ahxenta promised she would do what she could and then authorised shore leave for as many of her crew as she could spare. They wouldn't have much time, she cautioned them, but some was better than none.

Amid the suppressed glee on the bridge, Apnis cocked her eye at the captain, grinned knowingly and mentioned that she'd better get on with chivvying marketing about the recent cargo drop-off and its fate. She slid out of her chair and made her way off the bridge without as much as a stray glance in her direction.

The outer belts were strung, like vast three-dimensional thin donuts made of glistening spun candy strands in myriad colours, around the small and seemingly distant world of Merkat Three. That shone like a blue-white diamond in the centre, whilst the inner and middle belts hung fire between, a blaze of tiny stationary and moving lights netted within the confines of their distinct but all-embracing latticework. The interminable star-spangled darkness beyond seemed dimmed by the radiant glory of the artificial skies that had been created around the small planet. Only Merkat Primary, the yellow sun of the system, was brighter, but in the vast docking and repair belts that constituted the outer strands of the Web it was hardly a candle in the night.

The small craft ferrying the scuff and buff teams of Blue Shift out to the stanchion rigs where two Friskianx League loaders waited for attention were late: staff shortages in the Guild meant that jobs were taking longer and the Friskianx were way down the list of ships that mattered. Ships that mattered were those who would pay bonuses for work finished ahead of schedule or who would refuse to pay if jobs were left undone or completed late. Or those whose captains were inclined to scream and dance in rage and tear strips off whomever they could commandeer at headquarters. The pilot cum team leader of the first of the two repair craft was optimistic.

"I checked the logs; this shouldn't take us long. The bots can be sent in to assess and list dented areas and begin scraping," he told his team. "Just you lot make sure your suits and your harnesses are fully operational. And your comms, we don't want to lose one of you in the dark. You all right, Hardstone? You know what you're doing?"

"Well yes, Chief. I cut my teeth on the rigs out at Polstarn Repair Base and though they're not a patch on the set-up here, the systems are similar," responded the bright orange clad form of the latest recruit to the crew, Leffy Hardstone.

"I've worked with her before, Chief, she'll do," grumbled Kit Biernop from the back of the craft. "Just let's get on with it, I've a session in the sim-suites booked and I don't want to miss it."

There were similar rumbles from the other four members of Blue Shift present and a handful of derisory comments about the distance out of their present assignment. Not that the Friskianx would worry if the job was done in a hurry, as they were itching to get back to whatever it was they did, according to one of the Blue crew team. He had met one of their junior weapons officers in the *Green Diamond*, an insalubrious hostelry located in the outer belts, the other night, he told them. The man was shooting his mouth off about having scores to settle out in the ether beyond Dryssicon Minor.

"I told him that the *Arianrhod* was in and if he wanted a score to settle, he should start there and we'd all stand back and watch him," Red Hinks guffawed.

"What did he say to that?" Leffy Hardstone demanded.

"He said she'd get what was coming to her, but he was looking over his shoulder as he said it. He didn't stop long after that."

"Okay, here we go, cut the chatter people," called out team leader Chief Bark Barker. "We're starting on this Friskie boat; Karina's mob will start on the other and we'll wade in as and when to get both jobs done. We're mooring at the starboard rig here; make sure all the bots are in deploy mode."

After an exchange or two with his opposite number aboard the second repair runabout, Barker docked his own small vehicle swiftly and deftly alongside one of the plentiful scaffolding ramps and began organising bot deployment and gear unloading by his six crewmen, exhorting, cajoling and generally bullying them into action.

The Friskianx cargo vessel assigned to them was a large ship and sported a goodly number of weapons' emplacements over her hull. Her twin detachable cargo pods were also substantial and from what Hardstone could see from her viewpoint, the near one had sustained heavy denting.

"She didn't do that loading and unloading at her last stopover," Kit Biernop observed, waving an orange-clad arm as he manoeuvred his suit in the right direction. "That's old damage, that is."

"Old pods," Hardstone replied, grabbing for the other end of the vacuum float that would be used to smooth out smaller dents before the hull surface scoring was repaired. "Doesn't match the main hull," she added as she and her partner set their retros and rose smoothly over the edge of the closest pod like a pair of twin suns rising.

"Whatever. Here's our area of ops. Our bots have marked the first of the outlines. It looks like it's not too deep so we should be able to get the needful done without much trouble."

Some hours later, team one of Blue Shift reported back to base in the inner belts, its schedule completed and its members ready for a well-earned break in the aptly-named *Port in a Storm*. Hardstone intimated that she could not stay for more than an hour but would remain long enough to hear her crewmates let off steam about the drawbacks of working the outer belts. Barker jumped in first with his opinions of the failings of the Friskianx when it came to telling the truth in their maintenance logs. It appeared that the few scratches resulting from a mishap with their loading gear at their last port was way worse than reported and several deep dents had had to be fixed, not to mention scoring that was older than that. The extent of the damage logged was way off beam, declared Barker, and it was just as well that all the repair runabouts at Merkat were sufficiently well-equipped that they could carry out the necessary without several return trips to the sheds to restock with extra gear. The fact that his and Karina's teams had finished to time was beside the point, in his expert judgment.

Hardstone agreed to it all and shook her close-cropped dark curly head at the ebullient Red Hinks as he winked at her and asked how she had found her first shift.

She treated him to a coldwater stare out of her piercing blue eyes, but smiled as she replied in her strong brogue, "I've quit better jobs than that. Hope the next will be better."

"You'll be lucky to get an easier shift, smartarse. But I'm off, my mate and I are playing roundball at the sports diamond later and we have dates in the *Anchor's Rest* after that. See you guys the next shift."

Amidst various rude remarks and calls for more ale, he strode off, closely followed by Kit Biernop and Leffy Hardstone, who had just recollected business elsewhere.

"Got what you wanted?" Biernop asked quietly of his companion as they trod the narrow way down the corridor that led away from the *Port in a Storm* on green level six of inner belt two.

"I did. I owe you. I may want another trip out, so I'll be in touch. I'd be grateful if you could keep your ears open for anything about the Friskianx or their disreputable friends. If anyone asks, I've heard that my brother's been injured out in the Belts and I'm waiting for news so I won't put my name in for another shift at the moment."

"Got you. Nice get up by the way; I hardly recognised you."

"Thanks for that. There *is* one more little thing that you could help with, by the way…"

Captain Ahxenta was less complimentary than Kit Biernop about her first mate's appearance when she surveyed her later aboard the *Arianrhod* in the privacy of an isolation suite in medbay.

"Lose the hair and the eyes and take the cheek pouches out for hell's sake: you look like a moon-faced space parrot."

"I'll be glad to get rid of this gear. It's tight and the extra weight skin-suit makes physical work twice as hard. Azular got anything on the hull scrapes or the visuals I got?"

"He's working on them. But what about the repairs that you and your buddies carried out?"

"The cargo pods were very old ones bolted on, which isn't that unusual I guess, with all the travelling that pods have to do and given that cargo pods are the things that are usually looted first, so they do get knocked about. But it looked odd that a pair of new or newish loaders had such old pods attached. Got samples of the pods as well, by the way," Apnis went on thickly as she hauled out the cheek pads that were stretching her face uncomfortably.

"Are you sure they were new ships?" asked the captain.

"We were told they were and it looked that way. Azular should be able to verify the extraction date of the metallic elements of the hulls fairly accurately and tell us how recent they are and where they came from. I suggest we go over the probe scans of the hull plates as far as we've got them. I couldn't probe too deeply as the hull of the ship I worked on first was studded with surveillance gear and I bet a lot of it was pointed at the repair crew. And I only had a short spell close to the second boat. But I did manage to lay my paws on a copy of the repair schematics from the docking lacunae that the two Friskies were allotted; each lacuna has a set of total-ship scanners to ensure that the complete surface areas on the berthed vessel are checked over for damage – or at least those bits that are not shielded. But the shields don't hide shape. So thanks to my buddy Kit, I've a pretty good set of external blueprints, or as near as dammit, to check against our and the *Comet's* data from our recent little incidents."

"Good going, Tallica. Here's Azular now."

The Berzic science officer ambled in at his apparently effortless pace bearing a holo-pad under one arm, which he unfolded on the nearest flat surface. With half a glance at the dishevelled first mate, he got down to business and soon a hologram of one of the Friskianx League loaders was spinning lazily a few fractions above the table.

"Looks a tad more polished than the bunch we came up against," Ahxenta remarked, "And bigger, from what I can see. But what's a Friskie cargo doing with phase cannons the size you usually find on a warship with a grudge against half the mapped galaxy?"

That had also struck the science officer as unusual and he pointed out various other anomalies incongruous with the type of ship. There were long-range scanners of impeccable pedigree that appeared to derive from the master instrument makers of Hervesta Tertius and were more often found adorning the skins of explorer ships destined for deep-space missions; the proliferation of comms gear was such as might be expected to equip a small spy satellite; and the complex and novel externally-mounted shielding would provide some protection to a small moon, should it be in a situation of such need. But most telling was the meta-jurillium alloy of the hull plating. As expected, it had its source on Beta Zegonia 68c; that its signature was identical to that of the two Friskianx ships that had recently launched a surprise attack on *Arianrhod* was interesting. The latter samples were of course closely akin to the meta-jurillium alloy scraps that the *Green Comet* had captured after her own incident, Azular pointed out needlessly.

"Now we come to the ship's shapes," he continued with barely a flicker. "A new design, if the schematics data we have in our files on Friskianx merchant and military fleets is accurate. I compared these with the less-detailed ones we got during our own little fire-fight with the Friskies. There are many similarities, although *our* opponents were a good bit smaller and carried no cargo pods."

"Jikelleli did wonder if they were really new-built Friskie boats or if they were damn good counterfeits," Apnis said.

"The telling thing, of course," Azular observed, "Would be the crews. Are the personnel aboard these alleged Friskianx ships actually natives? Most Friskie ships are manned by home-grown crews."

"That could be faked as well," Ahxenta cautioned.

"Not easily."

"I agree, but it's possible. So how do we find out if the crews, or the majority of them, really are biologically Friskianx?"

"I wouldn't go asking probing questions, not even late at night in the *Half Moon*," Apnis said. "But where there's a will there's usually one way or three," she twinkled mysteriously at the other two.

"And just which way do you suggest?" Ahxenta demanded.

"We go along to the *Green Diamond* and pick a fight with any Friskies in for a jar."

The *Green Diamond* was a seedy eating and drinking hole located on one of the less well-travelled routes of the Web's outer belts. It had taken time in one of *Arianrhod's* older and less used shuttles to make one of the small docking bays for craft visiting outer nine's blue level seven. Wearing casual clothing but sporting their usual arsenals, the captain and first mate stepped through the dingy portal, an ancient veiling holo of a rare green diamond, a gem few could claim to have seen, and those that did were usually lying. They made for the bar.

At this early hour the *Green Diamond* was sparsely populated and the bored attendant pointedly ignored the twosome by polishing the face of the gaming station he was studying.

Ahxenta purposely walked up to a point opposite him and tapped his sleeve. "Two jars of house ale," she demanded.

"Just a minute, I'm busy."

"I said two jars of house ale," she repeated dangerously.

"And who the hell do you think you are, mate?" he hurled across the space between them, eyeing her sourly.

"Captain," she responded, smiling harshly. "*This* is my mate."

"Want me to get them, Cap?" Apnis queried lazily, removing a small stun pistol from an inner pocket.

"And set me up a tab," Ahxenta continued. "Here's my ident."

The flickering holo emanating from her palm as she extended it towards the man caused his eyes to widen, his jaw to drop and his hand that was halfway to an emergency button that summoned a pair of heavies from some grimy corner to freeze in horrified recognition. He looked from the holo to her face and back again to the holo.

"I wouldn't try it if I were you," Apnis warned as his hand unfroze and began its creep towards the button. "You wouldn't want a big mess to clean off your nice and squalid floor, would you?"

"Two jars of house ale. On your tab," the man said, slowly raising his hands to show that they concealed nothing more than a deep scar along one palm and a set of filthy fingernails. "Don't see you in here often, Captain," he added nervously as he poured the goods.

"You never see me in here," she corrected him. "Except when I have business out here. Which is usually never."

"Who *do* you get in here?" Apnis asked conversationally. "Not many by the look of it. Who are those guys over there, for example?" She waved her pistol at a small group at one distant table.

"Dock-rats from out the inner belt repair sheds," he responded uneasily. "They come in now and then near the end of their shifts – when they've finished early," he clarified.

"So they can have a jar before they report in for the end of their shift," Apnis explained. "And who else have you had in recently?"

It was obvious to their quarry that the two were fishing for facts but what they wanted to know eluded him. He excused himself on the pretext of having to collect used mugs and ambled off at what he hoped would pass as an easy stroll to one of the furthest corners.

"Oh look, Cap," Apnis observed in a carrying voice, pointing to the counter-top. "Our friendly barman has set the recording cams off and he's loosed a floating hover-cam to spy on us from above. Now isn't that just a teeny bit unsociable?"

"It is," Ahxenta responded, calmly removing a phase pistol from her upper pocket and taking careful aim.

The barely airborne hover-cam exploded with a hollow bang, to shower the already littered floor with myriad shards of synth-metallic particles. They settled gently, glittering like some shimmering exotic snow. The man's steps checked and he half-turned. Deeming it better to keep going, he ignored the second bang that told him that one of his recording cams had been dealt a similar blow and set off again, his shoulders hunching apprehensively against the next attack.

"Proximity alert," Apnis muttered as the barman, by now unable to carry any more used glassware, had no option but a return to post. In the interim a young servitor had materialised from some unseen lair and was hovering by the counter, tying on her apron.

"See to these," the barkeep growled at her, rattling the drinkware. "You're late as usual. That's more customers just come in, go and see what they want."

The girl looked nonplussed, as well she might at the conflicting orders. "Mugs first or customers first?"

"Don't get smart with me or you'll be for the chop."

Shrugging, the girl made towards the tall trio that had come in and was heading for the far end of the bar. She had heard it all before and was unimpressed: any den as downmarket as the *Green Diamond* was unlikely to sack one of the few who would apply for the job. She was more rare and precious than any green diamond and she knew it.

Ahxenta turned casually away from the counter to face the door, her first mate's back and the dim lighting the *Green Diamond's* owners considered suitable to hide the dirt and the poor quality of their beer shielding her from all but the most sharp-eyed of any new arrivals. The proximity alert Apnis had sounded was the response of a cleverly concealed bio-scanner that she had placed at the portal to the bar to warn them of the approach of any being remotely resembling a native of Friskianx. The receiver was a button that vibrated against her inner wrist and it had been triggered by the advent of the threesome.

"Passed Azular's first test, then," Apnis noted in an undertone. "Scanner suggests they're Friskies or closely related."

"Don't look as if they've got bio-cloaks and their uniforms look to be Friskie mercantile issue," Ahxenta returned equally quietly.

The three had decided to stand at the bar rather than opting for a table, their orders already taken by the efficient assistant. She quickly slid in behind the counter and began to punch in the required drinks at the auto-console. Three frothing mugs were set out on the bar in no time and she extended her hand for a credit slip.

"Set me up a tab," the tallest of the trio directed in a surly tone.

"*Please* set me up a tab," the waitress responded smartly. "And the answer's no. Hand over the credit or no beer."

"Intending to stop us?" the lanky individual sneered.

Her answer was the swift removal of the two closest mugs, which she set on a shelf below the counter. As she reached over for the last, he snatched it away and, grinning at his mates, swallowed a mouthful. The girl quickly pressed the emergency button and a noise over in the back gave notice that help was on its way. The man grabbed her wrist with an oath but let it go as her free hand closed on a handy empty mug and it sailed into the air to land smack against the side of his head. He howled, grabbing at his deafened ear as his jar of ale slipped out of his other hand and was expertly retrieved by the waitress.

As the bartender growled ineffectually for an end to the fracas and pounding boots from the murk beyond announced the advent of the heavy mob, the man found his next attempt on the girl floundering as Ahxenta grabbed his nearest arm, spun him about and landed a sock on his undamaged ear. He staggered back and fell over a stool. Apnis was there before his two pals had halfway reacted and by the time back-up arrived, all three were damp heaps on the floor.

Ahxenta raised the head of the nearest prone body. It flopped back to ground level, groaning.

"I'll need compensation," she informed the two bouncers, whose unsteady gait and dribbling chins indicated that they probably would have been of little use anyway. "Look at the state of my gear."

"Take it out of their hides," one of the two scowled.

"I intend to, believe me," she responded, making a search of the nearest pocket.

"Oh, oh!" warned the waitress. "Here come their reinforcements."

"That really *will* be the end of this suit," Ahxenta observed wryly, squaring up to two more uniformed individuals who had appeared on the threshold.

The following day at fourteen hundred hours found Captain Murmur Fleetskup seated in the command chair on the bridge of the *Tallulah*, scratching his head and perusing a memo urging his attendance at a meeting of the captains and first mates of every PSS vessel in the Web. The cause of his perplexity was the location: the meeting was scheduled for sixteen hundred in the bucket-bay of the *Arianrhod*.

"It sounds underhand to me," he said to Commander Goodsocks. "That's in two hours, so she's not giving us much time. You'd better find Toadflax – she'll need to cover for us."

Lieutenant Commander Primrose Toadflax, the *Tallulah's* second mate, was happy to take the conn; both she and the first mate knew that not only would she do a better job, but she was more popular with the crew. At least she was known as Looty Primrose behind her back: the captain's epithet was Mumble Whatsup.

"And only we two," Fleetskup went on to Goodsocks as Toadflax signed off. "Get me Ahxenta. I'll need to bring Buntle along."

"Why do you need Lieutenant Buntle?" the commander asked. "We don't know what this meeting's about, but if Captain Ahxenta specifically says thee and me, then thee and me she means, not Mr Buntle, however useful you find him."

Melly Goodsocks herself found that a very little of Thomas Buntle was more than plenty in any period of twenty four standard hours but prudently did not inform her captain of her opinion.

"I want him there," Fleetskup insisted, more because he liked to have his own way than for any other reason.

The first mate dutifully put the call in. Ahxenta was denied as she was busy, but Tallica Apnis informed her counterpart that command officers only were invited, adding that the others there would be Sarie Jikelleli of the *Green Comet*, Jury Djassi and Gallisty Tynissel of the *Equinox*, the *Hexameter's* Bee Lyvy Coxen and Rosee Charellis and Adhara Peakfrost and Exalyn Goldenfield of the *Quarkstorm*. The *Obsidian Sky* had not made it in for reasons unknown.

"I take it Ace Periwinkle's still out of action, then?" Goodsocks asked Apnis sympathetically.

The commander nodded. "*Comet* will have to fly her next mission without him when her repairs are finished, as she has targets to meet. He'll be left in Merkat medbay: Captain Jikelleli's taking no chances."

"Wise woman. Well, the captain and I will see you at sixteen hundred," Goodsocks confirmed, tabbing shut the comm link before Fleetskup could comment.

"Huh!" was all he said.

Apnis eyed her captain, who had been conning over data streams at the science station. "D'you think we should get Murmur Fleetskup a comfort blanket? He won't have Tommy Buntle to hold his hand."

The bucket-bay of the *Arianrhod* was in fact a briefing room tucked away near her secondary bridge, the command centre from which she could be operated if her main bridge had been rendered inoperative. All the invited officers were remarkably timely given the deliberately short period of notice of the meeting, and took their places around the large table upon request.

"I'll get straight to the point," Ahxenta began as the doors closed, the guards stationed outside straightened to attention and the privacy shields were activated.

The captain had set up a holo of one of the two Friskianx League ships that still held position in the Web and began to give a succinct account of Azular's findings on the craft's external gear as the image rotated, pointing out the phase-beam and torpedo ports and pulse cannon emplacements, the high-tech long-range scanning and comms arrays and the outer shielding of innovative design.

As that sank in, Ahxenta regarded her fellow officers unsmilingly. "Now for the most interesting part: we've now confirmed that the two Friskianx ships here now have the same meta-jurillium alloy in their hull plating as we found in the hulls of the Friskie freeloaders that ambushed *Arianrhod* not so long ago and the hull samples that Sarie's people picked up from the ships that attacked the *Comet*. The molecular signatures match, Beta Zegonia 68c is the source and the ore was recently mined. So all of these ships were recently built, or at least recently completely re-hulled and refitted."

As she indicated the holo, Jikelleli called. "You got a sample!"

"Tallica got the samples."

"How?" Fleetskup was openly annoyed.

"Not your concern," Ahxenta responded sharply. "What *is*, is that these ships are not what they appear and they're newly hatched. The Friskie ships here are novel models that my team haven't seen before, they have more surveillance gear than God and they're armed to the hilt. But on the face of it, they're Friskianx. And the raiders that hit the *Comet* looked to be raiders but their design subtly suggests that they're not the usual run of the mill scumbaggers that attack out of nowhere, grab what they can, destroy their victims' ships and clean up their own dunnage to hide their trail. So we're left with a mystery, and not a very nice one. I've not had news of more attacks, but I suspect it won't be long until I do."

Jikelleli was pondering over Ahxenta's words and looking closely at the still-spinning holo.

"So if they're not Friskianx, Cinnabar, who are they?" she asked.

"Oh, they're Friskianx, Sarie, or at least some of their crew are," she replied with a queer smile and a tilt of her head.

"And just how do you know that?"

"Tallica and I acquired samples of genetic material from five of them and all five have been verified as native Friskianx by my chief medical officer."

"I'd sure as hell like to know how you did that," Captain Bee Lyvy Coxen of the *Hexameter* put in wryly.

"You and me both," Jury Djassi nodded.

"I'll bet you would. And I'm not going to tell you. Suffice to say that we did."

"Wouldn't be related to that little scrap over at the *Green Diamond* the other night would it?" the *Quarkstorm's* Captain Peakfrost asked slyly. "First thing my supercargo was told by the mercantile liaison after we hauled in and your name was mentioned in the passing."

"No comment," Ahxenta told her. "But that's what the current situation is as far as I'm concerned. If any of you have more, I'd like to hear it. Adhara, you're the latest in, have you heard more out in the deep that we've not had news of here?"

The captain of the *Quarkstorm* tapped her lip. "Not what you'd call hard evidence," she admitted. "But a couple of small transports that were running scared into Heligon's main repair station had a story of some massive ship of unknown configuration that they'd glimpsed out near one of the remoter deserted worlds over by the outer edges of the Starglass Nebula. They'd no doubt been out that way to lift some archaeological detritus that the officially sanctioned teams had missed or left behind and weren't going to hang about in case they were caught."

Heligon was a small planet with a handy and well-equipped repair station that catered mostly for trading or exploratory craft and whose other function was as a market centre for rare, luxury or expensive goods. It was quite a way from the Starglass Nebula, which was a diffuse but bright object beyond the edge of currently charted space, outside the far-flung ISP-majority sector of galactic zone Zeta. The nebula was, however, in fairly close proximity to several ancient, deserted worlds that were generally held to have once been populated by technically advanced but now-vanished civilisations. Over the years a number of archaeological expeditions had been mounted, ostensibly to gain a deeper understanding of these peoples and their cultures. The results of these quests were little known, being closely guarded by the bodies that had paid for them in the first place and who thus considered themselves entitled to first dibs on anything potentially valuable uncovered, and everything else as well. Artefacts from such deserted worlds were much sought after and many fakes had surfaced. Those certified as the genuine articles were sometimes found in open markets, but the specific purposes of these rare pieces were usually unknown.

Ahxenta looked at her colleagues again. "As no-one else appears to have anything else to add at this point, I may as well bring up another matter. No doubt you recall the sly Spendle Doosbak of the Coalition suggesting that one of us transports his shifty chum Bick Micklemouse to Dryssicon, to show our unity, or however he tried to put it. I've had words with one of the Trades reps and the overall opinion of the TA is that it's as much in the dark as we are as to why, and obviously as suspicious of motivation. That being the case, and as you've all expressed your opposition to the plan, I'm prepared to give him – and his little boat – a berth on the *Arianrhod*, at least until I can figure what his game plan is."

Ahxenta held up a hand to forestall interruptions as the company stirred in surprise and a degree of incredulity. "Anyone else willing to volunteer, you'll have your chance, but hear me out. Of all our ships here, we've recently been repaired and upgraded and we're close to full complement. We're headed in the general direction of Dryssicon anyway. And as I don't trust Micklemouse, his Coalition friends or his ship, and given the fact that he's Friskianx and I trust all his kind even less, I want him where I can see what he's up to."

"This should be further discussed; what's in it for you?" Fleetskup demanded belligerently.

"A whole load of trouble as far as I can see," was the cordial reply. "You want him? You're welcome. How do you plan to accommodate him and get him to Dryssicon?"

Fleetskup had obviously not figured that far and began to mutter about liaising with his exec. Commander Goodsocks cut in decisively to inform the company that their next cargo, soon due for delivery, could not wait and a trip via Dryssicon would have to be later rather than sooner; and as far as she was concerned, *Tallulah* had sufficient on her plate without a passenger of such dubious credentials as Bick Micklemouse. Although furious at the interjection, her captain had no option but to agree.

"However, Murmur, I can of course see your point," Ahxenta butted in smoothly and with an attempt at diplomacy that sat ill with her. "But time's short and we all have contracts to fulfil. We still have one of your medics, Dr Greenwing, aboard and if you want to leave him with us as an observer, I have absolutely no problem with that."

As Fleetskup chewed that over, Ahxenta called on the others for their reactions and any alternative offers of a berth for the Friskianx trader. The consensus seemed to be that the *Arianrhod* was welcome, rather her than any of their ships and a berth in a garbage scow heading nowhere would probably be more fitting as accommodations for the said Mr Micklemouse. Given the reactions, Ahxenta had no compunction in wrapping up the meeting and calling for escorts to lead her visitors back to their own ships.

Captain Fleetskup had of course to waylay the two from the *Arianrhod* and demand audience with his medic. Ahxenta left Apnis to deal with the *Tallulah's* captain: she had other web to weave and a short talk with Melly Goodsocks as they walked behind the other two led to their diversion into a small office just off medbay.

"Well," Apnis said later to the captain as they waved the two officers off. "I wouldn't say he's overjoyed at the deal, but he thinks he's gained something. Greenwing's delighted he's staying on; I had to pay his way, but that's life; and I've promised Fleetskup that I'd meet up with him again sometime soon for a drink. How about you?"

"We've got Greenwing on a semi-permanent basis. Goodsocks has more or less agreed to it, as *Tallulah's* medbay is well-staffed. She'll talk Fleetskup round, as he's always up for saving credit here and there. How much did you have to sweet talk him anyway?"

"Too much," the first mate grimaced. "I *will* have to take him for a drink sometime. But let's go and tell Micklemouse the good news. Best have him locked in, in case he makes a run for it."

Micklemouse had obviously been half-hoping that the nightmare was over and that he would not be invited aboard a PSS on a short trip to Dryssicon. He confessed as much to *Arianrhod's* captain when she and Apnis intercepted him on a heading to the marketing suite of the inner belts to inform him that they had found him and his one-man yacht a ride. His eyes popped when his vessel was mentioned. The fact that his ship was to be commandeered, however laudable the reason, concerned him: he had planned to leave her behind at Merkat and how disruption to the arrangements he had made would sit with the docking reps on Merkat he did not know, he told Ahxenta glibly.

"Then let's find out," the captain said tersely, collecting his elbow in a vice-like grip. "Where to? We can speak to them now."

He squirmed out of that with admirable cunning by pretending an assignation with the relevant people in a little over half an hour. He turned the subject by hoping that he was not holding the captain or the commander up in any way and requesting the name of the ship in which it would be his privilege to travel.

"You'll be riding with me," Ahxenta declared grimly. "So let's see this boat of yours and arrange to have her shipped up to *Arianrhod*. I don't have all day to hang around, so the sooner we get it sorted the better. I'm assigning you two of my crew to help you with the prep. They'll no doubt be able to smooth things over with the docking reps here. Let's to it."

Having successfully pulled the rug from under his feet, she went on to pull the wool over his eyes by dealing him a fictitious account of her final duties in port and the plans for *Arianrhod's* departure. As he was wringing his hands in real or pretend distress and eyeing her sideways, Ahxenta hit him with a final blow. He would have no time to make any subtractions or additions to his ship before they left: she had already agreed with the Trades Alliance and the Port Authority to have docking control assigned to her. Doosbak had approved. With the TA and local Port Control as well as the *Arianrhod's* captain breathing down his neck, the trader had little choice but to comply.

Ahxenta had received confirmation from the repair squads working on it that Micklemouse's one-man Comet Six was ready for removal from their repair sheds. With no more credit to be made out of the man other than docking fees they preferred to have the space for clients with ships that needed work for which they could charge. The old prospecting craft, with its small bridge and habitation areas atop, its engine sections aft and its freight holding bays below, was a well-known design and this one to an untrained eye looked little different. But Ahxenta had brought along Crizz Cottontail as her aide to look over the vessel and decide how best to quarter her aboard *Arianrhod*. The ship's chief engineer had cut her milk teeth in an unremarkable running repair dockyard out at Larrikon Seven, where her folks had run the yard and their planetary smallholding in tandem, and she knew small craft like the Comet Six inside and out, having used them and pieces of them as playgrounds when she was a child for lack of better facilities. Her critical eye, the captain knew, would serve her better than any set of everyday scanners.

Micklemouse sat up front in *Arianrhod's* shuttle and indicated his craft with what appeared to be proprietary pride, Ahxenta thought. It certainly looked well-worn despite its recent cosmetic overhaul at the hands of the Web's repair crews. Cottontail, with the schematics that they had managed to twist out of the trader's grimy paws in front of her, ran experienced eyes over both the craft and its owner.

"These don't match the ship," she said flatly. "Those bulges in her skin aren't listed and no Comet Six ever had that boxy underside."

"The schematics are the old ones, before I had her renovated and strengthened less than six months ago," Micklemouse said nervously.

"So where are the updated schematics?" the engineer demanded.

"The work was done at Mellifly in one of the minor orbital repair sheds," he responded. "They don't tend to be too particular about record keeping."

"Those bulges are...?" the question hung in the air for a moment and Micklemouse licked his lips as he looked at Cottontail's less than friendly but very sharp eyes.

"They're additional storage bays with extra shielding for delicate cargo. I sometimes have to carry instruments and the like. And the extern latches are for securing carrier pods when I have them."

"Really?" she retorted derisively. "She's reading structurally sound but there are shielded areas aboard that our scanners can't penetrate. Care to explain why?"

"I have as much right to my privacy as you have," he indignantly announced. "I have a duty of care to my customers just as you have and I need to keep protected areas aboard my ship – you as pirates, eh, Privates, should know that."

Ahxenta laughed soundlessly at the slip and let her chief engineer carry on.

"The repair crews have used top-quality rad-repelling coating and applied it as a mighty thick skin," Cottontail noted as she checked her readout. "And those weapons weren't fitted as standard when you coughed up the credit for that old bucket. I've seen lesser armaments on an ISP cruiser."

The Friskianx man refused to be more forthcoming however, and Ahxenta gave the order for the transfer of the small craft to one of the *Arianrhod's* outer docking bays. As far as was detectable from the readings they could take, the ship was sound and not liable to blow up in their faces as a result of defective engines or wayward weapons capability. The captain had left her supercargo in charge of lodging the owner of the craft, with strict instructions that his quarters were to be as near to security as possible and that a discrete guard was to be posted at all times.

The transfer was accomplished without too much trouble, apart from complaints from the trader that he had business to finish on Merkat and the precipitous departure of the *Arianrhod* would not enable him to do so. Ahxenta was unapologetic: she had no intention of letting him loose to report to whom he saw fit and the less he knew of her ship and her business the better. As soon as the Comet Six was aboard and her own dealings completed, she gave the order for departure and the great vessel slipped her docking traces. With a final farewell from Port Control, the *Arianrhod* made her slow way out of the Web and into the space lanes, where she could set for her next destination.

"Forty minutes to the bypass, Captain," Helmswoman Romanna Dox announced. "Set for Dryssicon Major?"

"Dryssicon Major, aye," confirmed Ahxenta. "Best speed once we hit the bypass, Ms Dox. And now I need to see Cottontail, Azular and Flintlock. You're with me, Tallica; we'll use briefing room five. Lieutenant Commander Earbleat, you have the conn."

"Aye, Captain," the weapons officer called from her station, rising to make her way to the captain's chair.

Ahxenta closed the door and set privacy: even aboard her own ship, this meeting required as few chances as possible to be taken and she had set security guards on the outside. The company was invited to sit around the small table and all took their places swiftly. The trader Micklemouse was perched miserably between Chief Cottontail and Dr Azular, who had been designated his minders: he had no illusion that his hosts had now had all the time they needed to fully examine and explore his ship, and given the captain's ill-concealed wrath they had no doubt found one or two of its secrets. Just how many he was not prepared to guess, but he could hardly claim duress and his rights as a member of a free trade association. Captain Ahxenta was not one to be fobbed off with threats of legal action over privacy invaded.

"I expect you know why you're here?" she began.

"Captain?"

"Don't play me for an idiot, Micklemouse," she warned. "Your strangely shaped secure storage compartments are for one helluva lot more than stowing expensive bits of kit out of everybody's sight and temptation's way, are they not?"

The man shuffled but remained silent.

"Well? Are they not?"

"What do you expect me to say, Captain?" he retorted with assumed bravado. "I'm a private trader, same as you."

"Hardly," Tallica Apnis snorted.

"I need somewhere to store my more delicate pieces of cargo, as I think I told you before."

"It's more than the highly protected and shielded sections aboard your ship that concerns me and my officers, Micklemouse, as you're no doubt aware. It's what you're carrying in those compartments at the moment that we're here to discuss – amongst other things."

She was giving nothing away and the man was wary. Had she or had she not been able to breach his shields and get through the various blocks he had in place? And if she had, how far had she got? The small but grim smile on her face gave him the impression that the captain knew something but he was not one to hazard a guess as to what and how much.

"You have two clear-cut choices at the moment, Micklemouse," Ahxenta said finally. "The first is this: you tell us the whole story in your own words. Let's start with why you had those shielded sections built into your ship in the first place and why your ship's been fitted with technology and armaments that are not only so far in advance of the galactic norm but in nature and extent, you'd normally only expect to find their like on a war cruiser bent on system domination. Your little boat packs a mighty big punch for its size, mister. A meta-jurillium alloy skin ten percent thicker than standard that despite its apparent scarring is so recently done you can see your face in it, and a premium rad-repelling coating that's thick enough to keep you safe in a fallout zone?"

"In my trade you need all the defences you can get."

"Or can afford, I expect. And you can afford rather a lot, can't you? Your expenses are quite phenomenal but you seem to have no trouble paying your bills. You must have interesting customers."

"My customers are my business, not yours," he spluttered. "And their details are private. You know that, Captain – you know that I can't divulge any information…"

"Your ship, Micklemouse," Ahxenta persisted. "What's the story behind the upgrades you had done – more recently than six months ago, as you told us. And as a matter of interest, where were they done and by whom? The products of Beta Zegonia 68c don't come cheap and they're not the usual in one of the minor orbital repair sheds at Mellifly. That was the place, I recall, that you mentioned earlier when we looked your ship over in the dock Web-side."

"I can't tell you."

"Can't or won't, you little weasel?" Crizz Cottontail interrupted.

"Can't. I don't know." The man's face was pale and greasy and he licked his lips. "Look, my ship needed repairing big time and one of my clients told me that if I would make her fit for his requirements, he would foot the bill and give me a job or two. It was out at Mellifly. All I know is that I agreed: the ship was shot, I couldn't afford the repairs as I'd let my insurance lapse and I was owing some guys big time. I needed to pay my debts or I'd be in real trouble."

"So you're saying you got suckered into letting someone have free rein to fix your ship up the way they wanted and use you as a casual operative to do their dirty work for them?" Cottontail went on. "And at Mellifly, that well known centre of enterprise and expertise? And at which one of the minor repair sheds at Mellifly was this work done?"

"One out over the northern polar region, they said. They had their own repair dock thereabouts, they told me," he said dully.

"They? It's they now, is it?" Ahxenta asked coldly.

"My contact had associates; he called them in when I agreed."

"And who is your contact and who are these associates?"

"I don't know! I never met the associates."

"Your contact," persisted the captain. "You called him *one* of your clients, so you'd known him some time?"

"This is blood out of a stone, Cap. Why don't we just fry the little weasel or stick him in the brig?" Cottontail demanded.

"I got rights!"

"Aboard my ship mister, you don't," Ahxenta apprised him. "Your contact was well known to you?"

"No, I'd only just met him. He was asking about a contract job and we got talking."

"I bet you did. And how does Doosbak fit into this? How did you get to know him and your other strange friends in the Coalition?"

"I've known Doosbak for years; he's Friskianx, same as me. He was an independent dealer at one time; well, he still is, but he runs a much bigger operation now. He ran a small fleet of short-range cargo boats out of his base at Lonagan Four then. That's close to Friskianx and I helped him out now and again, whenever my ship was laid up," Micklemouse told her, his eyelids flickering rapidly.

Ahxenta folded her arms and waited, eyeing the trader with disgust. Realising that his answer was cutting no ice and that he was not going to be able to wriggle out of the question, he looked at her.

"I took a rap for him once," he admitted. "Contraband cargo that got picked up by the Lonagan authorities. He'd just got onto one of the Coalition trades committees and was set to get into its inner circles in a big way; I was an unknown and had no previous offences. So I got off with a caution, only I lost my licence for a time. He gave me work until I regained the licence, got me a place on Friskianx…"

"Even though you're not quite Friskianx," the captain stated.

He started. "How do you figure that! I'm Friskianx, I…"

"Your genetic make-up's been altered. Oh, you'll pass as native Friskianx: we're all much the same this side of the charted galaxy, so it doesn't take much. But you're no more pure-bred Friskianx than I am, Micklemouse. And Spendle Doosbak owes you so much he gets you in as part of a Coalition delegation to Merkat Three and into a high-level meeting. Just how much *does* he owe you? And I'd like to know who's pulling *his* strings and why. But we haven't finished our talk about your ship. Why the number and size of the armaments?"

"My customer was calling the shots!"

"Pretty big shots, given the size of the guns," Apnis noted dryly.

"And was this customer also responsible for those shielded units to keep interested parties out, so that they couldn't figure just what you got up to in there?" Ahxenta demanded.

"Up to?" he repeated warily.

"Up to, Micklemouse; I want the whole story and whingeing 'I don't know' is not part of the equation. Let's put it this way: we're damn well sure, so do you confirm or deny?"

"Confirm or deny what?" the man whined.

"He's stalling, Cap. I vote we fry him anyway, or let him know the second of his clear-cut choices – that may change his mind for him," Cottontail said, a harsh smile on her face.

"Well? Are you going to tell us precisely – and I mean precisely – what you get up to in the largest of those storage units?" the captain snapped.

"I can't tell you!"

"Then we have no option but to take the second option."

"What second option?" the trader queried with a nervous swallow.

"We launch your ship into space and blast it to smithereens."

"You can't do that!" he gasped in horror.

"Want to come up to my bridge and watch me?" Ahxenta asked him. "Your choice, mister: take it or leave it."

Micklemouse surrendered. "I'm a sentient data-logger, part cyber-enhanced and an observer and recorder of everything I'm exposed to. My sensory systems record my experiences: what I see and hear; and things that I'm subliminally aware of..." he trailed off. "My systems and their genetic and mechanical components need recharging from time to time so that I can function efficiently."

"A walking super-spy, an info-sent, just as Doc Flintlock and Doc Azular suspected," interrupted the chief engineer. "And what do you do with the data once you've got it?"

"Doctor?" asked Ahxenta of her chief medical officer.

"It has to be downloaded," Axellina Flintlock said. "To all intents and purposes the storage space of an info-sent is near limitless; in practice the information is usually required long before that and as it can be hijacked, it doesn't tend to be left in situ for longer than necessary, as that would pose a danger to the info-sent."

"So this little pipsqueak is no doubt still recording everything around him?" Cottontail demanded.

"Not exactly," the Berzic science officer put in. "We doctored his lunch and he swallowed a systems inhibitor. It won't completely stop his programming, but it will make the data intake fuzzy."

Micklemouse looked at him aghast. "You what?"

"We couldn't take the chance you'd escape our clutches and make it back into the belly of your little lifeboat," Ahxenta told him. "That *is* where your download and storage facility is, isn't it? And it *is* where your operators can access it, if they get close enough. Your puppet-masters must have a lot of very high-level contacts Mr Micklemouse, to get you into the circles you run in. And now you're on my ship. What in the galaxy am I going to do with you?"

That question was also bothering the trader big time. He had now no illusions that the officers of the *Arianrhod* were well aware of what he was and how he operated. And it seemed that they knew about the cosy cocoon aboard his own ship where he was reprogrammed and downloaded on a regular basis. But what else did they know?

As if in answer, Ahxenta spoke again. "You *do* know what's in your other storage sections, I take it? The twin ones adjacent to your cyber suite?"

"Operations and comms units," he replied. "They're sealed on the inside as well, so even I can't get to them."

"And I bet you've tried," Cottontail butted in.

"That's the reason, Micklemouse, that we're still considering the second option we spoke about," the captain informed him.

"But you can't! I've told you all I know!"

"Surprisingly, I believe you. I also believe that you've no idea that those other compartments house enough firepower to destroy not only your ship, but much of mine. And your finger's not the one on the trigger. That's why, mister, we will be getting rid of your ship."

The trader's face was ashen. "But you can't!" he repeated. "They would kill me!"

"Rather you than us," was Cottontail's ungracious riposte.

"So you are now going to tell us all about your ship's recent refitting at Mellifly and who and where and what. Aren't you?"

The gleam in Ahxenta's eye boded no good for the trader and he swallowed rapidly. "I'll tell you what I know."

In the event his account came as near to truth as could be expected of a slyboots who was as used to deception as Micklemouse. Ahxenta had made sure of that by placing her senior science officer, Azular, next to him: very few people outside Berzic were aware that certain of the Berzicon were telepathic and in rare cases the talent was highly developed. One reason that Azular had sought a career away from his own world was that his inborn skill was so beyond average that even amongst his own people his ability gave rise to a degree of disquiet. With someone such as the trader, Azular had little problem picking up on the shades of his mind that let the science officer separate the essence of truth from downright lying.

Micklemouse indeed knew little beyond the fact that some months previously he had been approached by a potential customer who was as smooth as the average business person and who, in most respects, looked humanoid: most of the peoples in the charted galactic zones and sectors shared a large number of physiological and psychological characteristics, the result of widespread organic seeding coupled with colonisation in the early stages of galactic expansion. This man had held out the proverbial lifeline: he and his business partners would repair the trader's vessel and make her fit for their business, which related to the transfer of highly confidential technical and political information. They were also prepared to pay substantial fees for the services rendered. These services were not onerous, the trader had been assured, and would interfere very little with his own dealings.

The nondescript and beat up little Comet Six had thus been taken from him to his clients' repair shed and rendered spaceworthy and far in advance of any ship like it that Micklemouse had ever seen. He had actually become extremely proud of her. His own transformation into the sentient data-logger, or info-sent as the conversion was known, at a private underground medical facility on Mellifly, had caused him some concern as it meant that he would be trackable by a signal sent out by his implanted cyber systems. He had been reassured that only his immediate clients would be able to track him, that his biology was particularly suited to the procedure and would cause him minimal disruption and in fact it would assist him in trade. At that point he was so far under the influence of his initial contact and owed him so much that he felt he had no way of backing out and the remuneration he received did give him entry into certain social spheres that he had only dreamt of in the past.

There were other matters in relation to her passenger and his ship that concerned *Arianrhod's* captain, however, of which Micklemouse was not made aware. The jurillium alloy components of the hull of his craft had conclusively proved a match to the skins of the two Friskianx League ships in Merkat space dock that Apnis had sampled. The inference was that the person or group who had set the trader up as a spy was linked in some way to those responsible for the attacks on the *Arianrhod* and on the *Green Comet*. And Ahxenta was reluctant to keep the Comet Six aboard her own ship because of the danger posed by the lethal explosive devices that her extremely talented chief engineer and senior science officer had detected through the layers of tamper-proof plating and shielding that protected them; but she was also highly loath to get rid of the ship. The latter would alert whoever was manipulating Micklemouse to the fact that the devices had aroused suspicion at the least and discovery at the most. But neither could she render the contents of the ship inoperative, as that would inevitably lead to the same conclusion.

The captain was likewise not certain that incarcerating the man in the brig would serve any purpose other than to alert his masters that he was under more than natural suspicion on her part. And according to Azular, Bick Micklemouse was rather an advanced info-sent, as his cyber implants gave him more than the recognised info-sent capacity of infiltration and data capture. In Azular's opinion, the trader was potentially capable of connecting physically to data sources, which would allow him not only to utilise them but possibly to disable them, although he seemed unaware of the facility. He was thus an info-sent to be treated with extreme caution.

Once Micklemouse had been escorted under guard to his quarters and a watch posted on him, the captain faced her senior officers.

"We've quite a haul in front of us still and we're housing a major headache with that damn boat. Your task, Crizz, is to disable those internal volatiles without disturbing their shielding; Azular will help. And Doc, I'm afraid that you're faced with disabling Micklemouse or at least his capabilities, without interfering with his cyber implants. And I want it done before we get to Dryssicon. Good luck, people."

"We sure as dammit are going to need it," Cottontail sniffed. "Thanks for that Cap. Any more miracles required while we're at it?"

Ahxenta let her have the last word.

6: OUT IN THE DARK

The huge ship was black against the blackness of star-spangled space. She hung like an immense creature carved of solid shadow, angular but smooth, her glistening hull limned with a cold blue-black fire.

"She looks like a ghost from hell," Commander Apnis remarked conversationally into the silence. "Just as well she's one of ours."

That the ship was a PSS was obvious, with her name and registry clearly visible on her upper hull. She was *Vanguard* class in design, as were nearly all the ships in the PSS fleet, and she bore as her insignia the distinctly-emblazoned shell-pink skull and crossbones that was the flag of the Trades Alliance, under which she flew. The device was integrated into the floors of her enormous outer cargo and landing bays; those flanked her massive inner bays, which in turn were set either side of fascia-covered main habitation and service areas. Those were set amidships and ran the length of the ship from stem to stern. Her reactor core, drive and fusion cell units were also set centrally.

"She's a bonny vessel," Crizz Cottontail observed from her station at engineering, a touch of envy in her voice. "Not a patch on ours, of course," she added lest offence be taken. "But what's she doing in this neck of the woods? I thought she was headed into Merkat for the Trades Alliance meet, but she didn't make it."

"Long-distance scans still show no other ships close by, Captain," Lieutenant Gliss, the senior tactical officer called.

"She's not dead in space, Captain," the duty science officer added. "Her life support systems are operational and her crew complement seems to be animate, judging by the lifeform readings I'm picking up. In fact I read at least twice the number of crew she should have; it looks like she's hauling live cargo," Lieutenant Greffy continued in a puzzled voice. "She's got no shields up and her energy levels are low but I can't detect any obvious damage to her hull beyond a fair bit of recent scoring. Her weapons systems are intact but they're running hot – it looks like she's been using them not so long ago."

"Only one way to find out what the hell's going on," Ahxenta declared, stroking her chin. "Open a link and let's see," she ordered the comms officer. "This is *Arianrhod* to *Obsidian Sky*. What's your status? Do you require assistance?"

There was a few seconds of crackling static before a scratchy voice replied, "*Obsidian Sky* to *Arianrhod*: we're still in one piece, mostly. As for assistance, Captain: as much as you can spare would be good. Hold on 'til I get a visual up…"

After a pause of several seconds, as the image on the main holo-grid expanded downwards into the well of the bridge and cleared, the *Arianrhod's* crew could see their counterparts aboard the *Obsidian Sky*. At first glance the situation seemed as usual, but Ahxenta was well acquainted with Captain Grey Bluejohn and she could tell that there was strain behind the level eyes that looked across at her.

"What's the trouble, Grey? It looks like you've had an argument with someone."

"A frigging great battleship ambushed us out of the Orriga Two asteroid field; unknown configuration, though she looked to be an offshoot of the raiders' usual strike cruiser mould. Only bigger, one helluva lot bigger; and with armaments that could take out a small moon, by what we could read of her tactical spec."

"And you didn't take her on?"

"Not this one, Cinnabar; not when I'm carrying a shipload of refugees from the Marridan System."

"Refugees?" queried Ahxenta.

"I guess you didn't hear: a fleet of unidentified ships jumped off the bypass at the Marridan beacon, three or four standard days ago. They took out two orbital defence platforms before the planetary authorities could turn around. Left four of their number to blockade the place and the rest took off into the dark. The Marridani couldn't track them as half their orbital recon systems were taken out as well. We met our passengers racing in the opposite direction to home with a raider on their tail. They were on a pleasure cruiser returning from some ceremonial pilgrimage on one of their colony worlds and were warned not to try to come in. They ran and made hyperspace but the raiders must have got wind of them and sent a small war cruiser onto the bypass after them. The Marridani sent out an emergency call and we picked it up. We took care of the raider but the Marridani ship was so badly damaged she couldn't be salvaged and we were already so late for our stop off at Merkat Three that we gave that up and had to head out for our next cargo collection out at the Outer Reaches Archipelago."

"Which is close enough to the Orriga Two asteroid field to be called neighbouring," finished Ahxenta.

"That's about it. I'd planned to pick up our cargo and then drop the Marridani off at some safe haven on the way back into more habitable parts. But then we ran into that bloody battleship and it started firing at us as soon as it saw us. There was no way I'd stand and fight as we were seriously outclassed, and I mean outclassed, Cinnabar: that thing was huge. But we smacked up a few asteroids in its vicinity with our long-range phase cannon and made a run for it while they were sorting themselves out. We took a convoluted course out of the Orriga sector, dropping reflector flak and scatter mines on the initial part of our route. We didn't take the chance of heading for our next port in case they'd figured what that might be."

"What help do you need?" Ahxenta asked practically. "We're fully refitted and in prime condition."

"Weapons recharge modules and as many large energy cells as you can spare. Our injuries from our argument with the raider war-boat were minor so our medics can cope there, but if you have a couple of dozen berths that you can set up for some of our passengers, that would help. I'd planned to offload them at Selliden Central as there's a big medical facility there and an ISP local office. The Marridani are ISP so it's about time the Protectorate took a hand."

"You got it," Ahxenta told him promptly. "Send me over the list and we'll get on it. I'd like all the tactical and science data on both your little spats, Grey, if you don't mind. I'd like to know what we're dealing with here. I'll shuttle over a team with the gear and they can bring back a few of your visitors on the return leg. I'll see about spare berths as soon as I can. We were heading out elsewhere, but we can detour via Selliden Central and pick up our lost time later. And the ISP should recompense us anyway."

"You should be so lucky," Captain Grey Bluejohn grinned wearily at her. "But I'll make out a full report and get it circulated pronto and on a tight beam to our lot at least. The TA will want to know about it as well. My supercargo will contact yours about the weapons recharge and energy cells. Standard charges?"

"The hell with that, they're yours. And if ever you can return the favour one day…"

"Understood and thanks, Cinnabar."

"They've had a rough day or two then," Apnis observed ironically as the *Obsidian Sky* linked off.

"Sounds like it. Best see what we have in the way of spare berths, Tallica. Some of ours may have to double or triple up: we're not rigged for luxury cruise passengers."

"We're not rigged for luxury, much less passengers, Cap. But we have a couple of empty inner cargo bays that can be set up as billets: we've done it before, so I guess Lindell still remembers the ropes."

"Good idea. I don't know a lot about the Marridani or what they'll need, but we'll cope. Mr Box, plot a course to Selliden Central. We'll match our tracks with the *Obsidian* once we're on the move, helm, but for now get us in tight enough to get a shuttle over. And all stations, keep your eyes and ears wide open, I want to know if anything out there's heading in."

The next few hours were a helter-skelter of making something out of nothing. The *Arianrhod* was a trader and had never been designed to cater for more than a handful of paying passengers, but those crew assigned to the duty of making a few empty holds look like inviting temporary homes took to their tasks with gusto and with engineering supplying the necessary power, waste and water systems, a reasonable pseudo-hostel was soon assembled. Axellina Flintlock had insisted on a rapid medical review of those Marridani who were to be their guests before they set foot anywhere out of the arrivals bay lest they were carrying some unknown malady that could infect any of *Arianrhod's* crew, a procedure that made the harried newcomers feel even more agitated. Added to that, catering was hard put to find sufficient and suitable food and drink from the stock of provisions that the ship held and its team was letting fly strings of complaints to any ears that had time to stop and listen. The *Arianrhod's* supercargo, Lieutenant Lindell, who with his second Ensign Helly Pinkhorn was responsible for the apportionment of much of the cargo that the ship carried, had a good handle on what could be spared and was given the job of supplying the needy as economically as possible.

Ahxenta was also concerned that delays in the vicinity might enable the ship that had attacked the *Obsidian* to pick up her trail and therefore that of *Arianrhod*: by what the captain had heard from her opposite number, she was not inclined to have a confrontation with such an enemy, given the condition of the edgy civilians she was bringing aboard. In consequence, she supervised the recharge of her fellow-vessel's weapons arrays herself and set her first mate on the resupply of their engineering decks with energy cells. The bulk of the *Arianrhod's* repair-bots were also redeployed to assist those of the *Obsidian Sky*. Ahxenta's tactical, science and weapons stations were conning over the information that the *Obsidian* had been able to get on the intruder. Unfortunately, there were no tangible pieces of evidence to glean apart from the stray weapons signatures that could be extracted from the scoring on the black ship's hull, Whisper Earbleat, the weapons officer and *Arianrhod's* second mate, informed the captain, but they were also running comparisons on the tactical and science data from both the incidents in which the *Obsidian* had been involved.

The Orriga Two asteroid field was some distance away from their current position but the nature and level of any damage taken by the enemy ship could not be estimated without knowing her capabilities, particularly her defence shields. If she was anything akin to raider strike cruisers in make-up she would be a tough nut to crack and could well have survived intact a peppering with sufficient small rocks to seriously disable a standard cruiser. It was likely that the ship carried not only deflector arrays for the usual junk that littered space, but close-proximity disruptor beams that could be deployed in case of near-contact collisions with debris. The arms that Bluejohn judged could take out a small moon sounded ominous enough and implied the presence of lesser weapons arrays as standard.

It was two hours before Captain Bluejohn was back on the comm; he had hurriedly put together the promised report, less than full but of a depth that was likely to cause a degree of unease in those for whom it was intended. He did not propose to circulate it until the *Obsidian* was ready to depart, lest his adversary intercept the transmission and track it back to source: raiders were adept at such manoeuvres. His ship was almost back to power enough to move out, hull repairs were ongoing and the transfer of passengers to the *Arianrhod* was complete bar the final shuttle load that was on its way over.

Ahxenta had concerns of her own. She had ordered her senior science officer to update on all the information he could in relation to the attack on Marridan by the fleet of hostiles about four days before, according to Bluejohn's news. It seemed that the Marridani were still under alien control, judging by the few reports that had leaked past the planetary blockade. The intruders had set up a massive local jamming field but one or two small and intrepid fighters had slipped out with schematic and tactical readouts and were assiduously alerting nearby systems. Descriptions and scant visuals of the blockading vessels had also been obtained, which Azular had enhanced, utilising the data he had been given by the *Obsidian Sky*. He had then conjured up a series of impressive though superficial profiles of the invaders.

The Berzic officer also took the trouble to enquire among the

Marridani and had found a couple of them willing to assist. One of the latter was able to verify that the profiles looked oddly similar to that of a strange ship that had been sighted close to one of the outer colonies to which the man had been attached a month or so before. The sighting had been logged of course, but as there had been no contact, nothing had been done. It thus seemed that the strangers had scouted the territory before sending in their big guns to take Marridan. What was exercising both Ahxenta and her senior science officer was that the Marridani had also been able to confirm that the invading ships bore more than a close resemblance to the massive battleship that had ambushed the *Obsidian Sky* out by Orriga Two. They were somewhat smaller, he believed, but shape-wise they definitely looked similar. More importantly, Azular had worked out from the tiny amount of data he had that their ion trails were practically identical.

As Bluejohn listened to Ahxenta and watched the relevant holos flow past his viewscreen, he shook his head, sighing deeply. "It's little enough to go on, Cinnabar," he told her. "But it looks like there's a new kid on the block and he's a bully."

"My head needs a reprogramming," groaned Micklemouse. He lay in a disordered heap on the floor of his quarters, moaning dismally.

"Allow me," Captain Ahxenta told him acerbically, eyeing the man with increasing disgust. He smelt like a sewer.

Chief Medical Officer Axellina Flintlock was unrepentant. "My brief was to render his recording abilities defunct."

"And was making him so roaring drunk that all he can do is puke and piss the only way?" the captain demanded. "Call yourself a doctor? What about do no harm and all this stuff you're supposed to sign up to at medical school?"

"Needs of the many, Cap. And at the moment that's us. Besides, I got Greenwing to double-check the dosage and it's strictly controlled. If you like I could use it as an excuse to get him into an iso-chamber where he'll have no opportunity to record anything – but that might of course alert his lords and masters that I'm liable to pick up on what he actually is, if they're close enough to detect him and link into his systems. However close that is. Your call, Cap."

Ahxenta shrugged, grimacing. "Our next port is Selliden Central where we'll be offloading our Marridani passengers. Greenwing has certified them all as physically able to be unleashed from his care. I've already contacted the Interstellar Systems Protectorate local office chiefs so they're prepared for what's coming in and they'll have the medical facility on standby to take them in anyway. I'm hoping not to be there too long as the quicker we get to Dryssicon the better I'll be pleased. If the ISP decides it's time it got involved in the problems in the Marridan System, the fur should start to fly. Bluejohn's going to stay there until his ship is back to rights, but he still has his cargo collection out at the Archipelago."

"He's going? But what if that ship that attacked him is still in the vicinity of Orriga Two?" asked the doctor.

"He's taking the chance; and he'll have to warn the worlds out in the Outer Reaches that they may have a problem anyway and he sure as hell won't be doing that on an open channel. He'll keep us all updated, but things are getting mighty hot around our local galactic zones and sectors."

The captain again looked down at the bundle on the floor. "The Zidexallians say guests and fish stink after a few days and they're so right. Keep him here for the duration but get him cleaned up. I've got to see Crizz and Azular."

The chief engineer and the senior science officer had worked long and hard on the problem left with them and were slightly further on. They had hauled in Dr Greenwing to assist: his nickname of Puzzle was well-bestowed, as he was famous in some circles for his grasp of the unusual and his response to such. With broad military experience and having travelled across more of the known galaxy than most, he was proving to be an invaluable assistant.

"We now have some degree of containment," Cottontail informed the captain. "Azular suggested we fabricate a thin skin of transparent keratinaceous hard-set gel around as much as possible of those twin storage bays of the Micklemouse boat. That should afford a degree of separation from the rest of the ship, and we've infused the gel with super-absorbent crystalline meta-jurillium. Dr Greenwing advised us to scrape the outer hull with nano-tomes to get a source and he knew how to create pico-particles for the infusion. So with luck, any probe should think it's all part and parcel of the boat itself. We're thickening the skin slowly, but if the process triggers an explosion, at least there will be some degree of suppression."

"Some degree?" questioned the captain. "How much is some?"

"Not enough," admitted Cottontail. "But, as Puzzle pointed out, if you can't do more to the boat, then do more to *Arianrhod*. I want your go-ahead to seal off that bay as far as possible and set charges to loose all the restraining struts and bolts in the whole section."

"What!!!"

"It's only a precaution, Captain," Greenwing interrupted.

"It's only a precaution," repeated Ahxenta. "You want to blow out a chunk of my ship and it's only a precaution!"

"We can set the whole section to blow out, so if the worse comes to the worst, we'll have minimal damage to the bulk of *Arianrhod*, her cargo and her crew," the engineer argued. "We'll have to remove the hard-set gel skin before we let Micklemouse and his ship free at Dryssicon, I guess, but we can re-soften it and suck it off with a vac extractor. I'd like to plant a locator bug aboard so we can keep tabs on the little sod, but I guess that might be picked up."

"Given the degree of tech his ship has attached, I'm sure it would be picked up," the captain said dryly. "But your next job," she went on, ignoring the groans, "Is to abstract what Micklemouse has picked up during his stay here and replace it in his cyber system records with harmless memories of a pleasant trip. You'll have to leave what he's picked up about our rendezvous with the *Obsidian*, but that can't be helped. That's probably more your areas of expertise, Greenwing and Azular, and naturally you'll have to liaise with Dr Flintlock, but Crizz can assist on the technical aspects if need be. Then we set him loose at Dryssicon. We've got no reason to detain him but at least we know what he's about."

"And we can forewarn the other Privates," Cottontail put in.

"No we can't," Ahxenta said firmly. "Sorry, Crizz, but until we know the extent of what's going on, the fewer that know the better, even if it does compromise some of our associates."

"Well, given we have to count the *Tallulah* and Fleetskup amongst them, I suppose you have a point, Cap," the chief engineer conceded. "What about Captain Bluejohn?"

"I'll be speaking to him," Ahxenta told her.

After some thought and discussions with her senior officers, Ahxenta finally authorised the sealing off of the docking area around the rogue ship and let her chief engineer and weapons officer set the minimum number of charges possible that would blow away the section in an emergency. She ordered a ship-wide amber alert meanwhile, more as a means of keeping Micklemouse quiescent in his quarters and out of everything than maintaining the alert status of her crew.

Captain Bluejohn and the senior officers of the *Obsidian Sky* were made aware of the additional passenger *Arianrhod* carried, and of the danger that he posed, in a short meeting en route to Selliden aboard the former vessel: Captain Ahxenta was wary of discussing anything about the situation anywhere near its subject. On her Berzic science officer's advice she also said nothing of his added capabilities. None of the *Obsidian's* officers had had any contact with an info-sent before and could offer no useful advice but all had heard of such individuals. Bluejohn was grateful for the warning and agreed to keep quiet about the trader and to keep his sensors on *Arianrhod's* relevant bay for the duration.

The drop-off of refugees at Selliden Central was carried out with little fuss. Most of the Marridani, dazed at what had happened to them and their system, were glad to be planetside and together in relative comfort after the spartan facilities of the PSS vessels. Little more had been heard of the current situation on their homeworld, other than that communications were still being jammed and no other authority had sent ships in sufficiently close to get a clear picture, for fear they would be next on the unknowns' target list.

In view of the incursion and blockade of Marridan, the Interstellar Systems Protectorate office on Selliden had already called in advisers and representatives from its closer affiliated planetary systems to organise fleet deployment. Ahxenta was, however, adamant that she had time to present only a quick overview of her involvement in the matter: with Micklemouse aboard, she wanted as little as possible to be stored in his augmented recording system. Whilst info-sents were so rare that their full capabilities were practically a mystery to all but a handful of people, she had heard enough to be highly suspicious of what he might pick up, even if caged in his quarters for most of the time. She wanted him and his ship gone as quickly as possible and her next port of Dryssicon Major was hence her prime objective.

To that end, *Arianrhod* spent as little time in orbit around Selliden as was feasible, halting only to take on extra supplies and ensure that the *Obsidian Sky* was safely berthed. The trip to Dryssicon would take several days and she had already lost a substantial amount of time in supporting and escorting her sister-ship and in ferrying the Marridani refugees to safety. It was with relief that she bade Bluejohn goodbye and wished him and his crew a safe onward journey.

"Dryssicon Major, and as much speed as we can muster without blowing up Chief Cottontail's engines," Ahxenta ordered her flight team at the navi-helm console.

"Best speed to Dryssicon Major, aye," Lieutenant Dox echoed as the PSS broke free of her moorings and set her head out of the Selliden system.

"Any particular route, ma'am? I've calculated a couple that might shave a few hours off," Navigation Officer Box stated.

Ahxenta studied the navi-holo closely. "We'll cut across to Ferris from Lesser Kirrin and then make for the node off Vreskota Two: I don't want to come near that worm pocket off the Helix Cluster."

"Course set," Box confirmed. "If we hit a problem, I'm sure Chief Earbleat's phase cannons can handle it."

"Good. And now I need to see Azular, Flintlock and Greenwing about our pet weasel, Tallica, so you have the conn."

The senior science officer and both medics had put their heads together to come up with a way of dealing with the trader. After his last experience with Flintlock, he had very little inclination to partake of anything stronger than fruit juice by way of quenching his thirst and was inclined to look suspiciously on everything that appeared on his meal tray. His augmented senses meant that he could and did judge the quality and content of every mouthful and Dr Flintlock had been hard pressed to supply innocuous food and drink. In the end she petitioned the captain to allow the trader to eat in the crew's mess at least once a day, ensuring in advance that the only crew there at the time would be well-briefed and observant. Azular had been obligated to accompany Micklemouse each lunchtime, a duty that the Berzic officer found tedious but it gave him the opportunity to take full measure of their unwanted guest. The situation had the added benefit of rendering the man grateful to him for the company, everyone else aboard tending to avoid the trader like the plague.

It was during the course of a couple of meals spent with him that the science officer had come up with a means of replicating and downloading the data that the trader had picked up since his advent aboard *Arianrhod*. Azular had discussed his idea with the two senior medics, both of whom had been horrified, but had eventually agreed that it was feasible. It was no less than temporarily to turn Azular himself into something akin to an info-sent and abstract the relevant information using the Berzic officer's strong telepathic abilities. The data could then be reworked and replaced within the data-logging system of the cyber-enhanced little man by overwriting the original. The latter part of the procedure still had to be worked out, but given that the information harvested by an info-sent was meant to be downloaded and could be hijacked, it should be possible.

"There's little option but basically to partially brain-wipe the little perisher, Cap," Cottontail growled when she had been brought in to share the discussion over the technology that would be necessary. "We need to remove all the information about our ship's spec and systems and our missions that he might have picked up."

"Not to mention the working over we gave him to abstract the material about him, his ship and his clients," Ahxenta put in.

"In that case, the little sod ought to be grateful. If we remove all the info that incriminates him regarding passing on the goods about his very dangerous associates to us, he won't get the fatal pasting he's expecting once they find out," the engineer snorted.

"Dangerous criminals and those unfortunates that have suffered partial or permanent memory loss *can* be reprogrammed with false or replacement memories," Greenwing said slowly. "It's not a perfect system and the memories have to be sourced, but it can be done. My only concern is the superior capabilities of an info-sent: subliminal messages, feelings and so on have to be taken into account."

"I can help there, Doctor," Azular told him. "My people have used that kind of capability in medical circumstances and I'm familiar with the concept at least. I think our main problem will be the actual reprogramming: he'll have to remain unaware of the exchange."

"Morph gas while he's sleeping," Cottontail said shortly. "We can flood his quarters. That should really send him under. But given that his super-duper extra-special cyber system is operative at all times, does it record his dreams as well and anything that happens while he's not conscious?"

No-one could answer that, but with only a couple of days left until they reached Dryssicon, they could not waste time in finding out.

7: SAND AND STORM

The enormous asteroid to which the Dryssicon Major ore-processing station was anchored hove into view. The helmswoman's skills were put to the test in docking *Arianrhod* safely, for Ahxenta firmly refused to hand manoeuvring control of her precious ship to Port Control. A number of large ore-carriers were in for unloading, their chains of ore drones strung out behind them like lines of obedient ducklings, but few other trading vessels of note were visible. The proximity of the Dryssicon stations to the Belts and their location within the large Coalition-majority area of zone Alpha probably had much to do with it: few ships calling tended to stay longer than need be, especially if they had no links to the Coalition or to the Interstellar Systems Protectorate, the second main authority in the zone.

A couple of heavy cruisers that bore ISP insignia were positioned just off the network of large docking bays that hosted the facility's ore-carriers, no doubt because the governing council that directed the operations of both Dryssicon stations had requested ISP aid. If there were any ships from nearby systems providing extra military cover they were well hidden, for the *Arianrhod* could detect no sign of them.

Bick Micklemouse had intimated that he was eager to depart his current berth with his ship as quickly as possible, but his next port of call he was in no way eager to divulge. Ahxenta looked askance at her first mate and then looked the trader in the eye over the comm-holo.

"Weren't you, as a Coalition representative, supposed to fly with us to Dryssicon Major to indicate to whoever is causing the mischief out here that the Coalition, the Trades Alliance, Merkat's governing body and the rest of the good guys are all one big happy family and jointly seriously put out over it?" the captain asked him. "We should in that case have a quick meeting with the Dryssicon Council to bring them up to date. And we can bring in the ISP, as there *are* two ISP heavy cruisers hanging off my port bow."

The man gulped, clearly having forgotten his purported directive, but held firm. "I have deadlines," he told her. "As you have, Captain. Aren't you headed out to Burr Two for a cargo pick-up and then on to Veximer Prime?"

Ahxenta let go an inaudible sigh of relief as she gave a confirming nod: the reprogrammed patch that her medics and her senior science officer had used to overwrite the info-sent's data-log had evidently worked. She only hoped that the systems inhibitor that had been slipped into his last meal was also operating and was confusing his current data intake, as she did not want him picking up subliminal messages from her or her crew.

"I am," she said. "We'll take you over in a shuttle and transfer your ship to whichever of the berths Port Control assigns. I'll let you deal with the docking fees and the details of your ship's manifest with the port authorities yourself. I'll let you know when we're ready to go. Ahxenta out."

"He didn't like that," Apnis noted, grinning. "He wanted to fly her out himself."

"I bet he did. And he owes us for a berth for the *Gadfly*: she's still at Merkat and her overhaul's nearly complete. I'm tempted to send Azular down with the little sod, to make sure he has only pleasant memories of us," the captain said quietly. "He and Crizz have cleaned off whatever they coated his boat with, so it's ready for shipping. Lindell has agreed it with Dryssicon Port Control: they've apparently heard of Bick Micklemouse, so he's either a regular client or they know something about him that's worth remembering."

"Azular's still semi-cyber, so he may be able to figure it, and as he is what he is, he won't give anything away," Apnis stated. "He's also cleared for piloting all our shuttles. It would prevent one of our pilots unintentionally letting slip that our next stop isn't Burr Two."

"And if we do the transfer, whoever is controlling Micklemouse may just be convinced that we had no idea that his ship was in any way a danger to ours."

"Possibly," the first mate said doubtfully. "But if they're as smart and nasty as he thinks they are, I suspect they'll be quick to run their hands over it and him, just to check that they're both in the same state as previous. If we didn't have that stop-off at Vreskota Two and then the run to Xerophyte IV to do, I'd be tempted to stay here and watch developments."

"Can't be done, and that would only raise suspicions about us. We throw him out and go," the captain told her. "I'm also of a mind to link in with the Protectorate ships, but I'll let that hang fire as well. Lieutenant Gliss can get the usual updates on current events from the Dryssicon authorities and then we head out."

The Berzic science officer was deputed to ferry the trader to his destination whilst Chief Cottontail supervised the transfer of his ship to the bay assigned to it. Unable to attach a tracking device to the vessel lest it be discovered, she instead inserted a drone tracker into the energy cell that was used to power the transfer pod and suggested that the pod remain in the Dryssicon docking bay until *Arianrhod* was out that way again. It might not be of use stuck in the back of a small mooring station, but given that Micklemouse was first and foremost a shady dealer, she reckoned he might filch it or its energy cell before he left the station as a comeback for his enforced trip with them: the memories that Azular and the medics had inserted were a little less than pleasant, as it was no part of Ahxenta's purpose that the info-sent should relish a second voyage aboard her ship.

Azular on his return had little to report. Micklemouse was relieved to be at the end of his trip and was intent only on checking out his ship, picking up a consignment and getting as far from Dryssicon as possible. He intended to head for his usual hidey-hole of Mellifly, he had told the science officer, as he had a friend to see there. Azular was certain of the destination but sensed that the friend he spoke of was not someone he was looking forward to meeting. They parted on friendly terms – Azular had been the only one aboard the *Arianrhod* that had shown him any consideration at all was the trader's point of view, and he was glad to be shot of the lot of them.

As the science officer took up his station on the bridge and all boards glowed green, Ahxenta sighed.

"Let's get the hell out of here. Plot a course for Vreskota, Mr Box, and get us there as fast as possible, Ms Dox. It shouldn't take us too long and the drop-off will be quick," she added to Apnis. "Pycorp's orbital agro-station is set up to collect the gear and we've dealt with them before. Lindell can sort out the clearances and the fee transfers before we make port and our unloading teams will be ready. And as soon as we're clear of Vreskotan space, flight, set for the Drosophila Twelve planetary system and Xerophyte IV, best speed, avoiding any potentially hostile places, people and objects that we can."

"Vreskota Two and then Xerophyte IV, aye," Navigation Officer Box sang out as he set his initial coordinates. "We can make up time across zone Epsilon as there've been no recent reports of trouble and it *is* ISP. We can make for the Idledott beacon and then cross direct to Barfit at the node there. You've no hazards along that crossing," he added to his mate at the helm.

"Just take care we don't cut the edge of the Silverglass Nebula," was the reply. "And Drosophila's in Coalition space, so get the latest from comms on anything we need to look out for well before we get there and have jump lines programmed in. It's a long way and a lot of empty space. And you'd be surprised what can hide out in empty space," Romanna Dox informed him tartly.

The great ball of Drosophila Twelve hung incandescently yellow-white in the velvet black of space, extinguishing the fainter stars that spotted the vast starfield. It was the immensity of the empty spaces that caught at the heart strings and pulled the breath from the body, Cinnabar Ahxenta thought as, chin on fist, she watched the holo expand out over the forr'ad bridge section and down into the well of the bridge. The mantle of dark swept around the bright shape that marked *Arianrhod's* position on the expanding light grid that defined the space highways, netting the ship in a vast web within a nebulous starry shroud, and she seemed to be little more than a tiny pinpoint, moving no closer to her objective for all the minutes that dripped by like so many drops of syrup off a cosmic spoon. The ice-cold gleam of starlight unmasked had no warmth, no friendliness in it when it was merely the backdrop to nothingness.

"Steady as she goes," Ahxenta said almost automatically. "What's our ETA for orbital insertion, flight?"

"One hour, sixteen minutes, Captain," Romanna Dox responded.

"Good; let's have another look-see at the manifest and check that we have all the bits our customers ordered," Ahxenta said to Apnis. "Meanwhile, all stations, scanners at max and keep your eyes peeled: I want to know if we're the only major payload transport in the area. And keep a note of any traffic in and out of planet four's space, or hiding in any other nook and cranny within the system that our scanners will penetrate. If there's a whisper of an ion trail out there, I want to know about it."

A chorus of assent echoed around the bridge and the captain turned her attention to her own board, calling up the relevant holos and spreading them out before her with a flick of her hand.

"Interesting stuff Thystal Communications has ordered this time around, and there's a lot of it," she remarked to her first mate.

"The company's been on the level from the dealings we've had in the past, but we haven't been out this way in a long, long while and the reps are probably new. But the cargo's expensive and I agree it pays to keep tabs on these things, especially given the current galactic unrest. I'll have Gliss trawl through the planetary open comms systems to see if he can spot anything untoward."

"Cook it," responded Ahxenta, returning to the cargo manifest.

Xerophyte IV was a dry, desert-like world, sparsely settled and still primitive; it orbited as the fourth planet out from its primary like a golden yellow ball. The star system itself, Drosophila Twelve, had ten other planets, all of which were seriously uninhabitable and hardly worth exploiting for their mineral and other riches, a situation which did not appear to deter some of the more disreputable locals or a few less local aliens from nearby systems that often tried their luck, to the detriment of the more law-abiding natives of planet four.

The inhabitants of Xerophyte IV, or the Xerophytics as they were known, were on the whole a hospitable people. Their planet's main saving graces as a viable place for exploitation, apart from the almost endless sunshine, were vast deposits of useable mineral oil a long way beneath the surface and several highly-prized gem mines closer to the ground. Oases of greenery were dotted here and there, particularly near the planet's northern and southern limits, and these formed the chief habitable parts. The main continent was titled Xeroph Comma and the foremost settled area on a world of few such areas was Xeroph Township One and its ring of satellite villages. The township itself was unattractive, stretching like a dirty crumpled cloth across the desert landscape, its mostly single level dwellings hewn from various lumps of native rock that had not crumbled to sand over the millennia.

"The *Red Sunset's* the best place for a night on the town," Ahxenta reminded her first mate, stretching luxuriously as she released her cramped muscles from the confines of her command chair after signing off the last of the accounts. "The brew's half decent and the food's not bad either. At least that *was* the case when we were last here, but that was a few years and a few wrinkles ago now."

"As long as you're paying, I'll follow you to the gates of hell. In fact I have done on several occasions, if I recall," Apnis responded. "Lead on, Captain."

Their cargo of costly crystal comms components had been safely delivered and what was more, paid for, an hour or so before and the captain had decreed a spell of shore leave for as many crew members as had requested, on a rotational basis, as *Arianrhod* was not due to her next pick-up spot at mining station Brown Amber for a few days by ship's chronometer and they had time in hand. She and Apnis were fitting their furlough in early, in order that their heads would be in one piece for the onward journey.

Leaving the bridge in the capable hands of second mate Whisper Earbleat, the two officers headed down to the crew levels to collect their planetside gear from their quarters. In short order, they made their way to their ride, joining a handful of fellow crewmembers who were packing themselves into one of the smaller shuttles. The craft slipped quietly out of one of the *Arianrhod's* rear docking bays and made for the outer reaches of Township One, where landing facilities were available for a reasonable fee and various transport options were accessible for onward travel.

The *Red Sunset* was a small bar-restaurant down one of the dusty side streets out from the central and more crowded series of main squares of Xeroph Township One. The dark had fallen suddenly, as it always did on most of the settlements of Xeroph Comma, and the night life of the place was beginning to revive after the heat of the day. As they walked through the door of the place, a solidly real door, unlike the holo entries of many bars, the jangling noise of a musical instrument being tortured by the musician attached to it hit their ears.

"Nothing changes," Ahxenta murmured to her companion as she led the way to a small table at the far side and sat down with her back to the wall to survey her surroundings.

"Don't recognise any of the staff, but then I can't recall who they were the last time I was here," Apnis called out above the racket.

The captain tabbed the menu, scrutinised the contents and made her choice. The first mate did likewise.

"Keep your hand on your gun," Ahxenta advised. "I'll have to go order and pay up front at the bar: this place is as far from civilisation as you can get on a dark night in the middle of nowhere."

The food was hot and spicy when it did arrive and the beer was as good as promised. With the exception of a few curious glances at the unfamiliar uniforms, the two were left severely alone. Apart from one or two local ships, the *Arianrhod* was the only other vessel currently in orbit and it must have been obvious to the majority of locals that the two hailed from thence. After about an hour however, a couple of other customers had thawed sufficiently to approach and exchange a few words; they were also possibly taking stock of the newcomers and gauging their chances of dunning them out of a few credits. One recognised the insignia that both women bore on their jackets; the fact that their badges clearly said *PSS Arianrhod* was almost certainly the giveaway, but it was in a way gratifying that the *Arianrhod* had been heard of even in this neck of the galactic woods.

The two were joined by a few crewmates, including Dr Flintlock, and soon the place became more comparable to a friendly session in their own ship's mess. A handful of natives added to the company and the tales and the beer went round as customers came and went and the odd spillage and breakage was cleared away. Apart from one bout of fisticuffs that was competently dealt with by the *Red Sunset's* resident heavy mob, there was no overt trouble and a couple of hours passed away pleasantly.

The captain and first mate had booked rooms at a nearby hotel as they had meetings with their principal client earmarked for early the following planetary day. Their client's head rep had indicated that his company would like another consignment of comms modules and had invited them in to discuss details. Proposing to check up on the availability and cost of such freight with her supercargo, Ahxenta had decided to call a halt sooner rather than later and so bid goodbye to the crowd around the table and set off alone, eschewing the company of Apnis and Flintlock and saying that she would see them later.

The hotel was a few blocks away, down narrow and dusty streets and on the edge of one of the larger of the central squares. Looming buildings still held in a goodly amount of the heat of the day and the air was warm yet and tinged with desert dust. A few windows faced into the raised sidewalks that edged the streets but all were uniformly shuttered in some opaque material that ensured that passers-by could not peek in. The Xerophytics evidently had reliable eyesight, for the roads were badly lit, but remembering her way the captain strode forward confidently.

The blow was unexpected and Ahxenta turned, stunned, to see a face she did not recognise looming over her. In the dim light she could see that it was light in colour, had one dark diagonal streak across it and the mouth was smiling crookedly, but otherwise it looked human enough. That was all that registered as the captain automatically struck out in defence. One too many or not, she was still capable of putting up a fight when necessary. The being's smile vanished, to be replaced by a spurt of blood, but another blow caught the captain from behind and she staggered. The second assailant squealed loudly as Ahxenta's boot-heel caught him. He stepped back, and drawing a small gun, he fired. She gasped in pain, hearing the first of the two thugs rasp out in a hurried whisper,

"Get her off the damn street!"

A large dark shadow emerged from against a blank plate in the wall that was obviously a door and grabbed the *Arianrhod's* captain in a vice-like grip around her waist, heaving her easily off her feet. "In here!" it said urgently.

All four tumbled through the door, which shut like a hissing snake behind them. The floor felt dry and sandy to Ahxenta's groping hand but she had no time to do more than turn and lash out at her closest assailant before she felt her senses reel from a blow to her head.

"Cut that, damn you!" bawled one of the three who had caught the end of the swipe. "Get her weapons – she'll have plenty."

The captain struggled as her phase rifle was taken and two pairs of hands began a search of her clothing for other arms. She was pulled into what seemed to be an inner room, but it was barely light and she had trouble adjusting her eyes to the gloom. With a final kick she was thrown against a wall and the light slowly grew as the three, dressed alike in dark and enveloping clothing, stepped backwards and away from her. A very large armament of some sort in the light-faced one's hands was raised menacingly.

They were rather tall by normal Xerophytic standards but looked humanoid nonetheless. As far as she could tell the three were male. The illumination was too poor to make out details, but Ahxenta had no illusions: they were a nasty trio and a pleasant discussion was obviously the last thing on their minds. She made it to her feet, but before she could raise a hand a fizzing sound hit her ears and with it a tight beam of dazzling energy that hit her like a blast of hot air.

It was akin to being borne down by a great weight of atmosphere that was getting heavier second by second, a mantle that wrapped and tightened, constricting effort and impeding flight. Breathing became laboured, sweat poured out of every pore and the burden of the body became a burden of the mind. As she dropped to one knee, a corner of Ahxenta's brain sparked into life and she forced her numbed hand to unzip and creep inside her jacket and into a concealed underarm pocket. The small device she abstracted felt cold and metallic as she clasped it within her palm. She forced her hand out, up to her mouth, compelling her frozen fingers to operate. With her teeth she pulled the clip, tearing it away as she pushed up the activation switch. At the same time she bunched up and hurled herself with the last of her strength at the three dark-clad figures, trying to take them down like ninepins. She could almost hear their laughs as they avoided her with ease, jumping out of the way and turning back towards her as she rolled past them, the tall one raising his weapon for another blast of the stun beam.

Boom… The dull bellowing thud seemed to come from all around as it echoed off the walls. It was all the time she needed. Her upper weapons they had taken: the small but deadly phase pistol in her boot they had missed. It was out and in her hand and she had no intention of missing or of checking to see if it was set to still or kill. Her rigid finger tightened on the grip and a blue beam seared across the space between her and her adversaries. One down… Two down… The fractional delay of the third was his undoing and he caught the third shot on his shoulder. It spun him round and he dropped.

Ahxenta scrabbled up her sleeve to set the distress on her wrist communit and then dug another tiny sound bomb out of her pocket: she was taking no chances that the three on the floor had friends in dark places and that reinforcements were on their way. The pain of the stun beam was lessening and she swept the room with her eyes. Her weapons had been thrown down by the door. She collected them hurriedly, crawling around her erstwhile assailants, all three of whom were completely out cold.

After taking the time to disarm the other weapons she could see and to search the bodies for those she could not and treat them likewise, the captain stepped warily through the door into the murk of the outer room, her heart thumping, achingly aware of every blow and still numbed by the stun beam. A moment to adjust to the low light level and she sealed the door at her back, sliding along the wall to find the street exit. The rising hum of her communit warned her of company close by and she paused, raising her phase rifle.

"It's the Cap," Ahxenta heard the relieved voice of Tallica Apnis call from beyond. "Stand back, Cinnabar, it's us."

A short hiss and flash denoted the destruction of the door plate and its lock. The first mate of the *Arianrhod* appeared in the opening gap, to be met with a rifle in her face.

"It *is* us, Cap," Apnis assured her.

Ahxenta lowered her weapon and groaned in relief.

"We're getting out of here," the first mate said. "There's a bunch of feet heading this way and I don't like the tune they're playing on the sidewalk. I'll freeze this door but it won't hold. Flintlock and Hanx, get the captain between you. We're moving now."

The quartet moved swiftly but quietly along the street and away from the approaching footfalls. Whoever they were, they stopped just outside the door that Ahxenta had lately departed. Apnis led the way, with Ensign Hanx keeping one eye on the captain and the other on their rear. Deeming it unwise to make directly for the hotel, the first mate ordered *Arianrhod's* berthed shuttle to stand by and directed her team to make for the nearest hover-stand to capture transport.

The hover owner at first assumed that his potential passengers were drunk, but the business end of a phase rifle in his face soon convinced him that they were merely in a hurry and he allowed them to board, stipulating only that they paid in advance. He made good time to the shuttle in its bay out at the end of the less settled area of town and dropped them off close by the small craft.

Once safely sealed inside the shuttle, Apnis left Flintlock to check the captain out and called the situation in to Earbleat, ordering her to contact their crew on leave and warn them of potential hostiles in their vicinity. As the captain had clearly been targeted, the first mate had to assume that other crew members were also in danger. Ahxenta was able to add in the few details that she recalled of her assailants, but where and how they picked up her trail she could not tell. They may well have followed her from the bar, but she was fairly sure she would have been aware of them: wary as she habitually was, she was not one to miss that sort of detail.

Security Officer Hanx suggested that the captain's departure may have been noted by a person in the bar and the information passed on to others elsewhere. A discreet questioning of the bar staff of the *Red Sunset* would be a good place to start, the young ensign hinted, his eyes lighting a fraction.

"No you don't, Ensign," Apnis told him. "Not unless you've got one of your senior officers or Dr Azular with you. How do you feel, Cinnabar?" she added to the captain before he could argue the point. "You look like you took quite a pounding."

"I'll live," was the gruff response as she removed the doctor's hand and its attached soothing wipe. "But I want to know who those bozos were, why they went for me and who put them up to it."

"Micklemouse…" began the first mate.

"Would hardly have had time to get back to his den on Mellifly, but that can't be discounted. But hell knows we have enough enemies without him. One roughneck had a light face with a dark stripe across it, so that would be a place to start. His mouth was twisted as well; there can't be many with that look, though the face may have been a disguise. And they were all pretty tall for locals. They didn't kill me, so they wanted me alive. Find out what you can about the place they dragged me to. I couldn't make much out, but it was empty and the floor was gritty – there may be traces under my fingernails, so check it out, Doc."

"I reckon there are traces of a lot of things under your fingernails, Cap," Flintlock responded. "I'll see if I can pick up any bio-indicators that might give us a clue to your attackers, but it's probably a long shot. So who knew we were headed to Xerophyte apart from our crew and our main clients?"

"Depends what the clients told their staff, their other suppliers, other clients, the Port Authority, their grandmothers and their friends in the bar, to name but a few," Apnis said sourly. "Half the township has probably known for days. And who's that knocking on the door?" she added irritably as the external link buzzed loudly.

"Lieutenant Kelsitt," Hanx told them, eyeing the viewer.

"Let him in, he can pilot us back aboard," she ordered.

"We've got hotel rooms booked," Ahxenta said thickly.

"Too bad, Cap, you're heading back aboard so that the Doc can get you properly looked over. Some of our crew down here can use the bookings; I'll let Lindell know."

"I concur," Flintlock put in. "I want you in medbay for the next several hours."

Knowing when she was beaten, the captain agreed.

Early the following morning, Ahxenta, Apnis and Lindell shuttled out to meet with their clients, whilst Azular, with a pair of security guards as back-up, set off for a meeting with of the staff of the *Red Sunset*.

Late the night before, the science officer and two of *Arianrhod's* security team had made it their business to quiz the regular workers in the *Red Sunset* for any clues as to who might have carried out the attack on the captain. All had emphatically denied knowledge of the incident and refused to give their opinions as to who might be behind it. The only one in Azular's view that was holding back was one of the *Red Sunset's* watchdogs who kept the peace between patrons whilst mopping the floor and collecting glassware. Outwardly a hard-faced woman, she had shrewdly scrutinised the inquisitorial officers but kept her mouth tightly shut. Azular had not pursued the issue at that point as he was sure that there was more to Ms Molli Warweft than met the eye.

Whilst questioning the one or two topers who had been unable to make it out the door at closing time, the science officer had scanned his environs, including the tall guard. She appeared to be Xerophytic but was smarter than most, as she knew exactly what he was at and was understandably annoyed. She had suggested the tryst in a quiet moment and had passed Azular a token of her legitimacy. He had recognised the insignia immediately and agreed.

The small apartment was tucked in at the back of a store that sold cheap clothing and was accessed by a constricted lane down one side. Like many dwellings on the planet it was hewn from the local dusty yellow stone and was barred by an old metallic door that slid into the wall. Azular and his aides, who were in casual wear, were greeted by a curt nod and directed to seats at a central table. Warweft evidently meant business.

"I expected your commanding officer," she said abruptly to the science officer as the four sat down.

"She's busy; she sent me," he replied equally curtly and then made straight for his point. "What's a member of ISP Intelligence Division doing rounding up drunks in a downmarket bar like the *Red Sunset*, Commander?"

She curled her lip at the *Commander*. "You've been checking up on me. How come you have access to that kind of information?"

"We have access to a great deal of information: our lives depend on it," Azular told her. "And you haven't answered the question. This place seems a long way off the beaten track to be of interest to the Interstellar Systems Protectorate, unless something big is going on."

"Something big *is* going on. Your people will no doubt be well aware of the recent spate of attacks on various shipping lines from here to the Belts and all points between and beyond."

"Here?" he questioned.

"Yes here. At least, here might be one of the places where these raiders pick up some of their supplies. It's out of the way, its currency is often untraceable gems and certain of the locals don't tend to ask too many questions or report their hurts or losses to authority. As a native of these parts once, I was considered a good candidate for a recon detail and I've been here for about thirty standard days. You're Berzic, aren't you?"

"You know I am," Azular said icily, his eyes narrowing shrewdly. "You've been scanning all three of us from the time we turned off the main street. And you'll know we're armed and have implanted locating pins, which *are* being monitored by our own people. So what does the ISP think is going on, and what has it to do with our ship and our captain? Why was she attacked?"

"How is your captain?" Warweft asked with apparent solicitude.

"Fine. Please answer the question; you were the one who asked for this meeting after all."

The woman grimaced. "The ISP has little clue as to what exactly is going on. The attacks are being carried out by unknowns, as far as we can tell. Both Coalition and Non-Treaty Alliance governing bodies are crying foul and scrutiny of debris in areas where alleged attacks have taken place have suggested, but not proved, that our ever-nasty quasi-local raiders may not be the culprits, unless they've suddenly come into seriously new tech. As the bags of scum have taken some losses recently – one or two at the hands of the *Arianrhod* – it's unlikely they've got the funds for either new fighters or new base ships. So that leads us to knowns that have suddenly and very quietly come up with the tech, knowns that have been developing it in secret for quite a while, or unknowns. You're either a very good hand at poker or this is not news to you."

"Why was our captain attacked?" Azular again demanded.

Warweft sighed. "Quite frankly, I'm not certain. But your cargo of pricy crystal comms components for Thystal Comms has not gone unnoticed in some sleazy backwaters around here and I understand that Thystal wants to talk new business, presumably for the supply of more components."

She held up a hand to forestall the question. "People in bars talk. Why do you think I went there for a job? And Thystal is practically on the doorstep. It's possible that Xerophyte IV is one of the sources of supply for these marauders that have recently surfaced in almost every zone of the mapped galaxy: they would have to find resources and dealers somewhere and this is as out of the way a place as most. And they're not likely to draft in ships that fly under the Trades Alliance flag to provide them, or in fact any regular mercantile line. Where *do* you get the supplies you bring in anyway? You have to get them someplace that lets you sell them on at a decent profit or it wouldn't be worth your while bringing them all the way out here."

"That's none of your business," the Berzic officer told her.

"Fair enough. But it *is* one possible reason that your captain was targeted: ransom for a supply of classy goods or information on the same. Or maybe it was retribution for *Arianrhod's* part in putting the scuppers on raiders and others of a vicious persuasion – your ship's rather well-known for putting up a good fight and usually winning. Are you any further forward on who the attackers were?"

Azular looked at the woman, reading her as far as he was able. She had been well trained and had some skill at keeping her thoughts and emotions to herself, but he was sure that she was trustworthy, at least to some extent.

"There were three, male, tall for Xerophytics and strong. One was pale-faced, with a dark diagonal streak from his left eye, across his nose to the edge of his lip, and he had a twisted mouth. They were packing heavy weaponry and the captain was taken to a lodging one street down from the *Red Sunset* that was empty and had been out of use for some time as living quarters. The three had accomplices that were close behind but we don't know if the attackers sent a message for reinforcements or it was planned in advance."

Warweft pondered. "The face I don't recognise but it may have been altered. There *is* a twisted mouth that's been in the *Red Sunset* a couple of times recently and it's been attached to a lanky roughneck wearing dock-rat fatigues, though half the customers that come in are off-duty dock-rats: Township One is the major port around here after all. The guy in question has been in with one or two mates but they haven't caused trouble, at least when I've been on duty. I'm back there in a couple of hours: I'll see what I can find out. I take it you'll be around that long?"

"We will," Azular informed her. "If these people are not locals, who are they likely to be?"

"Tall for Xerophytics? That's not much to go on, but all three were tall, you said."

"Yes. As you are," the science officer pointed out.

"I am. One of the reasons I left home: I got singled out for fights rather too often for comfort. But I *am* Xerophytic – your perps may not be. I'll get back to you."

Azular nodded briefly. "You know where to find me."

8: COURSE CHANGE

The *Arianrhod* sat serenely in her assigned dock. There had been no hint of trouble either planetside or in the near reaches of the system, apart from the usual scuffles of the lower orders that were always to be found where people gathered, but the crew remained at full alert. Ahxenta had called a meeting of her senior officers to discuss her mission to the surface and the results of her science officer's meeting with the ISP operative.

The captain had gone into the Thystal Comms company offices more cautiously than usual: she knew her chief client, having done business on previous occasions, but several of his team were new to her. Apnis and Lindell were equally wary and without giving away the events of the previous evening, they all took close stock of their hosts during the talks. That Thystal wanted a quantity of extra comms parts was a mystery in itself and the chief negotiator would not divulge the reason. In Ahxenta's opinion the man was nervous and rather in awe of one of his associates, Hoxiz, who when called on to contribute, had pressed forcefully for a good price and early delivery.

The astute Lindell, having sourced the necessary goods and well aware of the cost to the *Arianrhod*, played his part calmly and quoted the top price that he and the captain had agreed between them, to take in collection, storage, shipping and the inevitable risks run in the cargo trade. He made play of the growing levels of hazard to vessels in the space highways as a result of the attacks by raiders and others with eyes on the sometimes expensive consignments carried. This cut no ice with Thystal agent Hoxiz, who seemed to be a poor choice of representative, far from diplomatic and belligerent. The talks ended in stalemate, as Ahxenta refused to sell her crew or herself short and had other business in hand in any case.

Azular had received no word from Warweft but was not unduly concerned as her current shift would last for several hours. He, with the agreement of *Arianrhod's* security chief Jay Goldwash, had sent two officers in civilian attire out on the streets; they were due into the *Red Sunset* shortly. As he had not told the ISP agent that analyses of the samples that Flintlock had abstracted from various areas of the captain's anatomy implied that at least one of her assailants was part-Friskianx, he awaited her comm with interest.

Further tests by Flintlock and Azular had revealed that the dust residues Ahxenta had picked up from the place she had been taken were indicative of packing material originating from Keystone Kell, the natives of which were known in some circles as suppliers of first-class arms. In fact, some of the heavier hand weapons carried by *Arianrhod's* crew had been sourced there. One of the inferences from that nugget had to be that the place was or had been used for the storage or transfer of weapons or similar.

The captain was clear on business as far as Thystal Comms was concerned: no deal would be struck. Both she and her officers had registered the tense quality of the meeting and the company premises seemed to be full of scurrying individuals intent on keeping a low profile. There was an atmosphere of fear that had not been lost on the three visitors, none of whom were able to fathom the reason. That being the case, it was possible that the suggestion by Warweft that Xerophyte IV might be a supply source for the faceless attackers that had recently and ominously emerged to harass the local galactic sectors had some basis.

It was as they were discussing this idea that the expected link came through for Azular from the ISP officer, who seemed to be back in her own apartment. After introductions, Warweft made straight for the point: the tall man with the twisted mouth that she had noted had shown his face in the *Red Sunset* only an hour ago; he was dressed in the habitual outfit of a dock-worker and was with two others, also tall and garbed as dock-rats. One of his friends displayed a bruised face and an unhealed cut to his left cheek. From their talk, they had just finished a shift in docking bay Red Seven, unloading a freighter that had recently come in.

"Red Seven?" Crizz Cottontail repeated. "One over from us. Now isn't that handy?"

"I didn't get details of the cargo they were shifting but I got a bio sample from twisted mouth. I've run it and it checks out as Friskianx, but there are traces of various substances in the sample that suggest he's got cyber implants."

"An info-sent?" Apnis demanded.

"No, I don't think so," Warweft said. "Not with the attitude and the amount of ale he was swigging. I recorded tiny amounts of meta-jurillium absorption products, probably from the implants. But he also had traces of serocepcin in his system."

"What's that?" Ahxenta enquired.

"A drug that's often given to genetically-altered individuals after treatment to aid them in adaptation to their new status," Azular said quietly, raising a mobile eyebrow. "What kind of sample did you have?" he asked the agent. "It must have been quite sizeable."

"Urine," was the wry response. "And don't ask how I got it. I also noted dark stains on his hands that may have come from skin paint; micro-traces transferred to the mug he used. It's a common cosmetic colour, if my auto-sampler read it correctly. So he may be one of your attackers, Captain. But as to the motivation for the attack on you, I'm no closer. I did not bug them, nor did I scan them: I'm sure it would have been spotted and I've no intention of blowing my own cover. For all their hard drinking, all three kept one eye on the door."

"What do you know about arms smuggling in this system?" the captain put in suddenly.

Warweft might have been surprised by the change of tack implied by the question but answered equably that it happened. Wherever there was a port facility open to anyone that paid docking fees, illegal weapons trafficking was one of the known problems. Xerophyte IV had the added advantage of being off the beaten space highway and hence was well away from the majority of judicial eyes and ears: the perfect place to outfit ships clandestinely.

"But not build ships," Cottontail put in, shaking her head.

"Not build. Somebody would notice," Warweft grinned. "But it would make sense to outfit new ships close enough to the sources of equipment they would need. Like comms components. How did your meet with Thystal Communications go?" she asked.

"Didn't you pick that up in the main bar of the *Red Sunset* earlier?" Apnis interjected.

"No. I may do shortly, on the late shift."

Ahxenta had been considering their new acquaintance astutely. "No deal. And there won't be. They're not offering enough for me to stick my neck – or my crew's – out. But something or someone at Thystal has got half the staff running scared. It might be worth your while to check it out."

"I see. Do you have a name?" Warweft asked.

"Hoxiz – a confrontational type and nasty with it. Nothing else."

"Thanks. I'll catch up with you later."

"You won't. Once we've run our systems checks, we're leaving. We have other deadlines."

"Then I'll hope to see you again some time, Captain."

"Likewise, Commander Warweft – if that's your real name."

The only answer was a smile as the ISP agent signed out.

After a pause long enough to ascertain that the connection had been cut, the first mate turned to Ahxenta.

"Once we've run our systems checks? Once all the crew's back on board you mean, Cap," she said.

"I know. So you'd best recall your two scouts, Azular. And Crizz, I want you to run discreet checks on our next door neighbours. Their freight manifest you won't be able to get, but their size and origin you might. Lindell, you help: you'll have your own sources. Everyone else, dismissed. We have a ship to ready for departure."

The freighter in docking bay Red Seven was a typical vessel out of Drosophila Two, a bordering system with one inhabited planet that majored in agricultural produce, much of which was circulated locally as food concentrates of various forms. It was Cottontail's opinion that almost anything could be hidden in a shipment of essential chow and very few would look at such a ship or her manifest with overt interest, but despite Lindell's assistance, the engineer's poking around came to naught. The two security personnel that the senior science officer had commandeered for his own purposes had little more to report than that they had missed the three dock-workers spotted by Warweft. They had, however, got into conversation with another brace of dock-rats who had little to say on the freighter in Red Seven but much to say on the attack on the *Arianrhod's* captain.

It was apparently common knowledge that Ahxenta had been captured and detained for a short time the day before by three thugs intent on robbery but she had beaten all three to a pulp and made her escape without a shot being fired. Her street-cred had been upped again, as it was also a well-known fact that she had been seen about her business that morning without a scratch. The two barflies refused to name their sources and had no view on what the captain's business was. They were likewise in no way curious: they did not want to find themselves on her hit-list of people to be kept in order.

Such being the state of play, Ahxenta gave the orders for slipping *Arianrhod's* moorings and setting a heading for Merkat's commercial space dock. The latter was to fool any would-be trackers or any leaks in communications. Their actual heading of the Brown Amber station would be set later, and during the initial part of the journey, every spare member of the crew was set to scour the outside of *Arianrhod's* hull with short-range scanners lest something had been planted that had outwitted ship's security.

The copper glow of gem mining station Brown Amber lit the dark like a beacon. The crew of *Arianrhod* knew the place; they had been there numerous times to haggle over a bucket-load of raw diamonds or other valuable crystals that, once cut, polished and array-set by a friend of Captain Ahxenta's on Freskat Six, could fetch a fair profit on several open markets. And if profits were high, bonuses were good: Ahxenta rewarded her crew well for hard work and honest labour, especially after a visit to a place like Amber, a little further from the edge of the Belts than the majority of mining stations and hence not in the most salubrious location as far as outside intrusion, particularly that of raiders, was concerned.

"Keep the outlaws off our backs for as long as it takes to agree the price of what the Brownies have in hand to peddle and we're credits in," navigator Box remarked to his companion at the helm.

"Tactical and weapons best have their eyes peeled and their hands at the ready in that case," Romanna Dox replied good-humouredly.

Box and Dox smirked at one another and cast speculative glances at their comrades at the relevant stations.

"I heard that," Lieutenant Commander Whisper Earbleat at main weapons called out in the carrying voice that belied her name. "You two do your jobs and we'll do ours."

"Cut it," Apnis directed them from the command chair. "Comms, keep close tabs on the captain and the team on the station: little as I trust the Brownies, I trust many of their clients even less and there are a few in at the moment I wouldn't have as shipmates."

"Aye, Commander," was the response from chief communications officer Lieutenant Lynxi Bellfish. "The captain and Ensign Hanx are now in the main marketing suite with two others as far as I can tell, but the Brownies have suppression systems in operation around all their installations so I can't get much more than their life signs."

"Keep a close watch on those, Mr Bellfish; you too, Azular."

Ever since the captain's encounter on Xerophyte IV with the trio of undesirables, the first mate had been adamant that all off-ship missions be accompanied and that each crew member wore a locating pin. The current pick-up was not expected to take long but they were taking no chances. As well as Hanx, Apnis had assigned two other security guards to the captain's party. They were perforce stationed outside the marketing area: the Brownies were a tad touchy when it came to numbers, preferring that they had more of their own and those more heavily armed, in view of the nature of most of their merchandise, but they tolerated customers' reinforcements within reason. Bellfish reported that their two additional crew were also still animate and in their rightful positions.

"Good. Keep monitoring ship to surface comms as well and every commercial channel you can," Apnis ordered. "I don't want to miss anything. Science and tactical, check out our neighbouring vessels to see who they are and what they're up to: it might be a long shot but I'd like to know what this gang of no-goods is doing at Brown Amber. A lot of them don't look like the usual gem-grabbers."

By the time the captain had returned to the ship the limited data collected by ship's stations gave the senior staff something to chew over. Apart from the usual dilapidated one- or two-man traders out to scrape a living by buying and selling small quantities of gems from minor-league prospectors, a couple of their companion vessels were both more heavily-armed and newer than the usual run of freighters that hove into Brown Amber. From what the inquisitive Azular could make out, most of the larger ships were trading vessels, a fair number from Coalition and Non-Treaty Alliance systems and one or two independents, but almost all chose to keep their identities and their business under wraps. The senior science officer had noted that *Arianrhod* was the object of scanning by at least two other vessels, but her shields were sophisticated enough to foil their probes.

Bellfish had kept a close watch on detectable comms to and from vessels in the vicinity, but little had leaked out. The industrial news channels were majoring in the rising numbers of attacks on shipping and the resultant impacts on trade, and skirmishes in nearby sectors between various opposing factions. One local network had included an item on an upsurge in shipbuilding in a number of worlds allied to both Coalition and Non-Treaty Alliance parties. The former included Jurgall Three, a remote colony world of the Friskianx League. Jurgall was known as a minor source of meta-jurillium ore, the abstraction of which was time-consuming and hazardous. The planet supported a small processing station and operated on a shoestring, but as it was obliged to charge a sizable fee for its products, it improved its credit-rating by manufacturing small hull sections in situ and shipping them elsewhere. It now seemed that the colony was expanding its remit.

The comms officer was curious and had tried to dig up more on the Jurgall Three outpost and its trade but apart from advertising promoting the colony as an alternative source of meta-jurillium and as a place actively recruiting mining and associated workers, he found little. Lynxi Bellfish was no fool and checked over the jobs on offer. Construction workers with experience in large-scale projects such as space dock assembly were wanted for various areas in the Friskianx League, but all applications were routed through a central office and location could not be guaranteed. Nevertheless, it was an interesting development and something to think about as the *Arianrhod*, her cargo uplift complete, set off for her next stopover, which involved a long haul to the ISP-majority area of zone Lambda.

The home and business of Captain Ahxenta's contact was located on Freskat Six, a world of many small scattered settlements. The system itself was some way off the more well-travelled space highways but commanded prestige as a novel travel destination by its proximity to the spectacular Ginseng Nebula. Several pilots used the place as their base and could be relied upon to produce a yarn or two when off duty. Whilst the captain, in mufti, took a small shuttle down with the goods to spend a little time with her friend, talk terms and catch up on local gossip, assorted members of her crew were already in the main settlement to take advantage of the short spell of shore leave she had sanctioned.

The news in the Freskat neck of the galactic sector mirrored that elsewhere, but the Freski were no more than marginally concerned, as their system had intrinsically nothing of great value apart from the view from its peripheries. That other worlds were gearing up for action on some frontier or other was now common knowledge across hyperspace comms channels, but apart from a little increase in trade for one or two local concerns that specialised in minor engineering components, little was felt there. The only nugget that Azular picked up from a sortie to a local bar was that one pilot, who had been ferrying a bunch of small-time archaeologists back from a long-haul trip out by the Starglass Nebula, had reported that his passengers' base station had been buzzed by a tiny ship that looked like some sort of fighter, but the craft had veered off when it realised that it was being scanned and had not returned. As the pilot was rather reticent about the identities of his passengers, Azular could only assume that they were not part of an authorised expedition.

Arianrhod had departed Freskat space several standard days before and was almost at the crossover from zone Lambda to zone Beta and on a heading for Merkat when Ahxenta received an urgent link, to be taken in private. As the captain returned to the bridge from her office with a thoughtful look, the bridge crew furtively glanced her way, their ears at full attention.

"Change of destination, Mr Box," she instructed her navigator, raising an eyebrow at her first mate as she slid into her chair. "Set to bypass Merkat and make for the Orriga sector, best speed."

"Orriga sector, aye," Box responded, making a face at his sidekick at the helm.

"Best speed, aye," Romanna Dox echoed as she complied.

"So what's up, Cap?" demanded Apnis.

"A request from the main planetary affairs office of ISP HQ out at Skyrtek Key: they want a supply of processed beta-jurillium that's waiting at Orriga Two's Helleborus Station and they need it quickly. It's to resupply their shipbuilding dock off Skyrtek Prime."

"Interstellar Systems Protectorate's upping the fleet ante, then?" Apnis shrugged. "The Friskies seem to be building more docks, other Coalition and Non-Treaty Alliance systems are in a frenzy of boat-building and even Freskat's into the supply of smaller ships' pieces; and the systems that aren't in the middle of all this are arguing with each other over territorial rights and what have you. The galaxy's going to hell in a hurry, by the sound of it. Which means trade picks up for us I guess, but all this mayhem means it's a helluva lot more dangerous out there. But we're a long way from Helleborus; you'd think they'd have called on some ship nearer in. And where does it leave our scheduling? Skyrtek's in central zone Epsilon."

"Our schedule's on hold. And the ISP won't know where we are, or shouldn't – our business is our own concern. I'll go and discuss things with Lindell and see how we go from here. You take the conn and I'll see you in a bit."

Requests from bodies such as the ISP were rare enough, Ahxenta pondered as she made her way down to the supercargo's office, but given the urgency of the appeal and its nature, she had no thought of refusing the contract. It was as well to keep on good terms with the ISP and the captain strongly suspected that the reason for resupply of the Skyrtek Prime shipbuilding dock was that the apparent spate of shipbuilding and similar military activity that was currently ongoing had a lot to do with the upsurge in the number and ferocity of the recent attacks on ships and the annexation of the main planet of the Marridan System. Her supercargo concurred, and they set themselves to rearranging *Arianrhod's* flight and cargo schedules to minimise their losses time-wise.

The Orriga sector contained amongst other areas of interest the

Orriga Two asteroid field. This area of space was located at the more populous end of the Outer Reaches Archipelago but was still remote. It had been settled by miners and their associated trades for decades, however, because of the wealth of rare ores contained in many of its constituent bodies. One such ore was beta-jurillium, the processed version of which was prized in shipbuilding as a less costly substitute for the preferred meta-jurillium alloy as hull protection.

It would take the ship many days standard to reach the Orriga sector even at best speed, Ahxenta knew, and that being the case she decided that apart from readying the outer cargo bays for the load, it would be a good idea to ensure that the ship's armaments and her shuttles and ancillary accoutrements were in tip-top condition. A bit of tactical drill would not go amiss either, she informed Apnis. Even though the *Arianrhod* was a private vessel, she was run on military lines and her captain was adamant that her crew would not be found wanting in any situation.

"Damn shit!" The expletive rang around the bridge as the duty officer bawled for the red alert and demanded the presence of the captain and the first mate at the double. "All crew to battlestations!" was his next order.

Moments later, Ahxenta, with Apnis, Cottontail and Earbleat on her heels, pounded onto the bridge. The main holo-generator was set up in full view and the four took their places amid the wails of the alert and the calls of crew that all shields were at maximum and that phase cannons were powering up.

"It just popped out of hyperspace, Cap," duty officer Lieutenant Pollux Gliss announced as the ship reeled to a sonic shock wave that hit her hull. "Saw us and the guns started blazing."

"Evasive!" Ahxenta bellowed at the helmswoman. "Expand the view and get me full tactical! Earbleat, get a bead on that and hit it with the best you've got. And I want fighters standing by."

"Cap, you're not going to launch fighters against that?" Apnis asked as the enormous black ship swept across the field of view as the *Arianrhod* banked and swerved.

"Not unless I have to. Tactical, get me the lowdown on that ship. I want to know everything you can read from her. Azular, you get all you can and check for anything remotely like it in our databanks."

"She's shielded so completely we'll not get clear readings. But I think I've seen that shape somewhere before…" Apnis said grimly.

"You and me both. Unless I miss my guess, that's the frigging battle-bucket that ambushed the *Obsidian Sky* – or one out of same pack. Tactical, compare your readouts with the *Obsidian's* data."

"Matches what we got from the *Obsidian*, Captain," Gliss verified. "Same configuration and I have no other records that match those."

"Confirmed," Azular concurred. "Nothing in my databanks either. There *are* parallels with raider cruiser or dreadnought types but she's at least three times the size of anything we've met before, bar cargo and transport vessels."

"Armaments appear to be phase cannon and slicer beams and she's bristling with more than enough torpedo emplacements to take us out twice. She's targeting!" Gliss warned.

"Launch deflecting drones! And target her surface comms, I want her blind and deaf!" Ahxenta ordered the weapons chief, her eyes darting across the massive shape as all the information that the bridge stations could glean were displayed across the bridge holo.

Apnis had inserted herself into an auxiliary weapons station next to Earbleat and was targeting what she deemed to be the fighter bays of the attacking ship. The last thing they needed was an assault by smaller craft released from the mother vessel, she told the second mate. Judging by the size of the thing, she was more than capable of housing a small fleet.

Ahxenta ordered one of her gunnery crews to concentrate on the detectable communications relays of the ship. The other teams under Earbleat would be used in broader sweep attacks on the larger targets of shields, weapons and hull.

"She's trying to take out our drones!" Whisper Earbleat yelled out. "And she's launched a breaching pod! Targeting… I've got it, but that was close!"

They all felt the vibration as the breaching pod exploded. Ahxenta cursed volubly: *Arianrhod* was a cargo vessel and although she was far better equipped than almost every other private starship in the fleet and had a well-trained crew used to obeying orders, she was not military and not built for either manoeuvrability or sustained attack. The captain could hear her own voice to Bluejohn: "And you didn't take her on?"

No wonder he had not taken her on, if this was the same or a similar ship. *Arianrhod* was not about to win this encounter any time soon, not without a deal of subterfuge. The ship shuddered to the onslaught as a pulse from one of the enemy phase cannons smacked her hull and a second struck a glancing blow.

"Shit! One of our aft shields has taken a hit and she's out!" Crizz

Cottontail called from engineering.

"Getting reports of casualties on the lower outer decks, Captain," the comms officer informed her. "Doc's got it covered, but she says it's not good."

"Repairing hull damage," Cottontail cut in harshly. "But another shot in the same place and we'll lose the plating.

"That's the last of our drones taken out, Captain!" Earbleat sang out loudly. "Launch more?"

"No, let them think that's all we had. Helm, get us some distance from that ship and keep them guessing but easy as you go, not full speed; make as though we're limping. Comms, send out a general distress, local only, and put me through to Lindell. Earbleat, get your crews to round up a few close-proximity charges, big as you've got. Crizz, get ready to power up those engines. Lindell?"

The supercargo looked up at her from the link. "Captain?"

"Have you got any wrack that you can dump overboard? Any excess that we don't or won't need any time soon? Good. Liaise with Earbleat and put it in with her charges – put it in torpedo tubes if you have to. Crizz, got those engines running hot?"

"Running hot!" echoed Cottontail. "Sealing the outer breach, she'll hold a bit. My team's on it."

"Helm?"

"She's not letting us out of her sight, Cap, she's matching speed. She thinks she's got us on the run and she's manoeuvring to get a better targeting position."

"Keep our distance but keep limping. Slow down on the weapons, Earbleat, but you keep up the targeting of those bays, Tallica, I don't want a fleet of fighters on our backs as well."

A couple of minutes ticked by as Earbleat and Lindell made ready their cargoes.

"Box, set us a course around the edges of the asteroid field and Dox, get ready to hit it, no holds barred. Crizz, you ready?"

"You'll get all we have and more, Cap!"

"She's closing!" bawled Dox from the navi-helm station.

"Let her get closer still, just a little closer…"

"She's powering up more weapons and she's targeting our main engines!" Gliss called as he refined the tactical holo.

"Launch charges!"

"Bombs away!" bellowed Earbleat.

"Get us the hell out of here, helm!"

"Getting us out of here, aye!" Dox responded.

Arianrhod streaked away at a tangent, her engines groaning, as the close-proximity charges she had left in her wake detonated and the bloom of blue-white lit the dark behind her. This close to the Orriga Two asteroid field was not the best place to be for a less than sleek cargo vessel but the *Arianrhod* had one or two surprises up her sleeve that very few other ships, even military strike craft, possessed.

"Put us on a line for the Helix cluster and lay a false trail, Dox," Ahxenta ordered. "How's our cloak?"

"Alive and well," replied the helmswoman, complying. "But it may not hide us from whatever tech that beast has got on board."

"It might take them a while to figure that we've got a cloak. We'll hold it in reserve for now. Meanwhile Box, once we get as far as Spiral, set us a convoluted course back to the asteroid field."

"You're taking us into the asteroid field?" Apnis queried, resuming her rightful place at the captain's side. "Isn't that the stuff of space derring-do and the last hope in all the worst adventure epics you've ever experienced?"

"Where else do you suggest that's close enough to lose them? Besides, the larger asteroids are so far apart they won't be a problem and as for the debris that's been blown off them over the centuries, I trust our short-range deflector arrays…"

"Whose signals could be read by any ship with the right scanning gear that's close enough."

"Not if we dump reflector flak as we go and don't maintain a straight course. We can use our close-prox disruptors for any larger bits that get in our way but we'll have trouble keeping our cloak in place. I want all auxiliary weapons stations manned, including those on the secondary bridge. We've been through worse."

"No we damn well haven't," Apnis contradicted in a low voice.

"Medbay, report on casualties."

"Nine out of action, Cap," Axellina Flintlock called out in a loud voice from whichever station she was at. "I'll send you an update on their conditions as soon as I get a minute. Flintlock out."

"We don't seem to have a tail, Captain," Pollux Gliss announced. "But how long that'll last, I don't know."

"I've analysed the tactical and schematic data that we've picked up Captain, and compared it with all known ship designs in our files," Azular informed her. "There are similarities to raider profiles, but there *are* subtle differences. Which doesn't mean they're not raiders," he cautioned. "They may be an updated specification."

"Raiders aren't going to redesign a bunch of their ships and start sending them out on sorties. They'd upgrade weapons before they'd upgrade ships, surely. We've still had raider attacks using their usual weapons systems – these weapons are different and more than one step ahead of typical raider designs," argued Ahxenta. "And Jikelleli was adamant that the fighters that attacked the *Green Comet* were no way raiders *and* they had a mothership and sweepers for debris. No, I'd trust Sarie Jikelleli's instincts on this one and that ship out there is on a par with the ships that attacked her and the nightmare that ambushed the *Obsidian*."

The crew was crushed back into its seats as the pressure increased and the grav compensators shifted to high mode to cope. Azular and Gliss had every sensor *Arianrhod* possessed looking in every direction possible. The starfield visible in the grid of the main bridge holo-generator spun as the ship altered course and then shifted again, her course showing as a thin line of light on the array.

"Here we go, Cap: the asteroid field!" Dox called as she brought the rectangular bulk of *Arianrhod* up sharp and skirted one large and a few smaller rocks bound together by a common centre of gravity that marked the beginning of a very hazardous course. "I'll skip in below the plane of the field and then go through – that'll give us the option of coming out above, if we can. That may just put a scupper on their sensors, but these bigger rocks are mighty far apart so unless we cut power, our systems may still be trackable."

"Our ion trail will be in any case, but go for it; it'll make their target practice more difficult at any rate," the captain ordered.

The mighty *Arianrhod* dipped and straightened as she was brought in under the vast sea of rockery that was the Orriga Two asteroid field.

9: SPACEWRACK

An asteroid field was not the safest place to be when you were flying at close to bypass entry speed and hiding out from adversaries: you might escape the scanners and sensors of whoever was trying to eat you for lunch, but you were almost as likely to be crushed to dust by the very rocks that you were relying on for protection. Fortunately for the *Arianrhod*, her hull was reinforced meta-jurillium alloy and her shields were the best that technology could produce. She also packed a mighty range of proximity sensory scanners and a net of efficient shield artillery, though these advantages could cope more successfully with natural dangers such as the asteroids that called the Orriga Two home than with technological threats like high-energy pulse cannons.

Arianrhod flitted through the field, dropping reflector flak in short bursts and in various directions. Azular had matched the flak to read as metallic ore in hopes that it would fox the enemy. As ominous thuds reverberated around, the bridge crew looked about anxiously: despite the plethora of short-range deflector arrays scattered over her hull, there was obviously a stray or two getting through.

"Well, lookee here," Apnis said softly, pointing to the bridge holo, where a luminous dark outline had materialised at the outer edge of the projection.

"Tactical, expand that area of the holo," ordered the captain.

Gliss complied and the projection blossomed outwards to take up a goodly section of the forr'ad bridge area. He enlarged the suspected intruder as a second holo and they could see that the ship certainly resembled the battlecruiser that had been on their tail. It was skirting the area, evidently seeking traces of its quarry.

"Cloak might be a good idea now, Cap," Apnis murmured. "Or even Cottontail's and Azular's new toy."

"That's not been tested and a battle situation's not the best place to test a new bit of tech that may or may not work in an area like this. And it uses up a fair bit of energy and a lot of spare energy cells we don't have: we gave them to the *Obsidian* and we haven't been able to get back to full capacity again, given all the little contretemps we've had since. But you're right, now might be a good idea to cloak."

Ahxenta gave the relevant order and even on the holo the icon that was *Arianrhod* winked out. The cloak was an expensive but useful piece of kit that the captain had had installed after a profitable cruise a year or so ago, in preference to dishing out a set of bonuses for the crew. They had grumbled at the time, she recalled ruefully, but they might be more grateful now if it saved their hides. Every eye on the bridge watched as the enemy ship skirted the asteroid field, moving ever closer. It was obvious to most that as they could see the alien, it was possible that it was picking up readings on them or at least finding evidence of their trail, despite the all-encompassing cloak.

"Seems the lights are fully operational but no-one's home," the captain remarked as she continued to scan the tactical readout holos. "They're veering off. Have they figured we've been scuppered or do they think they imagined us?"

"They might just be trying to outflank us, or keep us here while they send for reinforcements," Apnis warned.

"Keep an eye on them, Earbleat," Ahxenta ordered the weapons officer. "And steady as she goes, Box and Dox, I don't want to have to pay for new paint."

"It's not new paint we'll have to pay for if she comes in after us," Box remarked in a low voice to his companion.

"Shut up and set the coordinates," Dox retorted irritably.

Their pursuer was still visible as a structured spot of light on the tactical display and the captain pursed her lips. "They don't give up."

"They've backed off but they're still there and they know we're in here," her first mate noted astutely. "You think they'll launch fighters and send them in after us?"

"That's what I'd do. Their fighters will have more of a chance of spotting us and it only takes one. But that ship's big and though she's highly manoeuvrable, I can't imagine she'd come in, unless she had the firepower to clear a path through the field."

"Which she may very well have," the commander pointed out.

"And that would set off more than one alarm in this sector; there will be listening outposts on several of the larger bodies here, the Coalition will have seen to that, as will the Non-Treaty Alliance. The Trades Alliance might have a monitoring station here as well, I don't know," Ahxenta admitted. "What the hell's that?"

A small spot of light had detached from the main ship and was heading towards the asteroid field.

"She's launched something! It's too big to be a fighter: a sweeper or another craft?" Apnis hazarded.

They watched as the smaller spot swept across the field of view, releasing a trail that showed as a shower of pinpricks of light.

"Incoming!" warned Earbleat as Gliss echoed the same and the red alert siren around them increased in frequency.

"Bastards!" Apnis hissed.

"Unmanned fighters controlled from that ship she just launched," the tactical officer confirmed. "And they're packed with high energy explosives. The ship won't be able to detect us with our cloak up, but it sure as shells will see our distortion field if it can get in range."

A puff of red lit up space like a flame amid the circling rocks and blossomed outward in an expanding orb of light.

"One fighter down," noted the first mate. "But we can't outrun things that size in this field and they're dispersing in a search pattern. Whatever that ship has by way of scanners and sensors, she damn well suspects we're still here and haven't been smashed to bits. Now might be a good time to test Cottontail's and Azular's new toy. They get any closer and we'll have nothing to lose. Our cloak may deceive visual as they're unmanned but if one gets close enough to ram, we'll have to take it out and then the game will be up."

"Azular!" the captain called.

The Berzic science officer had been following the conversation closely and was immediately alerted. "I can have the decoy in place as soon as you give the word, Captain. Location?"

Ahxenta scanned her tactical displays again. "Below us in the plane of the field but as far as you can get to starboard."

The minutes ticked by as they watched and waited. A holo note from medbay lit up across the captain's board and she looked down, momentarily distracted. The news was not good. Ahxenta and Apnis exchanged glances. One fatality: young Ensign Scudder. The others were stable. For now.

Cottontail had joined the senior science officer at his station and their creased brows indicated that their operation was proving tricky.

"We'll need to drop the cloak, Cap," the chief engineer said at last. "Just for the initial projection at launch; the decoy unit's systems will take over after that but we won't have control once it's in position."

"Liaise with Dox to drop the cloak for as short a time as possible on my mark. Earbleat, have your teams ready to let go with all we've got, and I mean all."

The captain was on her feet, directing, exhorting, checking stations and watching the holo so closely she was almost part of it.

"Drop the cloak and launch decoy!" she ordered.

"Decoy away!" thundered Azular.

"Cloak back up!" Dox bawled from her station.

"Think they caught it?" Apnis asked. "That was a short window but that's a powerful ship out there. And we don't know what else her short-range fighter launcher's capable of."

"Decoy's projection successful, Captain," confirmed Cottontail as she returned to her station.

"Now we see if they bite," the first mate said slowly as the whole bridge crew sat in silence, waiting.

"The closest unmanned fighters are swerving away!" yelled Gliss. "One of them must have spotted the decoy!"

"But where's the main vessel?" demanded Ahxenta.

"Tracking," Gliss replied. "Larai, keep on those fighters," he told his second. "She's headed in closer to the field and she's shadowing her fighter launcher. They think they've got us, Captain."

"Once they find it's a shadow of us projected from a box that emits fake signals, they'll be pissed," remarked Apnis. "Helm, plot us a course out of here and in the opposite direction to that ship."

"Belay that, helm!" barked Ahxenta. "Who the hell said we're going to run? No bloody battleship's getting the better of *Arianrhod*. And it's payback time. They killed young Scudder and they're not getting away with it."

The captain's dander was up and the crew knew it: they had seen this mood before, not often but sufficiently so that they knew they were in for a rough ride.

The *Arianrhod* rose up out of the Orriga Two asteroid field like an avenging angel, cloaked to the boot heels and with every weapon emplacement ready to roar. Her torpedo tubes were packed and her engines were running so hot that the chief engineer was steaming.

Their adversary had evidently realised that it had been tricked and that the PSS they thought they had in their vice-like grip was no more than a very clever projection. And they had wasted several of their unmanned craft trying to take out a shadow. As Apnis had pointed out, they were pissed. Whoever was in command over there was running hot with fury. Ahxenta was ice-cold in anger as she scanned the mighty shape.

"Take her down!"

The manned fighters that the alien belatedly launched were little more than pin-pricks on the hull of the mighty *Arianrhod*. Her cloak dispensed with and all her energy concentrated in her weapons, she went in close, guns and phase cannons blazing. Dox, a helmswoman of legendary skill, slid her closer to the alien than it should have been possible to manoeuvre so large a vessel. The fighters and smaller craft of the huge attacking battleship were baffled of their target for fear of hitting their own mothership and could do no more than sting: the gunnery officers of *Arianrhod* had tracking down to a fine art and her smaller gun emplacements were both deadly and unremitting.

Up and down, around and across the *Arianrhod* skimmed, so close to the alien that they could feel the buffeting of her shields. Enemy fire searing her flanks, *Arianrhod* maintained her relentless attack. Shards of flak sheared off and were sent skimming away into the dark of space that was now as alight as a sunrise. The myriad rocks of the Orriga Two asteroid field glinted in their wakes likes a mighty flock of shadowing ghosts.

"This one's for Scudder!" Ahxenta hissed.

She took the shot herself and sent the largest torpedo her ship had left down the maw of the enemy craft. As the hull section exploded outwards in a searing ball of white-hot metal, *Arianrhod* swept up and over the top of her, rocking in the force of the explosion. The alien ship broke into three sections. As the pieces separated, a small fleet of arrow-shaped transports speared off from the flaming wreckage amidships and into the distance.

"Take them out!" ordered the captain.

"Can't," Earbleat replied. "We've no more distance firepower, Cap, we're totally dry."

As the fleeing ships diminished to a haze in the distance, a burst of hissing crackled across the deck and a voice cut through it.

"This is *Obsidian Sky* to *Arianrhod*. Do you require assistance?"

Ahxenta let out a small chuckle as her voice lanced through the static. "*Arianrhod* to *Obsidian Sky*: as much as you can spare, Grey. We've had one helluva day…"

"So I see."

Captain Bluejohn's ship had been forced into a protracted stay at Selliden Central as his crew and the teams at the planet's repair sheds had been obliged to wait for suitable parts. He had been able to reschedule his cargo collection at the Outer Reaches Archipelago and was thus only recently loaded and ready to head off to his next port. As he had spent time in discussion with a few of the settled worlds in the Outer Reaches to warn them of the *Obsidian's* close and almost deadly encounter with the strange battleship, he had been sufficiently delayed that he had caught the buzz of subspace comms and weapons discharge that had alerted him to the *Arianrhod's* situation.

"They may have got a call out for back-up before they launched their escape craft, Cinnabar," he warned. "I wouldn't stick around if I were you. I can tow you: we're heavy in the beam but we'll manage. And as we're fully operational, we can return the energy cells you lent us. I wasn't going to run the risk of hitting trouble, so I made sure we had a complete overhaul."

"We're sticking around long enough to pick up as many pieces as we can," Ahxenta told him. "We should get word out to the TA and the ISP that they should get in here and do the same."

"I'll see to that," Bluejohn told her. "Meanwhile, let us know what we can do. And be ready to shift: you've taken a hell of a beating."

"You're telling me…"

The Orriga Two sector was situated at the more densely settled end of the Outer Reaches Archipelago and was thus sufficiently close to the Belts that by the time the *Arianrhod* had reached safe harbourage, word had spread. It seemed that *Arianrhod* was not the only ship that had had a run-in with an alien vessel of novel design and descriptions of such hostiles and their latest patterns of attack were disturbingly similar. Against single or multiple ships the assailants were leaving no survivors, nor much in the way of evidence. Cargoes were being lifted but apparently destruction came before profit and if the ships put up any kind of a fight, they were taken down ruthlessly.

"Upping the ante," Ahxenta said harshly when she heard.

"Well, at least the legend that is *Arianrhod* lives on," Captain Grey Bluejohn told her over a hot drink in one of the massive repair bays of the neutral station Jurassa that served the outer area of the Belts. "She'll live to fight another day. And you're the only ship on record that's taken out one of these bastards, as far as we know. Even the Coalition's impressed."

Ahxenta released her breath in a short hiss. "We'll live to fight one or two more battles, but *Arianrhod* needs a complete refit. And that comes expensive, time as well as credit. Jurassa's a bit out of the way and they charge for every nut and bolt. Once we're spaceworthy, we'll have to make for the bypass in the direction of whatever's the most pressing of our assignments. My supercargo and his team are using their collective charm to keep our customers sweet. At least the hostiles and their antics are putting the fear of death on so many local systems that clients are not squealing too much, though some carriers are upping prices and quoting dangerous times as the excuse."

"If you need a cargo or two shifted, you know you only have to ask," Bluejohn assured her. "I'm off to my next drop-off spot but it's only four or five days standard. But any Private you ask will give you her eye teeth if you want them, you know that. You did good, Cinnabar – as usual."

"That's as maybe, but I still have to send word to young Scudder's folks. Good grief, Grey, the boy had only been with us for a year! And I've two more that are still on the danger list. And there's no med facility around here that my senior medic will trust to transfer them to. I'm just grateful we have Greenwing with us; he's been around the block a few times."

Bluejohn eyed her sympathetically, his hand closing on her arm. "We've all lost crewmen, Cinnabar: it goes with the territory. Doesn't make it any easier, I know, but there it is. Heard any more about your scheduled pick-up at Helleborus Station?"

"The *Green Comet's* just dropped a small cargo at Merkat Three, so Sarie Jikelleli has agreed to do the run as it's not too far out of her way. And she certainly needs the credit as Ace Periwinkle's still in the medbay there; his injuries are worse than they first thought. The ISP is okay with the change. But if you'd pass on Azular's analyses of the bits of alien tech we scavenged out yonder to the ISP and the TA, as well as the rest of the Privates, I'd be grateful; and get anything else you can in the way of more information out of them and keep me updated. Our comms systems are a lot less than fully operational and we need to keep emergency channels open."

"No problem, Cinnabar, anytime. I'd best leave you to it and get back to my ship: we leave in an hour."

One of Ahxenta's problems was restocking the *Arianrhod's* arsenal without giving too much away on the nature of her firepower to the repair crews at Jurassa Station. She trusted them, but only to a point. She was also working out how to retrieve the *Gadfly*, now fit but still taking up space and being charged fees at Merkat Three's space dock. The repairs at Jurassa were taking an inordinate amount of time and continuing to cause headaches not only for *Arianrhod's* captain, but for her personnel. Ahxenta had found herself continuing to play catch up on several commissions that she had taken on and having to assign some of her own crew to pitch in to aid station repair crews: every local system was on alert as a result of the latest attacks and there was no spare help to be called in.

Bluejohn had kept his promise of sending in as much information as he was able. Little headway had been made on the identification of the hostile that had attacked the *Arianrhod,* he informed Ahxenta, for the Trades Alliance and the Interstellar Systems Protectorate were so caught up in their own concerns that they had not despatched ships to scour the battlefield for any debris left behind. Analyses by Azular and his second had produced little more evidence as to the source of the materials used in the alien ships' hulls other than that the meta-jurillium signature was not that of Beta Zegonia 68c. The tactical data collected by *Arianrhod's* bridge stations had not provided any clues to the direction from which the alien had come, but that the mothership was capable of hyperlight travel was highly probable. And Azular had deduced that its ion trail was remarkably similar to those of the ships that had invaded the Marridan homeworld and the one that had ambushed the *Obsidian Sky* by the Orriga Two asteroid field.

Other contacts had brought in the news that the situation out at Marridan had not improved. No contact had been possible with the planetary authorities there as the whole area was being jammed by the four blockading ships and a couple of smaller ones that had put in an appearance. Attempts had been made to backtrack the ships that had left Marridan after the initial attack, using their direction of departure to gain evidence as to their point of origin, but these had been unsuccessful. All in all it was such a mess that the Coalition, the ISP and the Non-Treaty Alliance were now openly cooperating and the TA had sent its reps to the emergency meetings. And rumours from diverse sources suggested that whoever these new aggressors in town were, they were far too organised, well-equipped and informed to be able to operate without assistance from inside one or more of the affiliated organisations or systems. The implication was that they had allies, or at least dupes. It was a nasty situation.

Ahxenta was with her supercargo, Lindell, trying to work out the best way to appease the various clients that were waiting for goods to be picked up or dropped off when another business call came in. It was worth a look she decided, as it could be tacked on to one job in hand that had originally involved collection of cargo close to their current position and a trip to the Delta Iridium system for its drop-off. The captain had called in a couple of favours from her associates, one of which had been the transfer of the goods for Delta Iridium Colony to Jurassa and that payload was currently stowed in one of *Arianrhod's* smaller cargo bays. This new call meant a diversion to Brown Amber, but with a little manoeuvring the addition to their schedule would make them a quick stack of credit and their original commission to Delta would not be too seriously hampered timewise.

"Mind you, the story about our spot of trouble out at Orriga Two certainly seems to have done the rounds of many of the local star systems," Lindell told the captain. "And it's been embellished a bit. We could play on that as an excuse for late deliveries or pick-ups."

"That's not a tactic I use, as you know damn well, Lieutenant," Ahxenta rebuked him. "We have our reputation to uphold. But if we can make tracks once we've finished at Delta, we can catch up. I'd planned to head back to the Web to pick up the *Gadfly*, but we'll have to live without her for a bit. This refit and refurb will see us through a couple of months, unless we have to use our new stocks of energy cells and arms and that bothers me. Azular and Cottontail will go on working on the decoy unit. It saved our hides and if they can upgrade it, so much the better. And that means time and credit. Get them all they need in terms of stores and if you have to requisition what we don't have, do it, though don't let it interfere with our schedule."

"Anything else for my department?" he asked, raising an eyebrow.

"I want a comprehensive upgrading of our weapons capability as well. Here's the list."

"You want mayo with that, Cap?" Lindell demanded as he conned over the info-sheet. "We're almost up to full capacity," he continued hurriedly as he saw the dangerous gleam in her eye.

"I want our arsenal not only up to full strength but expanded and our emplacements and our weapons housings top notch as far as we can go without hauling in for specialist refurb," Ahxenta told him in a tone that signified no argument. "We've seen more military activity over these past few weeks than we have in the whole year preceding and I won't have the ship lacking anything that'll keep her running."

"Or fighting," the supercargo added.

"Just so. But let's go over this schedule again – if we can get more speed out of the engines and miss our shuttle pick-up at the Web, we can cut delivery times and get more or less back on track. But keep a note that we now owe a bundle of favours – I want them paid back as soon as and if you can find a way to do it, let me know."

"Aye, aye, Captain."

Three days later and *Arianrhod* was well on her way to the further-flung edges of her customary travel routes, heading again to mining station Brown Amber for their small pick-up.

"Okay, we offloaded the last batch at the Cap's buddy's place on Freskat Six, where's the drop-off for these once we've got them?" Box demanded of his mate at the helm.

"Search me, I only work here," Dox replied.

"Same place," Apnis notified them from her raised station behind the navi-helm console. "We've a new order for thin diamond wafers for comms links from Coronis Comms out at Delta Iridium Six and the Brownies have a suitable stack of crystals available. The captain's buddy can turn them over fast so we'll wait for them, as we've got the other gear for Delta that the *Hexameter* brought into Jurassa for us. You lot can pack in a few days furlough while we're on stopover at Freskat; you've worked hard enough. It's a speedy fulfilment of the Coronis Comms order and a bonus for us."

"That's what I call good business," Box smiled. "As long as we get paid on delivery."

"They don't pay, we don't deliver," the first mate reminded him. "And they'd have the Trades Alliance on their backs and their name tarnished to rust among the Privates to boot."

"Orbital insertion coordinates plotted for mining station Brown Amber," Navigator Box announced efficiently.

"Don't get up yourself, we're only half way there yet," Romanna Dox snapped. "We have to take the long way round, remember? We can't cross uncharted space – unless *you* know a safe way through."

"Nobody knows a safe way through. But move it; the quicker we get there, the faster the job gets done and the earlier *we* head out for the main settlement at Freskat Six and start our shore leave."

"Freskat Six isn't exactly the centre of the known universe, is it?" Dox complained. "We've been there plenty times and I don't recall a decent hotel in the settlement unless you count the *Halcyon*; and that's pricy, given Freskat's off the beaten track a bit. All it's got going for it is a nice view of the Ginseng Nebula and that's too far for a day trip even if you could afford the price of one."

The two continued to grumble at one another until the first mate ordered them to shut up or she'd have them up on report for annoying their fellow crewmen. But she smiled as she said it: it was obvious that the crew of the *Arianrhod* was getting back to normal after the trauma of the last couple of weeks.

The *PSS Hexameter* under the command of Captain Bee Lyvy Coxen had not only brought their original cargo for Delta Iridium Colony into Jurassa, she had also transported several large crates that she had picked up on her way in; they had been summarily stowed under top security in one of the best-protected holds in *Arianrhod's* inner cargo bays. The freight was exercising not only the talents of second mate cum weapons officer Whisper Earbleat, but of Chief Engineer Crizz Cottontail and her second, Lieutenant Gem Ferry. They seemed to be spending their journey time in close discussion 'tween decks with an array of gear and much coming and going between their usual haunts and the secure hold. By the time the approach to Brown Amber had been announced by the navi-helm crew, the trio had completed the task and the results had filtered out to the remainder of the ship's complement: the *Arianrhod* now sported upgraded phase cannons and several new outer hull installations that supported additional long-range scanners, torpedo launch tubes and drone deployment pockets.

"Turning us into a frigging battlecruiser," Pollux Gliss at tactical complained in a low voice to Lynxi Bellfish at comms.

"Get on with your reconfiguring and stop bellyaching," Whisper Earbleat commanded from her main weapons station, where she was involved in a similar operation. "And make sure our ops down in the armoury are on top of the new loading sims that Azular coded in. We get caught napping and you won't *have* a mouth to complain with."

"Aye, aye, Chief," Gliss responded, turning back to his post. "A dozen new emplacements and now we've a squillion new options for set-up and deployment. Just dandy," he continued under his breath.

The station Brown Amber glowed in multifaceted coppery shades in the main bridge holo, its vast and elongated body revolving gently to maintain the gravity necessary for humanoid comfort. Attached to its external struts in a metallic network were several ancillary platforms. These served the smaller vessels that plied the narrow spaceways into and out of the thin asteroid belt of the local star system that supplied much of Amber's raw materials, and were also used by the shuttles of bulkier visiting ships. Brown Amber itself was anchored to the largest asteroid of the system and far enough away from its neighbours not to be overly in danger of collision with any. Still, docking in the outer orbital bays for a huge cargo vessel like *Arianrhod* was a risky business and the approach required caution. Nonetheless, Ahxenta eschewed taking on a pilot for the trip in, trusting to her own crewmen and women to establish safe anchorage.

"It's quieter than last time we were here," observed Apnis. "But you're still wearing a locating pin and taking security down with you. And a pilot for the shuttle over."

"I'll get ready now. You link in with the marketing office and keep me updated. Everything should be ready for pick up if Lindell has got it organised," Ahxenta responded.

"We *could* arrange to have the shipment sent up here."

"No way; I'm not having the Brownies on my ship. And I want to check quality before I put my hand to anything. I'll take Azular: he can test the diamonds for flaws and he has other talents that might stand us in good stead if anyone's going to try a fast one."

"With our reputation, I doubt anyone would," the first mate said, "Even though there are a couple of large transports in that look as if they pack a punch. But Bellfish will be keeping tabs on all of you, so don't do or say anything you wouldn't want to be overheard."

"Thanks for that, Tallica. But I don't plan to be down there long; we need a quick exit and on to our next port. You have the conn. Keep her on standby and don't power down. If there's a need to get out in a hurry, then go. You do *not* wait for us."

"Understood, Cap. See you on the flipside."

The trip to the entry port of Brown Amber and into their allotted bay took only minutes. *Arianrhod's* shuttle docked safely and Ahxenta, Azular and their security were escorted through the maze of corridors to the relevant open section, where various corridors led off to the diverse marketing suites that dealt with the commodities of the place.

At the comms station aboard *Arianrhod*, Lieutenant Bellfish was keeping up a running commentary on their progress. "The Captain, Dr Azular and Ensign Hanx are now in main marketing suite green three and have met up with two others: their contacts by the sound of it; Lieutenant Kelsitt is still aboard the shuttle. There must be quite a few other ships here on business as there are a lot of personnel on the ground, judging by the comms exchange."

"Greffy, check what's going on down there," Apnis instructed

Azular's second at the science post.

"Amber's well-shielded but I'm detecting the lifeforms in main marketing," he stated. "I read at least twenty, some in small groups, a few solo. Several marketing suites are occupied, though I can't make out specifics. And yes, I detect a lot of comms exchange, short- and long-distance. Some of it is maybe from Amber to subsidiary stations out in the field or to clients aboard transports and smaller cruisers."

The commander pondered for a moment. "Any other craft in the vicinity apart from those we can see on the holo?"

"A couple of small shuttles off our beam holding position rather than heading in, but there could be a fleet at back of the station or on the other side of the asteroid that we can't detect," Greffy answered.

"Keep a weather eye out. You too, Gliss," she ordered the tactical officer. "Earbleat, get a bead on every ship in the vicinity that we *can* read, great or small, and on the main defence emplacements of the station that are in our sights. And get ready for targeting any one of them on my mark."

"Expecting trouble, Tallica?" Cottontail asked as a short murmur of surprise ran around the bridge.

"No. But taking precautions just the same."

"Ready for targeting on your mark, ma'am," announced Earbleat.

"Ma'am, there's a surge of power from Amber's main reactor core and from a number of her systems: she's getting ready for something or other," Greffy warned loudly. "And she's ordered an extensive diagnostics check on all off-station comms channels. That'll cut out long-range comms for a bit. Just as well we've got our own systems."

"Can't be warfare," Crizz Cottontail surmised. "She's a bit of a sitting duck if things did turn into a fire-fight."

"She has defence craft aboard," Earbleat pointed out. "No station like Amber could run without them."

"Unregistered transport vessel *Lambda Red Velvet* is powering up, but she hasn't requested departure permission that I can detect," Greffy notified Apnis. "And she's packing a massive armoury."

"Is that so? Send out a targeting systems testing alert to all vessels in the vicinity and to the station on an open local channel, Bellfish. Give that a moment to sink in, Earbleat, and then target the main reactor port on Amber and the main engines on *Lambda Red Velvet*."

"Targeting, aye," the weapons officer responded after a pause.

"We have a very annoyed security liaison on Amber asking why we're targeting their station, ma'am," Bellfish called over. "And the captain of the *Lambda Red Velvet* wants an immediate explanation."

"Inform them that we're testing our systems," was the dry reply. "We've just had them repaired and updated and this is the first chance away from the repair bays that we've had. Brown Amber's and the *Lambda's* security must surely be aware that we sent out the alert and that our weapons are not running hot."

Bellfish relayed the message but the station security officer was not appeased and informed them that he was calling the situation in to Brown Amber's management office.

"He wants to file a report and start a war, let him do it," returned Apnis. "And pass *that* on to the bridge of *Lambda Red Velvet* while you're at it."

"Aye, Commander."

The aggrieved security liaison officer replied with the request that *Arianrhod* cease and desist targeting station Brown Amber forthwith. Apnis refused and they were still engaged in a verbal battle when the call came through from Ahxenta on the shuttle's channel that she and her team were heading back to the ship, having quickly and fruitfully concluded negotiations and obtained the relevant shipment.

It was only after the shuttle was safely back in *Arianrhod's* bay that the first mate gave the order to stand down targeting systems.

Ahxenta entered the bridge and resumed her command chair. "So what was all the fuss about, Tallica?" she demanded. "You hacked off a few of the great and the good in marketing, there were alarms going off all over the place. They were getting rattled."

"So why were they powering up *and* cutting off-station comms? A semi-permanent structure like Amber doesn't power up her main reactor to welcome the sunrise, does she?" Apnis growled. "And why choose now to offline their comms? Just as we heave to?"

"Testing their systems," the captain suggested ironically.

"Just as we were; and as we told them beforehand, come to that. So why were they so upset?"

"They had important visitors. They were keeping it under wraps: part of the marketing suite was marked off-limits but top level talks were mentioned and Azular picked up one or two sparks of anxiety from a couple of the trading ops hovering in the main arena. And I got the impression that Amber management wanted it kept quiet that we had rolled into town, though we made no secret of it."

"Hence its shutdown of comms," inferred the first mate. "But that wouldn't stop private channels, so half the ships in dock will know we're here. And some of the reps in marketing must have recognised you and passed the news on. But a power-up of the main reactor core could blanket other power increases from sources outside the station that Amber didn't want inspected too closely, such as sources on the asteroid's far side. So who were these important visitors?"

"Unknown: they may have been Coalition but nobody was saying. Whoever they were, they were causing a bit of a stir and more than a little fear, according to Azular."

"Not nice people, then."

"Not nice people. And it struck me that the reactions around us were strangely similar to those *we* experienced at Thystal Comms on Xerophyte IV. What ships do we have in dock or close by that we haven't seen yet, I wonder?"

"*Lambda Red Velvet* is requesting leave to depart," Bellfish called over. "And she's filed a complaint with Brown Amber's management committee about our behaviour, according to Amber."

"Too scared to file a complaint with us directly," Apnis said with a grin. "So what's our next move? Chasing the *Lambda* out of dock?"

Ahxenta looked around her bridge. "We have what we came for, and though it wouldn't hurt to hang fire for an hour to check up on what's going on around here, we don't have that luxury. Set course for Freskat Six, best speed, but don't take a direct route away from this station: I expect there'll be one or two eyes following us."

"Freskat Six, aye," Lieutenant Box echoed as he set the required circuitous coordinates and his partner at the helm began the delicate task of withdrawal from the vicinity of Brown Amber.

"We won't be welcome back here after all this," the navigator muttered to Dox as the ship slowly turned and slid her moorings, to emerge into the larger freedom of space beyond.

"Their loss," she shrugged coolly. "I was never taken with the place anyway: too much skulduggery."

"Belay the chat," Ahxenta ordered. "All stations keep a close eye on everyone and everything related to Brown Amber until we're far enough from her that we can't see her tail lights."

The bridge crew continued to gaze mesmerised at the moving display until the steady voice of the captain brought them back to a veneer of normality. As the whirling mass of luminous star-spangled nebulosity slowed, its myriad colours coalescing into an all-encompassing blue-white and pink glow dotted by the gem-like stars that could be seen beyond, heads were shaken and eyes rubbed. The holo froze and at the captain's command began to home in on an area to the left of the whole. It was at that point that the crew realised what had caught the commanding officer's attention: plainly visible was a clear octagonal space that appeared to be within the billowing outer misty mass of interstellar gas and dust.

"That shouldn't be there," Box informed the bridge at large.

"Spot on, Box. Something's not right. I'm tempted to send a fleet of Azular's sci-drones in to see what they come up with," Ahxenta said to her first mate.

"If we lose them it'll cost us more than time," Apnis cautioned.

The magnificent Ginseng Nebula was as stunningly beautiful as always but a regularly-shaped disparity of nothingness, limned only by a thickening of the nebula's spangled blue-white luminosity, was definitely not right and a sense of unease began to creep down the captain's back as she watched, stroking her chin gently.

"How?" the first mate asked, puzzled, equally hypnotised.

"Get Azular up here pronto," Ahxenta ordered. "Maybe he's seen something like it before. No offence, Greffy, but he's got a whole lot more experience than you."

"None taken, ma'am: I know he has," the young man replied, sliding across to the secondary station and powering up the console.

"Bridge stations, stand by; I don't know what the blazes is going on, but given our recent mixed experiences in the back of beyond, it could be anything," the captain continued. "Helm, station-keeping – I don't want to go in any closer. And put our cloak up; we've got a damn cloak, we may as well use it."

"It'll drain our power, Cap," Apnis warned. "But until we know what we're dealing with… I've never seen anything like it before, and I've been in this sector a few times and then some."

"It's not flat," Greffy noted from his station. "It's definitely three dimensional, like a clear octagonal box in space – a massive one. You could hide a small fleet in there."

"Hardly, if it's a clear box," Box pointed out from his post. "We'd see it."

"Oh ha, ha," Dox retorted sardonically. "That one really made me wet my pants."

"It's like a pocket in space, as if the nebula parted to contain it and space has folded itself over or rolled itself up to create the hole," the science officer put in, staring at his viewscreen holo.

Azular strode onto the bridge and over to his usual station. Once briefed by Greffy he was equally baffled, but began his own scan. He disagreed with the captain on the use of sci-drones. In his opinion, if there was something or someone sentient or malevolent behind the anomaly, it would not be wise to alert them to *Arianrhod's* presence or to her technology.

"It covers a large area," he reported, scanning his readouts. "I *have* heard of ships hiding in hyperspace, in pockets created by hyperspace currents, but this is beyond my experience. Note the compression of nebular substance at the anomaly edges. It's as if nebular material has been pushed out of the way by a huge force field to create the space, but there *is* containment within the overall nebular area to prevent its expansion. But I get no unusual readings from the surrounding space and our scanners can't penetrate the anomaly itself. We'd have to get closer, but that may not be prudent."

"I agree," Apnis said. "We need to report it."

"To whom?" the captain asked. "The TA won't be interested as it doesn't interfere with trade routes. The ISP's the body that should take responsibility if it's a hazard to navigation or anything else, but out here the ISP doesn't appear to protect much. The Freski are left alone most of the time despite their one-man membership of the ISP Council; and the Freskat Navy protects local spaceways. It's a long-standing beef but because Freskat's off the beaten track, you'd have more luck asking the Interstellar Tourist Board to take a stance."

"Do we go in or don't we?" Apnis voiced the question that was foremost in the minds of most of the bridge crew.

"I'd like a closer look," Azular admitted.

"I bet you would; you always do. But I don't like the feel of it," Ahxenta said slowly, shaking her head. "It's not something that I can put my finger on, but I don't like it. I've been here in fair times and in foul and this is as foul as anything I can remember."

"I have a suggestion, Captain, but you won't like it," the senior science officer told her.

"Out with it."

"If I take a shuttle out, I can make a close approach and see if I can get clearer readings…"

"No way, Azular: you get far too curious about things and it gets you into trouble more often than not. And I will not endanger this ship or any of her crew needlessly. After what we've been through recently, another barney with something beyond our control is just not on. You can send in a probe and see what it picks up. If it registers nothing, we decide what to do next. But we have deadlines and we need to drop our cargo at Freskat Six."

"The cargo's not large, Cap — we *could* send it off in our fastest shuttle and stay here to keep an eye on things," Apnis suggested.

"Bang goes shore leave," Box murmured in an undertone.

"Negative, this ship is for Freskat and that's where she's going," Ahxenta directed. "Azular, ready a probe – and a back-up recording probe to follow the first one in."

"Aye, Captain."

"You realise if there *is* something sentient in there, they'll know that something is out here," the first mate pointed out.

"I know. But if something's going to jump out of that damn box the instant our backs are turned, I'd like to be forewarned."

The probe and its back-up were ready to deploy in minutes and at Ahxenta's command the two were sent off on a course towards the centre of the irregularity. They waited. And waited.

"Our lead probe has arrived at the threshold of the anomaly, ma'am, as far as I can tell," the Berzic officer eventually called. "But we've no readings, none at all. The probe can't penetrate it, which leads me to suspect it's protected by a force field of a kind that our probes just can't pick up on. I have readings from outside the space that show an increase in nebular density… wait… damn!"

Even from their distance they could see that what had been their first probe was now a ball of white light spreading outwards as a fine, mist thin vapour. Azular had pulled the second probe back at speed and was able to continue his readings.

"Our first probe's been vaporised and it's naught but dust. The second probe's intact but what took out the first I don't know."

"Just as well we didn't go in for a closer look, Cap. We deploy warning beacons and get the hell out of here?" the first mate asked.

"We deploy warning beacons and get the hell out of here," echoed Ahxenta. "Azular, retrieve our second probe and set up a relay of beacons this side of the anomaly. I don't plan on going around back of it to see what's on the other side. We report it to the ruling council on Freskat Six, give them our data and they can pass it on to the ISP and its committees. It's time they earned their bread. Set course direct for Freskat Six," she ordered. "We have a cargo to deliver."

"And a spot of shore leave to get organised," added Box as he complied with all speed.

11: BACK OFF

The captain, with the first mate and senior science officer alongside, took an unmarked shuttle down to the outskirts of one of the smaller suburbs of the main settlement on Freskat Six in order that Ahxenta could make a rapid solo detour to her friend's workshop with the goods for conversion into thin diamond wafers. The three then set off for a priority appointment that had come in only an hour after the ship had docked. Whisper Earbleat, as second mate, had been left to organise shore leave for as many of the crew as could be spared. Supercargo Lindell was charged with the care of the rest of the cargo and of organising their forward schedule. Delta Iridium was two days away in hyperspace but the drop-off there could be made in less than a day if everything went to plan. Three to four days after that should see them back in the Web at Merkat Three and in its familiar and comforting harbourage.

A detailed report on the massive octagonal anomaly within the Ginseng Nebula had been compiled by Azular on the way in and had been endorsed by Ahxenta before being passed to the ruling council on Freskat Six immediately the ship had docked. The captain of the *Arianrhod* was sufficiently well known by repute to the admiral-in-chief of the Freskat home fleet that she had made it her business to read the report minutely. That had alarmed her sufficiently that she had requested a meeting with the senior officers of the *Arianrhod*. It was thus barely two hours after their arrival that Ahxenta, Apnis and Azular were installed in the admiral's office to discuss the sparse data that their probes had been able to garner.

Admiral Zillah was as pragmatic as any spacer with forty years' experience, many of which she had spent in dealing with higher echelons that were more concerned with their reputations than with the security or comfort of their charges. In her opinion it was high time that the Interstellar Systems Protectorate took a hand in the trouble that was threatening to engulf their corner of the charted galaxy, if not the rest of it beyond their ken. The infighting between the Trades Alliance, the Coalition, the Non-Treaty Alliance, their hangers on and all the other mini-leagues out there that had banded together for one selfish reason or another would have to cease, even if only temporarily. Ahxenta wished her good luck with eliciting any more beyond the usual perfunctory acknowledgement of the situation and the promise that the matter would be dealt with in due course. Zillah, however, had her own methods.

"I'll copy it to every other of the trades and political and security bodies that I know about, along with the veiled intention of passing the information on to as many of the news and media networks that want it – which will be all of them. If that doesn't put a squib up a few arses, I'll be surprised."

"You're a woman after my own heart," Ahxenta told her, rising. "And now I have business to get on with. Keep me informed."

Apart from raised brows at the tone, which the admiral did not expect from an officer whose rank was well below her own, they parted with mutual assurances of goodwill.

"Think she'll get the job done?" Apnis murmured to the captain once their escort had saluted them smartly off the premises.

"I think she'll certainly pass it to the ISP and I'd hope its high-rankers will take note; but Freskat's always been seen as a backwater and it'll take something big to catch their attention."

"I'd damn well think that an unknown entity in the nebula next door that chews up and spits out innocent probes is enough to make the ISP Council sit up at least," the first mate responded.

"We'll see. But we have more tasks on hand. No furlough for the seniors, but it goes with the territory. Azular, one of your and Crizz's main jobs is to continue decoy upgrade. And see if you can find out if any other ships have reported or heard of strange goings on around the Ginseng recently; Lynxi Bellfish may have picked something up."

"Will do, Captain," he stated equably. "I can start here. It's often better to obtain news by word of mouth and it may be that some of the local pilots that fly nebula tours have noticed something strange."

"Good call," Ahxenta approved. "And I bet you know the bars they hang out in as well."

"I do; I'll let you know – and how much it costs me to oil throats to encourage talking," he laughed quietly as he made off.

"He should have been an ISP intelligence officer," she said. "He's an expert at digging stuff up and he enjoys it – too much at times, I think – *and* he'll hand his bar bill to Lindell. But back aboard for us, Tallica. The merchandise will be ready by late the day after tomorrow, Freskat prime meridian time, so I'm told. The original diamonds were good quality and sizeable, so cutting and mounting will be quick."

"Your friend reckons he can start immediately and he'll get the job done without a hitch, then?"

"It'll be done as a priority, he knows our needs," Ahxenta assured her. "I want to make sure our other cargo for Delta Iridium is ready for direct despatch on arrival there; and all our surface craft should be given a thorough going over. We didn't have time on Jurassa and as we're still down one shuttle, the rest have to be tip-top."

"Agreed. One thing: we still have two serious casualties and a few walking wounded from our run-in with those hostiles and even with Greenwing's assistance, Flintlock is overstretched in medbay, though she won't admit it. This place *does* have superior med facilities – well, superior to Jurassa at any rate."

Ahxenta nodded. "I know. But we don't have the credit to treat them here, nor will I sanction recruitment of additional staff from Freskat. Not that there'd be a rush of volunteers. If you get a list of gear and medical stores that would help ease the burden, I'll have a word with Zillah, now we're acquainted. She's a veteran with a fleet under her command and may have a supplier we can use on the QT."

Admiral-in-Chief Zillah not only had a pet contractor in medical and ancillary kit under her thumb, she demanded the list of supplies and sent in the requisition herself, on the proviso that she was granted a tour of the *Arianrhod*. The latest doings of the mighty private starship had evidently caused a stir in her own circles and she was sufficiently impressed that she wanted to meet some of the crew responsible. Ahxenta sighed and agreed, aiming to make sure that certain sections would be off-limits and that her visible crew would be primed with what they could and could not mention during the state visit.

"If that's what it takes to get our medbay up to top military spec, it's a small enough price," Tallica Apnis had soothed.

"The problem is that it's not the only price," Lindell complained. "We might be getting the stuff at good rates and almost immediately but it still has to be paid for. And they'll want the credit up front in case we disappear over the horizon never to be seen again, I bet."

"Thanks for that cheery prognostication," the first mate told him sardonically. "We'll just have to pony up the currency. You must have made a good impression on her, Cinnabar: one of her aides told me she doesn't suffer fools gladly, she assigns them to garbage scows at the back of beyond where they can do least damage."

"I know one or two that would benefit from that sort of billet," the captain replied. "But enough of this badinage. Have we enough in hand that we can pay for everything without depleting our coffers overmuch or sending our credit limits into orbit?"

"No," Lindell informed her gleefully. "But once we have the fees for both Delta Iridium commissions, we should be back on track; or at least our heads will be above water – just."

"Good. So see to it: payment on delivery *after* the goods have been checked out by Dr Flintlock. Or you'll be the first to lose your pay if we have to dock crew wages."

The two command officers left the supercargo grumbling and made their way to an engineering lab where Cottontail was modifying their decoy. Without Azular the task was progressing slowly but the chief engineer was sanguine that once fully upgraded, the device would be less liable to be exposed for what it was by enemy sensors and be able to defend itself to a limited degree.

"Just make sure it's nowhere in sight when Zillah comes by," the first mate instructed. "I suspect that she'll suspect we have a lot more tech than we're letting on about. She gets a whiff of that and she'll soon work out it's a piece of kit worth having."

"We've got the patent on it, so she can sod off," Cottontail said bluntly. "But I'm nearly done, so I'll store it in a shielded cargo pod and lock it down. When's she due aboard, Cap?"

"Tomorrow at ten hundred; she's coming in on a fleet shuttle. We won't have time for much more than a rapid run through most of the sections. But if any of your people are free over the next day or so, have them run more sims on power provision and equalisation for our new weapons and scanning systems. We don't want lack of practice throwing a spanner in the works."

"None of my people *are* free," the chief engineer protested. "The ones not on shore leave are up to their butts and liable to stay that way. But once we're on the trail, I'll get them working."

"Good enough. Let's see what catering can supply in the way of ship's biscuits for an admiral that has done us a favour," Ahxenta said to her second. "I have a strong suspicion that she won't forget it and will come by to collect someday."

"You and me both," agreed Apnis. "We'll just have to add her to the list of people we owe and hope the favours don't cost us more than we'd like to pay."

Admiral Zillah was punctual and accompanied only by a pilot, whom Ahxenta left in the capable hands of one of her own whilst she and her first mate conducted the tour. Their visitor was astute, inquisitive and attentive, firing a string of probing questions at the captain and the commander as they made their way round. Zillah had re-read with interest several reports describing a number of *Arianrhod's* recent encounters with alien and other ships. On that basis she made inquiry into the private opinions of both Ahxenta and Apnis on the recent aggression and its reported increases in incidence and ferocity, as well as its evidently expanding range of operations. One of the advantages that an admiral-in-chief of a planet allied to the ISP had was access to more information on certain matters than a private starship and as Zillah's questions seemed to be set on a specific track, Ahxenta asked her outright if there had been attacks in zones beyond the reaches of the Belts and its adjacent sectors.

The admiral shrugged and admitted that an unconfirmed report of a missing ISP ship had recently been received. The craft had vanished whilst investigating sightings of what was logged as a colossal starship of unknown profile prowling the empty spaces between the scattered worlds that skirted the edges of the Starglass Nebula. Ahxenta's eyes narrowed and the senior officer looked at her closely.

"Ah, I see you've heard something of it?"

"Not of the ISP ship, no; but one of our PSS captains told us of a pair of small transports racing into Heligon repair station with a story of some massive ship that they'd seen out near one of the abandoned worlds at the outer limits of the Starglass Nebula that they couldn't identify, more than a standard month ago now."

Apnis nodded. "Peakfrost," she concurred. "And the Starglass is as close as dammit to the edges of a galactic sub-zone where most of the systems are allied to the ISP."

"My senior science officer also reported a talk that he'd had with a pilot the last time we were out this way, not long since. The pilot had been flying a bunch of archaeologists back here from a long-haul trip to a deserted planet by the Starglass; their base station had apparently been buzzed by a small ship that looked like a fighter, but it took off when they tried to scan it. I don't have any more on *that* incident as the pilot was too canny to give much away. I expect his passengers were not on an officially-sanctioned mission."

"I hadn't heard that last one," Zillah conceded. "Not surprisingly, I suppose. But a big ship of unknown configuration has been spotted a few times now, out at the edge and beyond the margins of the treaty-bound systems where the ISP has interest; and as Freskat's in an ISP majority zone, word filters through. So it looks like these unknowns, whoever or whatever they are, may be operating at either end of the settled galactic sectors. We haven't had reports of ships taken out in our neck of the woods yet, but we *are* closer to the limits of charted space here than the majority of the unified systems, so it may only be a matter of time before something gives."

"Have you been asked to investigate the sightings out near the Starglass Nebula?" Ahxenta asked curiously.

The admiral laughed mirthlessly. "No, we're too far out of the way here. Arrissia Five would be the largest ISP-allied centre out that way. But as I copied your report as high priority to ISP Central, I've been tasked with investigating the anomaly in the Ginseng. ISP contacted me barely a couple of hours ago and asked me to despatch a ship. One will head out shortly to observe, but I won't authorise a close approach, given the fate of your probe. But warnings to keep your distance have been despatched via the usual military channels and I've deployed a few perimeter beacons to warn ships to keep away. It won't stop some but that's all I can do at present. So I suggest you avoid the area on your way out. What's your next heading anyway?"

"That's private," the captain told her equably. "Client business."

"Your call," Zillah responded composedly. "How are the upgrades to your medbay coming along?"

"We'll head that way next," Ahxenta returned, well aware that her guest was subtly reminding her of the strings she had pulled to allow the purchase of crucial gear. "But on the issue of the Ginseng, one of my officers heard of an incident out that way less than a week ago Freskat time: a pilot on regular repair run to Shearpoint Station said that a huge ship of unknown spec passed his crew at the edge of their systems-testing range, in normal space. It seemed to be slowing and its trajectory suggested a heading of the nebula. The crew were on the ground and had shut off their ship's ops for testing – Shearpoint *does* host a covert listening post – and so they probably weren't picked up by the unknown, if it *was* on the lookout. The pilot didn't report it officially as he didn't think he'd be taken seriously."

Zillah was taken aback that the captain was aware of the listening post and frowned sharply, but let it pass: she wanted details. Ahxenta could not provide them, as Azular's informant had been so well-oiled by the time he had found out thus much that he could find out little else. The other small-time pilots that the Berzic officer had talked to supplied little more than that the tourist trade was dwindling as news of rising raider activity in the more populous zones had been scaring off their clients, but the pilots *had* heard of the situation out by the Ginseng and were wary of heading in too close. The captain did not burden the admiral with that detail.

By the time the group reached medbay, Flintlock was in the throes of installing her upgraded facilities. She had been pleased with both the speed of delivery and the quality of the new systems and gear and wanted everything in place before the ship left orbit. Her reactions to the questions levelled at her by the admiral were cool, however: top brass did not intimidate her and never would.

If the visitor had been impressed by all she had seen aboard the *Arianrhod* she would not admit it, but she did compliment Ahxenta on running a tight ship. She also undertook to relay relevant updates on the findings of her own people in relation to the anomaly within the Ginseng, an assurance that the captain regarded a tad sceptically, wondering what the word 'relevant' actually meant. It was with relief that the senior officer was finally shepherded back to her waiting shuttle and sent off with a courteous exchange of farewells.

"At least she didn't eat all the biscuits," Apnis observed as she and the captain watched the craft exit the shuttle bay.

With their small but precious consignment of thin diamond wafers collected and safely sealed in a secure locker of an inner cargo hold, *Arianrhod* set course for Delta Iridium Six. The turnover on Freskat had been rapid, to the disappointment of some crew members who had hoped for a longer furlough, but Captain Ahxenta was adamant that no time be wasted. Their eventual destination of Merkat Three would provide sufficient facilities and time for leisure and as Coronis Comms had promised a bonus for the early delivery of their order, there was more than sufficient inducement for current efficiency. The original payload for the Delta Iridium system had also been safely stowed aboard the shuttle that was destined to take it planetside and the various obligatory manifests were in order. All hands hoped that this particular assignment would not be interrupted by any of the mayhem that seemed to be following the *Arianrhod* around like a lost hound. The ship appeared to have the proverbial albatross around its neck and it was proving to be a difficult bird to shift.

A narrow band Ultraviolet III hyperspace message to the captain from Freskat Six was the only interruption on the way to Delta. It was from Captain Adhara Peakfrost of the *PSS Quarkstorm*, who had business on Freskat Six and had been buttonholed by Admiral Zillah, who was well aware that the PSS fleet had a means of messaging denied to those in regular planetary space service. The comm was to the effect that the ISP had at long last decided to intervene in the ongoing unrest: the assistance of an ISP starship was promised to Freskat as early as possible and the ISP was marshalling its resources for activity elsewhere. This was possibly in response to the now-confirmed loss of an ISP ship near the Starglass Nebula.

"And so the fun begins," Apnis sighed when she heard the news on Ahxenta's return from her bridge office. "Does that mean that at every large port we make within a light year of an ISP-run zone, we're going to find herds of grunts from ISP troopships all over the place?"

"Depends how long it takes to assemble the relevant pieces and get them into place," the captain replied. "But it's going to take one helluva fine piece of organisation. ISP fleet ships haven't seen this much action since the last bust-up between the miners at Dryssicons Major and Minor and most of their big-time clients. And that was only over the low price of meta-jurillium alloy and the processing and freight costs, when some cut-throats were out for more than profit."

"We made one or two credits out of that," Apnis recalled.

"True; but somehow I think that this is an entirely different kettle of cookies. So far all we've made is busted heads and a busted ship and we're out of pocket big time."

"But we've survived and so has our reputation; that's what counts in this game."

"No it damn well doesn't," Ahxenta contradicted. "It's the profit that counts, and don't you forget it. Or the rest of you," she added, looking around at her openly eavesdropping duty bridge crew.

Delta Iridium Six had been reached without incident and it was with relief that *Arianrhod's* two cargoes had been delivered, after payment formalities had been handled. The ship remained in orbit until local clearances were completed and the crew spent its free time in tactical simulations, scrutiny of news channels and grumbles over authorities that had nothing better to do than delay departures over trivia.

Meanwhile, *Arianrhod* had heard nothing direct from Zillah over the irregularity within the Ginseng Nebula, other than a relayed link, again from Peakfrost, that the Freskat ship ordered into the area had circumnavigated the anomaly and set out warning beacons around it in one plane. The far side of the octagonal box-shape matched the face that the *Arianrhod* had initially encountered and although the interior of the space read empty to every form of scanning used on it, signals sent from the far side could not penetrate directly through it to receivers on the near side. Greffy had probably been right, was the opinion of *Arianrhod's* bridge crew: a small fleet could be hidden in the space and it was probably a nasty one, given the destruction of their probe. The information had been enough to cause a flurry within the upper echelons of the ISP, however, and a large science ship was en route to the area from the Skyrtek system.

"It might pass us," Apnis noted when she heard. "Delta Iridium Colony is part of the beacon system she'll have to use to navigate across zone Delta and into Lambda to reach Freskat."

"We won't be hanging about to say hello and ask exactly what they've been tasked with," Ahxenta told her. "Once we have the go-ahead to leave orbit, we're going. We have a shuttle to pick up."

"And shore leave to negotiate," the soft voice of Box from the navi-helm console was heard to mutter.

Arianrhod was well on her way back to Merkat and a rendezvous with her shuttle, the *Gadfly*, when a high-priority message came in from the Trades Alliance. The captain took it in her office. The news, imparted by a grave TA rep, had come from the Coalition Central Council. Given the long-running animosity as well as the internecine warfare that had disunited the rival bodies over the decades, that circumstance was surprising enough. Ahxenta was grim-faced when she returned to the bridge, and deeming that all her crew should know, she ordered her statement to be relayed ship-wide.

"You've all heard – and we in particular have suffered from – the depredations of what appears to be an enemy of unknown origin and unknown capability. The ISP has at last recognised that there's a problem and have decided to take a stand: a fleet of ISP ships has been mobilised and several systems-wide alerts are in place. I've just received an urgent communiqué from the TA upper chamber. You'll all remember the attack and sequestration of Marridan. The aliens have struck again using the same pattern: a small number of ships jump off the bypass at a local beacon, take out defence and comms and set up a blockade. Only the place they've hit this time is on one of our regular trading routes. The mining station Brown Amber has been attacked and is now under alien control."

Into the shocked silence came the quiet but plaintive voice of Navigation Officer Box. "Bang goes any more shore leave."

12: LIFE IN THE WEB

Debarkation was rapid at the main passenger-receiving facility that served the huge, utilitarian docking bays that formed part of Merkat Three Web's outer belt nine, and once past the obligatory name, rank and number checks at the entry to outer nine's habitation levels, the troopers of the Interstellar Systems Protectorate Starship *Trojan Horse* shook off their apathy and looked eagerly round for the quickest way to the nearest bar.

After a speedy scan of local schematics holos, the brighter of the advance wing set off at a trot to the elevator that would take them to sub-floor six and the *Frozen Sunbeam*, where, the holos assured them, a warm welcome and a cold beer awaited.

"One day we'll see the end of all these marching feet," murmured Jurry to his drinking partner as both cast wary eyes on the small army jogging by their lookout station behind a power pillar a little beyond the edge of the debark zone.

"Hope not," Malty said. "Think any of them are worth picking?"

"Not military types, unless you get one or two doofers on their own. In a bunch they get nasty and then you'll be sorry. Best head back to inner two and the *Half Moon*," Jurry advised sagely. "Some of them will no doubt end up there, once they start to find their way around. Outer belts are no fun and it's my belief they keep the heat turned down to discourage the likes of us from loitering."

It took the two some time to cadge their way around the vast Web that was the mighty Merkat Three commercial space dock to the cosy and relatively safe harbourages that comprised inner two belt. Their tenacity in seeking their objective was well-rewarded, for no sooner had they commandeered a small beer apiece and one of their usual tables with a good view of the door in the *Half Moon in a Puddle* than Jurry nudged his mate.

"Look there, Malty my lad. If that's not Grinsard Yellowfork, the *Tallulah's* senior science officer, holding up the bar, I'll eat my hat."

"You're not wearing a hat," Malty pointed out.

"If I was I'd eat it. But I'm right, it is, isn't it?" Jurry raised rheumy eyes to his friend's face and then cocked a wink at the lonely figure.

"You're right. What's he doing out on his own?"

"Drinking by the look of it. Drowning his sorrows maybe, and with Fleetskup in command he probably has plenty. But that means the *Tallulah* must be in. I hadn't heard she was due, had you?"

"No," conceded Malty. "But then we're never first to be informed on the transport in and out of Merkat. In fact we're never informed. In fact, it's my opinion that certain parties go out of their way to keep us in the dark."

"Your trouble is you're a pessimist," Jurry enlightened him. "But the Interstellar Systems Protectorate, the Trades Alliance *and* the Coalition all drinking in the same place? Now that's novelty for you."

"So who's here that belongs to all that lot?"

"That's a couple of Friskies over there, so that's Coalition; there's Yellowfork for the Trades and we've seen the ISP and it won't be long before a couple of them roll in. So there you are." Jurry set his pot gently on the table. "You think Yellowfork would stand us a jar if we asked nice?"

"We could try. Poor lad's alone, after all. But he's a pirate; they're only loosely linked to the TA," Malty disagreed. "All they do is fly the flag and cough up their fees so they can legally get port clearances."

"Same difference. Let's speak to the boy."

The senior science officer of the *PSS Tallulah*, Lieutenant Grinsard Yellowfork, was certainly in a low mood. Jurry and Malty had that figured ten seconds after sidling over to begin their double act with the opening observation that it was a busy morning in the *Half Moon*, was it not, and was the young lieutenant here on business?

Yellowfork was short with them but undeterred they continued with a mix of flattery and cajolery to break down his defences, going so far as to offer him a drink. Malty bought him the first one; it was tacitly understood that he would be shelling out for all the others.

The lieutenant was on shore leave as his senior officers had been bidden to an important Trades Alliance meeting. As ex-spacers, the two topers could well sympathise with the flurry of activity that a summons from the TA would cause aboard a ship like the *Tallulah*, especially, as Jurry delicately hinted, with a captain such as Murmur Fleetskup, who was known for his adherence to every jot and tittle of protocol. But interruptions to the day's activities such as unscheduled meetings no doubt had knock-on effects that caused other problems. Yellowfork's eyes blazed, his lips performed a sudden downturn and he let rip with a muted oath that led his two hearers to conclude that here was the source of the trouble: he was a victim of his captain's over-zealous attention to duty.

Ally lent his ears and his mouth to the debate as he served relays of cold beer and sound advice on the way to deal with a captain who would let slip the important matter of a young officer's promotion to first lieutenant and its resultant rise in pay for the trivial matter of a meeting about possible interstellar war. Shore leave, even in the Web, was no compensation for loss of rank and credit for no good reason but that Fleetskup liked to be first in line when the chance of a high-level pow-wow with prominent people was in the offing.

Ally was forthright. "Get a berth aboard another ship," he advised Yellowfork. "I see one of your senior medics managed to decamp to the *Arianrhod* last bout, and I bet he's not come back."

Yellowfork had to admit that such was the case. But they wouldn't want him on the *Arianrhod*: she already had a senior science officer who was much more skilled and highly ranked than he was, and a second who was way in advance of the typical products disgorged by the various science academies up and down the sector at the end of each standard academic year. Despite his high scholastic gradings and his consistently sound scores during his obligatory term of military service, the young lieutenant had been taken on as a cheap option by Fleetskup and he knew it. He continued to sip his beer morosely.

Within a secluded meeting room of the TA in that organisation's HQ in the Web, the subject of the captured station Brown Amber was the topic under discussion. Several TA reps were present, with trading partners from elsewhere and a number of the PSS fleet that had made it in. In addition to the command-rank officers from the *Arianrhod* and the *Tallulah*, those from the *Obsidian Sky, Equinox, Quarkstorm, Hexameter, Labyrinth* and *Karillion* were all there. The *Green Comet* was still out but her injured first mate Ace Periwinkle had hobbled up from the Web's medbay to show solidarity and share what he knew of the *Comet's* recent encounter. Captain Cinnabar Ahxenta looked around at the number of well-known and less well known faces that surrounded her.

"If someone wanted to take out a goodly number of the leading reps of the TA and its associates in one fell swoop, now would be the time," she remarked.

The TA chairman looked startled, but called for order. "Brown Amber," he began. "You've all been briefed so I don't need to repeat the story. We've no more than what you were told. But some of you will have been out that way recently and this meeting gives you the opportunity to bring us up to date on anything you know, or that you may have heard or suspect in relation to the attacks on Amber and Marridan, or on the assaults on shipping in local sectors and beyond, or anything else that may be related. The records will be passed to the Interstellar Systems Protectorate's Council once complete. Everyone will have a chance to take the floor."

"Hell, does that mean Fleetskup as well?" Apnis groaned in an aside to Ahxenta.

Unfortunately, Captain Fleetskup was included and was one of the first to his feet, but as his ship had neither been attacked nor had he much to say, the chairman firmly quashed him with a few polite but well-chosen words. Ahxenta of the *Arianrhod* and Bluejohn of the *Obsidian Sky* were the two most recently involved in skirmishes with what were now almost unanimously being recognised as unknown and definitely hostile aggressors, and the chairman quickly called them before Fleetskup could take umbrage.

Bluejohn, at a gesture from Ahxenta, began with his clash and the pieces he had been able to put together based on his own data and that provided by the tactical and science stations of the *Green Comet* and the *Arianrhod*. His science officer had put together various holos as to the similarities in the composition and structure of the attacking vessels and it was now almost certain that the ships were either new, or highly advanced versions of current technology.

"Which means exactly what?" demanded Fleetskup.

Which could mean, Bluejohn clarified, that the enemy might be unknowns from outside, unknowns from inside the mapped zones that had not shown their hands before and were advancing aggressive technologies in secret, or – and this was worrying – those responsible might belong to the known races of local galactic zones, sub-zones and sectors, possibly in league with powers inside or outside those areas that were either supplying superior technology, or the knowhow that allowed the development of such technology.

That last statement caused a flurry of argument and questioning that was obviously going nowhere. The chairman rapped again for order and demanded that speculation be left well alone until all the facts were garnered. He called on Ahxenta to speak, as her ship had not only suffered attack but was involved in the pickup of Marridani refugees and had also recently been to Brown Amber. Hers was also the only ship that had been known to have downed one of the enemy vessels single-handedly.

The *Arianrhod's* captain was in no mind to repeat all that Bluejohn had succinctly summarised but reiterated the details of hull structure that had led to the belief that some attacking ships had been built using locally-sourced means, however alien they appeared otherwise. This strongly suggested that the so-called aliens had either infiltrated one or more allied systems or that certain systems were involved, either willingly or unwillingly with them. This plain speaking caused ruffled feathers among her audience but Ahxenta was unrepentant. If the information was going out to ISP, Coalition and Non-Treaty bodies, then let them argue the toss.

The captain then went on to give an account of the assault on the *Arianrhod* and her escape from the larger and better-armed battleship in the Orriga Two asteroid field. She deliberately omitted to mention *Arianrhod's* cloaking system and the decoy projecting device that had been developed by Cottontail and Azular, but gave a fair account of the means they had used to escape and then to end their assailant's attack. The running so close against the enemy's hull that *Arianrhod's* guns could take out her surface emplacements was greeted with some incredulity but Ahxenta's ice-water glance quelled the doubters and she went on to describe the breakup of the enemy ship, the launch of the small fleet of what were probably escape transports and the inability of her ship to stop them. Here she paid tribute to Bluejohn and the *Obsidian Sky*, without whom they would have been left almost as sitting ducks for any other would-be aggressors.

The TA and the ISP had been notified of the incident but neither Ahxenta nor Bluejohn had had follow-up on any actions taken in relation to their joint request for these bodies to carry out in-depth searches amongst the scattered debris presumably still circulating out among the rocks of the Orriga asteroid field. This was more than important, given that *Arianrhod's* senior science officer had reported that certain hull fragments of the alien mothership that *had* been recovered bore a meta-jurillium alloy signal that was not related to the largest and most important local source of Beta Zegonia 68c.

The TA chairman looked askance at this and had to admit that he had no further information on anything that had been found out near the Orriga Two sector, but that no doubt they would be informed in due course. More than one person present recalled the earlier attacks on Dryssicon, where cargoes of raw meta-jurillium ore were targeted. It was apparent that these aliens were well capable of processing their own sources as well as stolen ore from elsewhere.

The *Quarkstorm's* Captain Peakfrost brought up the extension of hostilities to the further end of charted space. Confirmation had been received that the ISP ship lost whilst investigating sightings of a mystery starship lurking around the edges of the Starglass Nebula had probably been attacked: a prospector ship from Freskat Six scouting the area had picked up two ion trails of unknown type but indicating large vessels, and a trail of debris that crossed them. In the face of the evidence, the small ship had run for home, having no inclination to face whatever had left the trails. Peakfrost had not heard of any other incident whilst at Freskat, but the Freski themselves were concerned, particularly as the octagonal anomaly within the Ginseng Nebula first reported by the *Arianrhod* was expanding and had eaten up a couple of their marker beacons.

"Admiral-in-Chief Zillah of Freskat Six has despatched a couple of ships to the Starglass," Ahxenta interposed. "I had a communiqué copied to me that she'd sent to the ISP. They're scouting only, they have orders not to engage."

Murmur Fleetskup was immediately on the defensive. "Why did she copy it to you and not the rest of us?" he demanded.

"She's not an inter-system news service," Ahxenta informed him curtly. "We reported the anomaly in the Ginseng to the authorities on Freskat and she updated me as a courtesy. So what are we going to do about the problem under discussion? It's affecting our trading and it's sure as hell scaring the socks off most local systems and sending their militaries into a spin. We could be looking at galactic meltdown as well as our own losses."

The chairman cut in before Fleetskup could respond with more pique. "We've sent representatives to a high-level, confidential joint meeting with the ISP, the Coalition, the NTA and reps from various independent systems. They've still to report back, but we're getting updates and it looks like there will be some sort of super-alliance formed to combat the incursions, as we all seem to be affected."

"Who's this all?" Bluejohn wanted to know. "And how can any assembly, however high-level and hush-hush, bring in every affected body without bringing in spies or infiltrators from these unknowns, whoever the heck they are? You can't keep a secret meeting secret if half the damn galaxy knows it's happening and most of them have their own people in on the act."

"I agree," Fleetskup broke in. "We have very little knowledge of the Independent systems in zone Mu for example, and these invaders have now been seen in the area around the Starglass Nebula: not that far off beacon from zone Mu…" He paused portentously. "How do we know that the aliens don't hail from near there?"

"Hell, where did he learn navigation?" Apnis muttered to Ahxenta as a burst of indignation indicated that the Independent systems reps at the table had taken exception to the observation.

"I think you'll find that the Starglass is a tad closer to the edges of the furthest sub-zone of zone Zeta, and most of the major systems in that region belong to the ISP," *Arianrhod's* first mate corrected him. "Arrissia Five and Heligon Station are the nearest known outposts to the Starglass, and Heligon's far enough away. But have you any other news from Heligon, apart from what you brought in a while ago now, Captain Peakfrost?"

Peakfrost shook her head. "I've heard no more and it was just a tale at the time. A pair of transports hightailed it into Heligon's repair station with a story of a colossal anonymous starship they'd spied out near one of the far-flung worlds on the edge of the Starglass," she reiterated for the benefit of those who hadn't heard. "But we've now had unconfirmed reports of sightings of a large ship and a fighter that may or may not have something to do with it in the area. And now this loss of an ISP starship, so something sure as hell's going on in that neck of the galaxy. I'd say it's likely that these unknowns have an interest in the deserted worlds out by the edges of the Starglass and the attacks at the other end of the settled zones may be a way of keeping other people's noses out of their business – maybe."

"You've got a point there, Adhara," Ahxenta agreed. "It may be that the unknowns hail from one or more of the deserted worlds out beyond the mapped and settled zones. Star systems out that way have been known about for centuries but their planets were rumoured to be uninhabited or once inhabited and then abandoned. Maybe they're not all as empty as we thought, or some systems even further out are getting narky that their part of the galaxy is being encroached on. Hell knows there have been archaeological trips out that way for long and weary, with no doubt some interesting stuff being dug up. But on that point: I heard another unconfirmed report of a mystery ship, this one sighted near Shearpoint Station, close by the Ginseng Nebula."

"Until we have the reports from the ship or ships that have been sent to the *Starglass* Nebula, we won't be able to assess that situation, or any other related situation," Fleetskup interrupted. "But we're here to discuss Brown Amber and what we do about that, aren't we?"

"He sometimes has a point," Apnis remarked to her captain as the TA chairman called for an account of the *Arianrhod's* last visit there.

Ahxenta grinned at that and, skirting over their enforced sojourn at Jurassa for repair, she outlined their stay at Brown Amber, noting that as the station was within an asteroid field that made navigation hazardous, any rescue attempts would likewise be risky. The fact that the station had fallen into enemy hands was itself thought-provoking, given the dangers in the local area, and she for one was interested in the actual details of an assault that on the face of it was so speedy that it caught everyone by surprise. Jumping out of hyperspace and into the edges of an asteroid field was hardly an everyday event and must have required careful planning.

"I noted from the briefing we were sent that Amber's subsidiary stations out in the field were not attacked. There was no mention of what happened to their crews or any ships in orbit there."

"That's because we don't know," the chairman told her. "The attackers set up jamming and we've not heard. I would hope they ran, but we've had nothing. We're on alert; if something comes in we'll be informed. And as you know, the ISP has a presence here now, so it can be ready for deployment at short notice if the need arises. I hope," he added. "Go on, Captain."

Thus invited, Ahxenta quickly listed the incidents at Amber that had caused disquiet: the power surges from the station's reactor core and other systems; the diagnostics run that effectively cut long-range comms; and the high-level visitors that no-one would talk about. Azular's intuition that the visitors were causing the natives unease she omitted to mention but she did refer to the activity of the heavily-armed transport *Lambda Red Velvet*, docked alongside.

The final part of her input concerned the anomaly at Freskat that had already been reported and acted upon by the ISP: Admiral Zillah had seen to that. But Ahxenta had heard no more of the results other than that a ship had been sent to investigate and as Captain Peakfrost had said, the anomaly was expanding and destroying what was in its path, as it had the *Arianrhod's* first probe. The pilots that ran tourists to the Ginseng Nebula, she knew, were now refusing to do so until the matter was resolved. Not that the pilots cared: they had their insurance that paid up if trade was cancelled due to clear and present danger, and given that the ISP was on its way in, that counted as clear and present danger. Azular had found that out in one of the bars on Freskat Six and had told the captain before they left the system. That was another nugget she felt she had better not mention.

After various mutterings and grumblings about the known attacks there was little else to say and the meeting was adjourned, with the proviso that if more news came in, another session would be called.

"If they think I'm hanging on here in the hope that they'll have more to say in the next day or two, they can get lost," Grey Bluejohn told Ahxenta as the two and their first mates made their way along the corridor. "Unknown aliens or no, I have commissions to fulfil."

"As do we all. But I'm here for a couple of days, so I'll send on anything that comes in. Watch your back, Grey," she warned him.

"I'll be watching more than my back," he replied with a crooked smile. "Take care, Cinnabar. I'll see you flipside one of these days."

"Count on it," she smiled back as he waved a farewell and he and his first mate set off.

"Where to now?" Apnis asked her commanding officer.

"*Half Moon*. I need a drink."

"You paying?"

"I expect. Let's march; there's Fleetskup and he's got that looking for company to bore expression."

The *Half Moon* was half empty when the two officers strolled in. Ally looked over the top of a glass he had been polishing.

"Welcome," he said. "This one's on the house. We heard all about the doings at Orriga Two," he went on, slapping down two brimming mugs. "The legendary *Arianrhod* takes on the unbeatable enemy and sends them to hell. Care to tell me what really happened out there?"

"Only if you pay for the next one as well," Apnis told him.

"Deal. Take a seat and tell all. You two find your own space," he shot peremptorily at Jurry and Malty, waving a dismissive hand at the pair, who had slunk across from the far reaches of the bar on the off-chance of hearing something of which profit could be made later.

"Those two dunned young Yellowfork of the *Tallulah* out of half a day's pay only this morning," Ally confided. "Poor lad was up for his annual bootlicking, with the promise of promotion to first lieutenant and the chance of more pay and bigger bonuses, and then this Trades Alliance meeting comes up, so Captain Fleetskup cancels all his staff reviews for the duration and sets off to be first in line at the TA door. I told Yellowfork to find a new berth and suggested he asked you," he added, grinning wickedly. "Need another science officer?"

"No thanks," Ahxenta shot back. "Not one of Fleetskup's cast-offs anyway."

"You took Dr Greenwing."

"Greenwing my chief medic knew and vouched for and I needed him. More I don't. What are *they* saying happened out at Orriga?"

Ally enlarged on the stories that had come his way. The battleship was twice the size of a small moon and had a fleet of fighters that would make even Dryssicon miners back off, apparently. *Arianrhod* had of course legendary firepower and daring and had got so close to the enemy before opening fire that she could see the red of his eyes.

"So, tell me all, or at least what you would like me to spread about among my clients," Ally said, holding out another jar of ale each to the pair. "I've even had the middle ranks of the *ISPS Trojan Horse* in asking after you, all the way from their little bunks in outer nine."

The two were only half-way into the version of events judged appropriate by the captain to circulate to outsiders when Ally gave a low warning whistle. "Your best pal's just come in with his best pal at back of him," he told them, nodding towards the *Half Moon's* entry.

Ahxenta squinted over as Captain Fleetskup and his ever-present exec Buntle sailed through the holo-door. "I thought he'd gone back to the *Tallulah* to create chaos out of order," she groaned. "And where's Melly Goodsocks? Back aboard?"

"Lieutenant Yellowfork said the *Tallulah* was here for at least a week as they'd running repairs to their inner cargo bay doors to get done and Mr Buntle was arguing the toss with the repair crews about the cost," Ally told her.

"He'd argue with his grandmother if he thought it would benefit his pocket," Apnis stated baldly. "How he rates the rank of lieutenant I don't know."

The two from *Arianrhod* had instantly been spotted and Fleetskup and his exec made their way to the bar.

"Another memo from the TA Board Assembly out at Alto Finglas asking for our presence at a meeting tomorrow afternoon," Fleetskup announced. "It's about trading issues concerning the lower sectors of galactic zones Epsilon and Zeta."

"Another one?" grumbled his fellow captain. "You'd think we'd nothing better to do than jump every time the TA snaps its fingers."

"They're getting beyond themselves," replied Fleetskup. "The meeting will be in the TA meeting rooms here."

"How did you find out? I heard nothing," Ahxenta said.

"It came in as I was discussing meeting outcomes with the TA reps after our meeting earlier," Fleetskup said in what he considered a quiet tone, his face turned away from the bar, although Ally and everyone else within a stone's throw could hear clearly.

"You mean twenty minutes ago," Apnis pointed out. "What did you have to discuss that took so long, your part in this galactic action that's in the offing? *Tallulah* will be first on the firing line, will she?"

"We're a trading vessel, Commander Apnis, same as the *Arianrhod*:

we do not engage in hostilities unless absolutely unavoidable."

"You see a fight and run away, you live to take flight another day," the barman put in from the sidelines.

"Hardly!" Fleetskup snorted, put out. "We can and have fought when necessary and fought well."

"There's no point in looking for trouble but if you see it, get out quick. First rule of self-preservation," Tommy Buntle put in.

"How did you manage to get over so quickly, Mr Buntle?" asked Ahxenta. "You weren't at the senior officers' meeting, naturally."

"I was on ship's business elsewhere, Captain," he said smoothly. "I can't discuss it, obviously."

"Obviously. Well, thanks for letting us know, Murmur. Good of you to stop by."

The irony was lost on the redoubtable captain of the *Tallulah*, for he preened, told her she was welcome and offered to buy her and her first mate another drink. Ahxenta accepted as she figured she may as well try to prise out of him exactly what *had* been the discussion topics after the TA meeting. In the event, she learned little: it seemed that he had been filling the ears of the luckless TA reps with his own woes to ensure that his ship would not be the first called into action should the Privates, under the TA flag, be commandeered for any defensive or offensive activity that the governing powers deemed appropriate. It was an unlikely although not unheard of event and sanctions against those who refused to show willing was a possible outcome. The captain of the *Arianrhod* scented the manoeuvrings of Tallulah Tommy behind it all, but said nothing.

Captain Fleetskup eventually realised that he would get no further forward with his attempts to impress Tallica Apnis and at last bid the two officers farewell, telling them that he would see them later.

"He'll see us later," Cinnabar Ahxenta repeated mockingly to her first mate as the pair from the *Tallulah* departed.

"Not if I see him first, he won't," she replied.

13: PREP

Ahxenta and Apnis strolled wearily in the direction of the *Half Moon in a Puddle*. It had been a long morning in the outer belts arguing with obstinate Port Authority reps over docking fees and an equally long afternoon in the Trades Alliance meeting rooms closer in and both felt in need of a great deal of refreshment.

"At least we got rid of Fleetskup; he hangs around like a scarf," the first mate grumbled. "Makes us look like his minders, the way he always insists on walking between us."

"We give him emotional security," the captain told her.

"I'd give him a kick up the arse if I could summon the energy."

"He'd look on that as a mark of your undying affection. You'd never see the end of him," Ahxenta warned. "And this must be your turn to pay. I'm hungry. We may as well eat here; Ally's rations are as good as we get aboard *Arianrhod*."

"Don't tell chef or he'll sulk for weeks. What in hell is going on?" Apnis added as a shape rolled through the holo portal to land at their feet with a groan and an expletive that neither had heard recently.

"Fleet's in with a vengeance," the captain said, eyeing the badge of the snuffling figure. "First the *Trojan Horse*, now the *Argus*. It's always the same when the grunts heave to: no place to hang your hat and fights on every corner. Better hope Ally's called in reinforcements."

Ally had. His place was besieged and at least twenty pairs of eyes looked the two over as they made their way to the bar. The *Half Moon* was also well-lit for once: there was no chance that anyone would be hiding in the corners.

"What's with the illumination, Merry?" Apnis asked of the young woman behind the bar. "Ally come into some credit or is he afraid someone will sue him for ruining their eyesight?"

"He wants to make sure we can see any trouble before it finishes," Merry told her chirpily. "Merkat security's here as well as our own to keep the peace. What are you having, Captain, Commander?"

"Hey, we were here first!" The strident voice belonged to a non-commissioned type whose green fatigues and lurid badge showed that he was a member of the fifty ninth division of some troop or other.

"So you were," Ahxenta agreed. "Top marks for observation. Get the soldier a drink on Commander Apnis, Merry: he's a smart one."

Apnis sighed. "We've been here before," she said half to herself. "Just once it would be nice to drop into a bar for a meal without some heavy wanting to pick a fight."

A couple of the man's mates were at some pains to point out to him that although he was not dealing with a military officer, the pips associated with the uniform suggested that Ahxenta was a tad higher up the ranking scale than he was and perhaps it would be better if he let the matter be. The others were grinning in delight, clenching their hands in anticipation and hoping for a really good brawl.

"No weapons, tonight, Captain," Merry warned. "Not even stuns, security's orders."

"I saw the sign as we came in," Ahxenta assured her. "I take it fists don't count as weapons?"

"Yours sure do," Merry giggled. "Right, boys and girls, pipe down. And you, soldier, have a drink and shut your mouth."

She placed a quickly poured ale in front of the man and turned to get a couple more for Ahxenta and her first mate.

"Who the hell do you think you are?" the soldier persisted.

"I'm the captain of the *PSS Arianrhod*. Who the hell are you?" Ahxenta responded equably as half the company close to her backed off. Many of them had realised that she belonged to the *Arianrhod*, still being in a fit state to be able to read the badge she wore, but few had realised quite how senior she was.

The murmuring around the two officers swelled as word of their identities swept around the bar. Ally, it appeared, had been spreading rumours. Several customers unashamedly moved to higher ground, on tables in the booths at the edge, to get a better view.

Who actually threw the first glass was never ascertained but it took only seconds for another to join it and as Apnis ducked to avoid a third she felt a blow to her side. Her leg flicked out at her assailant and he tumbled like a ninepin. She could see the delight in the eyes of the grunts nearest her: this was the kind of night they liked, a bellyful of ale and a good punch-up. They waded in with arms flailing.

Heads rocked back as punches were levelled and bodies fell over the immoveable furniture, and all around could be heard the repeated thwacking of the rigid glassware in an attempt to break it. The *Half Moon in a Puddle* was awash with bodies, ale, food and blood and the yells could be heard three blocks away. Even the amplified bellowing of the *Half Moon's* security team, seconded by the drafted-in extras from Merkat as they pushed their way in, were but harmony to the melody. The whole was a glorious fusion of uniforms, boots and fists, a grand opera of the body physical.

There was a loud burst of what seemed to be weapons fire despite the prohibition and for a second the action froze.

"Break it up you grunts! Break it up or your heads'll be up your sorry arses!"

"Now that's what I call a voice," Ahxenta gasped to her first mate as the forms around them melted away, some sliding to the floor, some edging to the back and trying to look invisible. "It could shatter even Ally's crockery."

Commander Apnis stood up, wiping blood from her mouth. "You all right, Cap?"

"Been better. Nothing a good jar of ale and a hot meal won't cure, I hope. You?"

"I'll live. I expect."

Meanwhile, the owner of the voice, still roaring, had marched over to the main protagonist and his coterie to demand an account of who had started it. He had his own ideas.

"It was you, Fender, wasn't it, you thick-eared, flat-headed shithole!"

"No, Sarn't-Major!"

"You, Briggait, who started it?"

"I don't know, Sarn't-Major!"

This response was echoed by the next four or five battered faces. Everyone else in ISP uniform was enjoying the scene whilst trying to escape the notice of the sergeant-major, whose eyes were flashing like twin beacons around the bar. The eyes stopped roaming when they hit Ahxenta and Apnis, dusting down their uniforms and removing bits of teeth and other ephemera from their persons. The sergeant-major snapped to an upright position and faced the captain.

"Apologies, Captain. If you'll let me have a note of damages, I'll see reparations are made. The same goes for you," he added to the tallest of the *Half Moon's* security detail, deeming him to be in charge.

"Forget it on my behalf, Sergeant-Major," Ahxenta replied. "I'd say it was a pretty fair fight: the two of us against your half dozen or so." She eyed the line-up against the bar, raising a sardonic eyebrow.

"Yes, I don't guess they quite realised who or what they'd taken on," he guffawed, taking in her badge.

"Speak to Ally," the head of the *Half Moon's* security squad advised as the sergeant-major cocked an eye in his direction. "Up to him, it's his bar. And I guess they have enough of your lot in the cells already without wanting to add to it."

Ally rolled up, shaking his head. "Take them away, Sarn't-Major, but what you do with 'em is up to you. I'll let you know how much damage they've caused when I've worked it out. Meanwhile, back to work!" he addressed his staff in stentorian tones. "These people are thirsty and hungry!"

"He can say that again," Apnis observed. "Nothing like a bout of fisticuffs to give you an appetite. We'd better be first on the list for the eats or I'll be having something to say."

The two officers made for a small table at the edge of the bar with a good view of the entry: if any more trouble walked through it, they wanted advance warning. Their meeting with the TA representatives had given them and the other TA-linked Privates something to think about. The trading concerns relating to the distant sectors of galactic zones Epsilon and Zeta were chiefly that the areas were now listed as dangerous for travel. There had been no more reports from the ships despatched to the area around the Starglass Nebula, but rumours of minor attacks within well-habited parts of the region were growing. It seemed that the new bullies on the block were attempting hostilities on at least two fronts and that meant trouble. The two major areas of conflict were located at either end of the charted galaxy and thus a vast distance apart, indicating that the two arms of the attack forces were in effect autonomous and able to operate without joint supply lines, but there had to a communications network between them.

As a result the TA, in concert with ISP, Coalition and Non-Treaty Alliance governing bodies, had come to a degree of concordance on some of the action that needed to be taken. The major aspect that concerned the Privates was that if hostilities became more general, ships flying under the TA flag were liable to be called in as back-up to official military fleets. Not, however, in the front line, it had been stipulated, but as reserve supply and transport vessels. They would be compensated, naturally, for loss of trade. Most of the Privates were far from happy at this edict and had made their sentiments plain, but they were faced with the loss of their flag and the benefits they accrued from it if they resisted.

"We've been bloody drafted, is what we've been," Tallica Apnis complained as the privacy shield distorted at the entry of their rations in Merry's hands, the serving hatch being out of commission for the duration. "And you can bet that any war damage won't be insurable, and will the ISP and its band of new friends cough up if we sustain damage in their service?"

"I doubt it," was the dry reply as the shield reformed around their table. "Once we've finished here, we'd best get back aboard. I'll have to send the news through to Grey," she continued as she uncovered her steaming platter. "The *Gadfly* should be back aboard by this time if Crizz has got her team organised. It strikes me that if the ISP and all the other hangers-on could work out how these two arms of the unknown force can remain in contact with each other, they can cut their comms and cause them a mighty headache."

"Has it occurred to anyone that these two fleets or whatever they are may be completely separate and it's just coincidence that we seem to be fighting actions on two fronts?"

"Probably, but it's unlikely, given the similarity of ships and attack modes. It's also possible that there *are* more than two units of this attack fleet ready to jump out of hyperspace at the drop of a hat, or a planet. But it's their comms that concern me: there must be link stations or outposts within the settled systems network and they're damn well hidden. Hell knows there are enough empty planets and spaces out there that could function as listening posts and comms relay stations for a dozen enemy fleets, and if comms are properly encoded, who the blazes would know?"

"Tommy Buntle?" Apnis suggested half jocularly.

"That man I don't like and never have, but I don't think even he would stoop so low, nor risk his neck for that matter. And if he did, Melly Goodsocks at least would be aware of it. Fleetskup places far too much reliance on him, but a fair number of the *Tallulah's* crew is smart enough."

"Which is why a few of them want to sign on with us," the first mate chuckled.

"True," Ahxenta acknowledged "But back to the hostiles: given that they must have a complex comms network and plenty of spies within the settled regions, they'll surely know or at least suspect what this collaboration of all the major governing powers in our neck of the galaxy has been up to. Which means that the Privates will be as much a target as military ships."

"That's so. But we've been targeted already, so nothing changes. I think anything that moves is a target for these unknowns. They seem to take down anything in their path or out of it."

The captain considered for a moment, raised an eyebrow at her first mate and tapped a finger on the table.

"Come on, Cinnabar, I know that look. What's just occurred in that brain of yours?"

"Not here. Privacy shield we have, but I bet a few of the inebriates out there are damned good lip-readers. Finish your dinner and drink your ale. It's time we were back aboard anyway and I need to see Flintlock about something to put on my bruises – I'm getting too long in the tooth for this sort of daily bust-up."

At a distant table, Jurry sighed into his mug. "There they go," he said to his drinking buddy, indicating the exit. "No more punch-ups tonight then. Pity, Malty my lad; we might have been able to pick up a few bungs helping to sort out the walking wounded."

"Life always kicks you when you're down," Malty responded. "But on the bright side, there's another one of Fleetskup's disenchanted troop walked in. It's Lieutenant Inks. Maybe he's been passed over for promotion as well and wants a shoulder to cry on. Or at least a couple of ears to bend: I don't think Jesse Inks is a cry-baby."

"We can but try to spread a little sunshine."

"Tricky when the sun's so far away you can't see it, but let's try."

Back aboard, Ahxenta stopped in at medbay for an appointment with her chief medic, despatched the latest on the crisis to Bluejohn of the *Obsidian Sky* with the request that he pass it on to any he saw fit and then called a briefing of her senior officers. After a summary of the current situation, the increased risks that could pose hazards for trading trips to the outer edges of Epsilon and Zeta and the possible commandeering of the *Arianrhod*, she outlined the issues as she saw them regarding the comms needs of the unknown fleets and more importantly, the observation by Apnis that any ship that moved was potentially on their hit list.

"Comms? You have a point, Captain," Azular ruminated. "There *are* a lot of out of the way places in poorly mapped sectors with little of known value. With a covert system of relay stations, you could get away with quite a lot."

"Or you could batten onto existing systems and send messages using standard channels, but encoding them in such a way that only those in the know could access them," Crizz Cottontail put in. "The tech's available."

"Now that's sneaky," the captain said. "But is it possible, with all the usual security systems in place? Not to mention the villains out there who make it their business to find out other people's secrets and then sell them on to the highest bidder – they'd soon crack any channels that could be cracked."

"Commercial channels," Cottontail opined gruffly. "Who'd check? That reminds me, Mr Bellfish: those recruitment ads for construction workers and miners for various places that you picked up at Brown Amber on their news and business channels – you reported a lot of comms traffic. And there were a whole heap of ships docked around the place that weren't the usual freeloaders, though we couldn't fathom what they were up to, or even who they all were. But isn't it a coincidence that not a lot later Amber is taken over by enemy forces? Handy place as a base for gems supplies for crystal comms systems, and close enough to Jurgall Three that can supply meta-jurillium alloy and the wherewithal to construct hull sections, if not complete hulls."

"And also not too far from Mellifly," Azular put in, holding up a interrogative finger. "And there you have repair docks and sheds for any sort of refit, as our ex-passenger Bick Micklemouse informed us; and where his contacts have their own repair dock, come to that."

"I wonder how many more little rodents like Micklemouse are out there," the chief engineer muttered. "If he's part of this alien invasion or whatever it is, the known galaxy might well be scuppered."

"That's as maybe," the captain interrupted. "Our main concerns are delivering our cargoes and maintaining our business footing with our clients despite the crisis. To that end the comms situation needs a close eye: we don't want a raiding party popping out of hyperspace at our backs with murder in mind. And we have to keep abreast of local and extra-local events so we're not taken unprepared; that's your area, Lieutenant Bellfish. As for everyone else, we need every system at full capacity; that at least should give us some edge if we do happen to meet another of these starships. So our cloak and our decoy device are priorities for you, Chief, and you, Azular."

"Fine as it goes, Cap," Apnis interposed. "But back at the *Half Moon* a light went on, so there's something else isn't there?"

Ahxenta nodded. "This brings me back to your point that any ship is a target for these raiders, whether or not it has a cargo. It could just be terror tactics, but that beggars the question why waste the energy and time, not to mention the potential for damage to your own? They clear up their own dunnage so that little evidence is left about them. I suspect they're probably using any scrap they collect to repair their own, or possibly build new."

"They're basically garbage scows, but very dangerous ones?" an incredulous Lieutenant Lindell put in.

"It's only an idea, but why mine or filch meta-jurillium for your ships when you can steal others, strip them and use the bits to build more? But that's not my point: they seem to go for anything that moves, so if we become a target, we could give them a mark to aim for that would give us time to run or to mount a better defence."

"But that's what the decoy does, Cap!" Cottontail burst out.

Whisper Earbleat, silent to that point, tilted her head and tapped a finger on the table. "The decoy's a projection, an empty vision, and as the enemy's now seen it in action, they've no doubt told the rest of their fleet to look out for similar. It would be far better if the decoy was solid, steerable and filled to the gunnels with enough explosive to cause serious damage, but with effective shielding so that the target wouldn't clock it until too late. Yes, it would have to be small if we had to carry it aboard *Arianrhod*, but…"

"Any science officer worth their rations would figure it was a fake and there was no-one aboard!" the chief engineer argued.

"Not if obvious indicators and enough organic mass suggested otherwise, and that's doable, isn't it Doc?" the second mate appealed to Axellina Flintlock.

"I *could* simulate a pilot, but why go the trouble? Anything we'd be able to store aboard would be too small to be more than a pinprick to any sizeable ship. You could just launch a shuttle under auto control, which would give any attackers two targets instead of one. Okay we risk a ship but it would serve the same purpose."

"No it wouldn't!" Earbleat disputed. "Our shuttles carry our call-sign and are designed to keep us safe and secure in tight places. A decoy shuttle wouldn't need that and it could be fitted with a tracker so that if it was captured we could follow it!"

"Now you're getting out of hand; we're not the interstellar police force," the doctor responded.

"Enough," Ahxenta cut in. "The doctor's right, that's out of our league. My concern is protecting this ship and her crew. And the trick could be used only once; but if a hull signature was fuzzy enough that any enemy reading it would infer it as dense meta-jurillium and act accordingly, that would do it. And yes, it would be small, but small can be as dangerous as big in a tight place."

"If I may interrupt this highly interesting discussion," Lindell said.

"The voice of reason," smiled Apnis archly.

"Exactly. First, there are the materials; then there's expense, time, the skills needed. Not to mention impracticalities such as the storage of such a thing in the expectation that one day it might be used. It would use up valuable space that we need for cargo."

"Unless it *is* cargo, or at least cargo-carrying space," Ahxenta said.

"Excuse me?"

"I recall the *Green Comet's* clash with those unknowns – the scrap that left Ace Periwinkle in Merkat's medbay. Sarie Jikelleli maintains that the *Comet* got away because they could jettison their cargo pods with enough force to throw them in the enemy's face, said enemy not realising exactly what kind of cargo was inside. Her guns set off the fuel cells of the rock pulverisers in the pods and they exploded close enough to the enemy ships to make them back off. Now our outer hull cargo bay pods are detachable and manoeuvrable and we can operate them from the bridge."

"We could reconfigure and arm one as an extra vessel, with far more navigability, weapons provision, shielding..." Earbleat's eyes were shining.

"You've set her off," Apnis laughed. "The cargo pods are hard-alloy shelled sure, but not meta-jurillium and you'd need a helluva lot more in the way of engineering, retros, comms and such."

"It's something to think about, along of the million and one other things we have on our backs just now," the captain said wryly. "But I'm open to suggestions, wild or otherwise, that might just save our necks some rainy day, or at least give us a fighting chance if things seem to be turning out badly. But you'll all want your sleep; this has been quite a haul so far and sure as hell something else will turn up tomorrow that'll have us jumping. Dismissed, unless somebody has something that won't keep."

The captain's alarm woke her the following morning with a clashing cacophony that sounded like several metal objects having a barney in a rapidly spinning laundry basket. Ahxenta threw off her thermal covering, bawling "Off, you damned donut!"

"You got to catch me first," it responded, bounding out of reach.

"You'll be in the waste-disposal chute when I do!"

This was a ritual that was repeated at most wake-up calls. The alarm had been a present from her first mate after Ahxenta had been famously late for an important briefing after a rough night that had caused Flintlock to administer a barrage of pain relief medication. The doctor had also slipped in a narcotic that ensured several hours sleep, hence the late awakening. Flintlock had had a pay-cut for that one: the captain of the *Arianrhod* took no prisoners.

As Ahxenta crawled from her bed, she could tell that she was still suffering from the effects of last night's altercation in the *Half Moon*. She had had no serious damage apart from cuts and bruises, which her chief medic had assuaged by the usual pain relief sprays, but the strain over the past several weeks was evidently taking its toll. She located and grabbed the alarm, twisting it savagely to turn it off.

"Can't think why I bother," she said to herself, reasoning that there were easier ways of ensuring that she arose at the requisite hour than trusting to the quirks of a highly mobile and noisy timepiece.

There was a light winking from her comm, indicating that a non-urgent message had come in overnight. She ordered the unit to life and demanded that it play the message. A strange face emerged into the room and the holo introduced itself as Colonel Ellin Myrtleberry of the Interstellar Systems Protectorate Council. Ahxenta raised an eyebrow and ordered her security system to scan and confirm the ID of the caller and to check the message source. The results appeared in seconds: the stranger was who she said she was and the call had originated from a vessel treading the hyperspace highway somewhere beyond Merkat. That the colonel had not attempted to conceal either her identity or her location was a measure of her acuity, thought Ahxenta: she no doubt expected that she would be checked up on.

"Play message," instructed the captain.

If she had expected an important summons she would have been disappointed, Ahxenta thought to herself wryly, but the colonel had merely linked in to request a meeting with her and other PSS captains in the Web shortly after Myrtleberry's ship, the *ISPS Protector*, arrived in Merkat space. The *Protector's* ETA was in just over two hours from now, Ahxenta realised. She had better find Apnis, Earbleat and breakfast in that order and prepare herself.

The three senior bridge officers of the *Arianrhod* had been joined by Cottontail, Azular and Flintlock at the captain's request. She had no idea what was going to be disclosed, discussed or requested at the meeting, but she shrewdly suspected that *Arianrhod* would no doubt be heading into some firing line or other in the not so distant future and she wanted all her officers and their relevant departments in total readiness for whatever fate was about to pitch in their direction.

"Well, we weren't going to be doing anything in particular, were we?" Cottontail said sarcastically. "You really reckon it might be the call to arms, Cap?"

"No idea. But I can't imagine the ISP thinks it's totally ready for whatever the current emergency will throw at it next. I checked the latest status of the fleet here and in the local sector a few minutes ago and it's still status quo, but the ISP crews have all been recalled to their stations as far as Merkat's concerned, and they're rounding up the troops as fast as they can."

"So some balloon or other is going up?" speculated Apnis.

"That's what it looks like. But we have commissions to fulfil, so we're going ahead with that as of now. Lindell has got Pinkhorn to organise the schedule and we ship out tomorrow for a drop-off at Heligon – their main repair station is in need of some parts that we're picking up here – and then we're for Arrissia Five with their stuff, as they're not much beyond. That should bring us up to date with our orders. And now that we have the *Gadfly* back, all our pieces are in place. Lindell's negotiating some deals with a couple of brokers here on Merkat for our next cargoes."

"Nice to be back to normal, if normal you call it," observed Earbleat cheerfully.

"Don't shout too soon, Whisper," Azular warned her. "You can cut the air with a knife planetside and the docking belts are no better. People are worried and any more bad news won't help. Whatever this colonel has to say, the mere fact that she and her ship are turning up at Merkat will raise the temperature somewhat."

"Why must you always throw in a damp sponge?" was the sharp response.

14: DRAFTED

The *ISPS Protector* sat in her allotted docking bay in the outer meshes of the Web like a titanic twin-finned torpedo. The design was a new one, Ahxenta mused to her first mate as she ordered the pilot of the *Arianrhod's* shuttle to spin around for a better look.

"Her mid-section still spins to generate gravity, so they haven't got the artificial gravity problem licked yet. I guess she's destroyer class?" Apnis conjectured. "Who's in command? Not this colonel, surely?"

"Nothing in the link to say, but given her size she may be a troop-carrier and they're the ones under Myrtleberry's direct command; but she's ISP Council, which leads me to suspect she's more talker than tactician. I heard from Goodsocks that the *Tallulah* got the summons, so I guess all the Privates did. The *Comet* hove in last night so with us, *Tallulah*, *Hexameter*, *Equinox* and *Urania*, that's six all told."

"Well I expect we'd best head over to the meeting rooms and see what the ISP Council has got its hair in a knot over," Apnis shrugged. "I wonder who else will be hauled in to add their two credits' worth."

"Local TA reps but that's it, so the message said," the captain told her. "Make sure you have your phase rifle handy. You shouldn't need it, but the way this neck of the galaxy is twisting, you never know."

Once through the outer belts the shuttle slid smoothly into one of the bays close to the main marketing and meeting levels. Leaving the pilot to attend to details, the two made their way out and through the maze that led to the designated Trades Alliance meeting room. They were among the first to arrive: only Sarie Jikelleli and Ace Periwinkle of the *Green Comet* were ahead of them.

"I'm surprised not to see Fleetskup here," Ahxenta remarked after greeting her fellow officers and enquiring after Periwinkle's health. "He's usually the first with his nose in the trough for talks with high-rankers and an ISP colonel will count as one of those."

"He suspects that this might be the call to action and he doesn't want to seem too keen," Jikelleli snorted. "They don't waste any time do they? It was only the other day it was hinted that the TA might be calling in favours and we'd have to march to their tune or else. Ace briefed me about the meetings on the Brown Amber affair and the trading concerns in Epsilon and Zeta before we made it into dock," she explained. "I've heard no more on the Amber incident, so I guess the situation out there is still bad."

"There's been no word in or out, as far as I know," Ahxenta said as the entry parted to let in several more uniformed individuals and a brace of TA reps.

"Where's this colonel that arranged this then?" Jury Djassi of the *Equinox* enquired. "I haven't got all day; we're ready to ship out the second we get back aboard."

"And I haven't had breakfast yet," his first mate added, helping herself to rations from a nearby station. "I was on night watch."

"You and me both, Gallisty," Commander Rosee Charellis of the *Hexameter* put in. "This had better be worth it."

"Here's Mikbeam and Parlen from the *Urania*. I haven't seen them in a while but as *Urania's* home port is Delta Iridium, it's no surprise. But no Fleetskup," noted Apnis as she joined the crowd around the food station.

"Spoke too soon," Charellis returned, inclining her head towards the entry. "And I expect that stranger is the colonel."

Colonel Ellin Myrtleberry of the Interstellar Systems Protectorate Council was escorted by two armed guards, who stood either side of the entry while the officer scanned the room and its occupants. The numbers plainly tallied, for she nodded to her aides and ordered them outside to ensure that the meeting would not be disturbed.

"Thank you all for attending. Please sit," she began, setting a small device centrally on the table.

They all recognised the tool as a jammer to foil covert recording. It was followed by a thorough probe of the surroundings by a sweep scanner. The officers seated around the table exchanged glances but said nothing. The two TA reps looked a little startled.

"We're clear," the colonel announced briefly.

"May I ask what this is about, ma'am?" Murmur Fleetskup asked in order to get his mouth in early.

"That is what I am about to tell you," was the dry response as the colonel extracted an assortment of data shards from an inner pocket, sorted them carefully, and rolled one to each of the captains around the table. "Your orders as ratified by the TA: I *do* have permission from the Trades Alliance Council for this meeting and this approach, before there are any arguments. That's why the TA reps are present. Here's my authority."

As she spoke, the colonel set up a holo of the logos of both the

ISP and the TA Councils. "I'm here to outline what's expected of the private starships that fly under the Trades Alliance flag."

"Fly under the Trades Alliance flag we may, but the TA has no authority to give any PSS orders," Ahxenta pointed out acidly.

"Orders was perhaps too strong a word. But under the terms of your contract with the TA you *are* obliged to render military aid if the situation warrants it; and it's been decided that the current situation warrants it. Although you have, of course, the right to refuse."

Her tone implied that she knew the possible penalties for such refusal as she went on smoothly, "Those data shards you've been given remind you of that."

"Drafted!" muttered Tallica Apnis under her breath.

"You're all aware of the existing state of play with regard to the atrocities being perpetrated at both ends of the settled galactic zones. The latest you won't have heard: a rescue attempt on Brown Amber is to be made. Not that any of you will be involved – there are ISP and Coalition ships preparing for the assault."

"Why Amber and not Marridan?" queried Ahxenta. "*That* has a larger population, it's civilian and it's still blockaded. And it's ISP."

"We're aware of that and we're dealing with it as far as we are able. But Brown Amber is a centre of supply for various components and potentially could act as such for these invaders."

"Invaders?" Captain Sarie Jikelleli demanded in an icy tone.

"The ISP, Coalition and Non-Treaty Councils have now accepted that the present series of raids may signal major invasion, for what reason we have as yet no clear idea. Immediately before I came down I had a report of another attack and close to this sector of space. It was out in the Belts, on an ore-catcher belonging to the Friskianx." Myrtleberry's eyes swept the faces around her to gauge reactions.

"Taste of their own medicine," Ahxenta frowned. "So it looks like everybody, good, bad or indifferent, is being targeted. Which means we're inevitably looking at an enemy that's out of our usual league and that has it in for anything that moves, breathes or squeaks. And that's pretty powerful to boot. They seem to be taking on the entire charted galaxy."

"That's a new one at least," Apnis put in before the colonel could counter. "Galactic domination. Does that point to an extra-galactic opponent, then?"

"No," the captain said shortly. "Intergalactic distances being what they are, any civilisation with the tech to cross them would either be too smart to waste time and energy doing it to see who to conquer or would be so far in advance of us that we'd be toast already, never knowing what hit us. No, whoever these intruders are, they're home-grown; it's just that we don't know where they've grown, what or who they are or what their game-plan is."

"Captain Ahxenta, you and your colleagues are here to listen, not to put forward your own opinions," Myrtleberry interrupted tartly.

The captain of the *Arianrhod* was not used to being spoken to in such terms, even by a senior officer of a regular military body such as the ISP, and turned icy eyes on the colonel.

"We are here as a matter of courtesy and not on the command of the ISP."

"And I'm here to tell you what the TA Council and the ISP have agreed that the Privates could do to assist the war effort."

"So now it's war," the captain of the *Hexameter* snorted. "And just when did the TA agree to all this without consulting us?"

She glared at the two TA reps, one of whom began stuttering that the Privates had been informed only the other day that their services for the common good might be needed sooner rather than later.

"I must have missed that 'sooner rather than later' condition," Bee Lyvy Coxen shot back in response.

"This is getting us nowhere!" Myrtleberry interjected. "Those of you here have your immediate directives on the data shards, together with relevant clearances. We are now at the stage that we don't trust important messages on open channels lest they've been compromised and you are not authorised for linkage to secure military channels. There have been far too many attacks where our opponents seem to know exactly where and when to strike."

"And just what are these immediate directives you're so keen we follow?" Captain Coxen persisted.

"They are obviously specific to each ship, but in general you are being requested to assist in cargo transport, escort duty and rendering aid. For example there are several refugee ships on their way in from outlying Marridan colonies that will need escorting to Selliden and to other systems that have agreed to accept refugees. The ISP fleet can't spare ships for that type of work, nor can our allies in the Coalition and the NTA. Merkat, as a prime port, needs to be kept free of extraneous populations and available to us. I realise that you all have schedules to keep, but as we are not privy to those schedules, we have no idea of the level of inconvenience our requests may cause."

"For request, read require. Press-ganged," Apnis grunted.

"And what will the *Protector* be doing while we're doing all this?"

Ahxenta enquired.

"I have my orders and the *Protector* with my troops aboard is set to move in under four hours. So if you'll excuse me, I have work to do."

Colonel Myrtleberry rose to her feet, collected her instruments, made for the door and was through it before most of her audience could draw an outraged breath.

"She came all this way to tell us, like it or not, we're in it up to our necks and the TA will have our hides if we don't comply, is that it?" Captain Cobalt Mikbeam of the *Urania* rounded on the two TA reps, who looked as if they wanted to slide through the floor.

"We heard of it only an hour before you did," one admitted. "We had a communiqué from the TA Assembly at Alto Finglas saying that its Council had been in a closed session with the ISP and its allies and the outcome was that all their trades partners and associates would be encouraged to render any assistance possible. It looks like they're going to try to take on the unknowns that are holding Brown Amber, as it's near enough to here to have got them worried big time."

"I suspect the assault on Amber's about ready to start," Jikelleli put in. "Else why tell us? Spreading the word about it won't help it stay under wraps. If that's how the ISP normally keeps its secrets, it's no wonder there are leaks all over the place."

"Sitting here won't help," Ahxenta shrugged. "I'm heading up to my ship to see what's on this damned shard that the colonel thought was too important to send out using normal encoded channels. I'll no doubt be in contact later when I know more. You off, Jury?"

"I am. I've no time to hang about to wait for refugees or whatever is planned for the *Equinox*. I've a customer waiting for a shipment and I plan to deliver," Captain Djassi declared.

"My repairs will detain me here for another couple of standard days," Murmur Fleetskup announced ponderously as he looked at the data shard he had been rolling in his hand. "But I need to see all my senior officers immediately. Let's go, Goodsocks."

"Aye, aye, Cap," his first mate responded into the air as she prepared to follow him.

Ahxenta and Apnis accompanied Djassi and his first mate Gallisty Tynissel as far as the shuttle docking facilities close to the marketing suites, walking quickly to avoid the two from the *Tallulah*.

"I'm here until tomorrow, as far as I know," Ahxenta said quietly. "If I hear more on the current situation, I'll send a link out on the Ultraviolet III. I'll be sending the gist of this meet to the *Obsidian* and the *Quarkstorm* anyhow. I can't imagine Myrtleberry has fliers chasing them down to pass on their orders."

"No. But I guess the TA will catch up to the others soon enough. My ride's at the end of this tube, so I'll say goodbye now. See you on the flipside sometime, Cinnabar. You too, Tallica." With a half-salute, he and Tynissel turned and were gone.

"Wonder who assigned the acid-tongued Colonel Myrtleberry as messenger to the Privates?" Apnis asked as the two made their way towards their shuttle and the ride back to *Arianrhod*.

"She and her brood of troopers were no doubt scheduled to fly into Merkat for the jaunt to Brown Amber and the *ISPS Protector* has to be berthed somewhere. As one of the ISP construction docks is out at Alto Finglas, that's maybe where the *Protector* was built, but she can't have had much of a shakedown cruise."

"Best hope she doesn't go belly up when she sees action, then," the first mate replied. "I don't envy them an assault on Amber at any rate. It's a bit of a way off the beaten track though close enough in to the Belts, but the structures attached to it and its parent asteroid will make any attack risky, without having to face an unknown enemy that might have who knows how many more tricks down its socks or up its sleeves."

"That could work both ways, Tallica: defence will be as sticky as attack as there are too many ways in. But the resident population will have to be taken into account and as we've seen, these aliens don't think much of life in general, given what they've done thus far."

"Still need a workforce to run the place, I expect, but it won't be a pleasant experience," Apnis said, shaking her head.

The *Arianrhod* sat quiescent in her net of docking struts as the shuttle approached but Ahxenta's experienced eyes could see a gang of tiny hull repair bots sliding over her outer structure checking for damage. One of her gun ports was also moving, opening and closing under test. The crew was busy then, she thought approvingly.

Once back aboard, the captain made straight for her office on the bridge, nodding to her duty officers in the passing.

"So what's up, Tallica?" Whisper Earbleat enquired, vacating the command chair.

"Believe me, we'll all be finding out. What's our status as far as our cargo drop at Heligon?"

"Ready to run; Lindell's finished negotiations with the marketing bods planetside and he's struck a deal for an urgent cargo for Vellis Prime. We'll be in that neck of the galaxy in any case as it's en route to Heligon Station. Seems there's a distinct lack of enthusiasm for deliveries out that way right now and some local supply companies are refusing to go beyond sector ninety one of Delta Zone. Beyond Delta Iridium in fact."

"Earlier start than planned then, if we're to make Heligon to time. That'll make cargo pick-up tight."

"Lindell's got Ensign Pinkhorn on it. I routed out more hands to help with the loading and we've had to pony up a few extra credits to grease a couple of palms, but the profit margin's good on the Vellis delivery and it's small," Earbleat announced cheerfully. "The meeting went all right, did it?" she went on, fishing for information.

Several ears on the bridge pricked up but the first mate was decidedly unforthcoming. "No comment," she replied shortly.

Ahxenta when she reappeared was grim-faced. "Gliss, you have the conn, get the ship ready to depart. Apnis and Earbleat, you're with me. We're for Lindell's office; we're meeting Cottontail, Azular and Flintlock there. Mr Bellfish, keep your ears open to every comm channel in existence and if a message comes through for me I want it patched through promptly."

"Aye, Captain," Lynxi Bellfish responded.

As the bridge door swished behind the departing trio, Lieutenant Pollux Gliss made his way over to the command chair. "I want all the stations manned," he announced. "Lynxi, get Greffy and Gem Ferry up here pronto and check who's on the rota for second tactical and weapons and have them report for duty as well."

"Spoiling for a fight, are we?" Box called up from his station.

"Less of the chat, Lieutenant Box. You get ready to plot a course out of Merkat space. I reckon we may be heading out sooner rather than later," Gliss directed.

"Where to, Lieutenant?" the navigator returned efficiently. "Vellis Prime is the nearest."

"That'll do for a start. We were for Heligon Station and Arrissia Five, but that may have changed."

As the summoned officers appeared on the bridge, various orders were given for recall of maintenance bots and engine checks. Gliss sat back, scanning his ops boards and calling up various holos. "This is where the fun begins," he grumbled to himself as the crew around him exchanged various suppositions in whispers.

In the supercargo's office, Ahxenta called for updates on the state of play of *Arianrhod's* current orders and their sequence of despatch. Lindell confirmed that apart from the last minute pick-up of the cargo for Vellis Prime, everything was locked and loaded. A heading of Vellis for their first delivery within the next few hours would have them en route to Heligon in advance of schedule, where transfer of the bulky consignment of engineering parts could be made early. The remaining cargo for Arrissia was a military order for weaponry for planetary defence systems and thus under strict security, but Lindell was sure that early handover of that could be arranged.

"Axellina, how clear is medbay?" the captain queried.

"Couple of cases, both on the mend. Nothing long-term. Why?"

"Precautionary only, I'm hoping we won't need it but I want your team on standby at all times. Earbleat, you recall our conversation about reconfiguring and arming one of our outer hull cargo bay pods as a decoy vessel operable remotely?"

"Sure do, Cap. I've given it a bit of thought and I've consulted Chief Cottontail on one or two bits."

"It's not going to work without weeks of hard graft and a shoal of personnel that I can't spare," was Cottontail's contribution.

"If our cloak and projection decoy are almost up to scratch, both of you make a start on it. You have two hours to requisition what you might need from Merkat, but go through Lindell and class it as cargo. Azular, you lend a hand as and when."

The captain's face was hard in the harsh light of the office and Apnis looked at her searchingly.

"So what was in our so-called call-up papers from the TA?" the first mate asked. "You don't look as if you enjoyed reading them."

"I didn't," was the reply as Ahxenta tapped the data shard on the table. "As you know, Admiral Zillah of Freskat Six sent out a couple of ships to scout the region around the Starglass in response to reported sightings of a huge unknown starship lurking in the vicinity of the deserted worlds around the nebula edges, and of course the missing ISP ship sent out to investigate in the first place. Her scouts are both safe and heading back. They made for the area where a prospector ship had apparently picked up two mystery ion trails and signs of debris, but found nothing of significance."

"But?" interrupted Apnis.

"But they did pick up the faint signal of an emergency beacon that seemed to come from a region further out, where the only marginally habitable planetary system is listed as Kelfennig. There have been a couple of archaeological expeditions out there, years ago, apparently. They captured the signal and headed back in: they weren't equipped to do much more. The signal's now been analysed by ISP experts."

"And?" the first mate prompted.

"It matches the call-sign of a ship that crashed on Kelfennig Four years ago, a science vessel on a legitimate archaeological exploratory. The ship was a write-off, though the crew pulled out in a shuttle and made it safe back. But this signal seemingly has an overlying booster signal that's much more recent in date and military. The suggestion is that some of the crew from the missing ship, *ISPS Nomad*, made it to Kelfennig in an escape craft and are calling for help."

"My suggestion would be that somebody's found that old ship and is pulling a fast one, reactivating the signal to draw rescue ships in," Apnis said bluntly.

"That's my reading as well. But the ISP wants it investigated as a search and rescue mission and can't spare a warship to do it. We just happen to be headed in that general direction."

"Pardon me for asking, but how the hell did the ISP figure we were heading in that direction?" the first mate cut in. "Our flight plans are none of their damned business, as I think Myrtleberry was at some pains to point out."

"Arrissia Five is ISP, on the edge of ISP-controlled space, and our payload is for their defence department. Given their closeness to the Starglass, they're no doubt worried and are in constant contact with ISP Central, hence the link. The directive *Arianrhod's* been dealt originates from the office of a senior ISP admiral. I haven't sent my response as yet. What are your feelings about the mission?"

"Did they ask nicely or was it an order backed by the TA heavy mob?" Apnis asked. "Do it or lose the right to our flag?"

"It was framed rather more like an order than a request, with that subtle underlying threat, but the promised compensation for loss of business is respectable."

"How about compensation for loss of life and ship?" Cottontail put in angrily. "Sounds like a set-up if ever there was one, and why can't they send in this ISP ship they've despatched to assist the defence of Freskat Six?"

"Because it's a long shot. Even the admiral making the request admitted that much. But so much for ISP and TA promises that PSS involvement would be limited to cargo transport and escort duty."

"And rendering aid, if I recall," Apnis pointed out. "That would be running the gauntlet of these unknowns to see if a spurious signal that might be a fake is really a cry for help or a massive set-up to see how dim we are. If they swallow this, they'll swallow anything."

"I could analyse the signal to see if I can find something," Azular volunteered. "They *did* copy it to you, Captain?"

"They did. Play shard, section thirty four," Ahxenta instructed, setting the data shard into the holo port of the table's multi-console.

The senior science officer watched the resultant holo projection closely before using the console to carry out a search for matches of specific aspects of the signal to known sources. He then manipulated the results and added in various commands of his own.

"The call-sign *is* that of the *SS Palynia*, lost four point two standard years ago on Kelfennig Four. The crew of sixteen got out by shuttle and were rescued by a trader scouting the area two days later. What the records don't show is how and why the ship crashed, and there's no note of any later salvage missions," Azular stated. "I'm surprised there haven't been a dozen ships in and out trying to get their hands on something for nothing."

"Unless there has been and they didn't get out either," Earbleat posited darkly. "Place might have a rep as a ghost planet and all those in the know have been well warned to keep clear. Here be dragons and all that."

"I'll leave you to check out that aspect," Azular informed her. "I *am* detecting the booster signal superimposed on the original but I'm also picking up a parallel wave, as if there's another message buried in there somewhere. The ISP must have registered that, surely?"

"Maybe it was missed, or the ISP smart-alecks hoped we wouldn't find it," Cottontail spat sourly. "But then they don't have your talent, or our resources come to that. How clear is it?"

"Not clear," the Berzic officer admitted. "It's on a wavelength a fraction or so off the one used for the booster transmission but it's coming up as a regular pulse. If there *is* a message in it I can't read it, but something's nagging at the back of my mind. Another thing: if an ISP evac ship or pod did manage to escape an attack and make it to Kelfennig, how come their own call-sign isn't part of the message?"

"To keep the unknowns guessing? Damaged as they crashed?" the chief engineer hazarded.

"Keep working on it," the captain told the science officer. "But now to our main question: do we take on the mission and retain our reputation with the TA and everyone else to boot, or do we tell them to shoot off and risk losing our right to the TA flag?"

"They've got us over a barrel and they know it," Apnis grumbled. "Why is the *Tallulah* never hauled in for this type of face-off?"

"How much is the payment for the assignment?" Lindell queried practically.

In reply, Ahxenta tabbed a figure up on her hand-held pad and passed it over. The supercargo whistled.

"They're either desperate or they have too much credit," was his opinion. "That's certainly compensation."

"Because no other PSS is cocky enough to take this on, probably," Crizz Cottontail said tartly, peering over her colleague's shoulder. "You're thinking of agreeing, aren't you, Cap?"

Ahxenta nodded in the affirmative. "It would clear much of our backlog of debt for the refit of the *Arianrhod* that our insurers refused to cough up for, provided we're not shot to pieces in the process."

"I'll start gearing up our big guns," Earbleat beamed. "After I've checked out outer hull cargo pod four. That's got the thickest skin and it moves like a missile once you set it off."

"So yet again *Arianrhod's* in the firing line. I'd better see that my engines are up to it," the chief engineer sighed.

"Looks like there's no dissention. You'd better let the crew know, Cap," advised the first mate.

"After I've contacted this Admiral Piskettle who seems to think it's such a good idea. I want to clear a few things up with him. Like payment in advance for a start."

"And compensation for our next of kin if things go cock-eyed," muttered Cottontail as she sailed off to the main engineering deck.

15: TRICKS

The Starglass Nebula, Ahxenta thought. Everyone had heard of it, although few had been close enough to appreciate its full beauty. The nebula was small but shone like a blazing beacon in the dark to light up one of the most remote areas of the galaxy mapped thus far. Its proximity to several worlds held to be long abandoned by the race or races that had once called them home was sufficient to give rise to a plethora of ghost stories and legends, but from what the captain had heard, there was foundation for the tales. Long-deserted worlds that once were home to technically-advanced cultures, signals that cut in and cut out with no warning, artefacts unearthed that reputedly had strange powers – the rumours abounded. It was an unusual mission. But the pay in advance was generous.

The *Arianrhod* was well on her way to Vellis Prime and her captain had been assured that the current mission for the ISP was top secret and no-one but a few of the upper ranks knew anything about it. The TA was also in the dark as to specifics, allegedly. Ahxenta had taken that with a double pinch of salt and had made sure that a few tales about *Arianrhod's* latest mission had been spread around the Web to muddy the waters. One concession she had pushed for was a private channel to the ISP's tactical relay system to enable her to keep up to date on the military position as far as action in the area for which she was heading was concerned. She had no intention of flying her ship into the middle of a confrontation.

The captain had decided to take a longer route than necessary to their first port to keep within ISP-majority space. *Arianrhod* had thus been ordered to head for Delta Iridium and from there set for Vellis, with minor deviations en route to foil any would-be pursuers. Vellis was close to the boundary of zone Epsilon where it crossed into the small ISP-controlled region at the edge of zone Zeta and their next two stops were within that area.

Earbleat had meanwhile spent much of her time and that of two of Cottontail's engineers in refitting outer hull cargo pod four, using meta-jurillium hull patches that she had shamelessly persuaded out of a buddy that worked in the Web's repair docks. Their cost had been added to the bill for the *Gadfly's* refit, as had the credits to line her friend's pockets. Leaving her conscripted engineers to figure the best way to coat the maximum area of pod hull with the minimum layer of meta-jurillium, the second mate had then got down to re-tuning every thruster and overhauling every control circuit. Her proposal that two of the patients in medbay be drafted in to work from their sickbeds on means of directing the pod from a dedicated station on the bridge was vetoed by the furious chief medic, but Flintlock did release one of her staff with expertise in cybernetic limb replacement to assist in setting up the pod's auto-control systems. Azular and Cottontail had in the interim been left with the tasks of upping the potential of the decoy unit and the cloaking system.

One of the advantages of a private channel to ISP's tactical relay system was that the start of the assault to retake Brown Amber could be deduced. Once ongoing, the captain calculated, aggressors at her end of the galactic arena would focus their attention away from what was perhaps a local base of operations and leave a breathing space for her mission. To that end she had instigated a constant comms watch and as the ship hove into Vellis, the consensus among her officers was that the assault was imminent.

Offloading was rapid and the Velli clients grateful that their urgent order had been delivered ahead of schedule. It had not resulted in a bonus, Box pointed out sadly to his sidekick at the navi-helm, but at least the *Arianrhod's* kudos had been upped, as regular transports had been avoiding the area. The next stop of Heligon Station would also be earlier than projected and Lindell had agreed with his associate there that cargo discharge could begin directly on payment of fees. Although it was straight route and then a short hop over the Epsilon-Zeta boundary to the station, the course brought the *Arianrhod* closer to the Starglass and as Heligon was achieved, the misty brightness of the nebula had begun to illuminate local space.

"Pretty, pretty," Romanna Dox observed as she brought the ship in on final approach and the bridge holo lit with the nebular glow.

"Pretty dangerous you mean," Box sniffed, feeding in coordinates. "At least we only get the edge here: it's mostly in unmapped space."

Ignoring him, the helmswoman announced that docking had been achieved and that she had initiated station-keeping.

Transfer of the large shipment of engineering parts was begun at once as it would take several hours of run time, half of the station's transport craft being down. Ahxenta had approved limited furlough for the handful of crew that had missed out on their due allocation at

Merkat, with the stipulation that they gather any news relating to local goings-on in the vicinity of Heligon's cosmic neighbour. She also sent Azular down: his talents would enable him to pick up more than his fellows and his seniority would keep them reasonably in line.

"Sheepdog to stop us straying," was the navigator's opinion when he heard. "He may stand us a jar, if we're lucky."

"Don't look at me if you're not," was the discouraging reply from Dox. "You still owe me from the last time."

The crew was forbidden the planet itself and had to make do with the restricted facilities aboard the orbital complex, but there was little grumbling. The local alehouse catered mostly for peripatetic pilots and crews and the dock-rats responsible for cargo-handling and ship overhaul and they were a critical clientèle.

Azular made his report four hours later. The majority of local pilots were aware of scouts sent out from Freskat Six to nosey around the Starglass in search of traces of an unknown starship and a couple had heard rumours of the active emergency signal that had been detected close to the Kelfennig system. Their reactions were unanimous: you wouldn't get them on a run to the system for all the credit in creation. Receipt of the signal had in fact convinced most that keeping a safe distance was more important than ever and any hard-nosed treasure-seekers that really wanted a look-see at anything in the vicinity could pilot their own craft. Half the reported happenings were hardly worth crediting was the science officer's opinion, but it would be wise to heed two or three accounts. One such was an unconfirmed tale that a one-man operated ship had recently been lost near Kelfennig, hence the reluctance of any pilot to approach any world in the same general direction. The identity of the lost ship and her pilot was unknown as she had bypassed Heligon, but speculation was rife.

It was as *Arianrhod* was departing Heligon that a perplexed Azular requested a private meeting with the captain. He had been conning over their mission data again and a thought had struck him, which he had followed up. The result of the talk with Ahxenta was the order that Apnis, Cottontail and Flintlock all join them in the bridge office.

"The booster signal overlying the original is standard military," Azular began. "But it could have originated from the *Palynia* because although a science vessel and part of a commercial concern, she was originally a military craft that had been decommissioned after several years' service. But this regular pulse that's been annoying me: I felt I'd come across it before."

"And you've just remembered where," Apnis guessed. "Well, let us in on it. The Cap looks peeved, so I guess it's not good news."

"You'll love it," Ahxenta said briefly.

"It's a tracking signal sent out by certain implanted cyber systems and also by the cyber suite related to the cyber systems," the Berzic officer explained. "I checked it against our records."

"Micklemouse!" Cottontail hissed, her eyes sparking fire.

"It matches," Azular agreed. "It's likely to be part of the comms signal of an info-sent's ship so that whoever is controlling him or her can detect the ship from a distance."

"The little rat!" the engineer blazed. "But how could it be patched into a distress from a wrecked ship? And how did the little sod have the know-how to do it?"

"He would know how," Azular argued. "If it *is* Micklemouse, that is: it's probably common to similar systems. But if it *is* his ship, there may have been damage on impact and he's cannibalised the wreck of the *Palynia* to get a distress call out."

"A heck of a lot of ifs," the captain interrupted. "And so far we've no proof of any of it. But it's something that we have to take into account. We have our cargo for Arrissia to get shot of before we can head out to Kelfennig and that'll take time. Our clients will no doubt want to check every nut and bolt before they authorise final payment and we'll be under tight security until they do. Back to post all, but no sharing of this with the crew as yet. They'll know soon enough."

"Much as I hate to say this, Cinnabar, but it would be better if no crew from the ISP ship made it to Kelfennig Four if Micklemouse is there," Apnis confided to Ahxenta once the others had left the office. "He being what he is and working for an outfit that sounds as if it would sell its own grandmother to make a profit, anything that any member of that crew knew would be fair game."

"If they hadn't worked out what Micklemouse is and shot him, you mean," the captain said scathingly. "But it's all up in the air. We don't know it's him: it could be a fake signal, an ISP or other distress call or something else. And it still smells bad. As soon as we leave Arrissia Five, we remain on amber alert for the duration."

The cargo-drop at Arrissia was as fraught as Ahxenta had predicted and it took all of Lindell's charms to smooth over the annoyances. As the supercargo pointed out, the clients ought to have been grateful for not only receiving their goods ahead of schedule but for receiving them at all, in light of the reluctance of many ships to enter the area.

That the Arrissian military was jumpy was obvious and the crew from *Arianrhod* that had made the trip planetside were plied with questions over their theories concerning the current situation. The captain gave out that they were headed back to Heligon and when *Arianrhod* finally left orbit, that was the heading programmed in.

They were barely beyond Arrissian space when Bellfish called in that the first wave of the assault to retake Brown Amber had been repulsed with heavy losses on both sides and it looked like a standoff was in progress. The message had however been delayed for days as several relay stations were down.

"Maybe that's why we haven't seen much action hereabouts," Tallica Apnis surmised as the bridge crew digested the information.

"It could be, Commander," Bellfish agreed from his station. "But we might be getting busier soon: I'm picking up a transmission that I don't recognise, very faint, but it's there. General direction is beyond the border of ISP space and on the edge of the nebula."

"Show me," commanded Ahxenta.

"Just when we're about to go off duty," Box groaned dismally.

The pattern emanating from the holo generated by the lieutenant matched nothing that the captain could call up on her ops console, an outcome confirmed by Greffy at the science station.

"Triangulate and try to get a fix," Ahxenta ordered her tactical officer. "It's too close to be Kelfennig Four but there are a couple of worlds in that general area, if I remember aright."

"It could be a ship," Apnis broke in. "Although why a ship would declare its presence in this part of space is anyone's guess. Here I am, come and get me."

"Or here I am, just a bit closer and I'll be able to get you," Box grumbled to his mate in a low voice.

"Belay that," Ahxenta growled. "Though it *is* a possibility. Sound red alert: we'd best take a closer look. And keep monitoring, Bellfish, and let me know if anything changes. You too, Greffy: you may be able to make out specifics the closer we get. Earbleat, weapons on standby. Tallica, get Cottontail up here and make sure all stations are double-manned. We're taking no chances."

"You want outer hull cargo pod four on standby, Cap?" Earbleat asked eagerly.

"Desperate to give it a trial run," the first mate cut in, laughing quietly. "She'll be giving it a name and launching it next."

"Not yet," Ahxenta told the weapons officer. "Just make sure all our other weapons systems are running hot."

"Aye, Captain!"

The background panels pulsed red as the alarm wailed ship-wide. As all stations reported readiness, the noise was muted and *Arianrhod* changed course towards the source of the unknown signal.

"If it's a distress, it's not one I'm familiar with, Captain," reported Bellfish. "There's no date imprint, so I don't know how long it's been operational. But as this sector's one of the closest to ISP space, it surely would have been picked up long since by another ship if it had been going for a while."

Azular had reported in and was at his station examining the signal. He agreed with the comms officer and was sifting through the data he had gleaned relating to unknown craft encountered by other ships. The upshot was that he had been unable to find a match to anything that would suggest an origin for the transmission.

"It'll take us an hour at present speed to home in on the source but I want every station to remain at red standby," Ahxenta ordered. "Get our cloak up, Ms Dox; we're not going in with flags flying."

As the ship advanced towards the signal source, the holo in the well of the bridge updated in line with clearer readings and comms and tactical soon pinpointed the locus. It was a small planetary system on the outer edges of the Starglass Nebula that orbited an unremarkable star and was definitely beyond the edge of ISP space. There had been three reported missions to the place, Azular verified, but the results of the visits were classified, having been commercial.

"The system doesn't have a name," the Berzic officer said. "The star's designated by the sector and is recorded as Four One Two Alpha; the planet is the third one out. I *have* found a report of alien artefacts claiming to come from the place that turned up at a market on Vellis Minor but no specifics. It looks like there must have been inhabitants or at least visitors there at one time but they're long gone. The planet is categorised as uninhabited and uninhabitable, so it has no resources worth exploiting. I've no records of ships heading there and being lost, but I expect there have been secret stopovers in the past by prospectors or raiders out to make a quick credit."

"That's for sure," Bellfish agreed. "Every market you visit has a stall selling alien artefacts from all over the galaxy and they all come from uninhabited systems at the edge of eternity. Oops! What's this I'm getting? Another signal, Captain! It's much weaker than the first: an emergency beacon, military I think, and reads as ISP."

"Confirmed," Azular called. "I'm reading it as the *ISPS Nomad* –

the missing ship."

"Keep our cloak up and do *not* respond," Ahxenta directed. "ISP or no, I'm not taking it on trust. Try to get a clear ID on that second signal, Mr Bellfish."

"Confirmed as the *Nomad's* call-sign, ma'am, but her last known position wasn't anywhere near here," Bellfish told her. "It could be one of her escape craft."

"Do not respond," Ahxenta repeated. "I want to get a good bit nearer. This smacks too much of coincidence. Keep weapons systems running hot and sound the alert. All crew, battlestations."

The alarm sounded across all stations as the ship closed in on the third planet of the system. With scanner range at maximum, the holo-image expanded out of the grid, shifting as the viewfield changed.

"Orbital insertion achieved, Captain!" Dox called out as *Arianrhod* swung into position.

"That ISP emergency signal's growing stronger, but the original's cut out," Bellfish reported.

"Someone damn well knows we're here!" the first mate seethed. "Cloak or no, someone's picked us up!"

"I'm not registering debris on the planet anywhere near the signal source, Captain," Azular put in loudly. "Nor an obvious ship, but if it's small we might not be able to detect it."

"Local hyperspace field's just shifted, Captain!" Lieutenant Gliss warned from tactical. "Something's coming through!"

"Damn! Shields to maximum, all weapons online. Chief, get our engines ready to roar. Gliss, full tactical readout on what's coming in! Earbleat, get a bead on it! All pilots to fighters!"

"Hostiles on approach vector!" Earbleat bawled across the bridge. "Two of them and they're big!"

As two huge black warships hove into view, Azular swore loudly. "There's what looks like a listening or tactical relay post down there and they know where we are! They've launched a missile spread!"

"On it!" Earbleat yelled. "Station three, wide field: take them out!"

"Uncloak us, helm. Tactical, report!" Ahxenta barked.

"They're shielded but readings match what hit us last time and what the *Obsidian* faced," Gliss answered. "Similar spec but smaller vessels, around half the size."

"Confirmed," Azular verified. "And they're armed to the teeth. Sending readings to grid..."

"They're targeting... powering weapons!" Gliss bellowed.

"Take them down! I want them out of my sky!"

"Deflecting drones away!" Earbleat yelled. "They're in my sights!"

"Tallica, take main weapons! Earbleat, ready your cargo pod for launch, we'll need it. Dox, evasive! The second beast's trying to outflank us. All weapons stations, target anything you can get!"

Ahxenta was on her feet, her eyes fixed on the bridge holo as the second auxiliary weapons station confirmed the launch of an enemy breaching pod and the loss of two of *Arianrhod's* drones.

"Got the breaching pod, but here comes another!" Apnis called.

Ahxenta cursed as *Arianrhod* juddered to multiple hits from enemy fire and Dox pulled the ship out of the path of the closer warship.

"Lost an aft shield, Cap!" Gliss announced.

"Repairing damage but our plating's taking a beating!" Cottontail's voice rang out harshly above the din.

"So's theirs, but that's all our drones gone," Apnis reported. "You want more launched, Cap?"

"No, hold for now but target their fighter bays, I don't want them launching. That other ship is hardly touched and she's coming in to support the first. Earbleat, ready your pod for launch."

"Target?" Earbleat demanded.

"That second ship. Send it right down their throats!"

"Launching, aye. She's away! They've seen her and are targeting! Increasing speed and plotting evasive!"

As the captain watched, the streak that was the cargo pod wove an intricate course to keep the enemy guessing, her speed increasing as the weapons officer fought with her controls. The warship had turned to gain a better line of fire on the approaching craft, allowing Earbleat to choose her mark. As the pod closed with the enemy, she loosed a torpedo. The hostile reacted with a burst of close proximity charges but the pod immediately veered up and over in a sweeping arc at a speed that would have incapacitated any live pilot aboard.

"Surprise!" Earbleat crowed as she increased the speed still more, straightening out her course to send the pod straight down the maw of her adversary's main engine.

The great ship exploded in a bloom of fire that lit the dark like a supernova. Both the *Arianrhod* and the first enemy vessel were caught in the backlash but the PSS had been prepared and Dox had already set to outrun it, spearing across the planet and into the dark of space.

"Damn, that was close!" Cottontail called out from her station as the ship screamed in the shockwave and the bridge crew were flung about in their seats, their safety webbing straining to cope.

"What's our status?" the captain demanded, climbing to her feet.

"Better than theirs," the chief engineer told her. "We're holding."

"Enemy vessel is turning away… I think she's trying for a low orbit!" Gliss barked.

"Bet she's trying to pick up the ground crew from that blasted surface station," the first mate snapped.

"Turn her about, helm! Nobody kicks my ship in the teeth and gets away with it," Ahxenta instructed. "Get us on a line of sight; and comms, notify fighters to prep for launch."

"You're not setting our fighters against that thing?" Apnis called over from main weapons. "They won't stand a chance!"

"No. They'll take out that surface station, once we've dealt with the ship. We still have to find out how they were able to send out a distress beacon with an ISP signature, the *Nomad's* one at that."

"Reckon they're trying to make a break Cap," Gliss stated.

"Reckon they're trying to trap us," the captain countered. "Get us in close, helm. Main weapons, target their comms: I don't want them sending a distress, nor do I want that station asking for help. Azular, prep the decoy. I want it where they won't spot it immediately. Even if they're not fooled, that ground station might be," she ordered.

"Decoy ready to deploy, Captain. Position?"

Ahxenta scanned the tactical display holo. "The other side of the planet and as far from that ground station as possible. Deploy on my mark: I want to make sure that ship's too busy to notice. Earbleat, get our forr'ad phase cannon set to go with a parallel torpedo spread and once we're in range, you fire."

"Aye, Captain! Almost there… almost there… forr'ad batteries, fire! Torpedoes away!"

"Ready decoy for launch… mark!" the captain called.

"She's targeting us again!" Gliss called. "She knows we're up for a fight and she's let loose unmanned fighters carrying high energy explosive cells!"

"All stations, get those fighters in your sights and blast them to hell! I don't want even one getting through!"

The *Arianrhod's* gunnery crews immediately locked to their targets and streaks of fire from every hull emplacement shot across the narrowing gap between her and the small fleet of brightening dots.

"Torpedoes heading in as well, Cap!" Apnis yelled. "On it!"

"I want a hole in her hull!" Ahxenta roared. "Punch it!"

"Punching, aye!" Earbleat bellowed in response. "They just don't stop for a break, do they?"

"Hell, they're sending out sweepers to round up the debris from the other ship! That's crazy! What is it they don't want us to find?" demanded Pollux Gliss. "The ground station's spotted our decoy! They've sent up missiles to intercept!"

As the second warship imploded with a searing gout of contained flame and pieces of her hull expanded outwards, the captain ordered a search for escape craft lest any had crept past their view.

"Nary a one, Cap," Tallica Apnis reported.

"I agree," Gliss confirmed. "I'm not getting a single indicator that could be an escape pod, nor even a sweeper that made it. But these two were smaller than the last beast that attacked us; fewer crew maybe?" he guessed.

"Or none at all," Azular said, straightening up from a prolonged scrutiny of the secondary science console under Greffy's command.

"What?" demanded Ahxenta.

"That ground station's out of weaponry, I figure," Earbleat put in. "Nothing else coming up."

"Don't count on it," the captain told her. "That could be a foil to draw us in. Helm, hold position and Gliss, you get all the data you can out of it; send a probe down. Commander Apnis, do not loose fighters until I give the go-ahead."

"Aye, Captain!" was the joint response.

"Azular, what have you got?"

"I've had Greffy get as much data on those ships that he could, including sending in probe beads to get a clue to their biology."

"And?" Ahxenta urged.

"Precious little. Either she's cloaked internally and we can't get readings, or she doesn't have a crew that registers as any lifeform we know. Or the crew have personal shields to hinder scanning."

"Or they're only partially organic," Greffy cut in.

"What's that, boy?" demanded his senior.

"I *did* get traces of organic material, look. Not enough to suggest a shipful of animate crewmen but there are a lot of bio-traces that are so mixed up with various metallic moieties and what look like energy generation processes that they're difficult to separate out."

Whisper Earbleat had been listening in and gave a small hiss to indicate her thought processes. "Lieutenant Zaiklyn Oak: one of Dr Flintlock's team that's expert in cybernetic limb replacement. He helped us set up pod four's auto-control systems. Get him to once-over the data and see what he makes of it."

"Captain, confirmation that the ground station is practically out of firepower and they're digging in; I don't think they'll surrender anytime soon," Gliss called over from tactical.

"Wonder why?" Apnis asked the air. "Really don't want us finding out how they operate, do they?"

"Somebody or something on that station spied our distortion field and figured we were a cloaked ship," the captain said tersely. "They expected a rescue attempt in answer to that damn signal and were ready to take us out once we'd swallowed the bait and showed up."

"Bet they were sorry when they found out it was the *Arianrhod* that had done the swallowing," Box grinned.

"None of them left to be sorry now," Dox noted.

"Wrong," Gliss responded. "I'm reading lifeforms on the ground, so there are sentients alive there. But they're reinforcing the shields around what I think is their habitation unit."

"Scan the whole place; you too, Azular," the captain ordered. "Given their sneaky behaviour thus far, that could be another blind. Recall our decoy but remain at red alert in case we have a damn fleet of them heading in. Stand down fighters for the moment but hold them in readiness."

"Hell, they've blown the whole shebang!" Gliss called out as he rotated the tactical displayed by the bridge's holo-generator.

"Scan for lifeforms!"

"One ship heading for the far side of the planet! She's trying to make a run for it!" called out Azular. "She's manned."

"Launch two fighters and take out her engines! I want that crew alive and kicking!" thundered Ahxenta.

"Maybe not kicking," Box muttered as a flurry of activity heralded fighter deployment.

After several nail-biting minutes, the crippled craft was towed into *Arianrhod's* line of sight by the brace of fighters and then hauled into an outer cargo bay, where the captain waited. Security had been set around the ship to deactivate any live weaponry but none was found. Azular's scanning confirmed three aboard and animate but he could learn little of their genetics. The atmosphere was an air mix, however, and from that the science officer deduced that they were humanoid and probably not wearing breather units.

The captain ruminated and consulted her chief medic. The upshot was that a penetrative hull breach was made and sufficient morph gas to knock out a platoon pumped in. Flintlock, monitoring the readings closely, finally declared that they indicated deep sleep. The ship was forced open carefully and the three unconscious occupants strapped into gurneys and taken to medbay whilst Azular remained to check over every scrap possible of their craft.

Apnis meanwhile had ordered scanning of the planet's surface from the bridge to check for other structures or signs of occupation, as the probes she had sent out had come up empty. A couple of what looked like long-abandoned workings were spotted but nothing apart from the ruins of the wrecked station gave any clue to recent activity. Once Ahxenta had returned and had been informed, she decided that they would waste no more time searching.

"I don't want to be anywhere close when the owners of this place check in to see what's happened to their little outpost. And I suspect it won't be long."

"What about our new passengers?" Apnis questioned.

"They'll be out for hours. Flintlock will keep us up to date and Azular's going over their ship to see what he can pick up. I'm sure as hell not taking them with us to Kelfennig. We'll head into Heligon but meanwhile I'll call up our ISP contact. The planetary affairs office at Skyrtek must have some ship they can send out to pick them up. They can do all the necessary: we're not their fizzing police squad."

"Their mess, they can clean it up, you mean," Apnis smiled.

"They were the ones that lost their ship in the first place. Box, plot a non-standard course for Heligon Station and Dox, get us there as fast as possible. Meanwhile, I'll link through to the ISP and then we'll go over what we lost in terms of armaments and equipment. Lindell can damn well bill ISP as it was their missing ship's call-sign we detoured to check out when we were hit."

"You'll be lucky," Apnis called after her as Ahxenta made for her bridge office to put through the call.

The first mate began to call up the necessary inventories and had them ready when the captain returned, successful. A short time later the two were part way through their task when they were interrupted by a link from medbay.

"Cap, I think you should get down here," Flintlock told her. "You are going to love this."

16: MYSTERY

Arianrhod's medbay was a restrained hive of activity when the captain marched in. Several medics were busy at duty stations and two armed guards stood outside of one of the iso-bays. Dr Flintlock strode over, a forbidding look on her face.

"I see you've drafted in security," Ahxenta noted. "Not usual in your neck of the woods."

"I thought it might be wise. A precaution, for when our guests wake up. We'll talk in private."

"So what do we have out there?" the captain asked when the two were seated at a side console in the chief medic's office.

Flintlock called up a holo of one of the three inanimate forms, all of whom had been locked into med-cradles.

"They're all pretty much the same. Note the ironmongery integral to the bone structure and this prosthetic patch under the hair on the skull. Even Greenwing's seen nothing like it before and he's knocked around the galaxy a bit."

"They looked humanoid enough when we took them out but that looks like enhancement. Cyber?"

"And then some," the doctor told her.

"So what were they, genetically, before this stuff was implanted?"

"Friskianx."

Ahxenta's eyes widened. "I see. I think we need to talk to Azular."

The Berzic science officer was quick to arrive as he was already on his way to the bridge. He had intended to call the captain once he had carried out thorough scans of the captive vessel inside and out, but his preliminary findings had given him sufficient food for thought that he had decided to inform her immediately. He sat down beside the other two and set his holo-pad on the table, calling up a detailed spec of the craft's hull.

"Now why does an escape shuttle have more concealed firepower than a mid-range cruiser?" Ahxenta mused, scanning the holo. "And long-range scanners capable of detecting a flea up an alien's armpit, quite a collection of comms gear and what looks like highly efficient external shielding. What's her hull structure?"

"Meta-jurillium alloy sourced from Beta Zegonia 68c," Azular told her, raising an eyebrow. "Not a hairsbreadth off the stuff that coated the Friskianx ships that attacked us, and those ships that Commander Apnis sampled in the Web. But there are two hold units built into the outer hull here that my scanner can't penetrate, nor can I open them. I didn't want to use force as they may have explosive trips. But given the weight of the craft, I don't think they're empty."

"Interesting; it's maybe ops gear or extra weaponry. The crew of that boat," the captain asked Flintlock, pointing to the holo, "Just how cyber-enhanced are they?"

"Cyber-enhanced?" echoed Azular looking from one to the other.

"Show him," Ahxenta instructed.

After a rundown on the three beings and a close scrutiny of their implants, the science officer leaned back. "They're not as advanced as info-sents but they'll pack a punch, their prosthetics will see to that. And I suspect they can be monitored from distance. Do any of their implanted mechanisms emit detectable signals, doctor?"

"Not that I could figure; not long-range, that is. I *did* detect ops parameters so I was going to get Zaik Oak to help. He's going over the data from those attacking ships with Greffy, isn't he?"

"Yes, but it might be wise to call him in," Ahxenta agreed. "I want them in separate units and a guard posted on each. Friskianx! They used to be small fish in the Coalition pond but they're growing, in more ways than one. They're prowling the spaceways with new tech that's in advance of anything they could develop on their own, they're targeting big ships and acting the bad guys. And now we find *them* as well as their ships kitted out with hardware that makes them nasty to play with. It must have been going on for a while as it looks like these aliens have infiltrated Friskianx or their colonies, probably with inside help. And now they're moving into new territory and becoming more aggressive. But they've hit Friskianx ships: I wonder if the Friskies have got themselves in over their heads and are now regretting it."

"Our erstwhile associate Micklemouse was originally Friskianx," Azular pointed out. "And he seemed more than wary of these clients of his that had him genetically altered to fit in with their own plans."

"They scared him to pieces you mean, and you're right," said the captain. "I want you to check over those three out there and see what you can find. Axellina, you call in Dr Oak. But I don't want them waking up. The quicker they're off *Arianrhod* the better. There should be an ISP ship waiting for us at Heligon – they've rerouted some cruiser that was heading out to Kellybar One."

"Kellybar One? The only manned outpost that we know of in the ISP enclave in zone Kappa that keeps an eye on the Independents in zone Mu and their ore-running ops on that side of Kappa?" the science officer questioned. "I thought the ISP didn't have a warship available for this mission to Kelfennig Four they've sent us on and one of their ships is headed this way?"

"I've no details on the ship or its mission, Azular; it may not be a warship. But I want all the details you can gather on that shuttle and its crew, as well as what we have on the ships that attacked us, before I hand that lot and their boat over. I'll be passing the bare bones of what you find in a report to the ISP Council, and to the PSS fleet via the Ultraviolet III, in case they find themselves in trouble."

"No peace for the wicked," Flintlock sighed. "One thing, Cap: if I were you, I'd authorise as much rec time as possible for the crew. They've been through a heck of a lot recently and who knows when we'll see more furlough."

"Don't think I haven't thought on it. But we'll just have to hang in there for the time being. You have four hours before we dock at Heligon station. Then we'll see what we will see."

What the captain and first mate of the *Arianrhod* saw when the ship had safely achieved docking around the repair station at Heligon was a plethora of small and large craft, most of which seemed to be trying to find a safe route elsewhere. The abortive attempt to retake Brown Amber had been confirmed and the locals at this end of the settled galaxy were starting to worry that one of their worlds would be next. Rumour had it that the aliens were striking without warning further afield and it was said that the ore-carriers of two of the independents in zone Mu had fallen victim to hostile attacks. As Kellybar One was the closest Interstellar Systems Protectorate base to that zone, it was possible that they were arming in earnest to repel boarders, hence the rerouted ISP ship, which had already docked.

Ahxenta and Apnis had taken a shuttle over to make contact with two senior officers from the *ISPS Crusader*, the ship sent to collect the three prisoners and their vessel, who were apparently on the station on business. Neither the captain nor the first mate had heard of the *Crusader* and figured that she was one of the new war cruiser models off the production line. From the view they had of her as *Arianrhod* made orbit, she was sizeable and well-armed and probably maintained a small fleet of fighters.

The sight that greeted the duo as they walked into the meeting space of the station they did not expect: Colonel Ellin Myrtleberry of the ISP Council. She turned to greet them.

"Captain Ahxenta, Commander Apnis, I believe. I presume you remember me?"

The captain confirmed that they did, but refused point blank to discuss business until they found a private space. As they walked into one of the many small meeting rooms, the two from *Arianrhod* were introduced to Myrtleberry's companion, the *Crusader's* chief medic, to whom the care of the prisoners was be entrusted in the interim. The *Crusader* had been ordered to escort the three and their ship to Vellis Prime, where they would be handed over to ISP agents who were currently on their way out from the Skyrtek system.

Myrtleberry was rather perfunctory in her thanks over the detour to investigate what appeared to be the *ISPS Nomad's* distress beacon but demanded details of the ensuing firefight and of what *Arianrhod* had uncovered to date on the surface station, the captured aliens and the escape craft. Responding in kind, Ahxenta gave her a brief report and handed over a data shard of the relevant technical information. It was agreed that the prisoner and ship transfer would take place as soon as possible, a shuttle being sent for the humanoids and grapples being used for handover of their craft.

Despite it now seeming even less likely that *Arianrhod's* mission to Kelfennig Four would yield any trace of the missing ISP vessel or its crew, Myrtleberry was adamant that she should continue: there might be another listening post that would be better destroyed. The *Crusader* was manned by a shakedown crew under the command of a Captain Flute and her current assignment of the transport of Myrtleberry's detachment of newly-assigned marines for deployment at Kellybar One had been deemed a training run. That being the case, the ship was unsuitable for a rescue mission, but that was all that the two from the *Arianrhod* could find out.

Ahxenta was less than satisfied with the outcome of the discussion but only nodded curtly and made her farewells as civilly as possible. She was more forthcoming on the way back to her ship.

"Using us as cannon-fodder," she fumed to her first mate, who was in the pilot's seat. "It sounds as if the ISP's pretty stretched if it's using shakedown crews this far out, even if they're only transporting grunts: that's a coffee and cake run if ever there was one."

"True," Apnis agreed. "And manning outposts like Kellybar One with rookies right out of boot. But where are these troops from the Coalition and the NTA that were supposed to be fighting side by side with the ISP?"

"Too busy on their own fronts: Myrtleberry wasn't exactly clear on how things were going," the captain observed.

"Badly, from what we've heard. But you weren't exactly giving too much away, Cinnabar. Don't you trust the colonel?"

"No I don't. A colonel in charge of a squad of rookies sits oddly and right now I'm not inclined to trust anyone. As I don't know who her associates are or how far I can be sure of them, I'm not about to let anything slip, including how we managed to foil those damn raiders that attacked us."

"Nor that we've figured that the aliens must have a link to ISP tech to be able to send out fake distress calls and get hold of data on the disposition of ISP ships," Apnis added.

"As they now know the three we captured are Friskianx, they'll no doubt do their own digging and come up with one or two answers. At least Azular has verified that the signal *is* a very clever fake, but I'm not about to tell anyone that, or let out how he did it."

"Yes, you don't admit to having a telepath of *his* ability as part of our crew. But I'll be glad to see the back of that boat and her crew. Though you realise that our mission to Kelfennig Four could already be compromised, and a fleet there ready to take us out?"

"I realise, Tallica, believe me. But one thing at a time; Myrtleberry and her recruits can look after our ex-passengers from here on in."

"You don't think she'd be irresponsible enough to wake them up, do you?" the first mate asked.

"Her lookout if she does. We've given her Flintlock's opinion on the level of danger they represent and they'll be sound when we hand them over. The *Crusader's* medics just better bring their own med-cradles across, they're not having ours. We've already had to replace energy cells and torpedoes we lost on ISP business. And we haven't been reimbursed for them or for ship's damage," Ahxenta added darkly. "I'll get Lindell onto that as soon as I get back."

"Good luck with that, Cap. But here we are. I'd best order a full check-up on all our fighters and other craft before we leave Heligon, in case we need to buy in gear. At least with ISP back-up, we're one of the first in line for any stock the repair sheds have."

The transfer of the three recumbent passengers and their ship was handled smoothly as far as the *Arianrhod* was concerned, although the captain had made sure that her security was highly visible. She also had Azular standing by to deflect awkward questions and maintain a wary eye on the visitors from the *Crusader*. She treated the ISP crew with distant chill: her request for reparation for damages at Four One Two Alpha had been denied on the basis that the losses had been incurred on a mission not sanctioned by the ISP.

Remaining docked for as long as it took to repair the worst of the hull damage and to resupply, the *Arianrhod* headed out. Once away from local beacons, she set for the far side of the Starglass Nebula and Kelfennig. The journey would take two standard days as much of it would be in normal space. Meanwhile, ship's business continued.

Whisper Earbleat had spent her free time in Heligon's repair bays sourcing the means to convert another of *Arianrhod's* cargo pods. The lost pod, recorded as detached as a result of enemy action, had been replaced by an inferior one which Earbleat considered inadequate for the job. Ahxenta had given grudging approval: the same trick twice was rarely successful in her book and she was not sanguine as to the efficacy of the ruse if used again.

"It keeps her out of trouble," the first mate had consoled. "She'd only be playing with the aft torpedo bay controls otherwise."

"She'd be better helping Cottontail with our cloak: it didn't do us many favours in the last firefight. If this signal from Kelfennig *is* a trap, we'll need it operational and as far as possible undetectable."

"Tell that to the universe and it might change the laws of physics for you," Apnis snorted. "But weren't we told by the almighty ISP that this mission was top secret, no-one but a couple of their senior brass knew about it and even the TA was unaware?"

"And we've seen how that worked in the attempt to retake Brown Amber," was the reply. "Those aliens that overran it not only knew that they could, they had people in place well in advance. We sure as hell figured something was going on when we were there."

Earbleat had been busy on another matter and had sent an update round as they were half way to their endpoint. She had delved into the loss of the *SS Palynia* and had dug up an obscure report that suggested that the ship had not crashed on Kelfennig Four but had been pulled in by an unknown force and had been unable to extricate herself before her systems went down due to instrument malfunction. The small shuttle in which the crew had escaped had only got away because it seemed that the power that had pulled their ship in could only deal with one vessel at a time and in the short window of non-operation open, the shuttle made it out, the crew realising that their ship was not spaceworthy. There had been unverified reports years before the *Palynia's* loss that several ships in that area had vanished without trace. That was why, Earbleat guessed, that the *Palynia's* crew had been quick to hightail it off the planet and that there had been no salvage mission nor a rush to loot the remains by the usual suspects. Your ship might get in, but it was unlikely to get out again.

Azular had meanwhile reanalysed the recorded distress provided by the ISP to separate out the parallel signal wave he had detected to see if he could pluck out additional information, but could find little. As a tracking signal sent out by implanted and external cyber systems, it was meant to be detectable from a distance but what that distance was, the senior science officer was unsure. He did however suggest that *Arianrhod* search for it well before her approach to Kelfennig.

Comms had been adjured to keep wary eyes and ears open for any untoward transmissions from any direction and *Arianrhod* was within an hour of her destination when an exclamation from Bellfish caused all the duty officers to look up. Apnis requested an explanation.

"Picking up a tracking signal, Commander," the lieutenant stated in obvious puzzlement. "But it's ours."

"What do you mean, it's ours?" she demanded.

"Confirmed," chief tactical officer Pollux Gliss stated roundly. "I recognise it. It's a tracking signal from one of our drone trackers."

"Captain to the bridge! Find out if we're missing a drone tracker and if so, where it's gone."

"On it!" Gliss responded as Ahxenta sprinted in from her office demanding an update.

Moments later, the tactical officer began to laugh. "It's reading as the tracker that Chief Cottontail set into the energy cell that we used to power the transfer pod we hooked up to Micklemouse's ship when we moved it – the pod was left at that Dryssicon mooring station."

"You what? So what's it doing out here?" Apnis demanded.

"At a guess, some pocket-dipper stole the cell and probably the pod from Dryssicon and didn't check it for bugs," Gliss answered.

"I wonder who that was," Ahxenta cut in dryly. "From here on in, we cloak. This is getting more surreal by the minute. Are we picking up anything else from our target, comms?"

"Nary a thing, Cap," Bellfish answered. "I'm not even getting the signal that Dr Azular locked in. Ah! I have something now."

"Show me!" demanded the captain.

In response, the bridge holo-generator grid opened out to show a pair of pulse waves, the info display indicating a match.

"So we're detecting the same signal the ISP did and that Azular untangled," she noted, stroking her chin as she leaned back in her chair. "Still operational and being sent out multi-directionally."

"So whoever or whatever was down there still is," Apnis said as the senior science officer walked onto the bridge. "Or it's an auto-distress. If it's somebody, they must be getting desperate by now; either that or pissed that nobody's swallowed the bait."

"Even money says it's a set-up," Box whispered to his mate at the helm as the holo display rippled to show the starfield to which they were headed, the *Arianrhod* winking out as her cloak took effect.

"Usually is," Dox replied brightly.

"I wonder," the captain mused, ignoring the exchange. "I was just going over a report from the ISP tactical relay and things are hotting up at the Ginseng; the anomaly's expanded again and it's taken out another couple of perimeter probes. There's still no clue as to what it is apart from the energy spikes as it expands, but signals can't cross it, suggesting that something's well-hidden in the interior."

"Maybe it's the mouth of hell," Box suggested conversationally.

"However," the captain went on, "All the Allied Powers have sent a ship in apiece to monitor the situation."

"From a distance I expect," Apnis put in wryly. "Wonder who'll be sent in first if things get nasty. But we have our own little mystery to solve and we're getting closer."

"Exactly. I want all hands to stations and maintain silent red alert status. Steady as we go."

The Kelfennig system was in a remote area and the fourth planet was hardly habitable, although with sufficient atmospheric oxygen that it could be extracted. Cautious as ever, Ahxenta had sent in a probe to scan the place from a safe orbital distance and pinpoint the source of the signal that was now even clearer. It was as the location was being recorded that Gliss sent out an annoyed yell.

"Something's pulling our probe out of orbit! A tractor beam close to the source of that signal!"

"Life readings?" barked Ahxenta.

"Nothing detected," Azular called out from the science station.

"Then launch a damn torpedo and take out the tractor and the signal source!"

"Torpedo, aye!" Earbleat complied with alacrity. "She's away!"

Moments later and the detonation could be seen on the bridge holo, a gout of dust blossoming outwards.

"Got it!" she cawed gleefully as the captain ordered the cloak cut.

"Rescued our probe," the senior science officer reported. "It's maintaining a stable but lower orbit and is still fully operational."

"Good. Have it continue to scan. Widen the field as you go. I want to know if there are any other booby traps down there."

"That we can detect from up here," Apnis said a trifle sceptically.

"You have a point, Tallica. But if that's what brought the *Palynia* down years ago and it's still operating, was that what brought down the missing ships that were lost here before then and since? If not, there may be more than one of these devices, whatever they are."

"Or there have been new ones planted," the first mate said. "The *Palynia* lost her systems to an unidentified instrument malfunction, if that report that Earbleat dug out is anything to go by, so there may be numerous nasty surprises in store down there."

"I hadn't forgotten," Ahxenta told her. "We do several thorough sweeps by probe before we get any closer in."

"And anything we don't like the look of we take out?" asked the weapons officer eagerly.

"Keep our systems online but we don't let anything loose until I'm sure it's absolutely necessary," the captain said crisply. "We don't want to give away our capabilities if we can help it."

"Aye, Cap. By the way, I've done final testing on outer cargo pod two and she's good to go on your mark; although I don't recommend her for a surface hit: she'd make a bit of a mess if she crashed."

Ahxenta groaned and Apnis laughed quietly. "Doesn't miss a beat, does she?"

"Thank you, Lieutenant Commander Earbleat. Let me have the spec at your convenience."

"Aye, Cap. You'll note I've added a call-sign that identifies her as a small cutter out of one of the private yards near Velmbeach Major."

"I've never heard of Velmbeach Major."

"Doesn't exist," Earbleat announced jauntily. "Made it up. The cutter's called the *Echo*, by the way."

"I sometimes wonder what I pay her for," Ahxenta muttered in an undertone. "What's the latest on our orbiting probe, Azular?"

"Nothing unusual so far, ma'am. We *are* still receiving the original distress with an ISP trace on it, so whatever we destroyed down there wasn't part of it; however there may be more than one source. We've lost our drone tracker signal, so it must be on the far side of the planet and out of range. There are a few large surface structures, but all appear derelict. I've found evidence of underground constructions and they seem to go down a long way. They're accessed by fissures mostly but some probably have exits at ground level. Abandoned a long time ago, I guess. I suggest we send the probe in closer to pick out more detail. Ah, I'm now getting energy readings, nothing big, but from the far side. Our probe's now going out of range."

"Follow her round, Dox, but maintain our distance; we don't want to run afoul of anything that can pull us in. And keep all long-range scanners at max. If there's even a whisper of something out there, I want to know about it."

"Aye, Cap," echoed round the bridge as Dox pulled *Arianrhod* out to keep track of her probe as it circled the dark planet.

"Energy readings are increasing, Captain," Azular called. "Source is below ground and close to our tracker trace and the emergency call-sign – there must definitely be more than one source."

"Which sounds as if our energy cell is still in use and quite a way from where we left it," the first mate grunted. "And I can't imagine the other signal is in any way related to the *ISPS Nomad*. It smacks more of the fake signal that lured us into our last little firefight."

An hour or so later and the argument still raged. There was no other ship detectable within range, but that did not mean that a cloaked vessel was not out there somewhere. And the only way to complete the mission with which the *Arianrhod* had been reluctantly burdened was by sending down a landing party to investigate the signals, which seemed to be emanating from beneath the ground, some way below the ruins of a large, stone-built structure. Alongside the structure they had detected the remains of what seemed to be a ship, but it was not large enough to be a warship of any size.

Apnis was adamant: as captain, Ahxenta was far too valuable to risk on such an uncertain mission and should their ship encounter trouble or need to leave orbit, she would need her most senior officer aboard. The first mate was determined to lead the team and like it or not, the captain would be left behind, along with the chief engineer.

"Have it your way," Ahxenta finally relented. "But one sign of trouble, you all get out and to hell with the ISP contract. Are you absolutely clear on that?"

"As crystal, Cap. See you on the flipside."

17: DARK PLACES

The dark pressed around the small party like a living entity. They could almost sense its breath on the napes of their necks, a whisper of a breeze with a hint of iciness that froze the heart's blood. Kitted out in all-enveloping protective suits as the landing party were, the sensation was unnerving.

"It's here again!" whispered Apnis.

Her voice echoed eerily inside the helmets of her team. What *it* was, no-one was sure. They had left the shuttle beside the wreck they had detected, a standard small cargo-carrier that had long since lost its identity. It was not the *Palynia* or an ISP escape craft, of that they were certain. What was evident was that it had been stripped bare, possibly by more than one scavenger. It had no energy pods in place and the cracked hull was minus much of its plating. A breached cargo bay showed where its innards had been ripped out. Their own tracking signal, alongside the ISP emergency beacon, had been traced to an indeterminate depth below their feet and they had left the shell of the old ship to follow a clear path into the remains of a substantial, still partly roofed structure, much of which had fallen into enormous chunks of sand-coloured rock.

Within the vast hall they had found a ramped opening giving onto a downward incline that led into a wide tunnel. It seemed to be the only outlet to anywhere, apart from the way they had come. The first mate led the way with Earbleat alongside and Azular behind. They were escorted by security guards Hanx and Goldwash and a medic that Flintlock had insisted accompany the party. On turning a corner several metres beyond the opening, it was Flish Ma'Lappis who first noticed a faintly glowing orb high above their heads and out of the light of their torches. As the team looked up, all were assailed by a faint frisson of anxiety that wriggled up their spines.

They had followed the orb, which was heading down the only path. Apnis had called the situation in to the *Arianrhod* and had been directed to proceed with extreme caution, as the ship's scanners were reading a series of tunnels in their general direction. They had lost sight of the sphere when it turned a corner, but Apnis ordered them forward until the tunnel opened out into a wide circular grotto out of which two exits led. The first mate had sensed a chill before she spied the globe again, hovering at one of the two openings.

"I still can't get an internal reading on it," Azular announced as he swept the manifestation. "Apart from that it seems to be bounded by a fuzzy energy field."

"What else can you get of our surroundings?" Apnis asked. "The signals are below us still but this path's been twisting so we must have spiralled down."

The dim light of his scanner glowed pinkly as Azular probed the immediate vicinity. "We have. That building we came from is above us, though slightly to our left. But we're close to the signal source and it's reading strongly. And it looks as if our little guiding light wants us to go that way."

"Inviting us into a trap?" Earbleat suggested.

"Just keep your phase rifle primed," Apnis told her.

"Aye, Commander."

The *Arianrhod* was following their progress from the bridge as far as possible, but the specifics they could not make out. As the party moved closer to what they believed was the source of the signals they had been picking up, the captain advised care and ordered the ship in on a closer orbit. *Arianrhod's* long-range scanners were still showing clear but Ahxenta had despatched a trio of linked scanning probes to the far side of the planet to keep an eye on things there: she did not want to be surprised by something coming up on their blind side.

Below the planet's surface the landing party was descending still, down the wide tunnel that was in complete darkness apart from their torches and the glowing orb overhead. Suddenly Earbleat gave a hiss.

"It's getting light ahead, I'm sure of it!"

"Switch off the torches and let's see," ordered Apnis.

The weapons officer had been right: further on, a faint but steady glow seemed to emanate from close to the ground.

Azular, on the alert, had his scanner ready. "I'm reading what may be a shielded structure that seems to correlate with the source of the signals. We should see something just around that bend."

"Phase rifles at the ready. Set to heavy stun and shoot first if you see a problem," the first mate instructed.

"Permission to keep mine full on, just in case," Earbleat asked.

"Do it, but hold fire unless I give the go-ahead."

"On your mark, Commander."

The six made their way forward to the curve that hid the section ahead from view. The light was growing as the first mate reached a place that would allow her to take a cautious peek around the bend. Her exclamation caused Hanx to scurry forward, weapon raised.

"I doubt you'll need it, Ensign," she said dryly. "Take a look."

"It's a small ship! How did she get here?" he whispered urgently.

"Very carefully, I should think, and not the way we came down. Keep your weapons ready but do not deploy. Readings, Azular?"

"A one-man trading rig, based on the Comet Six design but with added capacity in the form of a number of carrier pods."

"One of which is reading as ours, I'll bet," the commander said trenchantly, eying the vessel.

"It is. The ship's very well shielded, especially the aft engineering sections, and she has substantial meta-jurillium and rad-shielding over the bridge and living areas atop. And she has an attempt at a cloak but it's not operational. She's been banged about a bit and she's got very little engine power. I doubt she'd be able to get out of here even with the spare energy pods she's got strapped to her freight bays."

"Which she salvaged, I expect, along with this stuff lying about," Apnis reckoned. "Send the details up to *Arianrhod*. Shall we see if anyone's at home, and how they managed to send that little guiding ball up there to us? The occupant must know we're here."

"What do we do, knock on the door?" Earbleat demanded.

"I wouldn't, the ship might be rigged to fry whoever tries it. Let's you and me get into the open, Azular. Mind our backs," the first mate added to the security guards. "One shot and you return fire, no holds barred."

The two made their way forward into the by now clear light and stood at the main cargo bay door of the small craft.

"Reading one occupant now," the science officer noted.

"Giving us the once over. He's no doubt aware we've got back-up and he's outnumbered. He's wondering if we're friendly."

As the two watched, the airlock entry slid slowly to one side and the nose of a rifle projected forward. A suited individual eventually peered out. Apnis tapped the side of her helmet, tabbed the external intercom link of her own suit and stretched out her gloved hand, palm upward, inviting communication. The small biped activated his own suit's comm link and waited.

"Hello," the commander said calmly. "Been here long?"

"Quite a time. Did you crash here too? My ship was pulled in and there was nothing I could do. I made it down here barely alive…"

Something clicked in the man's brain, for his voice petered out as he squinted intently at her, trying to make out the features behind her helmet's filtered face-plate. "Who are you?" he asked uncertainly.

"I was just about to ask you that," she responded softly. "And to ask how you got your ship down here: it seems a long way down for a beat up old ship like yours that crashed, leaving the pilot *barely alive*."

"There's a tunnel back that way that I found once I came to. I had enough in my energy cells to let me crawl through in hover mode and my life support was okay. It saw me through."

"I see. What's your name, Mr...?"

"Bloombusk," he told her. "Jerrin Bloombusk. I'm a trader out of Arrissia. I specialise in archaeological artefacts, which is why I was in this neck of the woods. I got a licence," he added, lest his questioner was some sort of trading standards officer. "Who are you?"

Apnis shook her head, laughing a little. "You are one lousy liar, Mr Bloombusk and you don't deserve to be rescued."

The man fell back in consternation, raising his rifle and repeating his question tremulously. "Who are you?"

"Don't even think about it, Bloombusk. I have four armed guards behind me and their guns are all pointing at you. Now tell me how you really got down here and be quick: I don't have all day."

In fact Apnis had no time for a loud chirp in her ear told her that she had an urgent comm from *Arianrhod* and she cut her external link to listen. Seconds later, she called the rest of her team into the open.

"Back to the shuttle, double quick. There's trouble and we need to get back aboard," she told them, releasing the external link.

"Are we taking him?" Earbleat questioned as she came up, poking a finger at the by now quivering Jerrin Bloombusk, who was looking from one to the other of his rescuers in perplexity.

"We're taking him, but none of his gear," the first mate told her.

"But I need my ship!" he quavered. "I can't leave without her!"

"You'll have to ask our captain, once we're back aboard. We've no capacity on our shuttle. Now move, unless you want to stay here and take the consequences of what's happening up there."

"What about our little guiding ball, Commander?" demanded Earbleat, pointing.

"Take it out."

"Nooooo!"

"Oops! Too late!" the weapons officer told him as she complied swiftly and efficiently and the radiant globe burst in a cascade of fire, spattering the Comet Six in sparks.

Apnis pulled the man from the shelter of his ship and prodded him forward with the sharp end of her phase rifle.

"Look after him, Goldwash; don't let him run away. The captain wants a few words."

"Aye, Commander," the guard responded, relieving Bloombusk of his weapon and passing it to Ensign Hanx.

A swift nod from Apnis to Azular sent the silent message that the science officer should keep both his eyes on the rescued trader as the party made their way at speed back the way they had come.

Once at the surface, the man gazed at the shuttle in utter dismay, immediately recognising *Arianrhod's* insignia. By now realising that his cover story of honest trader marooned by misfortune was probably well and truly blown, he was rather reluctant to accept the hospitality offered and was practically hustled within and strapped into a seat.

It took fifteen minutes for the shuttle to regain her berth aboard ship, where a security detail waited to escort the castaway to the brig. The man was divested of his helmet once through the airlock and in pressurised space. He blinked rapidly as he took in his companions.

"Well, Mr Micklemouse, we meet again," the captain greeted him. "Or have you changed your name to Jerrin Bloombusk?"

"I didn't know who you were!" he groaned. "You could have been anyone! I had to protect myself."

"You'll be escorted to the brig for the duration: that should offer you as much protection as you need. My officers are needed on the bridge immediately. Then we'll see."

"But my ship! I need my ship!"

"Too bad. Hell will freeze over before I'll allow that boat aboard *Arianrhod*," he was told. "Take him away. Azular, you go with them to make sure our guest is comfortable and then head to the bridge. Apnis and Earbleat, you're with me; the rest of you to your posts."

"Aye, Captain," was the joint response: all were aware that the red alert was now not muted.

"So what gives, Cap?" demanded the first mate in a low voice once the three were safely in a transport tube and headed to the bridge.

"One of our linked probes caught a signal that popped up out of the dark, so it's from something running silent that's just come off the bypass or it's a cloaked ship that's uncloaked for scanning or that thinks it's safe. It's headed this way."

"Sneaking up on Kelfennig Four?" Earbleat guessed.

"Seems so. Whether to land or not, I don't know. It reads as ISP but I won't risk trouble: we cloak. We're still getting signals from the surface and they're strong, whatever Micklemouse did or didn't do."

"Better hope it's not the ones that set them up and have come to see what their trap has brought down," said Apnis. "But what about our transfer pod that's still down there under Micklemouse's ship?"

"We leave it," the captain stated. "If anyone *is* checking up on the little sod and we take it, they may figure it was us here."

"Besides, somebody may have bugged our bug and could track it," Earbleat put in.

"His strange little pals, you mean," replied the first mate.

"Possibly; I'm not chancing it," Ahxenta said firmly.

"You have one suspicious mind, Cap," Apnis told her, smiling.

"In my trade I need it. Let's see what more our probes have got."

The probes were still netting data, which Greffy was adding to the bridge holo to produce a detailed image. As the two senior officers scanned the result, Azular appeared and settled at his own console.

"She reads like a ship but I don't detect a cloak, Captain. My guess is that she's dropped out of hyperspace. But she must be big as our probes are getting a profile," the Berzic officer declared.

"Warm up weapons, Ms Earbleat. If she detects our probes she might shoot first and leave us in the dark."

"She's maybe not spied us as she's come in on the far side," Apnis pointed out.

"She's detected one of our probes, ma'am, it's being scanned!" called Greffy. "I'm reading her as ISP. She's taken out our probe!"

"Recall the other two! Helm, get us in sight of her; I want to see what we have!"

"Aye, Captain!"

"Hell and damn and blast! I recognise that ship!" Apnis bristled as the sleek lines of a large vessel came into view. "What the blazes is she doing here and why has she shot down our probe?"

"I'd do the same if I thought it was scanning me," Ahxenta said. "But this wasn't her last course: she was headed for Vellis Prime and then Kellybar One. Hail them, Mr Bellfish, but don't identify us as yet. Earbleat, arm weapons but do not target that ship."

"They won't read us unless they get closer, Cap, we're cloaked," the first mate pointed out.

"She's one of the newest ships of the line and straight out of space dock: she probably has advanced scanning gear that'll at least detect our ion trail, if not our grav displacement. But what in hell is the *ISPS Crusader* doing out here?"

"Colonel Myrtleberry checking up that we're doing our bit for the glorious Galactic Alliance?" Apnis responded sardonically. "Training for her new troopers?"

"She wasn't in command of the *Crusader*, even though she was the ranking officer. I doubt she'd be able to change their mission. But even if the *Crusader* did have a quick turnaround at Vellis, she'd not have had time to make it to Kellybar One and be on the return leg. In fact, she'd hardly have had time to make it here unless she has some super-fast drive."

"She's a new ship."

"A new ship that's seen a scuffle," Gliss called as he skimmed his tactical readout. "Her aft shielding's damaged, but the output's rising, as if it's being repaired. And there's scoring on her hull. Her energy readings are low for a ship that size and her weapons batteries are half empty. And I'm reading excess heat in her fighter bays."

"Copy that," Azular concurred from his station.

"Any response to our hails?" the captain demanded.

"None, Captain. I'm repeating," Bellfish told her. "Just a moment: they want to know who we are. They refuse to identify themselves."

"Put me on speaker," Ahxenta ordered. "*ISPS Crusader*, this is the *PSS Arianrhod*. What is your situation?"

"That'll make them sit up," Apnis declared.

The first mate was right. In moments they had visual and a man in an ISP captain's uniform, looking surprised, faced them on the holo. "You must be cloaked, we're hardly reading you."

"But you *are* reading me," Ahxenta observed. "Interesting. What is your situation, Captain?"

"How did you know who we were?"

"You're reading as ISP and I saw your ship at Heligon a few days ago. And now you're here. I repeat, interesting. Do you require aid?"

"Not that he'll get it," Box muttered in a barely audible whisper.

The captain licked his lips. "You must be Captain Ahxenta. I'm Captain Jolion Flute."

"We figured," murmured Apnis in an aside.

"My crew is handling the situation but I would appreciate a couple of energy cells if you could spare them. I could send a shuttle over."

Ahxenta's jaw tightened. "I can't. As you no doubt know, I lost several in our last little skirmish on behalf of the ISP, for which I was not compensated; and now I've lost a probe at ISP hands. I can spare medical aid and other supplies. If you give me a list of your needs, I'll see what I can do. May I ask what you're doing out here and what happened to you? I understood that your heading was Vellis Prime, with the cargo that we handed over."

"I can't disclose that information, Captain," Flute told her sternly.

"I see. Is there any information you *can* disclose? Such as who attacked you? If they're still around, I'd like to know."

"We dealt with them. I'll make a list of my needs and get back to you. Flute out."

"Short and sweet," Apnis noted. "He says he needs energy cells but he could send a shuttle? What's going on? What's he hiding?"

"A whole lot. Maintain red alert and keep those weapons primed. Azular, did you pick up on anything?"

"Greffy's got details. The *Crusader's* showing more internal damage than external and she's lost at least three fighter bays. And Captain Flute is a very worried man."

"That I had worked out," Ahxenta stated dryly. "More internal than external damage?"

"You don't think Myrtleberry was senseless enough to wake up those three half-cyber Friskianx we handed over, do you? Or try to get into their ship?" the first mate asked.

"I don't know, Tallica; as ISP Council she's more bureaucrat than soldier. But Flute reckoned they'd handled it. Barely, by the look of it. No doubt we'll hear more when they call back with their list."

That Myrtleberry and her platoon of fresh-faced minions were still aboard the *Crusader* was not left long in doubt, for the colonel called less than an hour later. Ahxenta had used the time to order a sweep of the planet below to find and disable the sources of the emergency decoy signals and had just completed that task, despatching a pair of Earbleat's favourite beweaponed drones to take them out.

The colonel conveyed Flute's list of immediate needs and then told the captain that she had a request that was to be taken in private. The dialogue was long, for it was more than thirty minutes later that a grim-faced Ahxenta reappeared from her bridge office.

"You don't look happy, Cap," Apnis greeted her. "What's up?"

"Myrtleberry is up. Request my left boot! The *Crusader's* damage is so extensive that she's heading back to Heligon for emergency repairs and then to the fleet dockyard at Skyrtek Prime. So the colonel wants us to transport her shipload of rookies to the Kellybar One outpost."

"You what!"

"You heard. Naturally I refused, so she played the withdrawal of the Trades Alliance flag card again if we don't render support to the ISP if the situation calls for it. I called up the TA and they back her. Seems things are hotting up out there and they need all their pieces in the places they deem appropriate. Though what they think a bunch of beginners can do against these hostiles…"

"Desperation," Apnis shrugged. "So what did you tell her?"

"That I'd need to know the fine details of what happened to the *Crusader* that she's in such a state that she can't reach Kellybar One – not that she'd get much repair work done there. But I don't want us running afoul of whatever they came up against; there's a lot of Zeta zone between here and Kellybar."

"And?"

"As I half suspected: with the chief medic's grudging assist, she tried to resuscitate one of the Friskies. She wanted to question him about the surface station on the third planet of Four One Two Alpha that was sending out the *Nomad's* distress. She wanted to find out where they got it, how they did it and if there were more similar in the vicinity, given that she and her trainees were to be heading in that direction. They got more than they bargained for: the prisoner woke up all right and smashed the iso-bay to pieces before waking up his friends. Most of the damage was caused when all three shot their way out to get to their ship and once in it, blasted free of the docking bay. Myrtleberry says they followed the ship to take it out, to prevent it heading back to its base. That's how they ended up in this neck of the galaxy. But I reckon she doesn't know if a message got out before they put an end to it. Her people had gone over it as we did, to check that we'd given them accurate data. But Flute has got two dead on deck and a fleet of injuries, including his chief medic."

"We disabled as much as we could of that ship and Azular went over it with a fine-toothed comb. How come they could just blast free and fly off into the ether with smacked up engines and spiked weapons?" the first mate questioned.

"Those sections we couldn't access," Ahxenta reminded her. "The ones built into the outer hull. Remember those extra compartments on Micklemouse's ship with firepower enough to take out a vast chunk of *Arianrhod* and shielding to prevent breaking and entering? Their ship was maybe similar, with back-up emergency escape systems. We'll not find out now."

"I guess not. But did the colonel realise the prisoners were more cyber than humanoid?"

"We told them that, but I figure she thought she could handle it. Not that she'll admit it of course. But it looks like we're saddled with Myrtleberry as well as her fifty snot-nosed troopers. And as they're the relief for Kellybar One, there's a squad to be picked up there for taking out at least as far as Heligon, if not Skyrtek."

"We're not a fizzing transport service! We'd better be getting well paid for this, is all!" Apnis snorted.

"We are; Lindell's seeing to it. But he and Helly Pinkhorn are now busy sorting out billets for the brood of grunts. They'll have to make do with the hold accommodation we used for the Marridani: I'm not having the crew give up their bunks. Just as well we don't have much in the way of cargo at the moment. But I told Myrtleberry they can bring their own provisions; they're not having ours."

"We also have the small problem of our guest in the brig," her first mate reminded her needlessly.

"There he stays. He can like it or lump it. Azular can deal with the interrogation as he can manage it and Micklemouse trusts him about as far as he trusts anyone. But Azular and Flintlock are looking at ways to disable his capabilities."

"Permanently?"

"We'll see," answered the captain. "It depends on what he knows. Meanwhile, we'd best find out what aid we can render the *Crusader* before she sets off for Heligon."

"Myrtleberry given up on Kelfennig Four and the *Nomad*?"

"For the present, but I'm not counting on the fact that she'll let it slip. She knows we have an itinerant trader that we picked up there, but not who or what he is. Make sure the crew don't let out our dealings with him to her or any of her people."

"Will do, Cap. Maintain red alert?"

"Maintain red alert."

Ahxenta finally found that she had no option but to lend the *Crusader* two energy cells, to enable the crippled ship to reach Heligon. An ISP escort vessel was on the way, but there was no estimate as to when it would rendezvous and Myrtleberry was keen to make for Kellybar to discharge her troops. She would remain there, much to the relief of the crew of the *Arianrhod*. Her dictatorial behaviour was difficult to stomach and her troopers were argumentative, confined as they were to small hold spaces much of the time, the captain having made it plain that she would not allow them the run of her ship.

Bick Micklemouse on the other hand was more pliable. He had no wish to meet an ISP agent, or be hauled off to prison. He suspected that his food had been spiked with a systems inhibitor to impede his cyber abilities, but as his recent employers had sent no-one to rescue him, he was upbeat. At least the *Arianrhod* had liberated him from the lump of rock that he had imagined was to be his home for the foreseeable future, or at least until his employers or someone worse had located him and prised him off. Azular had been able to abstract thus much information but the science officer still did not trust the info-sent and recommended his continued incarceration in a very secure place, at least until they had time to deal with him.

Micklemouse was still emitting the tracking signal that was central to his implanted cyber systems and that allowed his manipulators to maintain remote surveillance on him. At what distance the signal could be detected was a mystery yet, but as an info-sent was rarely far from his source of recharge and download, it was logical to assume that it was not great. As his ship had been left intact however, his lack of link-up to it might conceivably alert his masters to the fact that he was no longer there. Azular raised his concerns with the captain and senior officers, particularly as Micklemouse was more than an average info-sent and had refused to disclose his business in the Kelfennig system. Azular had likewise no notion of just how much the trader's landing on the planet had been under his own cognisance or under someone's orders: he was clearly too terrified of his clients to say.

It was some days to the Kellybar system even at top speed and via as many hyperspace highways as possible. Captain Ahxenta had insisted on a convoluted course to deflect potential aggressors and had also limited Myrtleberry's access to the ship's main operational areas. The colonel was unhappy and made her feelings clear, but was summarily told to report it to her superiors at her own convenience. Ahxenta had been blunt, having had more than enough of the ISP and the TA and their joint interference in her business. As trade was not slack under the current state of galactic unease and her supercargo had had to turn down one or two potentially lucrative commissions, she was seriously put out.

In view of his captain's opinion of Myrtleberry and her foibles, Azular took it upon himself to cultivate her acquaintance as a change from his suzerainty over Micklemouse. As a Berzic he was more able than most humanoids to tune into others' sensitivities and he hoped to deflect a part of her unpleasantness from his crewmates. It was at the start of a short tête-à-tête with the colonel in the mess, where she had collared him after yet another argument with Ahxenta, that the science officer had become aware of a subtle emanation of energy from the ISP officer. Azular had been conning over the latest scans that he and Chief Cottontail had obtained of their pet info-sent and had been fine-tuning his mini-scanner at the colonel's approach. He left the device running as he courteously invited her to sit and asked if she would like refreshment. She did. She also wanted information on the trader that the captain had insisted remain in the brig.

With all the appearance of compliance, Azular informed the colonel that when they had rescued the man, Jerrin Bloombusk, they had found him in possession of one of *Arianrhod's* powered transfer pods that they had left at Dryssicon Major. He had no satisfactory answer for the presence of their pod in his ship. The captain was extremely displeased and in the brig the trader would remain until he had explained to her satisfaction how he came to have custody of the apparatus. As intended, Myrtleberry was rather amused that a small-time merchant had got the better of Ahxenta, particularly when she learned that the pod had been left with the trader's ship down on Kelfennig Four, as extracting it would have been costly time-wise.

With civil exchanges the senior science officer finally freed himself from his companion and set off apparently leisurely to his duties. His immediate task on return to his bridge station was a quick analysis of the data from his mini-scanner. The result was an urgent request for a meeting with the captain in the privacy of her office.

"We have a problem with Colonel Myrtleberry," was Azular's opening statement.

"What, only one?"

18: OLD ACQUAINTANCE

Dr Flintlock was surprised at the order that came her way via Greffy an hour later but lost no time in putting it into action. After some delicate subterfuge on her part, she sent Greenwing as a sociable and calm individual with sufficient superiority to outflank rebellion, to the outer limits of cargo hold nine. His task was to find any troopers with signs of the innocuous but uncomfortable Mizzen flu and haul them to medbay for further tests. Routine analyses of the air recyc system in cargo hold nine had shown viral traces and the doctor wanted it checked out. She also sent along a couple of the *Arianrhod's* more muscular security personnel as escort.

Flintlock's subsequent urgent report to the captain was relayed to Colonel Myrtleberry as soon as it was received, with the requirement that all personnel from the *Crusader* be subject to medical scrutiny as soon as possible. This included the abstraction of bio-samples from everyone that had come aboard from the ISP ship. Myrtleberry was livid, not only that her people had apparently missed the infection but that she was about to be obliged to the captain of the *Arianrhod* for the treatment of any victims.

A well-protected medical team was despatched to visit each of the holds housing the recruits in turn to take the samples, check for overt signs of the flu and administer a prophylactic as a preventative. The air recyc system was overhauled and purified and the *Arianrhod's* own crew ordered to submit to testing, since the colonel had not been confined with her team and may have inadvertently spread the bug through the ship. Ahxenta had Azular escort the colonel to medbay for examination, mildly surprised that her guest had not refused or at least caused some degree of fuss.

Arianrhod was only hours away from Kellybar One by the time the last of the troopers had been decreed disease-free. The two who had shown positive results were sharing an iso-bay and were under close supervision. Meanwhile, Myrtleberry had been induced to remain in her quarters and was whiling away her time communicating with any ISP stations within range. Azular had been spending his time in more exacting pursuits and the upshot of his findings was a meeting with most of the ship's senior officers in the captain's bridge office.

Ahxenta began with energy readings that Azular had inadvertently picked up from the ISP officer. He had seen similar before and his subsequent covert scans had confirmed that the colonel bore integral cybernetic implants. Azular had thus consulted Zaiklyn Oak, whose experience of cybernetics was greater than Azular's own. Dr Oak had agreed that the signals were not the usual emissions from substitute limbs or organs. The captain had ordered the science officer to carry out any further analyses necessary. As these had required bio-samples and the two were sure that Myrtleberry would not supply them on demand, a stratagem had been developed to obtain them, hence the cases of Mizzen flu found by Flintlock.

"Greenwing didn't deliberately infect those two grunts, did he?" Cottontail demanded a little incredulously.

"Certainly not!" the chief medic snapped. "We checked the med records we got with them and the two had been infected previously. The thing about Mizzen flu is that once the immune system has dealt with most of the viroid particles, any little sods remaining can hide themselves in the nerve endings unless they're flushed out by nano-sweeps; they use your own body's defences to manufacture protective coats so that they're not targeted by your white cells. Triggers such as stress can set them off again and deal you a moderated version of the flu, but it *can* be passed on to others and those not immune may get the full-blown version. We rigged the recyc log to show aerosolised flu particles – the flu's transmitted usually by inhalation of infected particles – and called the med alert."

"I had Azular run additional tests alongside while Myrtleberry was in medbay," Ahxenta told them. "Please explain what our friendly colonel's med tests show, Azular."

"That she has various elements in her system indicating that she has implanted cyber enhancements that are not run-of-the-mill," he said calmly. "As with those two suspects that we believe ambushed the captain out at Xerophyte IV, there were traces of meta-jurillium absorption products and serocepcin residues in the colonel's samples. You may recall that serocepcin is one of the drugs used as therapy to aid adaptation in genetically-altered individuals. The levels indicate that she's still within the recent adaptation window."

Most of the officers around the table sat stunned.

"You mean *she* could be the leak at ISP?" Apnis demanded. "She's one of the alien plants?"

"That's bugging me," the captain said. "She's not the pleasantest individual in the galaxy but she'd no hesitation in providing samples when she was told about the flu; and Axellina took the samples. If she was a mole, surely she'd know we'd find something untoward and would not have consented?"

"Unless she's such a damn clever mole that she's trying to make out she doesn't know she's been compromised," the first mate said. "But if she *has* been compromised without her knowledge, why hasn't this shown up on other med scans? She'd be subject to regular checks in her line of work, wouldn't she?"

Cottontail agreed: she and Myrtleberry had taken an instant dislike to one another and had clashed on several occasions. "We might have a whole bunch of nasty surprises waiting for us at Kellybar," the engineer grunted. "How do we know what she's doing, squirreled away in her berth talking to who knows who?"

"We know," Ahxenta interjected shortly. "Gliss isn't here because he's listening in to every word and will alert us if she links to anyone or anything dodgy. But you're both right: there could be subterfuge on her part and that's why I want her in on our suspicions. Her implants and adaptation may be nothing to do with the hostiles. The doc has gone over the medical records that came with her from the *Crusader* and there's mention of replacement joints, but that was in the past. She *has* seen action and she's been injured. But her record, as far as we've been able to access it, is exemplary."

"So why's she decorating a desk at ISP HQ at Skyrtek instead of out with a unit somewhere?" Cottontail demanded.

"That data is not available," Ahxenta told her sardonically. "But we'll call her into the level four briefing room and I want an armed security team on hand. She tries anything and we take her down."

"You can't take down a colonel of the ISP!" Flintlock exclaimed.

"Want to watch me? I've had enough of her on my ship. And we're doing it now; I don't plan to turn up at Kellybar One with this hot potato burning through my decks. And get that twinkle out of your eye, Whisper Earbleat: only on my mark do we disable her. But pack plenty knockout power, we don't know her full capabilities."

"Aye, Captain!" the second mate responded enthusiastically.

Not only were Earbleat and a security detail on hand, Ahxenta had a monitor set up to keep an eye on matters from a distance, lest she and her officers were subject to something with which they could not deal. Colonel Myrtleberry was in no way averse to a meeting before they reached their destination, and had in fact been expecting some sort of briefing before she was called in. The officers before her and the expressions on their faces alerted her to something amiss, but she sat down upon invitation equably enough.

Ahxenta called up Myrtleberry's medical data. That the visitor was surprised to see the holo of her prosthetic joints and other implants revolving above the table holo-generator was evident. That she was not disturbed was also obvious. She even congratulated Ahxenta and her team on their ingenuity in working out her superior capabilities.

"Meta-jurillium implants aside, we know you've also gone through recent genetic alteration. Care to tell us the extent, the reason *and* why you didn't mention it to the doctor when she took your bio-samples? You *were* obligated to disclose your current medical status." The captain's voice was calm but there was a dangerous glint in her eye.

The woman was smiling almost triumphantly. "No. It's none of your business."

"I see. Very well." The captain tabbed a comms switch. "Ahxenta to bridge: code blue alpha. Alter course and come about to one, one four by ten. Set to the local hyperspace beacon for Arrissia Five, Mr Box; and comms, I want a link to our contact at ISP Central. Ahxenta out. Security, return Colonel Myrtleberry to her quarters and post a double detail."

As the captain stood, Myrtleberry exploded in wrath. "We are for Kellybar One, where I have troops to relieve! You are under contract to the Interstellar Systems Protectorate!"

"But not to you personally, whatever you are. And I'm not about to compromise my ship by delivering an unknown quantity to an ISP base at the edges of a zone where hostiles are known to operate."

"I'll have you up on charges!"

"I'm not one of your lackeys, Colonel. I intend to consult with your superiors at ISP and take it from there. Lieutenant Commander Earbleat, escort our guest to her quarters and ensure that she stays there. If she resists, you have the authority to restrain her."

"Aye, ma'am!"

One look at Earbleat's drawn weapon and the colonel capitulated. "Have it your way. Yes, my prosthetics have been improved with the best medical science has on offer. And yes, I've been genetically enhanced, though how the hell you figured that out is beyond me: I was told most of the adaptive hardware was undetectable except to specialised equipment. My genetic adaptations are logged in my med record at ISP but can only be accessed at the highest levels. That doesn't include you."

"I see. And what exactly do these adaptations allow you to do?"

Ahxenta pressed for as the woman paused to look up at her.

It was Azular who replied. "They've enhanced her extrasensory capabilities amongst other things: she's trying to read you."

The colonel spun in her chair to look angrily at him. "What the hell's that supposed to mean?"

"Exactly what I said, ma'am. Your innate empathic abilities have been amplified, your intuitive powers if you like, allowing you to pick up on the mind-sets around you, the general atmosphere, and react accordingly. That's why you needle people, isn't it? To force them to respond so that you can gauge the situation."

"Was that why you decided to rouse one of the Friskianx we gave over to you?" the captain asked evenly, looking down at the officer. "You thought you could handle it. Only you were mistaken and you almost lost the *Crusader* over it. And now you've left Flute to pick up the pieces while you commandeer my ship and swan over to Kellybar One with your pack of raw recruits."

"The needs of the ISP must be met!"

"Not on my watch they don't. If I don't get answers out of the ISP, you won't be going anywhere. Lieutenant Commander Earbleat, you and your guards escort the colonel back to her quarters."

Apnis waited until the coast was clear before cocking a quizzical eyebrow at her commanding officer. "Code blue alpha? We're still headed for Kellybar, right?"

"Naturally. I didn't come all this way to turn back now. Azular briefed me on what he and the doctor had found. She might be more than humanoid but her underlings are the average products of three months of basic training. I suspect she was given the job of getting them out here so that she could use her talents to probe the local military and civilian authorities, and I guess that's why she's on the ISP Council and works out of ISP HQ, but who she reports to is anyone's guess. I checked her ID when first she called me and all our links say she's bona fide. But why her systems are similar to those of the dock-rats I ran into on Xerophyte IV is another matter."

"Meta-jurillium *is* the one of the better materials for strength and durability of implanted prosthetics, though it's not commonly used," Azular explained. "And serocepcin's used therapeutically in a number of situations. But the colonel's systems are not identical to those of the thugs on Xerophyte IV, Captain, and she has additional abilities, mental and physical. But I sensed she was holding something back."

"You and me both," Cottontail declared. "I don't trust her as far as I can throw her. *Are* you going to call ISP Central, Cinnabar? You realise that our transmissions could be intercepted even if you use priority channels and encode everything, especially this close to a base like Kellybar? And you might not get an immediate response."

"I know. That's why I've got Bellfish and Gliss working on a few things. Axellina, you and Azular go over all you have on the colonel in case there's something else; and Crizz, get ready to unload our cargo. We'll dock alongside Kellybar's orbital relay station and they can walk out; I'm not using our shuttles as ferryboats. Back to your stations, people."

In the privacy of her office, Ahxenta made the links that her comms and tactical officers had set up. She was some time and had ordered *Arianrhod* to slow to ensure everything was in place before their arrival at Kellybar. Myrtleberry had been denied access to any further communications, but Gliss reported that their guest had not attempted any external links but had spent her time going over as much data as she could find on the *Arianrhod*, her mission and her crew, which was precious little, as outsiders were not allowed to call up such ship's data. That little was sufficient that the captain had one of Cottontail's systems engineers rig a close-range data scrambler to scupper any data collection that the colonel had attempted.

"Who were you talking to that you were locked up so long?" Apnis asked inquisitively on Ahxenta's return to the bridge.

"Admiral-in-Chief Zillah out at Freskat: I wanted to check up on the latest at her end of the galactic zones – and if she had come across Colonel Ellin Myrtleberry before. She had."

"And?"

"All hell breaking loose at the Ginseng: ISP, Coalition and Non-Treaty ships have turned up and are causing local issues; two zone Mu independents that have been hit have sent ships in and some fool got too close and was wiped. But thus far no alien ships have been sighted there. As far as the admiral knows, there's been an increase in the numbers of confrontations with the hostiles in other zones but those attacked have tended to run rather than stand and fight."

"Cinnabar!"

"As for our friendly colonel, Zillah had heard of her through her ISP contacts way back, but only met her face to face after Zillah had sent our report on the Ginseng anomaly to ISP Central with a high priority tag, copied it to her contacts in trades, political and security parties and threatened to pass it to media networks. Myrtleberry hot-shipped it out to Freskat for a few words with the admiral about our report and about us."

"Now isn't that interesting?" the first mate observed. "You're sure our cool colonel isn't an info-sent? She's acting mighty like one."

"Azular says she's not but she may have implanted data recording facilities. Not that I could raise a thing at ISP. They all figured they'd their hands full with the current situation and nobody was keen to speak to me. It was only when I threatened to ship her and her band back to them that my original contact, Admiral Piskettle, told me if I didn't complete the mission he would have me for breach of contract and the ISP wouldn't pay, but given what he didn't say out loud, they know about her and her capabilities, they don't want to let on and they suspect ears are listening in that shouldn't."

"I thought we'd been paid in advance for this mission. Didn't Lindell clear that before we shipped the grunts aboard? Myrtleberry had the clout to make that happen, didn't she?"

"We did and she did. Piskettle said nothing about that and that's one of the reasons I think ISP has been breached; the upper echelons know it and they're doing their utmost to find out what's going on without giving the game away."

"So we're not much wiser and we're sure not the flavour of the month with ISP Central," Apnis sighed. "What do we do now?"

"We drop our current payload at Kellybar and pick up the troops there as planned. Once we've dropped *them* off we head out to our next assignment. At least our channel to ISP's tactical relay system hasn't been cut – I checked when I signed off."

"Have we got a next assignment? Our cargo pick-ups have been shot to hell with all this military shenanigans."

"Lindell has pacified most of our clients. We now have to transfer the squad down there at the moment to Heligon. I told Piskettle I'd take them no further and he could like it or lump it and that I wanted the two energy cells we lent to the *Crusader* replaced. Our next deal will be finalised once we're rid of Myrtleberry and her bunch."

"Micklemouse," murmured the first mate.

"I haven't forgotten him," Ahxenta replied.

"I bet he thinks you have."

The transfer of their unwelcome guests was relatively rapid and both sides were glad to see the back of one another. The colonel was furious, being aware that her implanted data-gathering facility had been tampered with remotely. Her protestations were met with the Ahxenta's steely stare and the information that she was welcome to raise a complaint with an appropriate authority. Ahxenta also warned her that since her crew, with far less facilities than a military outfit, could carry out such an operation at distance, there was good reason to believe that others could and it would be wise to take precautions. The captain of the *Arianrhod* had taken her own and had ordered Azular to observe Myrtleberry closely on the short way to the transfer point to meet with her opposite number from the station below.

Azular had his own reasons for not only watching the colonel but for monitoring her: he had intercepted the colonel's food orders to the mess and had slipped in a systems inhibitor and an innocuous sedative supplied by Dr Flintlock and was analysing the effects. He had not notified the captain as it would give her deniability lest their guest sensed something amiss and work out what it was. The science officer was fast coming to the conclusion that although the colonel was not an info-sent, she was possibly some sort of hybrid that was being developed by the ISP for undercover operations.

By the time the outgoing troops from Kellybar had shipped over to *Arianrhod*, Supercargo Lindell had worked out a contract with the authorities on Vellis Prime to transport a load of food from there to Vellisa Colony, one of their bases over the border in Delta zone. As the schedule was tight, Ahxenta gave the order for a straight run to Heligon and they lost no time once everything was locked in place.

The senior officer in command of the batch of seasoned troops leaving Kellybar elected to remain with his people, more to keep them in order than anything else. Ahxenta had made it clear that she expected no trouble and in lieu of the brig, there were plenty of empty cargo holds vacant for rabble-rousers. The captain did make a large area available for recreation and provided as much in the way of supplies that she could spare to ease the tedium. She waved away Lieutenant Gunn's thanks, telling him she would be billing the ISP for everything, including the ale.

The several days that it took the ship to make Heligon Station were tense. There had been no news of further major hostilities but neither was there any update on the situations in the Belts, at Marridan or at Brown Amber. Snippets that Admiral Zillah had sent through hinted that something was in the offing, with energy spikes detected arising from the Ginseng. Reports were also coming in of random attacks on shipping across Beta and Kappa and by Fivepoint, the convergence locus of five galactic zones on the edge of the Outer Reaches. The military was puzzling over the hits, as there was no obvious pattern to them and hence no way of predicting the next strike.

Heligon was a hive of activity, with several ISP ships in. Once docked, *Arianrhod* bid a thankful farewell to her visitors, who were set to commandeer whatever transport they could to the patch of galaxy they called home. It took time to cajole two energy cells out of the Port Authority as supplies were scarce, but mindful of the support given by the PSS fleet and the backing expected from the TA and any ships associated with it, the goods were finally released.

"They expect us to be grateful," Lindell grumbled to Ahxenta as he checked the cells in and set some of the crew under the direction of Ensign Pinkhorn to arrange the space for their next cargo. "We'll have to make good time to Vellis to keep their authorities sweet. I've heard that the harvest failed at Vellisa Colony and that's why they need the food shipment. Multiple dome breach apparently."

"Hostiles or stupidity?" the captain enquired.

"Won't tell us, even over a secure channel, so I reckon underhand activity. That's maybe why their own people won't take it on."

"Well, I'd best get the show on the road. There's a Trades Alliance office on the orbital docking facility at Vellis Prime; maybe somebody there will be able to enlighten us."

"There's also a Co-Scutter office," Lindell reminded her. "Since the Coalition has a small territory on the doorstep, it likes to keep a toehold in ISP space if it can."

"I thought we were all one big happy family now."

"Families may get to be big but they're seldom happy, it's all a myth," Lindell responded dryly. "Talking of which, when are we going to allow our little best buddy Micklemouse to pack his traps and leave the nest? He's eating and drinking and not paying rent."

"Oh he will. Azular's seeing to that. I'll be on the bridge."

The senior science officer was awaiting the captain with the same topic on his mind. Their non-paying guest's cyber functions were still operative to a certain extent despite the systems inhibitor and various drugs that Flintlock had dosed him with and he was still emitting the signal that alerted his operators to his whereabouts. Although he was anxious about the loss of his ship and thus his recharging facilities, he was sufficiently animate to be suspicious of anything and everything he was given. That had made it difficult to abstract and download the data he had been carrying when they picked him up and which had been exercising Azular's skills ever since the trader had come aboard.

"We think we have the bulk of it," the Berzic apprised the captain and first mate. "We have to work on him when he's partially under, but he *is* highly suggestible. As far as we can figure, his ship was pulled to the surface of Kelfennig Four but he didn't lose his comms systems, possibly because his ship was so well-shielded or because his comms and other systems were recognised by whatever caused the instrument failure that affected the *Palynia*."

"That's worrying," Ahxenta said into the pause.

"It is. But Mr Micklemouse does have some talents: he claims he found the remains of an escape craft that had nothing left alive in it, nor remains that might once have been alive, and that was emitting an ISP call-sign."

"The one we picked up?" she interrupted.

"Possibly," Azular concurred. "He uncoupled and removed the source and other pieces from the wreck and managed to reactivate the signal from his ship, which was what we picked up. His survey of the region in which he came down indicated one other source of the ISP signal; that wasn't linked to a ship but it *was* underground, apparently. He also found another couple of wrecks, one of which he thinks was the *Palynia*, but others had got there first and there was little left to recover or to identify it. He had hit upon the entrance to the underground tunnel system in which we found him and he was able to reenergise his ship sufficiently to steer her as far down as he dared. He was worried that whatever or whoever stripped the other wrecks would find him and do the same – they could obviously come and go with impunity."

"Have you found out what he was doing on Kelfennig Four in the first place?" Apnis put in. "And how long he'd been there?"

"He'd been there over four weeks and was getting edgy. He'd tried to contact his sponsors but had no reply. He says his business was salvage on his own account, but he may have been coerced: there was that intense orb that Dr Ma'Lappis spotted and that seemed to have some unaccountable psychological effect on our team."

"I wondered when we'd get to that," the first mate interposed. "It gave me the creeps, but our little creep seemed to be attached to it. And you couldn't read it."

"That's what set me thinking," Azular asserted. "My scanner could *not* read what was within the energy shell; it was as if it was enclosing some impenetrable emptiness. I recalled a comment by you, Captain not long ago out at the Ginseng Nebula, where there was something there that you didn't like the feel of but couldn't articulate it."

"A creepy feeling," Apnis remembered. "We all felt it – that block of nothing at the centre of the nebula! Our scanners couldn't figure what it was made of but we couldn't penetrate through to the other side, so it was something unknown to us."

"Exactly, Commander. So I rechecked the data that went into the report; but as we couldn't work out what we had, I came up empty on the nature of the anomaly. However, you recall the thickening of nebular material at its edges, as if the material had been pushed out by a force field to form the space? The field surrounding the globe also appeared to be dense, far denser than it should have been in the thin atmosphere of the tunnel system, hence the luminosity we saw."

"So how did it happen to find our landing team on Kelfennig Four and lead them to Micklemouse? And why was he so upset at the loss of it?" Ahxenta asked quietly.

"Loss of it?" Azular repeated. "Ms Earbleat destroyed the energy shell around it but as we had no way of detecting its essence, it may not have been destroyed – although Micklemouse *did* seem upset."

"Did you find out why?"

"No. All he would say was that it simply appeared a few days after he'd found his way into the tunnel system. He assumed it was some kind of ancient technology that was still operational but as it supplied the light that allowed him to explore the tunnels, he didn't consider it a threat. It even led him up to the surface to scavenge the materials from the wrecks nearby. We had to stop there, as Dr Flintlock judged that we had questioned him sufficiently and he was exhausted."

"I'd like to know if possible," the captain decided. "I'll leave it with you and Flintlock. His cyber signal is still emitting, I expect."

"Yes, ma'am. But we can't disarm it without surgical intrusion and Dr Flintlock is reluctant to take that approach; such intrusion might trigger a reaction that kills him or the surgeon or both."

"You know, if Earbleat's blast did destroy that light ball and it *was* the same material as the stuff at the Ginseng, that may be a clue as to what's needed to destroy or incapacitate that," Apnis ruminated.

"Possibly." Ahxenta did not sound convinced. "But we have our own business to run, our own people to protect. We find something, we pass it on. Meanwhile, our next stop is Vellis Prime and the pick-up of that food shipment for Vellisa Colony."

"And after that? Lindell has been mighty quiet about orders."

"He's working on it. For now, you take a break; you've been on duty for eight hours straight."

"Only if you do the same," Apnis grinned.

"Get out of here, dammit!"

Vellis Prime glowed red-gold in the light of its primary, a yellow star that was part of a small local cluster. Its main orbital docking station was the usual latticework of bays intersected by the service pods and link-tubes that provided office and work spaces. *Arianrhod* had been directed to an outer bay suited to a ship her size and was awaiting orders. The captain had been in lengthy talks with the reps in control of approving cargo transfer from holding areas to ships. A Trades Alliance rep was part of the meeting and Apnis, on the bridge, was mulling over the prolonged nature of the conference.

Ahxenta eventually called in from a secure link in marketing. The TA rep had registered a complaint about the nature of the food cargo and had slapped a delaying order on its loading. The captain was positive over the upshot of the argument: she had told those present that she had other business and was in no position to wait until the TA had sorted itself out

"He's not going to hang fire over releasing our payload," she said. "For one, he's no right: his fizzing badge only allows him to suspend work whilst statutory checks are made and the Port Authority has to carry those out. It's his self-preservation chip at bottom of it: he doesn't want his bosses to think he's slacking but as soon as the local dock-rats start to lose their overtime, their Guild reps start to scream. We're the only loading work they have at the moment after all."

"What if he tells us we've got to undock and move elsewhere?" Apnis enquired.

"I fry his arse. But there may be another reason for the delay so I want you down here pronto, and bring Flintlock and Azular with you. There's a Coalition rep here that's been asking for a meeting with me and I sure as hell want witnesses when we do see him."

"Why?" the first mate asked, puzzled.

"Because it's our old buddy and Bick Micklemouse's best friend Mr Spendle Doosbak, a Senior Executive Member of the Coalition's Central Council."

19: GAMES

Whatever were the suspicions of the *Arianrhod's* captain, she ordered her newly-arrived officers to show nothing but courtesy as the party crossed the hall to their assigned meeting room. She had met them at their shuttle, having taken the precaution of ensuring that each had an implanted locating pin fitted lest Doosbak had any surprises up his sleeve. Lieutenant Commander Earbleat had been left in command of the ship and of dealings with the obstinate Trades Alliance rep and Ahxenta expected that their cargo would be safely in place by the end of her conference with the Coalition agent.

Once through the door, the four from the *Arianrhod* realised that Doosbak had arrived early and had not come alone: his aide Grendle Treeshanks and an armed minder introduced only as Fencer were by his side. The captain was amused to note from Doosbak's reaction as she presented her crew that he had been expecting her to show with rather fewer than three well-armed supporters.

"I don't have much time, Council Member Doosbak," she began, placing a recorder on the central table as she and her team sat down facing the door. "Please explain the reason for this meeting. After all, we've had very little contact with the Coalition, so your summons *did* raise my curiosity."

The man took a seat, motioning Treeshanks to do the same as he cleared his throat and marshalled his thoughts.

"I heard you were on a mercy mission near the Kelfennig system," was the opening gambit, as the man turned wide eyes on the four in front of him in an attempt to look honest and concerned.

He failed utterly as Ahxenta raised a mocking eyebrow and gave a sharp glance. "And just how did you hear that, Mr Doosbak?"

"That's not important, Captain," he responded. "The point is…"

"Oh but it is important, Mr Doosbak, as our missions, whatever you believe them to be, are completely confidential and no business of yours or the Coalition's."

"I have contacts that pass on news when it concerns me, and your mission concerns me," he said with feigned confidence. "I can…"

He paused as Apnis stood, kicking her chair back as she hauled up her phase rifle. "One wrong move and you drop, mister," she coldly informed Fencer. "I suggest you put that weapon back in its socket and move away from the door."

"You have a hell of a lot of explaining to do, Doosbak," stormed Ahxenta, rising also. "I suggest you make it fast; I have appointments to keep. I also suggest you are honest, because if I find you are not, you will not like the consequences."

"You can't threaten me!"

"Isn't that just what you're doing to me with your armed guard and your concern in my business?" Ahxenta countered. "Make it fast: what do you know of our mission, how do you know it and why are you interested?"

"Look, I know you went to Kelfennig Four to search for survivors from that missing ISP ship – rumours fly everywhere these days and I *do* have contacts that have links into the ISP. They are..."

"I suggest you make it much faster, Doosbak, before your back-up gets here," Apnis said, raising her rifle again. "Or your friend Fencer is first and you're next. Oh my apologies, Mr Treeshanks is first."

The first mate let loose a shot as she turned and Treeshanks slid down his chair to lie in a crumpled heap under the table, the gun he had been trying to disengage from its housing falling from his fingers. The guard Fencer raised his rifle in response but immediately found himself hit with a stun wave that left him senseless and on the deck.

"Two down, one to go," Apnis stated. "Your call, Mr Doosbak."

"You won't get away with this!" the man howled, his face white with shock.

"I think we just have," Ahxenta said evenly. "You invite me here, your bodyguard *and* your aide pull weapons on us? I've logged the entire incident by the way, and this recorder is linked to my ship. So unless you want me to make this interview very public, I suggest you call off whatever heavy mob you've organised and start talking. I don't have all day."

"Mr Doosbak is sporting a deal of implanted hardware, Captain," Azular alerted her as he scanned the man from top to toe. "He's not quite an info-sent, but he *is* a walking data-recorder and is able to deliver a punch. I wouldn't get too close to his fists or his feet. And he certainly has an embedded download port for any data shards he can get his hands on. It's in his left arm."

"These two are fairly average humanoids," Flintlock announced, having examined the recumbent pair. "They'll be out for an hour at least and will have headaches when they wake up."

"Three armed individuals have just turned up outside this door," Apnis noted, consulting her wrist-mounted scanner. "Do we take them down and alert this entire facility to this business?"

"They read humanoid," the doctor reported. "Two more have joined them, but other than that the outside corridor's empty."

As she spoke, the door slid open. Immediately both Ahxenta and Apnis raised their rifles but their well-honed reactions cut in instantly to prevent them from opening fire. Three dazed humanoids were pushed in, followed by two security officers wearing the uniform of the *Arianrhod*. Goldwash and Hanx nodded to the captain and placed the weapons they had stripped from the three thugs on the table.

"Lieutenant Commander Earbleat ordered us down when she and Lieutenant Gliss picked up an armed transport shadowing our second shuttle and docking in the flanking bay. She realised from its comms that you might be in line for company," Goldwash told them.

"We've got more shuttles down here than we have on the ship," Apnis remarked. "What do we do with these scallywags? We can't put them all in our brig and Vellis Prime's law enforcers – wherever the hell they are – won't want them."

The three dark-clad unknowns had been subject to rapid scanning by Flintlock and her report did little to mitigate Ahxenta's wrath.

"They're definitely Friskianx."

The first mate raised her phase rifle a fraction. "Do we shoot them now or later, Cap?"

"The truth, Doosbak, or you and all your cronies will be handed over to the tender mercies of the Vellis Prime Judiciary and I *will* be pressing charges," the captain told the cringing man.

"Look, we were just hired to do a job," one of the three Friskianx put in. "We didn't know it was you."

"No-one asked you to speak and yes you did know it was me if you followed a shuttle from my ship," Ahxenta flashed back. "Last chance, Doosbak."

"I know you picked Bick Micklemouse up from Kelfennig Four," the man responded, licking his lips nervously. "I can't tell you how or why but I was sent to get him back. I'll take him off your hands for you and make sure nothing happens to him."

"Wrong answer, Doosbak."

"Look, Captain, as a Senior Executive Central Council Member of the Coalition, I pack a lot of punch. I can get you a…"

The captain's eyes blazed. "You dare to try to buy me off? You sit there and don't move a fraction or you'll be on the deck. Ahxenta to

Arianrhod: do we have our cargo aboard?"

"Just finished loading now, Cap," came Earbleat's gleeful tones. "We're reading you loud and clear. We have a full recording of events and our forward batteries are trained on the Friskie ship that let loose the shuttle that followed ours. Our fighters also prepped to launch."

That last was a lie and Ahxenta knew it but she did not bat an eye as she ordered her team to pack up for immediate departure. The look of relief on Doosbak's face lasted no more than a second for the captain continued in a grim tone,

"And prepare a comfortable cell in the brig: we'll have company."

"Aye, Captain," Earbleat sang out.

"Sorry folks, but we can't leave you to run for your shuttle the second our backs are turned," Ahxenta went on to the Friskianx trio. "You'll have to stay here awhile, but this won't hurt."

A nod to Apnis was all that was needed, for the first mate hoisted her rifle and before the three could blink they were treated to a wide-field stun wave that took them all out.

"You're crazy!" screamed Doosbak, evidently fearing that he was next on her menu.

"You *will* come quietly, Doosbak," the captain directed, trading a look with her science officer. "Dr Azular will keep you company and my two guards will be at your back all the way, just to make sure you don't slip. These five will be all right in an hour or two and none the worse for their nap. I'll send a version of events to Vellis Prime's Law Enforcement once we're off-station, copied naturally to several of my contacts. And I still intend to press charges against you personally as well as against the Coalition."

"Captain…" the man began desperately as Hanx prodded him with the business end of his rifle.

"Let's go, people," Ahxenta declared, ignoring him as she rescued her recorder from the table and sheathed her gun.

"Brig's going to be helluva crowded," the first mate observed as the party secured the premises and circumspectly made their way to a transport tube that would ferry them to their rides.

Flintlock, to Ahxenta's relief, announced that she could disable most of Doosbak's additional components without causing him undue harm. The chief medic and Azular between them had worked out that the techniques used to fit the devices were similar to those used on Micklemouse but there were fewer trips to prevent tampering, possibly because the man was not an info-sent and his data-gathering facility was less complex. Doosbak was, like his friend, unwilling to discuss his sponsors, but an in-depth series of questions had elicited the fact that he had recently returned to his home base of Lonagan Four via both Mellifly and Merkat Three. As a thorough search of his person had disclosed enough gem-ware to buy a small asteroid and three Primus Twelve Platinum Standard credit slips each differently encrypted, he had not come away empty-handed.

"Credit in politics," was Apnis' acerbic response to the finds in a briefing to discuss the issue. "Especially when the fingers are as sticky as the glue holding a Friskie boat's hull plates together and you have access to all sorts of interesting places. But our problem now is where we offload these two: nowhere's safe if the inner circles of the ISP and the Coalition have been breached. How did the little runt find out it was us that picked Micklemouse off Kelfennig and that we still had him aboard?"

"Azular hasn't been able to work that out as Doosbak's scared witless of his contacts and what they'll do to him if they think he's spilt any beans," the captain said, nodding at her chief science officer. "But whoever they are, they must now know we have him as well as Micklemouse. We can't pass them on to any authorities as that will make them targets. But these two, particularly our little rodent, seem especially precious to whoever's calling the shots. It strikes me that Micklemouse must be or have something that these unknowns want: why else are they risking the likes of a big mole like a senior exec in the Coalition Council to get him back?"

"He knows or has something they're afraid can be used against them?" Apnis postulated. "But he ends up on Kelfennig and they leave him? Why didn't they jump to his rescue if he's so valuable?"

"They tried to but failed, or they thought he'd be safe there until they could send in help. They or villains like them had booby-trapped the place after all, and they must have known about it. They didn't figure we could track him or that we'd outwit the planetary defence systems that have pulled ships in and stopped their comms."

"So why lure ships into such a hole in the first place and then try to keep them there?" demanded the chief engineer. "Okay, there are ancient structures that don't seem to have owners and that would pull in treasure-hunters or genuine archaeologists, I guess. But if the ships down there have been stripped bare, it has to be a scavenger set-up, though surely such an out-of-the-way place wouldn't get many takers. We followed an ISP beacon, or a damn good imitation of one, so that's how *we* ended up there."

"We were given the mission by the ISP so I'm not discounting the idea that *we* were set up," Ahxenta said. "A lot of people don't like us. But it could be that the hostiles, if they *are* the ones responsible for what's going on there, were trying to tie up the ISP and their allies so that they could hit elsewhere and hit hard, as they have done, judging by the reports filtering in. Or there might be something down there they have or need and they want to make sure that if anything gets too close, it disappears. That's one way of discouraging trespassers."

"Too many ifs," Apnis huffed. "But we found Micklemouse down a hole someone dug – someone with a lot of power and a lot of time. And Kelfennig *is* at the edge of the Starglass and allegedly the former home of a long-dead civilisation. Maybe they're not as dead as people thought and they've reanimated to find their world's been violated, battered by time and ransacked of everything valuable; so much so that they're peeved and want their toys back and are beating the crap out of the rest of the galaxy in an effort to recover them."

"Thanks for those pearls of wisdom, Tallica, but they don't help us now. But a lot of the clues we have are pointing to heavy Friskianx involvement: Micklemouse, the thugs who attacked me on Xerophyte IV, new and deadly tech on a number of Friskie ships, the three from Four One Two Alpha that we handed to Myrtleberry and her chums, and even Doosbak. He's Friskianx though he's based at Lonagan Four, and that's as close to the Friskianx home system as you can get. In fact it's one of their colonies, isn't it?"

"So Doosbak's base is Friskie as well," Cottontail grated. "All the rotten eggs are in one basket and now they're scrambling the rest of us. But didn't we hear that the Friskies were being attacked as well?"

"It's confirmed," Ahxenta said wearily. "But whether that means their own advanced meta-jurillium plated warships are being taken out I don't know. There's been precious little over the UV III link lately and I trust that more than the military or other channels we can get into. I've had Bellfish and his team running regular checks but so far nothing tracks. But Azular, it would help if we could blanket Micklemouse's call-sign. That way, we might be able to convince him and Doosbak that they're safe enough somewhere out of the way and then we can get on with our lives."

"Did you have anywhere out of the way specific in mind, Cap?" demanded Apnis suspiciously.

"I did, but I'm holding on to that just now. We're close to Vellisa Colony and I'd like to see this job finished before we start on the next. Lindell's got us a pick-up at Vellisa for Peascod Secundo, small stuff but local transport won't touch it for fear of interception. We may as well as it's en route to Delta Iridium and there's promise of some action there."

The authorities of Vellisa Colony were delighted to receive their food shipment, so much so that Ahxenta was spared the long negotiations and fights over additional levies that were often a part of the regular stresses at planetary import offices. She also avoided a clash with the local upholders of the law over her actions at Vellis Prime: *their* Law Enforcement officials were extremely unhappy about the five felons now taking up space in their orbital jail, as with no witnesses they could not be charged. The fact that a Friskianx ship was hanging fire as it waited for its citizens to be released was another sore point. The captain was unruffled: as her first mate pointed out, having pissed off half the mapped galaxy, one more port where it would be unwise to show their faces hardly mattered.

Their load of small engineering parts was already packed into two cargo drones that could be stowed in one of *Arianrhod's* outer holds and which would be straightforward to deliver. Payment was to be on receipt but as transport was difficult to come by, neither Ahxenta nor Lindell envisaged trouble, possession of the goods being a strong argument. Even so, the captain had her own team go over every speck of the drones before loading – she had lived so long trusting no-one but her own and had no intention of changing her ways.

The *Arianrhod* had slipped her moorings and was well on the way to the local bypass that would take her to the hyperspace highway and the Peascod system when Lindell appeared on the bridge. That was an unusual enough event to cause a few raised eyebrows and the comment by Nav Officer Box that here was trouble and would Dox please pass the coffee, as given the look on the supercargo's face, he was liable to need it.

"Trouble?" queried the captain.

"Not yet," was the enigmatic reply. "The offer of a cargo."

"Which smells like rotting fish," guessed Apnis.

"Exactly, Commander. It's the transport of a batch of processed meta-jurillium as hull sheets, but it's rather off our beaten track."

"From whence to where?" Ahxenta enquired.

"From Jurgall Three to Mellifly."

The two senior officers looked at one another and then back to the supercargo as a whistle from Earbleat cut across the bridge.

"The customers being whom?" the captain asked.

"The only information I have is that it's for a small repair dock at Mellifly," Lindell told her. "The marketing officer at Jurgall refuses to release client data until a contract is agreed."

"Why us? We're at the other end of mapped space. Not that they would know that, of course," the first mate put in ironically. "Is this contract out to tender or have we been asked for specifically?"

"That bothers me," he said. "The man wouldn't give me details. And the fee's generous for such a routine assignment, though it's a sizeable shipment, hence the need for a large ship like *Arianrhod*."

"Interesting; what does a small Mellifly repair shed want with large amounts of expensive meta-jurillium hull plate?" asked the captain. "And why Jurgall Three instead of the cheaper option of Dryssicon? As far as I know, *they're* still producing and processing the stuff?"

"Maybe not as hull plates," Apnis put in. "Jurgall Three's closer to Mellifly after all, and to Brown Amber come to that, and their dealers are known for not asking too many questions. And they're part of the Friskianx League. But why would some two-bit operation at Mellifly want hull plates unless they were into shipbuilding or massive repair ops? And why do they want the *Arianrhod* as courier?"

"Luring us into a war zone where our so-called allies are as likely to hit us as the bad guys," Box muttered from his station.

The first mate snickered but was quick to agree. "A minor repair facility at Mellifly rings a whole carillon with me, Cap," she added. "Wonder if it's out over the northern polar region?"

"That struck me too. Hang fire on any deal until we've had a word or six with Micklemouse, but try to get more data on the load itself and the destination."

"Aye, Captain. Another thing: the person I spoke to seemed ill at ease, as if someone was looking over his shoulder."

Ahxenta acknowledged that with a raised eyebrow as Lindell left the bridge and exchanged a glance with her second-in-command.

"Micklemouse?" said Apnis.

"Let's go have those words. Mr Bellfish, tell Dr Azular to join us in the brig, priority."

The face of the trader reflected his alarm when the three walked in, moans about his lodging dying on his lips. He could tell they meant business when he was pushed abruptly into a chair and bid be silent. The news that his erstwhile employers were apparently trying to take *Arianrhod* out with him aboard went a little way to instil terror into him and as his jaw dropped, Ahxenta pushed her advantage.

"These people and their facilities: I want to know all you know."

"I told you all I knew last time!"

"That was a long time ago and you've been a busy little bee since then, haven't you? You're not altogether a fool Micklemouse, given your survival on Kelfennig Four; so I suspect you've found out more about your so-called clients at Mellifly than you're comfortable with. And you're going to tell me. You're also going to tell me about your chum Doosbak and the nasty friends he's attracted, aren't you?"

"I haven't seen or heard of Spendle for months; I don't know where he is or what he's doing."

The captain smiled at him and not benignly. "Spendle Doosbak is in the cell next door to this. He and a posse of Friskianx heavies were trying to manoeuvre you off my ship and into his hands when we took him into custody a couple of days ago. So when exactly did you last have dealings with him?"

Micklemouse capitulated. He had seen Doosbak shortly before his ship crashed on Kelfennig. They had met in Rydderwild Township, the main settlement on the planet of the same name, in the Coalition-majority region in zone Epsilon. The trader had gone there to carry out a commission for his main clients, the delivery of a data shard to one of their contacts who was en route to zone Mu. He had come upon Doosbak and had mentioned that he was going to try his luck searching for ancient artefacts on Kelfennig, having heard from some source that they commanded a high price on the open market, as so few dealers would venture near the place.

"Yes, I'm sure," Ahxenta assented ironically. "Your clients, their nature, their business, their place of operation. Out with it."

It was some time later that the three left the wrung-out trader to a late lunch and the uncomfortable sensation that he had exchanged a frying pan for a fire. The captain and her two officers were far from comfortable with the discourse. Micklemouse remained in the dark as to some of his own capabilities, but that did not make him any less dangerous. As a physically and genetically altered being he was still an obscure quantity but it now seemed clear that he was well in advance of a typical info-sent, if such a composite individual could be called typical. As to the nature of his operators, he remained adamant that his first contact was essentially a regular executive, more forceful than most but as humanoid as anyone in that neck of the galaxy. One or two others with whom he had come into contact had left him with the strong impression that they were complex info-sents, dissimilar to himself but more powerful in that they were more highly cybernetic, but that was all. He had no names, but one description left Ahxenta and Apnis with the feeling that they had met it before in the guise of Thystal Comms agent Hoxiz, whom they had met on Xerophyte IV.

Jaw tightening, the captain had pressed for more details of these contacts, their business and their place of operation but all the trader could tell her was that they operated out of Mellifly as far as he knew and they scared the pants off him to the extent that he could almost scent them. His contracts had concerned the covert transport of data shards of what he was told was classified material to certain persons, or attendance at meetings such as the one with Doosbak in Merkat's Web, where as an info-sent he could soak up knowledge effortlessly and download it into the cyber suite aboard his ship. He was always given his task by personal contact with one or other of his clients and was warned in advance of the assignment.

The chance remark that Doosbak appeared to have been caught like himself and was part of his clients' operational chain alerted his hosts to another aspect of his talents: when probed further the trader let slip that he had realised that his long-term friend had been altered and was packing cyber implants similar to his own when he met him for the trip to the TA-led meeting in Merkat. In some way his system was able to detect and interpret the subtle signals given out by others and recognise them for reconstructed or mutated individuals.

The man's story disturbed Ahxenta but it was the admission that Micklemouse could sense his powerful and menacing clients when near them that was most significant. The captain called a briefing of her seniors to dissect what they could of the evidence. That the trader was Friskianx and much of the current trouble had originated close to and was centred on that League and its tributary systems suggested that those were the people first targeted. Azular reminded Ahxenta of an early exchange in which Micklemouse mentioned that his clients had told him that his biology was particularly suitable for adaptation as an info-sent. If that was the case, it could be one reason that the Friskianx had been selected as a test ground for seeding local galactic zones with infiltrators as a prelude to incursion and possible invasion. The predatory Friskianx nature perhaps welcomed the benefits of the advanced technology provided by the strangers and only when these newcomers began to overwhelm them and push them where they did not wish to go did they start to wonder if the alliance had been wise.

Ahxenta shook her head at her second's suggestion that they keep Micklemouse under for the rest of his enforced time with them.

"They can evidently detect him or his ship from distance. Once he was out of it, they knew; and they knew we had him as they sent Doosbak to lever him out of our care. So they're aware of his ability to detect not only those with implants like his own, but them. And that's why he's a danger to them and to us, though he's probably not realised it yet. He could also be able to detect the moles that have infiltrated ISP and other major authorities, so even if they can take out his ship anytime and they know it, he's too valuable a commodity to be let loose."

"But that doesn't track, Cinnabar," Apnis pointed out. "If he's so dangerous to them, why didn't they just fry the little creep and his ship when they were trapped on Kelfennig and then produce another one the same and with the same capabilities? He told them he was there after all, hoping they'd ride to the rescue. But they didn't."

"No: they sent him a guardian to keep him company."

"That globe of light?" the first mate asked, wrinkling her brow. "He *did* tell us it turned up in the tunnel system a couple of days after he did, but maybe he was lying."

"Or maybe he wasn't and when he crashed there the globe of light was sent to keep tabs on him and anything else that moved. It must have been programmed to link to him positively as he was upset at its loss, but it freaked all of you," the captain replied. "Some people or some forces that have a lot to do with this trouble that's kicking off around the mapped galaxy are sure as hell interested in Kelfennig or what's on it. Why else do they booby-trap the place to lure ships in and then make sure they can't get off again? Why was the *ISPS Nomad's* signal sent out from there? Or maybe…"

"Shit!" That was Azular and the oath was so outside his usual calm and so foreign to his nature that the whole team stopped short.

"*We* spotted wrecks down there and Micklemouse admitted that he'd found a derelict escape craft that was emitting an ISP signal but with nothing living or remains that may once have been living, in it," he clarified. "I took scans of the wreck near the tunnel system and I found no trace of anything that might once have been living tissue: it was as if the ship had been scraped so clean that any evidence of life was obliterated. As you just said, Captain, ships appear to have been lured in. But not for their tech, which can't be as advanced as that of these aliens we seem to meet more often than most."

"Are you suggesting it's the crews that are being targeted, not the ships or their cargoes?" Ahxenta exclaimed, aghast. "But for what?"

"Micklemouse's nature may be a clue. He's a very advanced form of info-sent, which means that although he's essentially organic, his cybernetic quality is highly distinct. The hostiles, what little we know of them, point to an origin that's not fully organic, maybe mechanoid for the most part. They've surfaced fairly recently, we suspect they've targeted the Friskianx as humanoids suited to alteration for their own ends – which seem to be an overthrow of order. But we find organic moieties that should be present on Kelfennig simply absent."

"I don't like where this is going," Cottontail said decidedly.

"Nor I," agreed the science officer. "And it *is* speculation on my part. But other ships are said to have been lost in the area in the past, before the *Palynia* came down. *She* was pulled in though her crew got out relatively easily, suggesting that whatever stripped the previous ships was no longer interested in the crews; but their traps were still in place and that was why the *Palynia* was caught."

"No longer interested in the crews? As in they'd done their tests on what they'd got and were ready to pull out?" Flintlock demanded.

"It's a possibility, however remote," Azular shrugged. "It might be worth running checks on earlier ships lost in the sector, to see if the crews included Friskianx. Micklemouse believed himself chosen on the basis of his suitability for adaptation and Kelfennig seems to be a focal point for *something* linked to hostile incursion; and *that's* rising."

"Why, after millennia of isolation when their cities turned to dust, did these – whoever – suddenly decide to up sticks and take on the galaxy?" Apnis asked. "Wouldn't they all be dead and gone as well?"

"The tunnels," Azular reminded her. "Hibernation may have been a chosen option as their world failed, for reasons we can't fathom. It was maybe linked to increased cybernation, given the results we've seen. With no way of leaving their world when they revived, they were stranded; but some of their tech must have remained. We know that relics of what are considered once highly advanced civilizations are scattered all over this region of space and several such are close to the edges of the Starglass. Slowly growing stronger and realising that their planet was being visited by others, they took advantage perhaps; or they were making sure that as they were still vulnerable, anyone who came in would not make it out to report what they'd seen."

"Are you suggesting that these aliens used humanoid bodies to increase their own capacities?" enquired Flintlock, shocked.

"Not necessarily, although they would have had to be able to pass as typical sentients when once they did emerge. And they would have had to be able to pilot any ships they reclaimed to leave the planet, unless they had their own buried with them. The technology of the ships we've encountered so far *has* been advanced, but it's been based on known systems. But the build-up to the present situation must have been going on for years, silently, secretly and not on Kelfennig Four, or we'd have seen recent signs."

"I hope that's the case," Ahxenta put in. "Because it's bothering me that if your conjectures are anywhere near the actual, there could be a whole colony of hostiles under the rocks at Kelfennig armed to the teeth and just waiting to pounce."

"It's practically uninhabitable even for a small population," Azular argued. "Our scans have shown that. I suspect that vast numbers of the original people wouldn't have survived whatever cataclysm ended their civilisation. Those ruins we've seen point to structures that were devastated either by natural or by sentient means."

"And if sentient, they now have more than average capacity for payback," groaned Cottontail. "So where are they hanging out now, if not at Kelfennig? If it was Friskie territory we would know about it, if as you figure it, they've been up to no good for years and years."

"Somewhere remote," the science officer stated.

"Like the Belts or on the edges of Beta," said Apnis. "It's where the trouble started, it's where we find Mellifly, Brown Amber, Jurgall Three, Treskk Primus and a host of other places where trouble seems to fly in at every window."

The captain shook her head. "There's always unrest in those areas but it's because it's a volatile region with a large number of aggressive populations out to make a quick credit – where trouble's fomenting all the time, there will be plenty to take advantage. But it's a hunting ground, not a hideout for building a fleet that can take on the charted galaxy. You'd need a remote and secret place where few go, but close enough to sources of everything you need and people willing to get it for you if you pay the right price or lick the right boots."

"In the middle of the Ginseng?" asked Flintlock.

"No, that's a recent phenomenon and maybe a hiding place, as I think Greffy once pointed out. Remember that pre-meet we had with the other PSS commanders that had made it into Merkat Three, just before we met with the TA and made the acquaintance of Doosbak, Micklemouse and various hangers-on?" she appealed to Apnis.

"Don't I just," was the response.

"Bee Lyvy Coxen of the *Hexameter* told us about rumours that the remoter systems at the far edges of sector sixteen of Beta had been buying in loads of comms gear, sending out carriers to pick up the cargoes, paying up front and saying nothing; and who knows what else they've been buying or stealing or for how long. Very few have had contact with systems in that sector for years as they're so far off the usual space highways; they've kept out of the way and kept quiet. But there've been so many recent contacts that people are noticing. And as Charellis pointed out, if they did have the tech to launch the hostile attacks we've had, they'd also have the tech to hide themselves and their ships if they wanted."

"And sector sixteen's a small jaunt from Mellifly if you head out through uncharted space, if you've got your own bypass and a damn smart ship that knows the way," Apnis mused. "You don't think our little pal Micklemouse has the nous to hide the fact that he's been there or seen something do you? They want him very badly, after all. Why else risk Doosbak, whose position in the Coalition makes him really useful as a plant to them, to get him back?"

"You've opened a can of worms, Tallica," Ahxenta asserted. "The other thing that bothers me is why they want Micklemouse so badly. As you said, they could have fried the little runt and wrecked his ship if they thought he was such a danger and then created another with the same capabilities. Perhaps Mr Micklemouse is even more than we – or they – suspect. He claims he can almost scent these hostiles, or the ones he calls clients. Maybe they *have* tried to create another info-sent with the same capabilities but they haven't succeeded and he's unique. And that would make him a valuable commodity to one heck of a lot people. We need to find out."

"Do we?" disputed Cottontail. "We're a PSS, a trading ship, not a fizzing avenging angel cleansing the galaxy of a bunch of no-goods. That's the ISP's job as well as others. Why else do we pay our taxes on every frigging load we carry?"

"We got drafted, remember," Ahxenta told her.

"You're taking this contract for Mellifly, aren't you?" guessed the first mate, scanning her commanding officer quizzically.

Ahxenta's enigmatic but grim smile was the only answer.

20: STRANGE CARGOES

The question of what they should do with their two passengers in the brig was exercising Tallica Apnis as she strode onto the bridge behind the captain. They were a risky commodity to carry if they could be tracked by unknowns. Her enquiries elicited little useful response, by which she inferred that Ahxenta had some plan up her sleeve. Once seated in her chair, the first mate repeated the question.

"Come on, Cinnabar, I know that face: what have you planned for the two pipsqueaks? They're more damn trouble than they're worth and they sure won't be doing us any favours if we keep them aboard. We'd be as well painting a bullseye on an aft cargo bay."

"Quite simple: we get everything out of them that we can, no holds barred, and then place them in a safe haven for the duration."

"That being?"

"Kelfennig Four. If aliens originating from or near there *did* alter them for their own ends, as Azular suspects, then they can damn well keep them for a bit. Micklemouse's ship is still there and we can leave them stores and equipment for oxygen and water extraction."

"And the bill to cover it, I hope," Box muttered from the depths of the navi-helm. "We're a trading ship, not a cut-price commuter run for criminals that cause nothing but trouble and drag us into military squabbles that upset half the known galaxy."

"Belay that Mr Box and plot us the fastest course there is. Helm, get us there double quick. We run silent, cloaked and with weapons primed. Everyone else, standby battlestations. I want eyes, noses and ears peeled for anything out of the ordinary. We shoot first and don't stop to ask questions."

"If that ball of energy was some sort of guardian and Earbleat didn't blast it to hell, the hostiles are going to know pretty quickly that he's back and that we dropped him off," Apnis warned.

"I don't think so, Tallica. It's a long way from the Starglass to the Belts and even further to sector sixteen of Beta, if that *is* part of the equation. Azular figures the aliens have to return to Kelfennig from time to time but they don't have an active presence there, though they may have close by. But I've had Bellfish and his team keeping an eye on all the comms channels and relays we can get into and things are growing quieter, especially out this end. Any actions we're hearing about are still random but seem to be mainly in zone Alpha and the sectors of the zones closest to Alpha. There have been one or two at the outer reaches of Kappa and close to the Enigma Nebula, hence the hot ISP presence at Kellybar, and independents in zone Mu have been hit, but that's it."

"I don't like it, Cinnabar. It strikes me that there *is* a plan there, whatever people are saying about the random nature of the attacks that makes it hard to know where they'll hit next. If these hostiles are avoiding certain areas, it's not because they don't want to spread their forces too thinly, it's because they've got something nasty planned and want it to be as big a surprise as they can make it."

"Ginseng Nebula," came the voice of the navigation officer.

"With ears like that, you should have made him comms officer," the first mate said ruefully as the captain sighed in exasperation.

"You have the conn, Tallica. I need to speak to Azular, Flintlock and Greenwing and between them let's hope they can extract enough from our unwanted boarders to give us a heads up before we hit the trail for Beta. Mr Bellfish, get me updates on everything related to the latest hostile strikes. Patch it through to my office. And I'll want the highest security on outgoing comms: I have messages to send."

"Cap's up to something," Romanna Dox muttered to her mate as Ahxenta strode off the bridge.

"So why isn't she telling us?" Box demanded, put out.

"With ears and a mouth like yours, I don't blame her."

"It's because we still have those two drones in the brig and who knows what they can pick up that we don't know about, or who they can pass it on to once they do, I'll bet," Box announced ominously.

"Shut up and plot us the most efficient course through the ISP-controlled part of Zeta, avoiding as much border space as we can. They've upped border patrols, hell knows why, and we don't want any awkward questions."

The captain was indeed up to something, as many pairs of beady eyes and twitching ears noted. She had spent time closeted with her senior science officer and the two medics, and she had called Cottontail and Earbleat in as support. She had then had a long chat to Lindell before making several long-distance links. The consensus was that *Arianrhod* was heading for trouble in a big way and the Cap was not going to go out of her way to evade it.

Meanwhile, despite the order to make best speed for Kelfennig, the navigator and helmswoman deemed it appropriate to plot rather a haphazard course to avoid pursuers and to put any stations picking them up off track. The result was a couple of hours lost, but orbit achieved around the fourth planet without any overt sign of pursuit or of ambush in the vicinity of the system.

Every crewmember breathed more freely once ship's complement was back to normal. Even those who had had little idea of what was going on felt the relief. Their two passengers had been unwillingly transported to the surface of the planet close to the long-abandoned wreck and left to their own devices. Both had been shaken to such an extent that they were claiming duress and threatening retribution, but their harangues fell on deaf ears: Ahxenta had seen to that. The officers escorting the pair were hand-picked security personnel that had been kept well away from the discussions pertaining to them and the trip planetside had been monitored every step of the way.

Once *Arianrhod's* shuttle was safely back on board, the order was given to break orbit and set for Heligon Station to take on a load of energy cells, arms and supplies that would be ready for them. The captain deemed it wise that once there, it would be made known that their next stop would be Merkat: many of the Privates used the Web as a base when not out in space, it was a natural objective and would take them in the broad direction of their next mission. The crew was now aware that the contract to shift a cargo of meta-jurillium hull sheets from Jurgall Three to Mellifly had been accepted, albeit at a higher fee than that set in the original offer. The fact that *Arianrhod's* increased demand *had* been met and that the client details were so sketchy as to be useless convinced Ahxenta that the whole thing was a set-up, but she had agreed and left her supercargo to deal with the minutiae as far as it related to Metal-Corp Industries, of whom he had never heard. Lindell had, however, secured another commission that meant a trip to Merkat for pick-up after the Mellifly delivery, hence their direction outwardly seemed in no way suspicious.

"Oh great!" sighed Box to his mate when the order came down to plan a course for Jurgall via zones Epsilon, Alpha and Delta to Skoon and thence to Duck. "Here we go again. It's a wonder my hair hasn't turned grey with all that we've been through lately."

"Will you shut up and chart the damn course, or I'll do it my way and that'll make more than your hair turn grey," Dox flared.

"There *are* quicker ways to Jurgall from Heligon than that," Apnis noted in a low voice as she scanned her station. "Got a reason?"

"Got several reasons," the captain told her, equally quietly. "Once my pieces are in place, I'll let you know. Our first business is taking on our supplies, as we had to leave quite a lot with our castaways."

"Not that they were grateful. The mouse should have been, given he's no longer trackable by his scary masters, though his ship still is, of course. What if they head on in to check up on it?"

"They don't seem to have thus far. Not our problem," Ahxenta declared. "We've done more for him than he deserved. I hope I don't regret not frying him when I had the chance."

"Not your style, Cinnabar. But that was some risk Flintlock took, going in to disable half his cyber systems."

"It was, but she's not getting a pay rise over it. She suggested it anyway. At least with the data we got out of them, we have a small chance of identifying one of these hostiles and maybe even one of their augmented moles, if we get within scanning distance."

"That's sticky: if we have to be that close, they'd be breathing down our necks. But Earbleat *did* destroy that energy globe and that's worth knowing. Though why the mouse was upset at losing a nanny his creepy clients sent out to keep an eye on him is anybody's guess."

"Azular doesn't think it was sent by his string-pullers. We can't be sure, but if it turned up only days after he crashed, unless they were tracking him and had it prepared *and* they were close to hand, it's unlikely. He felt an affinity to it, possibly because he'd been altered by aliens once native to the place and there was an empathy, but even he wasn't sure of its origin, only that it meant him no harm and it felt familiar. And our team did work him over pretty thoroughly."

"Needs must," Apnis sympathised. "But he'd some reaction when Earbleat blasted it. Maybe it sang him a lullaby every night. Can we work out how much energy it took to dissipate it? And are we sure it can't reform behind our backs, given it seemed to be pure energy?"

The captain raised an eyebrow at her first mate. "I wish you'd stop asking questions I can't answer, especially when one of the answers is liable to be relevant to taking action over something a lot worse."

"You mean the anomaly out at the Ginseng?"

"Precisely. But we're on beacon for Heligon, so I'd better get on down to Lindell's office."

The stopover at the station was mercifully short. Whatever strings the captain had pulled, their supplies were waiting for them and had been signed for immediate transfer and at remarkably sound rates. Her senior officers were impressed at the subsequent briefing.

"How?" asked Apnis.

"Who," Ahxenta corrected. "Admiral Zillah at Freskat Six: she has a lot of clout, I have a lot of interesting information, so fair exchange and absolutely no robbery. But now to business. She had one or two salient points to pass on regarding the current situation."

The current situation was that there had been a considerable lull in hostilities. Apart from minor skirmishes here and there, the hostiles seemed to have pulled back. Marridan and Brown Amber were still in enemy hands and little was coming out of them or nearby systems. At the other end of the mapped galaxy, the peaks in energy that had been detected in the Ginseng anomaly had quieted. The consensus was that it was the lull before the storm, the problem being no-one could predict when and where the storm was liable to break.

Ahxenta had informed the admiral of her team's calculations of how much power it had taken to dissipate the ball of energy they had found on Kelfennig and its possible resemblance to the irregularity in the Ginseng Nebula, but not of the issues related to its finding. The captain had also passed on sundry snippets, coded and on a very tight beam, of the cyber nature of their enemy and the likelihood of high-level infiltration in almost every interplanetary authority, but had refused point blank to reveal her data sources. Zillah was an old hand and did not press for more details, promising only to keep in touch.

"So all speed to Jurgall Three, then?" the first mate surmised.

"All speed to Jurgall Three."

All speed would take many standard days in view of the distances involved, the course plotted and the areas to avoid. The intervening time was spent by the crew on various tactics relevant to the ship and her safety. Having worked out the nature of the cybernetics that had augmented their late passengers and given them abnormal strength, Cottontail and Azular had set their teams to integrating their learning into detecting such altered individuals and their enhancements from distance and on the best ways of overcoming and incapacitating such as came their way.

Whisper Earbleat, crowned with triumph over the success of her decoy cargo pod four and of her follow-up conversion of outer cargo pod two into the *Echo*, was cheerfully renovating a replacement cargo pod four for use as another unmanned weapon, with more firepower that its predecessor. When asked what she intended to use to coat the hull of her latest creation, she had no scruple in announcing that she planned to liberate some of the meta-jurillium plates from the cargo that they were engaged to deliver to the repair dock at Mellifly.

Captain Ahxenta had her own business and she and the first mate spent much time in her office involved in long-distance comm-links. Noses twitching, the bridge crew watched every move but forbore to question: they knew they would be told when the time was right.

Having been ordered to give anything Friskianx as wide a berth as possible, Box had plotted a course to Spelter, from where they could cut across Epsilon to Selliden and then fly directly through Alpha and Delta zones via Bezel to Skoon and into NTA-controlled Beta space. The last part of her trip to Jurgall and closer to Friskianx interests took *Arianrhod* into a sector almost empty of settled worlds and thus ill-patrolled.

That the ship had met with no opposition, nor even with a passing vessel, during the lengthy trip out from the Starglass, had given rise to a few misgivings amongst the crew. Such calm was not their usual state of affairs and the advance to Jurgall Three was greeted with a little anxiety. None of the crew apart from Greenwing had visited the outpost before, it being a Friskianx League colony and not the most welcoming of places. The doctor was summoned to the bridge for his reactions as *Arianrhod* announced her approach and was assigned a route to her temporary berth.

"It's been a while," Greenwing noted as the holo in the well of the bridge expanded to show the bleak world and its adjacent structures. "But there's a heap more orbiting hardware here than there was last time I saw this place. Those rigs must be for building massive gear. And this is only one side of the planet."

"I *had* noted we were given a precise line to come in on," Ahxenta told him, scanning her board. "This is only what we're being allowed to see and there are off-limits beacons posted on every single berth other than the one we've been assigned."

"Being scanned from every angle, Cap," Gliss announced from tactical. "Just as well we've got jammers."

"Ask them politely why, Bellfish," the captain ordered.

The answer was that it was routine and would the *Arianrhod* please comply and lower her defences. The answer "no way in hell" did not go down well with Jurgall Three's Port Control but the operative at the other end of the link did not press the point when Ahxenta told him that she had a cargo to collect and if their marketing reps were not prepared to release it, she would register that with her clients and leave the area. She had better things to do than swap insults with a bunch of lackeys all day.

"Posturing in an attempt to gauge our reactions," Apnis reckoned. "But they *are* being rather polite all the same. Here come the release orders and Lindell's showing his boards as green," she said, tapping her ops boards. "They sure don't want us snooping down there. The manifest's just been sent in but a million eyes are watching our every move and they've sent tactical drones into position around us."

"Gliss, return the compliment and scan everything within range. Earbleat, target their drones but do *not* lock on," ordered Ahxenta.

"Targeting, aye," the weapons officer complied.

"They didn't like that, Cap; here's a formal complaint from Port Control," the first mate reported.

"Too bad. Lindell, what's the position on the goods?"

"Two payload pods are heading for our aft cargo bays via grapple drones," the supercargo responded from his office. "We're tracking them; it should show on your board, ma'am. Fine scanning shows content as almost pure meta-jurillium, standard packing materials and two additional signals from extraneous sources."

"So I see," Ahxenta said dryly. "Greffy?"

The science officer smiled over. "No danger to us, Captain. I'm relaying the details and my scans to Dr Azular."

"Get our tractors on those pods and haul them aboard. Make sure their grapples don't come within touching distance of our hull."

"I'm keeping an eye on them, Captain, in case they lob in any little extras," Gliss announced.

"They won't," Apnis maintained, "Since they've attached trackers to the payload pods, just to make sure they get to their destination."

Once the massive pods were safely aboard and the necessary data exchanges had been made, *Arianrhod* requested clearance to depart. It was swiftly given.

"Glad to see the back of us," Dox remarked as the docking struts retracted and she manoeuvred the massive craft free of her restraints.

"No rush, helm; we don't want them to think we're making a run for it," the captain cautioned as the ship turned in a slow arc towards the expanse of space beyond.

"Nobody seems to be waving us goodbye and wishing us a good trip," Box announced dolefully as he set in their forward course.

"You want the moon on a lolly stick, you do," the helmswoman told him. "Just be grateful they're not sending a parting shot across our bows to speed us on our way."

"Well," Ahxenta smiled at Apnis. "Shall we go meet Azular and Cottontail and see what the Friskies have landed us with?"

"Lead on, Cap. It'll pass the time 'til we run into the next hitch."

The four officers had prudently suited up for their trip to the vast outer aft cargo bays. They were open to space but when in flight, fine-meshed safety shields were dropped and pressurised tubes could be extruded for cargo inspection. It was in one of these tubes that the party made their way across to one of the two payload pods.

"What did you make of Greffy's analyses and the scans Gliss got?" Ahxenta asked the senior science officer.

"I suspect that whoever prepared those loads for despatch didn't realise that we're able to detect meta-jurillium components that are in contact with organic matter."

"Implants, you mean," Apnis said.

"Yes, Commander. Those grapple drones had more to them than inert mechanical and electrical parts and the readings we took of the adjacent structures, despite their heavy shielding, sent out signals that indicated the presence of what we suspect to be alien or altered entities, although not in large numbers."

"Just sufficient to keep the natives in line, then?" Cottontail asked.

"Possibly," Azular replied. "This pod has a fixed standard tracker but there's an auxiliary tracker with a distinct signature inside its hull. Its outer cladding is articulated and every section is linked to a central core monitor, so any tampering will be evident."

"Bang goes Earbleat's hope of purloining part of the payload for her new toy then," the first mate observed with a laugh.

"Not if we disable the core monitor," argued the chief engineer.

"I wouldn't recommend it," the science officer put in sagely.

"So what do you suggest?" Cottontail demanded with asperity as her eyes scanned the huge container.

"I suggest we work out the spec and range of the auxiliary trackers of both pods and on that basis figure who's responsible for them and thus might be following us at distance. I also suggest we decipher the codes for opening the pods legitimately and then open them."

The engineer shrugged. "The man has a point," she admitted. "In that case we'd best check the second one in case there *are* differences our scans didn't pick up. We don't have much time if we're on a straight course for Mellifly."

The second pod was a counterpart to the first, with no discernible differences. Azular returned to his main lab to work on the problems he had set himself as Earbleat fumed at the delay to her project. She spent her free hours devising a way to identify potential pursuers and eventually came up with the idea of dropping off a probe on the edge of a small planetary system they would pass en route to Mellifly. Any ship, ion trail or change in hyperspace field that suggested a cloaked ship passing sufficiently close would be picked up, scans made and the results transmitted to the *Arianrhod*. They could then match any traces received with what Azular had picked up from the internal trackers aboard the pods and the data they had gathered at Jurgall.

Ahxenta and Apnis took turns on the bridge and spent the rest of their duty time in the bridge office conning over the latest news from outside whilst making links of their own. Every other crewmember was at a high state of alert. Azular had reported that the auxiliary trackers had an extensive range and their design bore some similarity to the hardware they had now come to associate with hostile influences. His data was corroborated by Earbleat, whose probe had picked up a blip about five hours behind them whose readings matched the ships that had hit them at Four One Two Alpha.

Arianrhod's course to the drop-off at Mellifly had been plotted as directly as possible to avoid Brown Amber and a small Coalition-run sector of zone Beta, to make best speed without contact with other forces and to suggest to the pursuing ship that its presence had gone unnoticed. In the event she was unhindered, leaving some to suggest darkly that they were being monitored at every step and that a nasty surprise awaited them just over the next asteroid. The ship travelled uncloaked, at silent red alert and with every scanner set to wide field.

Their endpoint was a repair facility in a stable orbit over the northern polar region of Mellifly and at a distance from the planet so far out that any visitors would be marked well before they were on closing approach. *Arianrhod* had been given the final coordinates of Orbital Repair Facility Polaris X-4 as comms registered her presence and her business at the insistence of a marker buoy set a thousand kilometres from the perimeter of the repair installation's space. That perimeter was guarded by warning beacons but the ship was welcomed and sent the course to follow to her destination berth.

Arianrhod's long-range scanners had shown the place to be much larger than an average repair dock and the sight that met their eyes confirmed the analyses: the meshwork of a massive orbital docking station housed a fleet of part-assembled ships that sat calmly in space, each one a hive of productive technical activity. The facility was alive with diligent mechanoids weaving through the dark superstructures as they fixed, braced and welded plates, moved and reshaped internal structures and shifted countless small cargoes to and fro. The super-bright lights of myriad drones at work lit up the place like a tangled ball of netting strung with stars.

"There's a helluva lot of work going on there, Cinnabar," breathed Apnis. "And that's one huge fleet of ships. How come the planetary authorities haven't done anything? We've had nothing from them and there's been zip on comms – Bellfish has been keeping tabs."

"Get everything we can on what's going on out there but do not drop our shields or our targeting eyes," the captain ordered. "Warm up our weapons, Lieutenant Commander Earbleat."

"They'll ask why," the weapons officer warned as she complied.

"They may not," Greffy interposed in a puzzled voice. "I'm not reading life signs. Organic materials yes, but nothing that can be classed as humanoid, or even close."

"So what *is* down there telling us to come on in, doors are open?" the captain queried as the schematics of their assigned berth appeared on the tactical display that Gliss had sent to the main bridge holo.

"They're automated response and collection systems," explained Bellfish. "We're requested to dock at the marked berth and then to release our cargo to the grapple drones. Once the goods have been checked, the remaining part of our fee will be remitted."

"I wonder how? At the end of a torpedo with our name on it?" hazarded the first mate. "This berth must be the furthest out they have and well away from the action. Are we going to deliver, Cap?"

"We're going to deliver."

"And then we beat a hasty retreat?"

"Like hell we do. We collect our pay and then we blast the place to dust," Ahxenta declared firmly. "We'll have fulfilled the contract, but judging by what our scans are telling us, they're planning to slap those plates on enough firepower to wipe out a large fleet. And I bet this isn't their only dockyard. So we launch our little surprise and then we beat a hasty retreat."

"And you think we can take down an entire fleet?" Apnis was incredulous. "This time we may just have overstretched ourselves."

"Those ships are far from ready and none of them are armed," the captain pointed out.

"You hope," the first mate snorted. "They could all be booby-trapped with enough explosive to take out a star and all its planets."

"None of the ships I can read are operable, ma'am," reported Greffy. "Nor have they active weapons systems. Most haven't even their hulls in place."

"These are the ones we can see, what about the ones we can't?" Apnis persisted. "We've only got a partial view from here."

"Too late to worry about that, Tallica: we're slotting in place and here come the grapple drones. Lock us in, helm, but be ready to blast free on my mark. Get our tractors ready to push out the pods but hold onto them until they're well clear of the hull: I don't want those drones to get a toehold."

One of Cottontail's engineers had tractor control and manoeuvred the two huge units out of their bay in tandem and in the direction of the incoming grapple drones.

"Nicely done," praised Ahxenta as the payload was captured without a hitch and the drones retreated. "Lindell, send in the bill for immediate payment."

"We'll be lucky," came the voice of the supercargo. "I'll let you know the second they release it."

"Let's make sure we're set to release ourselves," the captain said. "We still have a ship five hours behind that I'm sure isn't friendly."

"Was five hours behind," the first mate corrected. "She may have picked up speed and called for reinforcements by this time."

"Thanks for that. They must be scanning those payload pods to make sure they've got what they ordered."

"The internal manifest shows that they have," Apnis chuckled.

"I hope that's all it shows," was the dry response. "Nice piece of irony: we deliver a cargo destined for ships that are liable to be sent out to take us down at some point."

"Some point's got closer, ma'am," asserted Greffy. "I read a build-up of peripheral power that could be ships about to launch."

"Captain, I have a request that you go down to their marketing office!" Bellfish called. "A question over the payment for the cargo."

"Decline gracefully and tell them I'll talk to them from up here," Ahxenta said into a swell of angry hisses from her bridge crew.

"A non-existent person down there evidently wants to speak to you," the first mate declared as the comms officer reported that the request had been repeated and that the captain was asked to head down in person. "That's novel."

"Tell them to remit our fee and I'll consider it."

"You are of course lying, Cinnabar?" Apnis exclaimed.

"Of course I am. Ahxenta to Flintlock: Doc? Priority one: I need you to grab sufficient organic material that will simulate an animate human and shove it into Earbleat's latest little toy ship. Immediately, we have no time to spare. Earbleat, get on down to medbay and help, then get back up here pronto. Bellfish, keep that auto chat-up system talking. All hands at silent battlestations; auxiliary teams to your posts and I want the emergency bridge manned at full strength."

The captain sat back and studied the bridge holo as duty officers, including Azular, sped in and made for their stations.

"Tallica, get our back-up organised as quietly as you can and let's hope they can't breach our comms," she ordered in a low voice.

As Apnis headed to the captain's office, Ahxenta straightened up. "Flight team, you two start plotting us a series of evasive courses that will take us out of here in whatever direction we need to go. Gliss, have your team keep tabs on that power build-up and maintain our long-distance scanners at full stretch. Azular and Greffy, link science arrays to tactical: we need to see anything before it sees us and know what it is. Weapons stations, run everything hot and get ready to deploy on my mark."

"Balloon's about to go up and I haven't had my morning coffee," Box groaned dismally.

"Shut up and keep plotting," Dox told him shortly. "Coffee would only make you want to pee anyway, and I sure as hell don't have time to manage your station if you have to visit the little officer's room."

In less than twenty minutes Whisper Earbleat had returned to her station with the news that her latest cargo pod was ready to launch on the captain's order and was sporting a call-sign identifying her as the *Loki*, a small one-man shuttle registered to the *Arianrhod*.

"That's nice and enigmatic," Box was heard to mutter.

"Here we go. Lindell, what's the position on our payment?"

"Sixty percent received, Captain. Once they've talked to you they say they'll release the rest," the supercargo reported.

"Fair enough, since we've only given them about eighty percent of their cargo. We'll take the rest out of their hides. Batten down your hatches, people. Bellfish, tell them I'm heading out, and Earbleat, you make sure that new little boat of yours is shielded every step of the way. All stations, report readiness."

Apnis returned to her usual seat at Ahxenta's side with a positive nod. As every station showed green, the captain ordered pod launch and immediately, Earbleat's voice echoed around the bridge,

"Cargo pod four alpha *Loki* away!"

As they watched, the small craft, looking for all the galaxy like a one-man shuttle, sped like a tiny missile from one of the *Arianrhod's* minor launch bays and towards the coordinates given as the location of the marketing office.

"Hold down the speed, Ms Earbleat, we don't want them to think we're overconfident."

"Aye, Cap."

"Power build-up increasing! Reading three sources!" called Gliss.

"Copy!" confirmed Greffy as he manipulated his boards and sent his readings to the bridge holo. "They match the alien warships we've met before and two are huge! Main weapons are phase cannon, torpedoes and slicer beams."

"Shields at maximum! Fighter pilots to bays and Azular have our decoy ready to go. Your new cargo pod still on course, Earbleat?"

"Aye, Captain; cargo pod two *Echo* also operational and can go on your mark!"

"Power build-up confirmed as three ships of hostile configuration off our port side and another's just appeared abaft of us: that damn beast that was trailing us must have put a spurt on and sneaked in by a back door!" Gliss barked. "They're holding position but all four have got a bead on us!"

"Target all enemy vessels and lock on! They need to know we mean business. Helm, move us slowly away from these damn struts and give me room to manoeuvre but keep us within firing range of that installation. They won't want to take out their own facilities if they can help it. All batteries prepare to fire, I don't want to chance more hostiles coming in on my starboard. Start reversing your pod, Earbleat, as if we're bringing her out."

"*Loki's* being targeted by an emplacement at what they said was the marketing office!" the weapons office bawled. "And they're pulling her in on a tractor beam! Bunch of bastards!"

"Bunch of stupid bastards," Romanna Dox corrected as she moved skilful hands over her controls to swing the enormous ship free of the docking struts and give her turning room.

"Have *Loki* return fire," ordered Ahxenta.

"Returning fire, aye. We're hardly stinging them, they're shielded so well. Launching *Loki's* twin torpedoes, increasing thrusters to disengage tractor. It's not working… they're firing on her!" Earbleat screeched. "She's hit!"

"Get us the hell out of here, helm, maximum burn!" yelled the captain.

As the *Arianrhod* swung in an arc and then dove to evade the trio of advancing warships and the fourth coming in at their stern, an expanding halo of fire erupted from behind them.

"Didn't expect that, did they?" the weapons officer yelled out to the bridge in general as she checked her boards and settled herself into the main weapons station.

Earbleat's latest meta-jurillium plated cargo pod enclosed its own surprise: a switch set to trigger on inner hull breach and detonate a charge that would blow the pod apart from the inside, releasing enough explosive to take out a small ship and sending the segmented hull plates into space as high-speed multi-directional projectiles.

"Activate the payload pods!" Ahxenta ordered.

"Activation, aye!" sang out the second weapons officer.

A double burst of flaming light from the holo told the bridge crew that the two recently-released payload pods were now an expanding field of space debris, as was most everything in their vicinity.

As the great ship streaked away from the intensifying energy that still spread outwards and the lesser bursts as various weapons systems caught and burned, the voice of Gliss rang across the bridge.

"Shit! Two more hostiles have just shown off our starboard! They've called in reinforcements!"

21: PLAYING WITH FIRE

The bridge crew hung on grimly, the speed that had been coaxed out of *Arianrhod* crushing everyone down into their seats. The drone of the overworked grav compensators rose to a high whine as they were pushed to handle the strain and maintain stability. Every sensor on the ship's vast exterior was sending in data, the stream coalescing into the image that spun within the confines of the bridge holo-generator field. The simulated starfield gyrated as the ship wove a convoluted course to escape the hostile ships moving in on several attack vectors.

"Three at least are faster than we are and one's getting closer!" panted Apnis, hauling herself upright. "The other three are smaller: holding back to finish us, I expect."

"Just another thousand or two…" muttered Ahxenta. "Set course for the beacon off Kifferbuck and maintain it as far as possible!" she barked at the nav-officer. "All batteries ready to go on my mark! Prep close-proximity charges and send them down the tubes! Earbleat, get ready to loose every frigging torpedo we've got, and I mean every last one! Target their bays with our big guns, I don't want them launching assault craft or fighters!"

Fear lent speed to hands over consoles and hours of practice left no-one with time to think. This was the worst firefight *Arianrhod* had ever had to face and she rose like a dragon aflame as the first assault wave began, her hull plates rattling in a rising crescendo as enemy pulses crossed space and spattered into stars on her hide.

"Launch deflecting drones, wide spread! And take out the surface comms of that nearest beast off the port bow!" the captain ordered.

"Shields holding!" Cottontail sang out. "Maintaining inner hull integrity so far – repair drones operational."

As the bloom of an exploding charge taken down by her guns lit the ship's upper sections, Dox pulled hard to port to outrun another wave of incoming missiles that lit the dark with deadly purpose.

"Auxiliary gunnery crews marking incoming fire! Maintaining our own against the nearest ship, but that flanker's coming in underneath! Breaching pods incoming, two!" Earbleat yelled.

"On them!" her second responded.

"Tallica, take main weapons! Earbleat, deploy cargo pod *Echo* and target that second big beast off our port! Azular, ready our decoy but do not deploy! Pilots, get to your fighters! Dox, turn us about to face that first ship. Forward batteries, target bursts of concentrated fire on every weak spot she has!"

The *Arianrhod* advanced, every gun emplacement thundering with lethal efficiency. Her torpedo tubes ran red hot as missile after missile launched. Earbleat screamed triumphantly as her small craft swerved and arced across the nose of the second advancing warship to smash into her main comms array. The massive explosion took out visible chunks of hull and shards were sent spinning into space. A third vast ship had now come into range off starboard and had sent its own devastating projectiles as a wide spread towards its target.

"Local hyperspace field shifting, Captain!" yelled Gliss. "Sending to grid: something big's on approach!"

Something big was indeed on approach. A huge dark ship, black as a hole in space against the blazing orbs of light that were incoming missiles being killed by *Arianrhod's* skilled gunnery crews, loomed through the ghostly light of the holo. As soon as the newcomer had got her bearings she switched course and made for the quartet of contending vessels, a spread of torpedoes lighting her path.

The third hostile had reached optimal firing position and her pulse cannons roared. A hit broadside from the approaching ship caught her off-guard and she rocked but continued her assault on her target. *Arianrhod* shuddered in the onslaught and Cottontail called out the loss of part of their shielding.

"Hull breach!" the chief engineer shrieked as their main adversary pressed the advantage and sent in a rain of torpedoes. "Teams on it, but we're losing air in two forr'ad sections!"

"Loose everything at the bastard!" Ahxenta yelled. "Azular, deploy our decoy to cover our underbelly."

As she called, the large ship off *Arianrhod's* starboard began to turn to defend her rear as another spread of missiles from the latest arrival spattered her hull with fire. Even as Gliss hollered out that the three smaller ships were on fast approach and firing blind, Greffy cut the air with a shout. "Two more coming in off the bypass!"

"About bloody time!" Ahxenta growled as the two blips coalesced into familiar outlines.

By that time Earbleat's target had all but broken up into lumps of twisted metal. The weapons officer had followed up the *Echo* with every piece of weaponry she could muster, targeting with deadly accuracy the most vulnerable areas. As the latest comers made for the smaller hostiles, two of which turned to fight, the *Arianrhod's* captain wrinkled her brow, checked her boards and made a swift calculation before giving the order for fighter launch. The tiny one-man craft would hardly sting ships shielded like the aliens, but they could get in adequately closely to take out salient systems and blow out opposing fighter bays and might slow the approach of the warship that was still outfacing *Arianrhod.*

"*Obsidian's* taken down her target!" Gliss hollered as the massive black ship appeared through the blossom of flame that had been the enemy warship. "She's setting her sights on this bastard here!"

As he fought with a shower of sparks from the tactical station and helped his second back into her seat, the great *Arianrhod* shuddered, scattering those on their feet like a set of skittles. Crizz Cottontail's explosive language cut through the fine dust of emergency quenching powder over discharges from almost every station as the power died and the red glow of the emergency lighting took over.

"Main engineering energy cell emplacement's been hit! Enviro systems down! Losing main bridge systems integrity!" bawled the chief engineer as the navi-helm console sent out arcs of blue light.

"Emergency bridge, take helm and navigational control and track all other stations! Engine room, get main bridge systems back on line, grav-compensator and atmosphere priorities! I need a medic on the bridge!" Ahxenta roared, clawing at her console as she fought to maintain her hold. "Status of hostiles?"

Gliss had made it back to his seat and was frantically tabbing his boards whilst tying himself in. "*Obsidian Sky* has engaged the hostile on our nose and she's got it on the run; *Hexameter* and *Green Comet* are holding against their opponents off our port and starboard but only just; our decoy's slowed the beast trying to undercut us! Updating grid-holo… something else on approach! I'm reading her as a PSS! It's the *Quarkstorm!*"

The advent of the latest Private proved too much for the attacking ships: whatever brain was behind the assault had evidently decided that discretion was better than destruction and the three smaller warships that could still manoeuvre turned as one and set off in the same direction at a speed that belied the pasting they had taken. The remaining large ship had veered off, but *Obsidian Sky's* torpedoes had hit their marks and she split apart amidships in a slow waltz of fire.

"Recall our fighters if our bays are operational!" Ahxenta's voice cut the air. "Stand down battlestations, but keep long-range scanners active, assuming we still have them, and make sure we keep well away from all that debris. Haul in the decoy if it's in one piece, Azular. Earbleat, keep our residual weapons systems online, just in case."

"I think we're down to phase rifles and handguns," was the rueful reply. "We could always chuck bits of superstructure down the tubes, there's plenty fallen off. Whoops! Gravity's back on!"

"Looks like," the captain agreed. "All stations, report!"

Cottontail's engineers had been able to stabilise most of the ship's systems and power was steadily being restored as standby energy cells were deployed in vital areas. The worst damage was the hull breach, the temporary fields that had been set in place using up a great deal of the available power. Much of the ship's shielding was also beyond her own repair capacity and would need replaced and various internal structures had taken a severe beating. Operational control had been returned to the main bridge and most systems were working, more or less, though at far from maximum efficiency. This included the crew, as several were sporting med-patches hastily applied by a busy medic. *Arianrhod's* eight fighters had made it safe in with minimal damage. Flintlock's teams were working flat out as Greenwing and two nurse-techs had been wounded whilst tending injured crew in the breached sections and were in medbay. Other trained personnel were dispersed all over the ship to provide aid but there were several serious cases that would require more specialist attention than *Arianrhod* could provide, though no fatalities.

"Captain Bluejohn requesting our status, Captain," Bellfish called out amidst the confusion that still reigned. "I can get a visual up. Captains Jikelleli, Coxen and Peakfrost also asking for updates."

"Link them all across," Ahxenta directed.

Bluejohn's eyes widened as he took in the chaos of *Arianrhod's* bridge. "Hell's teeth, Cinnabar, you've had quite a party! What immediate assistance do you need? We're minimally damaged."

"Field generators and energy cells to keep our hull intact until we can get to a repair dock for a start. And if one of you could spare some medical aid, I've a helluva lot of crewmen taken hits, including three of my experienced medbay staff. We're low on atmosphere as well," she added, checking her board. "Escort support would be a bonus, I don't have a torpedo or a drone left to my name and we're down to hand weapons by way of firepower. I plan to limp along to Merkat Three, if I can make it that far. I don't think we'll be welcome at any of the points in between."

"Your engines will keep you steady in the currents of the bypass?"

Captain Bee Lyvy Coxen of the *Hexameter* questioned.

"Just about, if we can maintain our hull structure and you can lend us some energy cells to patch into our engineering emplacements," Ahxenta told her.

"We're heading for the Web, so count the *Obsidian* in as escort," Bluejohn said firmly. "We'll use our main tractors to give you a bit of stability on the bypass. You're for Merkat as well, aren't you Sarie?"

"Yup," Jikelleli returned. "If you take starboard, I'll take port. My tractors on that side are still operational. I've taken a couple of bad hits but we're okay. I can send over my chief medic and an assist to lend a hand as well, our medbay's quiet."

Captain Ahxenta expressed her thanks as all four vessels tendered practical aid in the form of energy cells and other essential supplies. The Captains of the *Quarkstorm* and the *Hexameter*, after rapid debate, agreed to detour via Merkat to help bring the *Arianrhod* safe to port: Ahxenta had rendered them sufficient assistance in the past that it made some return. In view of the situation, it was deemed prudent to make as rapid a departure as possible. The debris that was once three massive alien warships was left to drift in space as the five starships, with *Arianrhod* at the centre, slowly manoeuvred into a formation that would allow support shuttles to cross with supplies and personnel. As the flotilla made for the nearest bypass and set to the local beacon for Merkat, Ahxenta began to count up the cost of the past few days.

Despite crippling losses in terms of damage to the ship herself and practically every piece of armoury she carried, the *Arianrhod* was still spaceworthy, though barely. The hull breach was repairable as long as materials were available at Merkat Three, and Ahxenta had set her supercargo Lindell, fortunately still in one piece and fully aware of the situation, into sourcing supplies of everything needed. The shielding of the exterior sections that had taken the worst hits would have to be replaced and the entire hull would need its remaining plating realigned and welded. On the positive side, a proportion of the meta-jurillium hull sheets that Earbleat had appropriated from the Mellifly cargo had not been used and being substantial and of good quality, they would go some way to making a start. Replacing the arsenal and the wrecked hull emplacements, as well as the comms and scanning systems that had gone, would be a headache, as over the years the captain had used her own sources to obtain superior merchandise. That she would have to count on advanced credit did not worry her unduly: Ahxenta was sufficiently sanguine to be aware that this latest exploit would have weight in terms of *Arianrhod's* notoriety and thus the willingness of outside parties to look upon her favourably.

The main trial that the captain felt she faced was her crew. She had put them through much over the past months and despite their inveterate cheerful grumbling, this most recent series of events had left them exhausted. Many were seriously hurt and needed extensive and expensive therapy, and of those less critical, several would need treatment off-ship. As she pondered the situation in the relative calm of their steady progress towards the Web, she became aware of the inevitable post-mortem of events at the navi-helm console.

"Why didn't they fire on the *Obsidian* as soon as they saw her? They could tell by her outline that she wasn't one of them," Box, his face heavily plastered by hastily-applied med-gel, was enquiring of his usual colleague.

"They must have thought she was our decoy: they'd evidently heard that we'd pulled that trick before and weren't going to be caught out with the same one twice," Dox said decidedly.

"Hah! More fool them," Box replied. "They must have really wet themselves when we *did* deploy the decoy; they wouldn't have known what was going on. We almost took the lot out single-handed, but I guess it was as well the cavalry came over the hill. At least the other Privates will be able to bear out that we took down almost a fleet of the bastards: the legend of *Arianrhod* lives on!"

"Good being part of a legend," Dox mused equably.

"It sure is," the navigation officer responded smugly, preening.

"I see you're planning to use your tattered face to capture a few ales at some bar, once we make Merkat."

"Where's the point of taking a hit when you can't use it to your advantage?" Box grinned crookedly.

Ahxenta looked over at Apnis, who raised amused brows and winked. The captain smiled in response. The crew would be all right.

"What do these damn aliens want with the *Arianrhod*? They seem to keep picking on us," Box went on in a loud and complaining tone.

"Good question," the first mate put in softly.

"A toehold in the best ship in the PSS fleet, Mr Box," Ahxenta told him. "As a PSS we have our own ways and our own systems not open to outsiders and we have practically free rein to any port in the mapped galaxy. And *we're* being targeted because we haven't been taken in by alien influences or shot out of the sky by alien guns. They no doubt reckon if they can get us, they'll be able to take on the rest of the PSS fleet without any trouble."

"Reckoned wrong, didn't they, ma'am? And that's five Privates they've let slip through their fingers; if they have fingers, that is."

Tallica Apnis nodded. "Fingers, toes, eyes, noses, ears; and if they don't, they have others who have. You know, I bet that was why Micklemouse was slipped aboard a PSS in the first place," she added quietly to the captain. "Just his luck it happened to be us. Wonder how the little rodent and his playmate are?"

"To be honest, Tallica, I don't give a damn. Once we get to the Web and into their best repair dock, then I might give it a thought. Lindell's sorting our docking and repair schedule and the transfer of what was to be our next shipment to another carrier. Grey's said he'll take it on if the clients and suppliers agree: *Obsidian's* here to pick up a cargo and he can add it in and drop it on the way to his next stop. And Flintlock's arranging medical transports to meet us and ferry our worst injured to Merkat's medical facilities as soon as we're in dock."

"What do *we* do when we ship into the Web?" Dox asked of her companion in a low voice.

"We head for shore leave is what we do," Box returned.

"Best idea he's had for a while," acknowledged Ahxenta. "You have the conn, Tallica; I'll be in medbay."

There were a fleet of eyes watching as the blip that was the convoy slipped into Merkat space. The buzz had gone ahead that five private starships were heading in off the beacon and that had been enough to raise the curiosity of the most incurious. Dockers' Guild reps were foremost in the queue for a look: the best-equipped repair dock had been requested for one of the inbound vessels and two others had sent word that they needed refit, and as the Guild would be charged with costing the repairs, supplying the means and doing the work, it had a vested interest. The usual swarms of dock-rats were also there, hoping for extensive repair and refit options to be agreed, as business had slacked off. Many were rubbing their hands at the thought of the extra tariffs that could be levied, and the overtime that might result, if the damage was sufficiently serious to tie up several docks.

The call-signs had identified the ships as Merkat's Port Authority processed entry requests and provided the necessary clearances. A trio of medical shuttles departing the inner belt area had not escaped the watching eyes either.

"Looks like someone's taken a bad hit," one docker remarked to the colleague next to him.

"I'll say," agreed Kit Biernop, his brow creasing. "But look at the colour of that ship's hide, what's left of it, in the middle of the bunch!

I'm damned if it's not the *Arianrhod*! I've a mate aboard that ship!"

"What's he do on the *Arianrhod*?" the other asked, impressed.

"She; and it's none of your business. But if that *is* the *Arianrhod*, she's taken one hell of a pounding! Let me at that comm!"

Two habitués of the *Half Moon in a Puddle* in inner two had coaxed the on-duty bar-staff to tune into the local comms net that broadcast such regular comings and goings and were also watching avidly.

"*Five* pirates turning up at once, Malty! That makes seven here, all told," Jurry observed after a quick scan of the fingers of both hands.

"Six," Malty corrected. "*Urania* shipped out last night. But Djassi of the *Equinox* was still here as of an hour ago. It looks like the one in the middle's a bit beat up. Which one is it?"

"*Tallulah*?" Jurry guessed, taking a sip of ale.

"Don't make me laugh! When's she ever stood to fight so much as a loose cargo pod? And if she did, catch four of her mates escorting her in. And she's not that shade of pink, what you can see of it."

"That's the *Arianrhod* you're talking about," a voice behind them that both recognised as Ally the barman said.

He sounded grim as he scanned the holo-screen and both topers adopted similarly serious faces as a show of sympathy and in the fond hope that free ale might be forthcoming.

"What happened?" Malty asked with seemingly ingenuous eyes.

Ally looked at him in disgust. "She banged into a loose rock off Dryssicon Major, what'd you think happened?"

He jerked his head at the image above the counter. "Got into one damn doozie of a firefight someplace or other; and given the surface damage, there was a heck of a lot more of them against one of her."

"There's four other ships there," Jurry pointed out righteously.

"And nary a scratch between them, I'll bet," the barkeep scoffed.

"They've scrambled med shuttles and medbay's on standby to take in casualties," one of Ally's underlings said at his back. "Two off-duty paramedics in here have just been recalled. Reckon it was a bunch of these aliens that have been taking on half the galaxy recently?"

"Bloody hell, she's not even docked and the rumours are flying!" Ally exclaimed in exasperation. "Get back to work. We'll find out in due course. And you two, mind your tongues. One day they'll get you into serious trouble if you're not careful."

"Hasn't happened yet!" Malty said jauntily to the retreating form.

The largest repair dock had been made ready to take in the crippled starship and as the docking struts were delicately deployed, Ahxenta breathed a sigh, if not of relief then at least of accomplishment. As they waited, each link was made until the ship was finally stabilised at station-keeping with an audible grinding of massive gearing.

"All green! Docking completed, Cap. The structure's steady and she maintaining her own," Cottontail called out, having supervised the procedure. "Permission to head to engineering and make sure the repair reps don't put their noses in where they're not wanted?"

"Granted, but make sure you take time out once you're done," the captain told her. "I'll have to see the Guild reps and start organising priorities for repair and resupply," she said to Apnis. "Flintlock and her staff are dealing with the urgent med casualties, but once all our injured are receiving proper care, Tallica, I want you to arrange leave. We'll need a skeleton crew in place at all times, but see if you can work out a rota that will give everyone time portside."

"On it," the first mate said. "You'll be at the top of my list."

"She'll ignore you," came the voice of Box from his station.

"And you'll be at the bottom," Apnis threatened as the bridge door closed behind the commanding officer.

Ahxenta's first stop was to check up on the status of her wounded crewmen. Medbay was far from its usual calm efficiency and she was hustled aside as a gurney with an inertia pod aboard pushed past.

"Two more to come and that'll be the first shuttle load!" the voice of Dr Zaiklyn Oak cut through the unusual racket. "That's one of the worst," he added softly to the captain. "Ensign Rob Lacewing, one of Chief Cottontail's. He got caught in a backblast when the forr'ad hull sections blew. Severe head trauma and he'll need a new arm, but he'll make it. Dr Flintlock's in iso-lab three: we're using it as a mini-theatre to treat minor surgical cases. Dr Ma'Lappis is dealing with the active walking wounded from a wheelchair in one of the side bays: she says there's nothing wrong with her brain or her arms so she may as well make herself useful. I've indented for more med supplies but so far zip. I'd hoped the shuttles would have had the sense to come loaded. Excuse me, Captain, I'd best get back to my patients."

Stopping only long enough to link through to her supercargo and get him on the case of additional medbay supplies, Ahxenta made for one of the side bays that housed the smaller craft used for personnel transport. Her heading was the main offices of the Dockers' Guild, located in the large habitation unit of outer belt nine, which dealt with the routine running of the main docking and repair facilities.

Ahxenta was greeted cordially: given the mess of her ship and her reputation, the local Guild worthies were in high hopes of a detailed account of the action that would earn them free meals when poured into the ears of their mates later. They were disappointed, as the captain had no time for chitchat. Her priorities for their Guild were the repair of her ship, the time it would take and the cost. As she pulled up detailed schematics of the damage and told them what she expected by way of *Arianrhod's* restoration to peak condition, half her hearers were amazed that she had managed to bring her into port at all. The other half was carefully calculating how much profit could be made on the refit, given that *Arianrhod* had nowhere else to go.

Well aware of how matters stood, Ahxenta was careful to press the point of where she had been attacked and the closeness of the Merkat system and all its prize facilities to the zone of hostility, which seemed to be expanding outwards. Ships of the size and integrity of the *Arianrhod* and her peers would be useful allies should the aliens turn their eyes in Merkat's direction and the quicker that agreement could be reached, the better. And as the Privates had been hauled into ISP service, the mighty ISP would no doubt extend the use of its own shipbuilding dock off Skyrtek Prime if necessary. Her trump card was the supply of meta-jurillium hull sheets that she was carrying: they might not cover all her necessary hull repairs but they would go a long way to making a rapid start.

Whilst the bickering over time-schedules and costs was underway, Commander Apnis called to request the captain's return aboard as soon as possible: an urgent appeal from ISP Central had come in for a closed meeting on the events at Mellifly. Ahxenta excused herself firmly and made for her shuttle without delay. She linked through to her first mate, commending the timing of the call.

Apnis shook her head warningly. "Don't gloat too soon, Cap: the caller was Colonel Ellin Myrtleberry."

"Pity we couldn't detect if we were talking to an enemy agent over a closed comm link," the captain grumbled, once she had digested the import of Myrtleberry's call.

"I bet Azular's working on it in his spare time," Apnis laughed lightly. "You calling him into this meeting?"

"You bet. She's asked for all my senior officers, but if she thinks she can say jump and we will, she's barking at shadows. She may just want to make sure there are witnesses on our side, or she wants us all in one place. I'll be having Bellfish monitor us in any case. You'll be there and so will Cottontail but that's it. Flintlock can't be spared as she's needed in medbay, Earbleat has plenty to do with the weapons, security is up to its ears and our tactical nets are scuppered – and as Snow and Larai are both on the casualty list, Gliss's team is down."

The colonel wanted clarification of what had happened at Mellifly. Word had come in from unnamed sources that a covert shipbuilding yard masquerading as a typical repair dock had been utterly destroyed by a single huge ship. That ship had been identified as the *Arianrhod*. Significantly, just after the conflagration, a fair number of anonymous vessels had been reported leaving the planet itself without providing forwarding addresses. Rumour had it that the *Arianrhod* had struck at what was believed to be a major base of hostile activity and had taken out a substantial proportion of enemy hardware. The port authorities at Mellifly were busily claiming blamelessness allied to ignorance, free trade being their justification, and lack of adequate resources as their excuses for being ignorant of the size and complexity of the structure on their doorstep. They were carrying out enquiries and the ISP had sent in two ships to investigate, whose results were awaited.

"*Arianrhod* is going to be so popular in hostile circles after all this that they'll be asking us for autographs before they blow us to hell," Apnis opined when she had heard the colonel's recitation.

"Be that as it may," Myrtleberry retorted. "May I ask what you were doing there and what happened? It *was* the *Arianrhod*, I take it?"

"It was," Ahxenta confirmed and carried on with details of their contract with the shifty Metal-Corp Industries of Jurgall Three, their equally furtive customers with no better descriptor than Orbital Repair Facility Polaris X-4, and the bare bones of the initial conflict.

"So you suspected it was a trap, Captain?" asked Myrtleberry.

"Of course I suspected it was a trap! With the pay offered and the lack of competition, they wanted *us* there. I wanted to know why and hoped to find out. But they tried to take us down before I could ask."

"Tried and failed."

"Tried and paid the price," Ahxenta crisply corrected. "Can you tell me why I was the target?"

"Jurgall Three is a Friskianx League outpost." The reply was tardy and was evidently not the first thought in the colonel's mind.

"That's not a reason and you know it. They're there to trade their meta-jurillium and are by repute a minor operation, yet there was one frigging lot of shipbuilding going on in the small area we could scan. We were given a fixed beam to come in on, every berth other than ours was posted off-limits and we were scanned from every possible angle. They sent tactical drones in as back-up, the cargo was delivered by grapple drones and we were sent speedily on our way on the same beam we had come in on. As that so-called repair facility at Mellifly was an enemy shipbuilding yard, according to your sources, it could be that Jurgall Three is a source of enemy supplies of meta-jurillium."

Myrtleberry pursed her lips. "You have a point."

"And you haven't answered my question: why was my ship the target?" Ahxenta repeated.

"I don't know," the woman said at last, veiling her eyes. "But you are well-known for your – unorthodox – methods and you seem to be able to deliver whatever the obstacles."

"You're mistaken. In fact I've just had to give up rather a lucrative cargo as my ship is in no fit state to transport it."

"I *had* heard that the *Arianrhod* had been badly damaged. How badly? I do have another mission that I had in mind for you."

"Forget it!"

"That's not the attitude. I'll remind you, Captain, that the Trades Alliance has confirmed that we can call on the independents that fly under their flag."

"That old song about threatening to take away our flag!" Ahxenta spat out, incensed. "I suggest you check with Merkat Port Authority, Colonel; I'm sure they'll be more than happy to fill you in on the reasons why my ship is at this moment unable to leave her berth."

"You met with stiff opposition at Mellifly, I take it?"

"They sent *six* damn ships after us!" Apnis cut in, unable to keep silent. "A third of our crew can't even stand up! And half of them are in Merkat's medbay."

"Belay that, Commander!" Ahxenta growled as Myrtleberry's eyes widened fractionally.

"If there is anything I can do to assist you, Captain?" the colonel said smoothly into the awkward silence.

"You can. We need weapons and other supplies that the Merkat yards are hard put to source. In view of the support the *Arianrhod* has rendered the ISP, it's a small return. I can link you a list."

The first mate's small snicker at the outraged expression did little to calm the colonel down, but she agreed to see what she could do and hurriedly cut out, saying she would be in touch.

"A small return?" Tallica Apnis repeated archly. "Think she will?"

"I think she's considering it, though she might send the bill with it. Azular, your thoughts?"

"She wanted your version of events, Captain. She already knows what happened at Mellifly, although perhaps not the specifics. She wants to know how you did it, but didn't want to ask outright."

"You think she suspects that her conversations are being bugged or she's being watched?"

"Possibly. Her body language suggested that. That we were faced with six attacking ships after our actions at Mellifly *did* surprise her I think. The fact that we survived probably surprised her even more."

"You didn't say much, Crizz?"

The chief engineer paused, her mouth pursed, shaking her head as she raised her finger. "I don't like that woman, never have, since first she invaded my ear space. But I've listened to the noises of engines, good, bad, indifferent for most of my life and I can tell if they're sound, damaged, in pain or just in need of a good oiling. And that's a woman in trouble and desperate to tell us something. I'd listen more to what she didn't say than what she did. I'd have Lynxi Bellfish and the best ship's psychologist go over every photon of that record."

The science officer had been listening and nodded in agreement. "There *is* a difference to the last time I spoke with her. I wonder who or what her unnamed sources are, the ones who identified *Arianrhod* as the attacking ship. If the installation was completely destroyed, few records would remain except those in alien hands, and they wouldn't be available to the colonel."

"And anonymous ships leaving Mellifly itself in droves? The bad guys running for cover, you think, or just getting ready for the next phase of the fight?" queried Apnis. "Or heading here to take us out while we're incapacitated."

"They'd need to take out Merkat first and it's far too valuable a resource for them to do that, given its size and importance," Ahxenta said. "But Crizz is talking sense. If Myrtleberry knows or suspects her comms are being bugged, she wouldn't pass on anything she knew or suspected on any channel. I'd like to know if it was her own idea to contact us, or someone else's. And if it was someone else's, that means someone higher up the chain in the ISP Council."

It was as the four were deliberating on the various echelons of the ISP and where leaks or infiltration would do most damage as far as they were concerned when Bellfish interrupted with the news that an urgent call, marked immediate and on a high priority coded channel, had come through for the captain from Admiral Zillah at Freskat.

"Hell! I seem to be more popular than a month of shore leave!" she muttered as she dismissed her officers and prepared to listen.

Whatever the results of her talk with Zillah, the captain was giving nothing away. She was extremely busy, the reports that were coming in relating to her crew, her ship and her access to resources taking up all her free time. On top of that, the planetary authorities on the Merkat home world and other less august bodies were clamouring for a word, given the proximity of Kifferbuck and the vast amounts of potentially salvageable material that was probably still drifting around there as a result of the firefight. Two days had passed before she was able to look above the level of her desk.

The first mate and the chief engineer were set to meet Lindell and the supercargo of the *Obsidian Sky* in the main marketing suite of the inner belts to discuss final arrangements with marketing reps for the transfer of their next cargo to their sister ship. Ahxenta had hoped to be present but a small explosion in the trading centre had resulted in an enforced delay to the schedule and the captain had decided to stay on board and then catch a lift on the last med-shuttle heading out to Merkat's medbay. The shuttle was set to transport the final patients for transfer to the Web's superior medical amenities. This would give Ahxenta the chance to visit her people already there and to check their progress with the local medics.

The reason for the trading centre explosion was baffling and the words *sabotage* and *alien retribution* were being bandied about, but the remains of an amateurish device had been found and the blame for overlooking it in the first place had been slapped squarely on Merkat Three's security. The members of that body had acted to amend their lapse and had cranked up their presence to the extent that Cottontail declared that they were hanging about the main marketing suite like a bunch of unwanted guests at a funeral, sizing up the estate of the deceased. As she and Apnis strolled into the small room off the main suite that had been assigned them they spotted their associates sitting alongside each other on an upended cabinet by the wall. All the room's furniture seemed to be askew. As they greeted Lindell and his opposite number from the *Obsidian Sky*, they noticed the rotund behind of a repair tech protruding from a large, low cubbyhole into which she was peering with intent.

"Looking for the way to the next level down?" Apnis enquired.

The tech's head appeared at the sound. "Looking for the holo-console that marketing swore was in here. They have client link-ups to make and some systems are still out of commission."

"Marketing really is flavour of the month: messing up bookings, missing trade openings, charging us over the odds. They seem to be run by Mizzle and Fizzle, the laugh-a-minute leprechauns."

"At least the catering console's online. Help yourself to something hot, ma'am," the operative invited. "I'll get the table set up."

"The repair crews will have a field day getting this place back to spec," Cottontail sniffed as she lent a hand to right a pair of chairs. "It shouldn't take too long, though; the damage looks cosmetic. Hope the damn coffee dispenser's working."

"Where are these marketeers we're supposed to be dealing with?" Apnis wondered.

"This small bang's scared them off no doubt," the engineer said as the two in question flew through the door. "Where's that coffee?" she added. "I've had a busy day already and it's getting no easier."

In the event, the transfer of cargo manifests and the obligatory clearances were arranged ably and without dissent. Lindell was a born diplomat and his counterpart from the *Obsidian* competent, forceful, and what was more important, in a hurry. The wreck of the timetable had incommoded him no end and he was eager to return to his ship. As soon as business was settled he shot out of the door like a shuttle off a pad. The two marketing reps cleared their throats, shuffled their info-pads and disappeared likewise.

"That's that," *Arianrhod's* first mate said, dusting her hands down her uniform. "Where to now, Chief? Lindell? That didn't take as long as I'd anticipated."

"I vote we head to the *Half Moon*. It should be quiet at this time of day," was Cottontail's opinion.

"You wish. The *Half Moon's* never quiet except when Ally shuts the doors after he's shooed the last barfly out and set the silencers. But drink up your dregs and let's get on over," decided Apnis. "The Cap came in on the last med-facility shuttle run and should be about done by now. I'll let her know and we could meet her there. You up for that, Lindell?"

"As long as you don't start any fights, I'll follow you anywhere there might be a jar of ale going," he smiled.

"No promises, but I'll do my best," she grinned back.

Ally was more than pleased to see them. Ever since the *Arianrhod* had hauled into the Web rumours had abounded and he had not been able to collar one member of her crew that would enlighten him as to what had actually happened. Three schooners of beer were set out on the counter by the time the three pairs of elbows had settled likewise.

"We heard you took out an alien fleet single-handed," the barman began after greetings and commiserations on the extent of damage to ship and crew. "They say there are scavengers headed to Kifferbuck to try to pick up profit already. So come on. These are on the house, by the way – as long as you give me the lowdown, or as much as Captain Ahxenta will let you."

There were other curious eyes that had noted the insignia borne by the three and their ears told them they had an audience, albeit a discreet one: no-one with sense would mess with any of the crew of the *Arianrhod*. Attention was cranked up moments later by the advent of her commander as she strode through Ally's hospitable holo entry.

"Got here then, Cinnabar?" the first mate greeted her, noting the tired but satisfied eyes. "Our people doing okay?"

"Okay," Ahxenta echoed, scooping up with a nod of thanks the jar of beer that Ally had produced at lightning speed.

"So, Captain," the barman began, settling comfortable elbows on the countertop. "Let's hear what you would like me to spread around the inner belts about your latest exploits."

"You will – as long as you get your chef on board with four hot plates of the best you have on offer and a private booth where we can eat without all these flies on the wall picking up every whisper."

"Done and done," was the swift response as her crewmen looked at their senior officer shrewdly.

They could tell when something was up.

22: REBUILDING THE BOAT

Once the four had come to rest in a large booth with a good view of
the door and no-one at their backs, Apnis asked the reason for the
early lunch and its hardly private setting. The captain only smiled and
began by outlining the current health of their most badly injured crew
and the treatment and time required for their recovery. Once the
food had arrived via the service hatch, Ahxenta pulled out a jammer
and set it purposely on the table, just in case, she pointed out, that
tables had ears. The *Arianrhod* certainly had: a number of concealed
data logging devices had been uncovered by her security officers and
traced to repair crews from Merkat that had hoped to exchange them
with news-hungry journalists on the trail of a story.

"Confiscated their hardware, boxed their ears and sent them back
with the suggestion that they apply for assignments elsewhere. But
this concerns you, mostly, Lindell: the call from Admiral Zillah."

"Ah! I wondered when we'd hear about that," Tallica Apnis broke
in. "She had news?"

"She had the offer of high energy torpedoes, pulse cannon energy
bolts, crates of deflecting and repair drones and any spare parts for
our weapons arrays that we might need."

"What!" breathed the first mate. "But her call came minutes after
our less than polite discussion with Myrtleberry!"

"Myrtleberry called *her*. Apparently said that she couldn't supply
our needs for the next mission we had for the ISP and asked Zillah as
a favour to find out our requirements and see what she could do."

"Zillah bought it?"

"Zillah was highly suspicious and called me to find out what the
hell was going on. I told her in very few words what had happened
but I didn't tell her our suspicions of high-level infiltration in the ISP
Council. I didn't have to; I got the impression she'd figured it. Said
she'd see what she could and asked for the list. I gave her it and told
her we'd no credit to pay for any of it. I've had confirmation that the
shipment will be here in ten days. It'll be listed as urgent medical
supplies in the manifest and will come in on a regular fleet transport,
though there'll be covert military assist. That's where you come in,

Lindell. Have your people keep an eye out and make sure nobody has the opportunity to scan it. Not that they should be able to as it'll be a pair of meta-jurillium plated cargo pods, which will be assigned to us. As the payload will have ISP clearances it should be okay, but take no chances. I'll give you the coding details once we're back aboard."

"You mentioned a next mission for the ISP, Cap?" Cottontail pointed out. "We don't have one."

"I mentioned *that* to Zillah. Her response was she thought we did. By that and her expression I gathered that she was hinting that we do our damnedest to see if we can find out anything about how far the ISP has been compromised – and do something about it."

"Great! Now we're mole-hunters for the blasted ISP! And when are we supposed to set off on this latest mission? We that don't have a ship that can fire as much as a pot!" the engineer hissed furiously.

"But we do have a large arms shipment with our name on it on its way that we haven't been billed for," Ahxenta said crisply. "Until it arrives, I want every crew member that's still fit to get in some shore leave. And everyone left aboard that can be spared will be drafted in as security to keep an eye on those dock-rats to make sure we have no more unwelcome additions or subtractions to the ship."

"I've got a mate in the Guild that got me into the shift that did the repairs on those Friskie boats," Apnis reminded her. "I'll put in for shore leave and scout him out on the QT to see if he can shed any light on the goings-on. He hangs out in the *Port in a Storm* on green six when he's off duty. You'd best take time out as well, Cinnabar. You need it as much as the rest of us. And as your second, you *do* realise I can get you classed as medically unfit and make you."

"You've convinced me. Once I've treated Grey and Sarie to the drinks I promised for their help at Kifferbuck. *Obsidian's* set to leave in a few hours and the *Comet* won't be far behind. I hear her repairs are near done. Crizz, I'll need you to stay aboard awhile, until the energy cell emplacement in engineering is back to full capacity."

"You don't think I'd let those amateurs from Merkat's dockyards loose on my engineering decks without me at their backs do you? That'll be the day!"

Two days later found *Arianrhod's* first mate in the *Port in a Storm* trying to have a quiet drink with her old friend Kit Biernop. The bar was remarkably busy, having been chosen as a handy refreshment stop by a bunch of bewildered ex-passengers from the luxury pleasure cruiser *Velvet Emerald*. She had had to make a run for Merkat to escape what had been classed as enemy activity near Beta Zegonia 68c and which had knocked out half the ship's systems. Their cruiser had docked in the outer belts to lick her wounds and her passengers, wary of the rough company there, had set up camp in the more salubrious inner belts. Now in the *Port in a Storm*, they were out to calm shattered nerves by sampling the local brews before finding transport to their various home planets at the expense of the luxury cruise company.

Hostile attacks were said to be rising, recent losses to their fleet only serving to piss the aliens off, was Kit Biernop's opinion. He had spoken to several pilots who had seen a slump in their livelihoods in the tourist sector and elsewhere as trade diminished and had thus cast up at Merkat to hunt for jobs. The latest rumour was that the Allied Powers, at the behest of the ISP, had listed Jurgall Three as off-limits to all but military ships in an effort to cut meta-jurillium quotas and close down enemy supply lines. Apnis snorted in disgust.

"All that'll do is give the hostiles a quiet spell to bolster supplies and make ready for whatever mischief is next on their agenda!"

"Well, two newly-rigged Protectorate ships called the *Protector* and the *Crusader* have been sent to Jurgall to keep a blockade going," Kit told her. "The *Protector* was docked here once; I remember the name."

Apnis also recalled the name. "Who told you that? The ISP don't usually publicise the names of the ships they send into war zones."

"A pilot that had been on a run between Alto Finglas and the ISP construction docks at Skyrtek," Kit told her softly. "It seems that the Trades Alliance at Finglas and the ISP are in close contact over the boat building industry. Trying to get more ships out that'll cope with the firepower these aliens seem to have, that pilot reckoned. He was over this way on a contract he couldn't talk about, so I didn't press the issue. He's gone now. But I guess your crew could give the ISP a lot more useful tips on how to tackle these aliens than most?"

The commander was not about to discuss private ship's business in an open arena like the *Port in a Storm* and turned the talk to the attempted bugging of sections of the *Arianrhod* by repair personnel appointed by the Dockers' Guild. Biernop was extremely concerned and promised to try and find out more. It was some time later that Apnis returned to her temporary lodgings in a snug dormitory wing of green level four. The hour was late but she decided that a talk with her commanding officer was in order, if she was available.

The restful setting of apartment twenty five's sizable bathroom was salve to the soul, Ahxenta sighed as she sank into the pure luxury of real water. The translucent blue-green sunken tub resembled a white sand-bottomed marine lagoon that she had once visited on Hespera Two, as the iridescent coral-pink rippled surface of the walls around her reflected myriad shards of crystal clear light and a gentle steam of sweet-smelling vapour rose around her in waves from the bubbling water. She closed her eyes and breathed deeply, allowing her mind to float into space and away from the cares of the past days. She could afford to: Apnis had insisted on posting guards outside the door and her apartment was festooned with an assortment of alarms.

It was not long, however, before, the present intruded into her busy brain and she regretfully brought herself back to wakefulness at the sound of the summons from the external comm. As she hauled herself out of the bathtub and into the folds of a luxurious drying robe, she called out her responses, telling her second to come on in.

"Sorry, Cap, I didn't realise you were in the tub. You should've stayed there."

"I'd have been a wrinkled prune if I had," Ahxenta replied as she stretched out to grab a towel. "Help yourself to a drink. What gives? I take it you had a… what in hell have you been doing? You've a cut to your face and patches that look like they'll be bruises by morning."

"Long story and I'll get something to cut the swelling shortly. But I did manage a few words with my chum Kit Biernop and thought I'd better pass them on. There *are* a bunch of new faces out in the repair shops as a lot of regulars are trying to make it home as hostilities are getting closer; and traffic flow into the Web's increasing at a rate of knots because ships caught out in the space lanes don't want to risk the smaller stops in case they're targets. So Port Authority and ID checks are not as tight as they were, hence our troubles with dock-rats and repair dudes trying to take advantage. But Kit reckons that two ISP ships have been posted to Jurgall Three as a blockade to halt traffic in and out. Boats called *Protector* and *Crusader* no less."

"The *Protector*? Myrtleberry's old ride? And the *Crusader*? She was hardly fit to be a colander when we saw her last. And they're now blockading Jurgall Three?" Ahxenta exclaimed. "That'll help!"

"That's what I thought, if it's true. They must be two of many, as two ships couldn't blockade what we saw there. What other bodies are represented Kit didn't know. But the name *Arianrhod* is being bandied about as being responsible for taking out an alien fleet, only she lost her captain and most of her hull in the process. There's also a whole heap of hogwash that makes it sound like the Privates are carrying out their own little war. Which is making the TA uneasy to the extent of thinking of revoking our flag."

"Nice to know I'm dead," Ahxenta returned with a grin. "But the TA wouldn't dare: the whole PSS fleet will tell them to go hang. But if I'm supposed to have bought it, who told? Whoever organised that set up at Mellifly were the only ones who knew that I'd agreed to go down to their fake offices to talk to them in person and then blew up the shuttle they thought I was on."

"That's what struck me. Your being here of course gives the lie to the whole story. But something sure leaked out from the very shifty Orbital Repair Facility Polaris X-4 before we blew it to hell that got as far as Merkat. I'm posting an extra security detail at your door."

"Are you hell. If they were that keen, they'd have got me before now. Go get your face looked at and I'll see you in the morning."

The *Half Moon in a Puddle* was strangely quiet next morning although breakfast time for many residents of the inner belts was passing. Ally put it down to new reports of hostile activity near Beta Zegonia and the fate of the *Arianrhod* only days before at Kifferbuck. Two usual hangers-on were, however, seated by the far wall but close enough to the bar to take swift advantage of anyone who might come in.

"Some chatter-merchants have been quick to profit hunt and are trying to make a few pocketsful out of these alien attacks," Jurry, with the authority of four jars of ale, informed his mate. "Heard tell there was one smartarse trying his luck on a good-looker that he thought came off the *Velvet Emerald*, that fancy cruise liner that ducked into Merkat to hide from the baddies; he figured she might pony up a few credits for some of his souvenirs."

"What souvenirs?" Malty demanded truculently. "Selling souvenirs to tourists is my stock in trade!"

"He should've made his something else," Jurry chuckled throatily. "After the flea in his ear and the sock on his snout, he got a boot up his arse that sent him flying out the door of the *Port in a Storm*."

"You what? Why?"

"You don't pick on dames you don't know in the *Port in a Storm*, especially when they're Tallica Apnis in mufti and you're trying to sell her what you claim are bits of shrapnel that came off the *Arianrhod*."

"Some people never learn, do they, Jurry my lad?"

"Nope. Not that that ended it, mind: he had a couple of heavy friends. But then so did Apnis. Quite a night. Let's find somebody's ear to bend with it and they might cough us up a couple of jars."

"Maybe not the two that have just come in," Malty said hastily, squinting at the door. "Eyes down and don't make any fast moves."

"Hardly a scratch," Jurry noted, ignoring his friend to furtively scrutinise the two newcomers. "Ahxenta's looking fit as well."

"*You* won't be if she catches you staring."

The two uniformed officers scanned the near-empty space as they made for the bar to order their meals and have a word with the host.

"Quiet this morning, Ally," Ahxenta noted.

"Quieter than the *Port in a Storm* was last night, so I hear."

"News travels fast," Apnis shrugged. "All this alien bucket-stirring bad for business then?"

"That's about the truth of it I reckon. Two for breakfast is it, or are you expecting company?"

"Just two," the captain said. "And quickly, we have a lot to do."

Soon after breakfast, Ahxenta and Apnis set off down to green three and the Web's main medbay. Two of their injured crew were due to be released and Ahxenta was keen to check on their fitness for duty. Dr Flintlock had gone over earlier and was to meet them there.

"Wonder how much they'll charge?" asked Apnis. "There was a bit of resculpting to do on Strawberry and Hanx took a nasty hit."

"I've already had the bill *and* paid part of it," the captain told her. "They wanted a deposit up front, so I didn't have much option. And let's face it, they were better in a decent med facility than on the *Arianrhod*. We're still as full of holes as a sieve."

"Getting there; and at least they've started welding the hull plates. Cottontail's crew are on their toes and every jack of the rest is doing their bit, though Earbleat's planning a new *Loki* using one of Zillah's promised cargo pods. And Azular's hidden scanners all over the place to keep an eye on dodgy dock-rats. But we'd better not get hit again: our insurers will scream that we're not covered for random acts of violence and our pockets can only take so much."

Dr Axellina Flintlock was happy to report that Ensigns Hanx and Strawberry were fighting fit and eager to get back on board. Medbay food was less than appetising, she reckoned, and that had a lot to do with it. Their other injured personnel were mending, a few slowly and one at least, Lake, would never be fit for active service again.

Ahxenta pursed her lips. "Let's see them. Tallica, check with Ally and tell him to bill me for two late breakfasts. We'll send Hanx and Strawberry over there once they're out and they can hang fire until our next shuttle heads up. At least Lake was due to retire soon and we can make sure his future's secure, but it's a hell of a way to leave a life of service in space. Those damn hostiles are going to pay a heavy price if ever I clap eyes on them again."

"We've got a ship to get into trading and fighting trim first. And resupply's going to be a problem even with our load coming in from Lambda, since Lindell's two down in his office, including Pinkhorn."

Flintlock gave a sly wink. "I've two crates of med supplies heading back with me. They're surplus as they've been classed as out of use due to faulty labelling; but there's nothing wrong with them. It pays to have good friends in every port."

"It does," the captain agreed wryly. "If your good friends need a tip, see Lindell: I'll authorise it."

"Affirmative, Cap. This way to the discharge lounge."

Ahxenta and Apnis were back aboard earlier than expected as Azular had linked to request an urgent briefing. His tone and face suggested sooner rather than later and the two, with Dr Flintlock in tow, took the next shuttle back up. The science officer had a holo set up when the three arrived. One of his hidden scanners in a small pocket of engineering had struck gold, he informed them as they sat, and he invited them to look closely at the recording. The image of two blue-suited repair operatives deftly replacing the contents of a blown-out energy housing in one of the bulkheads sharpened into clarity as their conversation, majoring in their off-duty plans, echoed clearly.

"They've tampered with the circuits?" Flintlock enquired.

"No. I had Chief Cottontail check their work when they'd done. No; it's this tall one with the dark red hair and the twisted mouth."

"I've seen that face before," Ahxenta noted harshly. "In the dark."

"My scans show he's Friskianx and that he has cyber implants, but then so have many dock and shipyard workers — it goes with the job. But his are extensive *and* they're emitting tracking signals. My analysis isn't detailed, but I'm pretty sure the pattern of the implants and the signals match those we've come to associate with alien alteration."

"It's a long way from Xerophyte IV to here," said Apnis. "But if he's not done anything, we can't get him pulled in for an interview."

"We can keep an eye on him and see who he contacts," Flintlock pointed out. "If he's Blue Shift, or whatever, he'll be back."

"It certainly looks like *Arianrhod* is being closely monitored. Why do they keep it up?" Apnis grimaced. "You'd think by now they'd have learnt to leave well alone."

"They want to know how we keep getting the better of them and what we have that other ships don't have," the captain told her.

"That's easy: a good crew with a vested interest in our business; a sound command structure; and let's face it, a crew that most military units would pass up as too maverick to keep under control," the first mate pointed out. "In other words, troublemakers. And as they're all uncommonly smart troublemakers, it works to our advantage. And of course we have the best ship in the fleet."

"I note you didn't mention the best commanding officer in the fleet," Ahxenta returned. "But you have a point. Now, what to do about our twist-mouthed spy…"

"Easy," Apnis said swiftly. "We set him up."

Three days later found the captain down on inner two green four, in Merkat's newly-refurbished main marketing suite, having just left a meeting. Several info-points and drinks dispensers around the walls were undergoing repairs, as was evidenced by the numbers of blue-suited techs trying to look busy as they searched around in tool kits, abstracted components and applied them to relevant housings.

Ahxenta stacked her kitbags on a small corner table next to the room from which she had come and looked around as her first mate followed her out. Apnis tossed a pair of data shards across and the captain caught them adroitly, sliding them into a small pouch that she then pitched negligently onto the heap of her belongings.

"That's about all the info, Cap. Fancy a quick coffee before the next meet? If the dispensers are working yet, that is."

They sauntered over to a station two metres away and made a play of examining the available drinks. Beakers in hand, they stopped to talk to a couple of officials who had just come in, motioning back to the room both had recently left. Another meeting had broken up and several more people poured out, milled around and stood talking.

It had been too tempting and the pouch was gone when Ahxenta strode over to pick up her gear once the crowd had dispersed. She made pretence of searching the table and floor and then shrugged.

"Someone's taken the bait, then?" Apnis said quietly as she traded a glance with the captain and nodded once at Kit Biernop, who stood discreetly in a corner with two men in Merkat security uniforms.

"Looks like. We'll give them a minute or so to find a hidey hole to see what they've got and then home in. Got your phase rifle handy?"

"I've always got my phase rifle handy. Not to mention another few bits of kit I'd rather be this side of. Including a nifty knock-out hypo that leaves no traces."

"Good. I'll set this scanner off and see where it takes us," Ahxenta stated as she hefted her remaining bags onto her shoulder and led the way through the exit into the almost-empty corridor, the three others following at a distance.

The scanner led them to a door in a small, dingy dormitory wing three floors below marketing. The readings indicated one individual within but he was more resourceful than they had given him credit for. As the two halted, a secure-cam popped out a fraction above eye level and pivoted. The motion had caught Apnis' eye and she hauled the captain away from the door as a beam shot out from the central insignia to smack the opposing wall.

"Plays rough!" Ahxenta called as the three behind came running.

By that time the first mate had blasted the door's opening plate without result. Kit Biernop reached over, pulled the casing away and slid a small flat card into a slot. The door slid into the wall and one of the two guards raced in, bouncing sideways across the floor. The lone occupant had raised a weapon to fire at the intruder, which was time enough for Ahxenta and Apnis to head in. There was no time to talk and in seconds the five newcomers were examining the prone form of the red-haired man with the twisted mouth.

"Are you all right, Lieutenant Goldwash?" Ahxenta demanded as the first man in stood up and dusted himself off.

"Aye, ma'am. A bit of bruising, but the suit took the blast," the young man responded.

"You breed them tough on the *Arianrhod*," Biernop observed.

"We do," Apnis agreed. "Appreciate the help, Kit. Now I really owe you."

"You help clear scum like this Len Lokterix guy from Guild repair teams, so fair deal," he responded. "How many more do we have?"

"That's four to date, but *this* one we really want," the captain told him. "We'll see if we can get more out of him and pass it on to you. The others that the Web's security bods have in the cells are small fry and not dangerous. *He* is and he's coming with us, temporarily. We'll render him less dangerous and security can have him back."

"I'll leave you to it; I don't want to be late for my next shift. And I won't complain if he gets lost in transit," said Biernop as he slid out into the corridor.

"Shut the door, Hanx, and if any twitching noses are out there, tell them security has it in hand and ask for witnesses: that'll make sure nobody saw anything," Ahxenta ordered.

"I hope he's worth three days of our lives pretending to talk shop with a bunch of marketeers with more profit in their pockets than we have," Apnis grumbled. "I'm giving him a shot of Flintlock's hypo, I don't want him waking up and latching onto anything."

The captain was undoing her kitbags and setting pieces out. Once slotted together, they made a typical transport trolley for large pieces of technical kit, complete with relevant labels. The unconscious Friskianx was bundled up with little ceremony and sealed inside.

"Right, let's get back to the shuttle. Goldwash and Hanx, you stay here and go over every atom of this place. Send your scans direct to Dr Azular using encoded comms. And get out of those outfits before somebody realises you're not Merkat security. Tallica, call up Azular and Flintlock, tell them we have the goods and have them stand by."

The trip back to the *Arianrhod* was made without trouble and their booty soon safely secured in a heavily-guarded iso-bay in medbay. Now more familiar with the process, Flintlock was able to inactivate many of the man's cyber-inclusions and disable his tracking system. Azular verified that he was not an info-sent but his implants were irrefutably alien in origin. The science officer was also able to trace the origin of the elements of a couple of the man's internal parts to a small crystal components processing plant on Mellifly. Given their delicate nature, Azular inferred that it was likely they were implanted close to source. Reckoning that questioning the man might prove difficult, he also suggested his immediate incarceration in the brig.

Ahxenta had ordered a briefing of her senior officers after the captive had been interrogated. The captain had not taken part in the questioning, electing to assign that to those better able to handle it and more importantly, to those Lokterix was unlikely to have seen before. The man initially had no idea he was aboard a ship, having assumed that he was in a secure facility on Merkat, a conclusion given credibility by his current berth in the innermost cell of the brig and the attentions of personnel wearing convincing replicas of Merkat security uniforms who knew his name.

Lokterix in some ways was similar to their former unwanted guest, Micklemouse, in that he was sharper than he had at first appeared. As intimidation had had no effect on his captors, he tried bribery. That cutting no ice, he resorted to silence, and when left alone, prowled his cell checking every nook and cranny, taking note of the exit, the secure cams and the trappings in terms of comfort facilities and food hatches. He had soon realised that his systems had been tampered with, but threats of retribution falling on deaf ears, he fell to scanning his guards closely every time they entered the space. That led him to the conclusion that this was no ordinary cell and that he had been taken somewhere unfamiliar.

An in-depth examination of Lokterix' berth on Merkat had yielded nothing useful: it was virtually as clean as a whistle. He had recently arrived at the port and apart from standard clothing that could have been bought anywhere, the single shred of evidence the team found was a handgun with the mark of a producer from Salt Three, the only inhabited planet of Drosophila Two. When faced with this, and the information that he was known to have been on Xerophyte IV some months previously, the identity of his keepers and his location began to dawn and with them the implications for his personal safety.

Azular had initially taken a back seat at the session with Lokterix and had scented weakening. Pushing the advantage, he had faced the man with his alteration on Mellifly, bringing in inferences relating to his controllers after their forced exit from there. It had been a tense and long stint, but the results had produced much to think about.

"What it seems to boil down to," Ahxenta told her officers, "Is that Mellifly is, or was, one of the places that these hostiles used for converting suitable humans into tools they could use to further their own ends. Micklemouse told us of a private medical facility there that he had been taken to and Lokterix confirms it and that he wasn't the only one at the time. It looks like the Friskianx were targets as they're suitable physically and mentally. It also seems that Jurgall Three is a prime source of meta-jurillium and other supplies for the aliens, apart from their thieving them from elsewhere. But our scumbag in the brig did insinuate that it was by no means the only one and traffic across the mapped sectors takes in planets of the Drosophila systems, likely Xerophyte IV and Salt Three, for its transport. That suggests to me that further supply sources exist on the other side of the known galaxy from here, possibly out near the Starglass, since so much goes on there. He wouldn't be drawn on the Starglass, but he squirmed when alien activity in that area was mentioned and Azular reckons he knows there's something in it. More importantly, he also hinted at bases in unmapped space that the ISP and their allies would never find. I'm tempted to send you back in, Azular, and see what reaction mentions of sector sixteen of Beta and the Ginseng Nebula bring out. But he's sharp and I want him away from here when our Freskat cargo turns up. And he may have friends that are missing him."

"So what do we do now?" Cottontail asked. "I know what I'd do."

"What would you do?" Azular enquired curiously.

"Scramble his memory matrix to make him think he was in a fight, get him roaring drunk and send him back to where he came from in the next available ship. You could send him off as a medical case that needs sedation the whole trip," she added suggestively to Flintlock.

"Mention sector sixteen and the Ginseng, *then* set him up with new memories," Apnis suggested. "It worked on Micklemouse."

"So did our scare tactics but they're not working so well with this guy, he's a nasty piece of work," Earbleat put in. "But that could work both ways: give him the idea his masters have reneged on the deal and are out to get him and let him loose to get them. He seems to have a streak of paranoia in him anyway."

In the event, an allusion to sector sixteen produced only puzzlement and mention of the Ginseng caused only a flicker of recognition and a militant look that Azular interpreted as scant knowledge allied to a stubborn refusal to be intimidated. Lokterix was thus sent under by a trickle of morph gas introduced into his cell and reprogrammed with substitute memories of a short working shift and a trip to the *Green Diamond* to meet with associates who would not turn up. He was then escorted in a dazed state to that unsavoury den in the company of Azular and two security guards in heavy disguise. Plied with doctored ale, the Friskianx was left in a secluded corner with a supply of brew and enough credit to keep drinking. Ahxenta did not enquire too closely when her crewmen returned more cheerfully than when they had set out, and smelling strongly of sour beer.

Meanwhile, having been unable to obtain the names of other light-fingered sinners among the repair crews, Apnis reported to Biernop only that their erstwhile captive had been dealt with and would be best left alone. Any more would be passed on to security as and when they were spotted. She had other matters in hand. The delivery from Freskat had arrived early and was being transferred over. As the captain had ordered that every fraction of the two cargo pods was to be checked out before they got within half a kilometre of her ship, *Arianrhod's* duty crews were hauled in and set to work. The captain herself was busy: with a wink from the skipper of the Freskat delivery transport, a third, smaller cargo pod, carried over by him in his favourite shuttle, had been left for Ahxenta with the compliments of Admiral Zillah.

23: ARIANRHOD AWAKES

The small cargo pod sat like a hunk of metallic ice in a forr'ad shuttle bay. A gang of curious repair techs had been effectively scared off by Earbleat, who had scented treasure and was stalking the perimeter of the container with a scanner in each hand and a blaster at her side. Ahxenta had linked to Zillah to announce the arrival of the cargo and had had confirmation that an additional pod had been sent out with some necessaries. Earbleat took that to mean hand-weapons and was seriously excited, despite the dampening prognostications of Box, who suspected it might be the resources to fabricate new uniforms or something equally as mundane.

"Get on with it, if it reads clear," the captain instructed. "I'll want you to start unpacking our other pods, after every person that doesn't belong to *Arianrhod* clears these decks. And I'll want guards posted at every entry as well."

"Bloody hell!" the second mate exclaimed as the pod's outer hatch was unsealed and she deployed her scanners. "Comms and scanning arrays! And beauties at that!"

"Just make sure they're not scanning us," ordered Ahxenta. "I'll get Greffy to give you a hand as Azular's on shore leave."

Earbleat was momentarily distracted. "You persuaded Azular to take shore leave, Cap? That's a novelty!"

"He said it was shore leave. I didn't believe him," the captain told her. "I'll be in my office. Make sure Lindell and his people have the manifest that goes with this and tell them to check out every single atom for traceability. I don't want to be accused of knocking off brand new state-of-the-art military technology."

"Aye, aye, Cap!"

Lieutenant Pollux Gliss had the conn and Chief Cottontail, having refused furlough, was directing sundry Merkat repair teams who were still overhauling and realigning power and distribution conduits on practically every deck. It was Gliss who took the incoming call and he linked it through to the captain's office in some puzzlement.

"I have a message for you, Captain; it's hedged about with every security device and scrambling code to prevent interception that you can imagine and it's come one helluva long way and on a very tight beam. I think you should take it privately."

"Why, who's it from?"

"Bick Micklemouse."

"What! I take it you're not joking, Lieutenant?"

"No way, ma'am. It's not a direct link; it's been bounced around half the known galaxy."

"Put it through," Ahxenta directed. "You will not mention this to anyone outside the current bridge crew. And if one of them passes it on their pay will be docked for three months."

"Aye, aye, ma'am. You got that people?" he added to his openly earwigging colleagues.

"My mouth is sealed," Box announced virtuously.

"The only thing that seals your mouth is a very large donut," Dox muttered. "But this time you'd better stay shtum or the Cap'll have your arse in a sling. And she'll charge you for the sling."

A short time later the captain called a briefing. Most of those present were reluctant, having been hauled away from their own matters, but the news was short and to the point. Once Cottontail had given over guffawing, Ahxenta called for serious opinions from her officers.

"I agree it doesn't deserve much attention, but given the trouble he's gone to in contacting us, it's either a massively clever ruse or he's in earnest. And he's not massively clever, as Azular would attest if he were here. And Doosbak doesn't seem to figure in what's going on."

"He wants to help us spot an alien when we meet one and says he knows how? He wants off Kelfennig is what he wants," the first mate said. "Doosbak's maybe not the good company he thought. How did he work out that traces of this zukivianite stuff will differentiate a hostile from one of their altered pawns? What *is* zukivianite anyway?"

Greffy was scanning his info-pad with a questing finger. He had never heard of it. "It was named for its discoverer, a chemist working with an archaeological expeditionary team many years ago. They were probing remnants of ancient civilisations in worlds beyond the outer edges of settled space."

"Which edges?" Ahxenta demanded crisply.

"The edges of zones Epsilon and Zeta."

Earbleat whistled piercingly. "Now isn't that a coincidence?"

"Too much of one, if you ask me," Cottontail remarked. "Our pet rodent's had help: the question is whose."

"It makes some sense if the aliens hail from these regions," Greffy put in. "I can't find references to the material from any of our other sources. It's a rare metallo-silicate that's been recorded on only two worlds in that area of space and if it's present as part of the physical makeup of these aliens independent of the cybernetic components they use on others, it's a possibility."

"So's snow on Hespera Two in high summer," Apnis shot back. "Point one, how do we test it? Point two, even assuming it's correct, what do we do about it? We couldn't pass on anything we got out of Lokterix and we sure as hell can't pass *this* on as some mole would intercept it and these hostiles would soon find out."

"Sorry, Axellina, this is your area of expertise. Once Azular gets back from whatever the heck he's up to, he can lend a hand to see if you can configure some sort of sensor to detect this zukivianite when it's allied to cyber-organic physiology. Greffy's needed elsewhere: I want these super-fast components that Zillah sent us up and running as soon as maybe and without anybody belonging to Merkat knowing about it, ditto our new weapons supplies."

"You trust this information that Micklemouse sent, Cap?" the first mate asked, a frown furrowing her brow.

"I'm using the data I have at my disposal."

"You won't send him a thanks and we'll see you soon, will you?"

"Like hell. I've ordered no response to the link, the record that we received it has been wiped and it's stored on a triple-secured shard. As far as you're concerned we've not heard from Micklemouse for a long time and we've no idea where he is or what he's doing. You stay and check over these inventories, Tallica. Everybody else, dismissed."

Once the coast was clear, the first mate spoke. "Inventories?"

"Convenient fib. You're right, we can't pass on any information we've squeezed from our recent meets with nasty people because we don't know how many outside organisations have been infiltrated nor how deeply, the risk being if the hostiles find out they stop us and they get around any weaknesses they apparently have. It's likely that Mellifly, Jurgall Three and two of the Drosophila systems have been infiltrated, and maybe other Friskianx League systems. The Ginseng's a part of it and possibly so's sector sixteen of Beta, though that got no reaction out of Lokterix. And if Micklemouse is right, this last one's a doozie. Which leaves us with a problem."

"How we take action on it," Apnis nodded. "Nobody'll pay us to go looking for aliens and then sorting them out, even if we could, though Admiral Zillah seems to think we have the savvy. Why else is she giving us presents that the ISP would never sanction, even if we could save its pants?"

"Now that's what I'd like to find out, that and other things. Which means a trip out, as no way would I trust this on any comms system, no matter how highly secure."

"Cinnabar, *Arianrhod* is as far from fit as our people that are still in Merkat's medbay. I know we got those meta-jurillium plates fitted with all speed and we didn't pay for them, but the hull's still minus ten percent of its skin and Merkat's short on supplies and charging us over the odds for the stuff it *does* have. Runs of meta-jurillium from the Dryssicon stations are way down, not least because of alien action near Beta Zegonia, and the military requisitions most of what gets out anyway. And according to Tallulah Tommy way back, Dryssicon was plagued by insider aid to what we thought were raiders when all this started, so anything earmarked for *Arianrhod* would never get here."

"I have an idea. But it's an expensive idea. I need to see Lindell."

The captain's expensive idea caused near-meltdown among her crew, all of whom were under the impression that the Cap had finally lost it. With the help of various parties, she had bought the major share in the luxury cruiser *Velvet Emerald*, now docked close to the *Arianrhod's* berth in the outer belts, and had ordered the systematic stripping of her outer hull to finish off her own ship's plating. The *Emerald* was a good deal smaller than *Arianrhod*, but she was clad in sufficient meta-jurillium to restore the balance of the large trading vessel's armour. The *Emerald's* other shareholders had been utterly dismayed but were too far away to take immediate action, and any legal sanctions would take months to organise.

Meanwhile the senior science officer had not been idle. Azular had called up an old friend whose supply ship had newly come into port at Merkat. His associate was Berzic in origin and was employed as supercargo on a Vreskot freighter from one of the agrarian colonies of Vreskota Two. The ship was in the Web to offload food supplies for the great port and space dock facilities. With a deal of persuasive talking, Azular had induced his friend and the Vreskot captain to divert some of their shipment *Arianrhod's* way.

When she heard of this latest annexation of supplies destined for others, Apnis half-jokingly suggested sending further crew members on fishing expeditions, to see what they could come up with by way of replenishing ship's stores and systems and bringing her back to an even keel. Ahxenta's enigmatic grin told the first mate that she had already set wheels in motion, and it was not long before Lindell had located and bid for a small batch of raw diamonds and other costly crystals. The cargo had been hanging fire for a while, having been one of the last out of Brown Amber before that station had fallen to the enemy. As the captain's contact on Freskat Six could re-set the materials into items such as thin wafers for comms linkages, it was a handy excuse to head out that way without exciting suspicion.

"This must be one of the fastest turnabouts Merkat's repair docks has ever seen for a ship as badly hurt as *Arianrhod*," observed Apnis, tapping the repair schedules she had called up on her board. "Dock-rats and other repair teams are pulling triple shifts to make overtime money and now we have a cargo to deliver to Freskat. But do we have a buyer once the gems have been turned over?"

"Military," Ahxenta said laconically. "Lindell sounded out various markets and the ISP's upper echelons at its shipbuilding docks off Skyrtek Prime and Alto Finglas are falling over each other for first dibs on any crys comms components available for the new warships they're churning out like hot cakes."

"And we're planning to be the suppliers?"

"Not necessarily: the local navy at Freskat is no doubt upgrading and repairing its fleet and if it needs the stuff, Zillah will have first dibs, we owe her that. But we have to get it there first and then it has to be processed."

"Not to worry you, Cinnabar, but where's the credit coming from for all the stuff we're having done? Insurance won't cough up. I've heard the local TA insurance rep is in hiding as war damage is classed as uninsurable and not covered by its contract obligations. There are a lot of very unhappy people that didn't read the small print."

"My buddy out Freskat way won't push for payment for comms link array production. And as for the rest of the essential credit, we've always covered our own backs; I've seen to that."

"True, but what about the crew? We've had a few back aboard but there are still more than a dozen in Merkat's medbay, a couple of them serious. That's costing as well."

"Greenwing's on the mend and he's helping out. I'll leave him at Merkat while we're gone to look after our people," the captain told her. "But I have an idea that might benefit our crew down there and our pockets. We still have around eight days here so we may as well make the most of it. Get our own people to overhauling as much as we can. They know the ship better than any outside repair crew and I'd rather our full capabilities were known to none outside our own. Security's hard put to keep our most sensitive areas shielded as it is. It would also be good if the ears around the Web were fed with the tale that we're in no way ready to depart in under a month: we don't want undue interest in our doings."

"Let Whisper pass it round – she's got a voice like a foghorn with indigestion," Apnis suggested.

"I heard that!" Earbleat sang out from her station.

"And ears like a cat that suspects it's going to be put in a bag. But seriously, we could let Ally know; that way it'll be round every one of the bars in the entire facility faster than a flea off the nose of a rocket. And if we're seen in the *Half Moon*, people won't figure we're getting ready for departure," the commander added with a knowing grin.

Azular had been intrigued on hearing of the link between zukivianite and the physiology of the aliens suspected of originating either on or near Kelfennig. He had heard of the material and in line with the captain's order he and the chief medic spent some time in devising an instrument to detect trace amounts of it. But the science officer's mind had also been whirring in other directions and Ahxenta asked no questions and gave only a resigned sigh when he announced that he planned to test the prototype device and set off with Ensign Hanx for one of the outer belt habitation areas. Both were in the garb of nondescript workmen and both packed a fair sized arsenal.

On their return four hours later, a senior staff briefing was called, where Azular reported that the hand-held sensor was able to detect minute traces of zukivianite and that at least one humanoid known to be altered by hostiles did not show traces of the substance. His test had been simple: he and Hanx had made for the *Green Diamond*, a place known as the hang-out of itinerant dock-rats, freeloaders and those of a light-fingered bent. There he had browbeaten a local dealer in dubious goods into providing a lead on the sale of rare items from strange places. One clue had led to a small-time trader in such objects who alleged that he had in stock fragments of alien material that had come from Kifferbuck. The trader claimed that his links to an official salvage company, regularly sent in on rescue and recovery missions, allowed his buying in of surplus pieces. He produced a validity permit so patently bogus that Azular had no problem in persuading him to admit that he and a couple of cronies habitually scoured areas of known shipwreck to see what they could pick up, and to take the two officers to his depository.

The two had seized several pieces from the large hangar in which the dealer's ship and stock were stored but let him go with no more than a kick and a warning, for both had noted their former associate Lokterix in the *Green Diamond* and were keen to return and confirm scan results taken in passing that had shown no trace of zukivianite in the man's system. Lokterix had not recognised them and Azular was able to take the necessary readings without causing a major ruckus.

Apnis was sceptical. How, she queried, could Azular be sure that the scraps he had got were alien and had come from hostiles that had met their end at Kifferbuck? Azular was quite sure: the remains were undeniably organic and fused to remnants of cybernetic material that matched data they had garnered over their several alien encounters; the zukivianite trace was clear and he and Hanx had recovered one sizeable fragment that supported his conclusions. He handed her a burnt and blackened piece of metal.

"So what is it?" the first mate demanded.

"A piece off *Arianrhod's* hull," Azular smiled mirthlessly. "It has a clear titanium-alloy signature. How many ships do you know that use titanium-alloy sourced from Aoria Six in their weapons arrays?"

"One: ours. But I don't like the look on your face. What's up?"

"Something else showed up on the organo-cyber fusion from the samples. Friskianx DNA – Dr Flintlock's confirmed it."

"Hell," Ahxenta said softly. "Did you figure this beforehand?"

"I suspected as much on Kelfennig. It *is* plausible that the sentient presence that survived when their culture ended was able to merge with or take over other organic material and incorporate it into what was left of their living tissue. We know the Friskianx were suitable: Micklemouse believed it and the other examples we're aware of are Friskianx – Doosbak, Lokterix, the three from Four One Two Alpha. Hence perhaps the early targeting of Friskianx populations."

"That's a lot of infiltration; seems like these aliens have made their way into practically every corner of the mapped galaxy," Apnis said in frustration. "Where does that leave us if they take the place over?"

"They haven't yet, and humanoids tend to be particularly resistant to interference," Ahxenta replied. "And now we know how to detect them, we have one advantage. How sensitive is your sensor, Azular?"

"It's reliable at close range but not at distance. Large accretions of zukivianite we should be able to detect, but trace amounts no. But we do have much more data on hostile vessels, their ion signatures, their methods of attack and the nature of their crews. What I've inferred so far from our evidence and that from the *Obsidian* and the *Green Comet* is that the ships are powerful, well-armed and well-armoured but that crew complement is low: the amount of organic material we find in association with other substances bears this out, unless the crews are much more mechanoid than humanoid."

"No way of working that out unless we find an intact ship with a live crew and do a head-count," Apnis said briskly. "And no way would I do that. But Cap, what in blazes are *we* doing in the middle of this? We're a PSS, a trading ship, we have our living to get and we find ourselves commandeered by the ISP for a war that's naught to do with us and now in possession of information that's enough to fry us. *Arianrhod's* been in tight places before but this beats all."

"I agree, and the sooner we get out of it, the sooner we get back to what we should be doing. But meanwhile, I want to check up on our people in Merkat's medbay in person, so I'm heading on in. But after that, we're for the *Half Moon*; we came off duty an hour ago and we have rumours to spread so we may as well start them off there."

Over the next days it was noticeable that the captain of the *Arianrhod* spent much time shuttling back and forth to the *Velvet Emerald* and to the inner belt marketing areas. She was giving nothing away but both Greenwing and Flintlock had been pulled in to assist. The crew was spending most of its duty time bringing the ship back to nigh on her former glory, although her outer hull was lacking its normal spit and polish. A flying visit by the *Obsidian Sky* had resulted in new engines for *Arianrhod's* few fighters and her pilots, all fair engineers, were hard put to have them installed in the short time allowed.

A late night visit to the *Half Moon in a Puddle* at the end of a taxing day had allowed Ahxenta and Apnis a rare chance to relax over a beer and hear the rumours that had been flitting around the Web, not only about *Arianrhod* but about the expansion of the alien incursion, which was now labelled War. The situations at Marridan and Brown Amber were stalemate still but the buzz was that there would be an all-out assault somewhere soon: the question was where and when. Aliens were supposed to be everywhere and listening at every door.

Although not giving credence to half they heard, the two were in a position to corroborate some of it had they chosen. Azular, in a further off-ship sortie, had verified the presence of two genetically-altered individuals that were cybernetically augmented, but minus the tracking systems that others they had examined seemed to possess. Neither was Friskianx, leading him to conclude that other worlds had been targeted for potential recruits, but as neither had had access to *Arianrhod*, no action was taken. However, their presence implied that others were nearby. The captain had retained access to ISP's tactical relay system and knew that hostile actions had slowed again, the ISP putting this down to the recent losses sustained at Mellifly and to the Jurgall Three blockade, but imminent assault was deemed probable. Veiled references to her ship had given her a touch of satisfaction.

Ahxenta and Apnis had, however, more than relaxation on their minds, and bidding farewell to Ally as he made ready to shut up, they set off for their shuttle. Merkat Three's Web of metal, light and power was dimming: the colossal structure kept the planetary diurnal cycle and although business carried on nonstop, night was observed by many residents who called the place home. Those whose business was not respectable were also inclined to welcome the fall of night, but few eyes would be turned towards the vast outer lacunae that provided harbourage for the titanic starships that used the port.

Arianrhod sat immobile, great docking struts holding her in place, the dim lanterns of her inspection and repair drones scouring every micron of hull and glinting like dull fireflies after a hard night's toil. Much of the ship was in darkness but shifting shadows cast by the subtly soft lighting behind the engaged fine-meshed safety shields of her aft cargo bays suggested that she drowsed rather than slept.

Once their shuttle had safely docked, the captain and first mate made their way direct to the bridge. Every post was manned. After a scan of her console, Ahxenta ordered a check station by station and then gave the order to recall the drones. To a frisson of excitement around the bridge, the command to ready engines was made. It was followed by the instruction to plot a course for Freskat via Delta Iridium. Only then was the call made to the Port Authority applying for permission to depart. As a sleepy operative awoke sufficiently to activate his boards, make the relevant checks and issue clearance, the great ship came to life, the pulsing of her engines slowly mounting and her flanks beginning to glow as each peripheral emplacement of comms, scanners and navigational gear made ready for engagement.

The external lights of the woven metallic lacuna in which she sat cast beams of light that picked out the plates of her pinkly glinting hull as *Arianrhod* broke free of her restraining docking struts and slid gracefully out into free space.

"Turn us about, helm and take us out," the captain instructed.

"Aye, aye, Captain!" Dox responded.

"You think our people will be all right down there?" the first mate asked softly, nodding at the retreating glow of the Web in the holo.

"We've done what we can for them and they have a safe berth. Greenwing, Ma'Lappis and the two nurse-techs are on hand and we'll be back this way to pick them up soon enough," Ahxenta responded. "We've said our farewells and they know our departure is on the QT and that we'll have to maintain silence while we're out."

The majority of *Arianrhod's* injured crew still under Merkat medical care, in company with a few from *Arianrhod's* own medbay, were well content with their current billets. Lest any larcenous denizens of Merkat's outer belts intended to exploit the depleted *Velvet Emerald*, the captain had ordered her own people that were well enough to leave the Web's medbay but unfit for active duty to take up their berths in the small but adequate facilities aboard the luxury liner and recuperate there, with medical personnel from *Arianrhod* on hand. As she was paying the bulk of the docking fees, Ahxenta reckoned that she was entitled to the greater part of the accommodation and it saved having to pay lodging for her crew in the Web itself.

"Lock onto the local beacon and set for Delta Iridium, best speed," she ordered. "And let's hope this trip's quieter than the last."

"You said it," Apnis replied. "But I recommend we run silent and cloak at the first cheep of anything we don't like the look of."

"You heard Commander Apnis, people! Silent running and long-range scanners to maximum."

"And hot coffee all round," Box added suggestively. "It's going to be a long night."

The following several nights were also long, for scanners had picked up other craft in the area as *Arianrhod* had dropped out of hyperspace to swop beacons en route to their destination. Opting to ignore the routine signals, the great ship sped onwards but kept wary eyes and ears open. One or two reports had come in via the ISP tactical relay that enemy activity was increasing again in sporadic bursts and on targets that covered a wide compass. It was as she was still half a day away from the Delta Iridium system that one message came over the comm that *Arianrhod* could not ignore.

"Distress call, Captain!" Bellfish called out. "It's difficult to read, but it's on a PSS channel!"

"Dammit! Red alert, crew to battlestations! Get our cloak up! All gunnery stations fully manned. Cottontail to the bridge. Do we know who it is yet and what they're up against?"

"Trying to get the details, Cap, but there's a lot of static!" Bellfish responded loudly.

Gliss was busily transferring his tactical display to the bridge holo-viewer, refining the data. "Cloak's not helping, Cap, but we have one large vessel, outline reads as PSS and two other smaller vessels – they read as hostile."

"It's the *Tallulah*!" the comms officer clarified loudly. "Two hostiles on her and half her systems out of commission."

"It would be! Hang Fleetskup! Drop our cloak, set attack vector. All shields at maximum, power up phase cannons. Azular, deploy our decoy once we're in visual and we go in high speed and all guns blazing! Earbleat, ready your new *Loki* but do not let her loose until I give the call. I want this short and sweet! Fighters on standby."

"They're a good deal smaller than the vessels we've met before but readings definitely match those previously encountered," Azular confirmed. "They're firing on the *Tallulah*! She's swinging round to protect her forr'ad shielding. Decoy deployed!"

"Their weapons are phase cannons, slicer beams and torpedoes. We've been spotted! One's turning to take us on!" bawled Gliss.

"Launch deflecting drones!" Ahxenta ordered the weapons officer as the tactical display expanded to take in the enemy craft. "And target her comms, I don't want half a dozen others turning up."

Apnis made for the auxiliary weapons station and set her targeting systems in operation as *Arianrhod* juddered to the repeated thwack of phase cannon on her hull. The hostile was highly manoeuvrable and flew over and around the larger vessel at almost impossible angles and at near incredible speed.

"All gunnery crews, open fire and take her down! I don't care how you do it! Launch fighters! All weapons emplacements, fire!"

"Got her!" crowed Earbleat. "But she's still coming on! What the hell's the crew playing at? They'll be smashed to bits!"

"One forr'ad shield hit and she's out!" Gliss called out.

"Throw everything at her, but not the *Loki*!" Ahxenta thundered.

"She's breaking up but she's set to ram!" Earbleat yelled.

"Evasive! Helm hard to port and get us out of here!"

"Aye, Cap!"

As the *Arianrhod* veered up and away, the smaller vessel exploded in a shower of flak, lighting the space around her like a beacon.

"Target second hostile. Fighters, get as far away as you can, she's not giving up. Earbleat, how fast can you get the *Loki* to that beast and how close?"

"She's heading off our starboard: our decoy's foxed her. But how can she move like that? *Loki* will be pushed to contact her."

"Give it your best shot! I want this ended now." Ahxenta was on her feet, her eyes glued to the tactical display in the well of the bridge as it spun with the ship's motion.

"*Loki II* away!" the weapons officer bellowed. "Hostile is targeting our decoy! On target… on target… Got you, you bastard!"

The second attacking ship burst like an exploding star, the energy wash flaming outwards and rocking the mighty *Arianrhod*.

"How are our fighters?" the captain demanded, hauling herself up off the deck and wiping a streak of blood from her nose as she made for the command chair. "I hope the hell they weren't caught in that."

"All reporting safe and undamaged," Bellfish told her.

"Reel them in. And get me a full damage report. Put me through to the *Tallulah*, she seems still to be in one piece."

"We're not too bad, but we've lost a helluva lot of our weapons supplies," the first mate reported as she resumed her usual chair and began to scan the readings flashing up on her boards. "No injuries to speak of, but how the hell could they manoeuvre so fast and at such steep angles? Those damn aliens must be near indestructible!"

"I strongly suspect those ships were unmanned," Ahxenta said sharply. "But how come the *Tallulah* got off so lightly? Given the power unleashed by those things, she should have been space-dust."

"Sued for surrender?" Apnis wryly suggested as Bellfish reported that Captain Fleetskup was on the comm and they had visual.

The large face of Murmur Fleetskup, a cut over one eye, formed within the confines of the holo-grid.

"Captain Ahxenta," he said formally. "I would appreciate your assistance. We've lost half our aft shielding and all our long-range scanners and comms are down. If you could provide us with a pair of energy cells and escort us to Delta Iridium Colony, I'd be obliged."

"You're already obliged, Captain Fleetskup," Ahxenta pointed out icily. "I have no spare energy cells but I will escort you all speed to Delta Iridium. You and I need to talk."

24: FIELDWORK

The orbital docking and repair station at Delta Iridium Six welcomed the *Tallulah* in graciously: it had not seen any new work for some time and the PSS would provide some very welcome income. Ahxenta had ordered her own ship into orbit and had registered her presence with the planetary authorities. She had much to think about and little time or patience to bestow on her fellow captain.

The readings taken by both Azular and Gliss during the firefight had confirmed her suspicions that the two alien ships they had faced were unmanned: no partially humanoid crew would have been able to withstand the forces imposed by some of the manoeuvres used by the attacking vessels and the fact that their decoy had deceived them implied that there were no sentient minds in control. It was likely that the ships were older models that had not been updated with the latest data on the *Arianrhod* and her capabilities, as her cloak and her decoy had both apparently been effective. The lack of back-up also implied that the ships were operating independently, which led the officers of the *Arianrhod* to wonder how many other autonomous hostiles were functional in isolated pockets of space.

Ahxenta and Apnis took a shuttle across to meet their opposite numbers aboard the *Tallulah*, firstly to assess her internal damage, and secondly to find out why she had not been blasted out of the sky the second the hostiles had become aware of her. Fleetskup and his first mate Melly Goodsocks were in the bay to greet them but Ahxenta was not impressed that Lieutenant Tommy Buntle was waiting in the briefing room when they walked in.

"What's he doing here?" she demanded.

Fleetskup bristled indignantly and attempted his usual defence of the utility of his exec, but *Arianrhod's* captain quickly silenced him and as soon as they were seated, she brought up the distinct lack of heavy damage to the *Tallulah*, given the nature of the emergency and the opposition that her ship had faced when she waded in.

"They popped out of nowhere the second we came in range of Elf One," Goodsocks put in as Fleetskup continued in outraged silence. "We'd planned to stop off there to refresh our air supplies as we were running low. They didn't attack at first; looking us over I guess. There was no communication but on the basis of their structure we figured them for hostiles, sent out a distress and took evasive action. That set them off. You must have caught our signal and were close enough to get here pretty quickly."

The *Tallulah's* first mate flushed as Apnis looked witheringly over at her. "You sent out a distress call *before* they fired a shot?"

"Well naturally!" Buntle put in. "They were recognised as hostile!"

"Who by?" Apnis shot back.

"This bickering is pointless," Captain Fleetskup snapped, banging a fist on the table. "The point is, you asked for this meeting, Captain Ahxenta. What is it you have to discuss? Naturally, I'll be grateful for any information you have concerning these hostiles and their actions, if it will add to the safety of my ship."

"I'd have thought you'd be grateful for the help you've already had from me," she retorted acidly. "I take it you scanned them before you bravely sent out a distress and ran away? If so, I'd like the data your tactical and science ops gathered. Our data suggests they were unmanned and possibly acting independently of a command centre."

"You'll have it," Goodsocks told them. "I'll have it relayed to your ship when I get back to post. But anything you can tell us would be a help, Captain," she added before Fleetskup or Buntle could interject. "And on behalf of the *Tallulah* and her crew, I would like to express my thanks for your assistance. Had you not fielded the flak, we would have been toasted. They were bent on destruction once they'd got our measure."

"But they did look you over before they fired," Apnis pointed out.

"They did, which gave us a chance to look them over."

"Strange," *Arianrhod's* first mate replied. "Maybe they were posted to look out for something specific and shoot down anything else."

"What would they be looking for?" Fleetskup enquired.

"Company," Ahxenta responded briefly. "More of their own – it's a short trip from Elf One to the beacon and bypass for a trip across Delta and into Lambda zone. That's why you stopped off at Elf One, after all. You could come off the bypass, top up your air for free at Elf One and hop on again. What was your destination anyway?"

"That's private!" spluttered Fleetskup.

"Drop-off here at Delta Iridium," Melly Goodsocks told her. "But air recharge costs here."

Ahxenta shrugged; she could understand that. "You dropped out early and they evidently picked you up and came over to give you the eye. Once they realised you weren't what they were waiting for, they tried to take you out before you could tell anyone about them."

Apnis looked expressively at her captain, the implications causing her eyes to widen, but she said nothing.

"But on another matter: I've expended a lot of artillery in coming to your assistance, all of which was spanking new and recently fitted. I've also sustained damage to my ship, which, if you're not aware, was fresh out of total refit. In fact I'm not even up to full strength, as I've left a fair number of my crew at Merkat, some seriously injured."

"We heard, Captain; was it that bad?" Goodsocks asked.

"It was that bad," she was told shortly. "I wouldn't normally ask for recompense, but *Arianrhod* was almost completely wrecked and I had to call in every favour I could to get her spaceworthy."

"Surely you were insured?" Buntle interrupted.

"War damage doesn't count for much with insurance concerns; you try it for this little bust up and see how far it gets you," Apnis cut in angrily. "We're traders. When you need *four* ships to escort you into port, it costs. And given we were the ones that jumped in to save your skins, your insurance should cough up."

Arguments were bandied to and fro but little was settled upon and the *Arianrhod's* officers headed back to their ship with little more than a pledge that the matter would be looked into. The only advance made was that the data promised by Goodsocks had been received and was being incorporated into their own information banks.

"But what were you doing fiddling with your info-pad?" Ahxenta asked her first mate as she brought the shuttle safely into the bay.

"Taking scans of Tommy Buntle; if anyone's likely to be under the influence of aliens, it's him. I'm sorry to report that he's as human as the rest of us, mostly. His conscience I can't vouch for. But back to business: aliens near Elf One and close to Delta? Close enough to the bypass across into Lambda and thence into ISP territory and…"

"The Ginseng. Yes, that struck me. And how many more route crossovers exist guarded by a pair of warships that don't give up and give no quarter? But why were they on the lookout? And why take on a ship that doesn't want to fight unless you're expecting company very soon?"

"I don't like the sound of that, Cap."

"Neither do I. Let's get back to the bridge and see how the troops are handling things. We need to get to Freskat on the double."

Most of the troops were assessing and repairing damage or busy with other duties. Earbleat was bemoaning the demise of her beloved

Loki II and calculating how to turn another of Admiral Zillah's cargo pods into *Loki III*. Lindell and his depleted team were hunting arms supplies to bring *Arianrhod's* arsenal up to full strength but were having trouble, as those with spare weapons were loath to part with them in light of the current troubles and even when they were, prices were steep. Cottontail was cursing Fleetskup and nursing her engines back to their normal state of smooth operation. Azular had set Greffy to dismantling one of the ship's long-range hull scanners to reconfigure it to scan for trace zukivianite. He himself was once more going over every piece of data he could get his hands on in relation to the aliens, their possible origins and the events on Kelfennig: a suspicion was eating away at the back of his mind that he had missed something and he was determined to find out what it was.

Ahxenta had approved the purchase of sufficient arms to fully re-equip the ship and had sent the bill to Melly Goodsocks, figuring she was a better bet than her captain to pay up. The tale of the fight at Kifferbuck had done the rounds as far as Delta Iridium Six and other provisions were offered at much better rates, as most suppliers were wary of running the risk that anyone from *Arianrhod* would come down to argue in person. One advantage accrued during negotiations: Lindell had secured a small contract to deliver an urgent consignment of new comms linkages from Coronis Comms to the Freskat Navy's supply depot. Terms were quickly agreed and in a little less than two standard days, the ship was ready to depart. With a sense of release, Ahxenta gave the order to set course for Freskat, best speed.

To the immense relief of the majority of the crew, the trip across zone Lambda to Freskat was made without incident. *Arianrhod* stayed well clear of the area close to the Ginseng Nebula, as word from the local tactical relay had come in that the outward edge of the anomaly had expanded once more. The captain had thus deemed it prudent to put an early call in to Zillah requesting a meeting and the admiral had confirmed, arranging to fly back planetside from her current station.

"Busy place," Box commented as he scanned the holo of the area around the planet. "There's a lot more here than last time and half of them military by the look of it. That must be the admiral's flagship."

"And how do you figure that?" demanded Dox.

"She's got the Freskat Fleet's insignia on her and her registration ends in one," Box replied. "And she's the biggest boat we can see. The *FSS Shieldstar.* Looks about the same as most heavy cruisers."

"Cap didn't take long to finish business over the crystals with her buddy down yonder at any rate; here's her shuttle coming in now," Dox said, pointing. "Must be an important meet, Commander Apnis and Dr Azular are already set to go aboard the *Gadfly* once she's back and they're all three heading down. No peace for the wicked."

"So I wonder when *we* get shore leave," her companion muttered in an aside meant to be heard.

"Next year," Lieutenant Commander Earbleat told them from the command chair. "There's a war on, in case you hadn't noticed."

"It's high summer in the central settlement at the moment and the sun's out," Box complained.

"It's high time you stopped moaning," the helmswoman told him. "Just be grateful we got here in one piece. How's *Loki III* coming along, Lieutenant Commander?"

By the time Earbleat had finished listing the virtues of her pet project, word had come in that their three colleagues were in closed session with Admiral Zillah and her second at Freskat Fleet HQ.

Ahxenta began by voicing her thanks for the supplies that Zillah had sent on, although as she had shrewdly realised at the time, the admiral did require payment in kind and much of that was the facts relating to *Arianrhod's* latest face-offs and every crumb of data that they had picked up relating to the hostiles that now threatened every zone of charted space. Azular had come armed with the relevant data shard, screened to omit a number of details that the captain had deemed too sensitive to pass on. Ahxenta trusted Zillah, but that was as far as she was prepared to go. A nod from her science officer had let her know that his scans of the admiral and her aide, Tealdun, read clear.

The main concern of the Freski officers was what was construed as an imminent hostile attack in their neck of the woods, in light of the growth of the local nebular anomaly and the increases in random attacks in every galactic zone. The latter were interpreted as a strategy to tie up a portion of allied forces in advance of an expected assault. The unmanned ships *Arianrhod* had met in zone Delta were an added complication. The captain's opinion was sought on the spread of the latest attacks, set out in a holo on the desk, despite her assertion that she was not military and would in no way sanction the use of her ship as a fighting vessel. Azular, listening and watching, pointed out what his acute eyes had spotted as the holo rotated.

"There seems to be little pattern," he said. "Most incursions have focused around the more populous areas of zones Alpha, Beta, Delta and Epsilon up here, or here in the ISP-controlled region of Lambda and beyond, but there *have* been incidents in ISP regions close to the Starglass and Kellybar, and others on the edge of charted space at Wester 287 and at Canna in Mu, near the Enigma Nebula."

"You'd expect densely inhabited areas to be hit more," interjected Zillah. "Where's the point of extending your fleet into sectors where there's hardly a ship to be seen?"

"Freskat *is* a fairly remote world," Azular pointed out mildly.

"My point: apart from this manifestation at the Ginseng, we haven't been too badly hit."

"However, Admiral – if I may – you'll note one sector that has *not* reported a hit within light years even though it's well-travelled, with many nearby colonies and outposts," Azular said, carefully fading out the places of known hits to leave a large area almost in the centre of the holo-array.

"Bang in the middle!" Zillah exclaimed.

"There have been no reports between Selliden and Rydderwild on one vector and from Elf One clear across zone Epsilon to the inner boundary of Zeta on the opposite vector," the science officer stated. "The Friskianx and Lonagan systems and their associated colonies haven't reported hits close to home; and that *is* a populous area."

"And look at what's in the middle of that space," said Apnis. "The Skyrtek system: ISP's HQ, including its main planetary affairs office on Skyrtek Key and its massive shipbuilding dock around Skyrtek Prime. And how many unmanned hostiles are sitting around there just waiting to butt in? Every available ship from Skyrtek sent out and an alien fleet steps in and takes out the largest shipbuilding dock in the entire mapped galaxy."

"That's one helluva speculation, Tallica," Ahxenta warned.

"But it makes a kind of sense," the admiral had to admit. "We *have* had reports in over the last few standard days reporting an increase in the frequency of minor attacks; and if we plot them in, they're in areas adjacent to this space. The attack on the *PSS Tallulah* at which you rendered aid was one of them, although you reckoned that the *Tallulah* was attacked because she'd come off the beacon at Elf One and the hostiles didn't want their presence reported?"

"That's what we figured," the captain agreed. "Which may suggest that an attack is impending."

"The ISP will have to be warned, although I'm a little reluctant to do that," Zillah grimaced.

"Because you figure the ISP has been compromised and there are alien infiltrators there," Ahxenta stated bluntly.

"I see you've reached the same conclusion, Captain," the admiral said wryly as her second's mouth dropped open. "Yes I do; which leaves me with a problem."

"I know what I'd do."

"I probably won't like it, but please go on."

"I'd have all the ships at the Ginseng pull out once you're sure the balloon's about to go up, but in the meantime, increase the number of probes around the perimeter and make sure they're jamming the spaceways with static in every direction. And I'd seed the perimeter with as many fusion mines as I could lay my hands on. If Skyrtek *is* the target, the most efficient route there from the anomaly could be estimated and the intensity of seeding adjusted accordingly."

"We couldn't set all that up!" Tealdun exploded. "Besides, there's absolutely no evidence to suggest that there *is* a fleet hiding in that irregularity, and that Skyrtek is about to be hit. It would be senseless to set anything like that up without more input. We need to wait until we have enough data to make sure there are hostiles there *and* that they're planning a strike."

"If you wait around for the universe to make sense, Commander, you're in for a long wait and you'll find yourself on the receiving end of a very nasty surprise well before that," Apnis told him. "If nothing happens, you reel in your remotes and save them for next time."

"How many Allied ships are there in the area, Admiral?" Ahxenta asked. "And more importantly, how many do you trust?"

Zillah's eyes blazed. "You don't pull punches, do you, Captain? But you have a point. Three ISP, two Coalition – one from Kanelian Juxta, the other from Friskianx – and two Non-Treaty from Lamella Four. The Lamellans are one of our closest major trade partners but I don't know the captains personally. A couple of independents have sent in ships to observe, but they're not equipped for heavy fighting. I *have* met with all the commanding officers but I'm not in a position to comment on their integrity. None of them struck me as unreliable, not even the Friskianx," she added dryly. "I *have* tacitly been given command of the situation as it's in my backyard and when I show them this they'll no doubt have things to say. Whether they *will* withdraw if your suggestion's the route I choose, I don't know."

"I expect they'll shift once you seed the space with mines," Apnis observed sardonically.

"That hasn't been decided!" Tealdun burst out.

"Button it, Johnny," Zillah instructed. "I'll give your ideas close consideration, Captain Ahxenta, after I and my team have gone over the data you've provided, and sooner rather than later: I think we're reaching condition critical. I'll keep you informed – and I hope you'll be around for a few days? Good. Before you go, tell me about the firefight at Kifferbuck and how you got out and got your ship back up to spec so quickly."

"I bet she's glad we're her allies and not her enemies," said Apnis on the trip back to *Arianrhod*. "And I figure she's worried, even with the heads-up we've given. But will the other ships' commanders buy it?"

"She's got the clout and she's been given the command. What do you think, Azular? You stayed pretty quiet at the end there."

"I think the admiral can convince her commanders that a strategic withdrawal is possibly their best option at this time, Captain. How she'll deal with informing the ISP's planetary affairs office at Skyrtek that its dockyard may be a major target is another matter."

"Through Myrtleberry, I expect," was the captain's view. "*She* was the one that gave her the job of outfitting us, though not directly. I suspect they understand and trust each other, up to a point."

"Nice one on the *Emerald*, though, Cinnabar, that was one doozie of a bonus," the first mate congratulated. "I half expected her to bite your head off when you suggested it."

Zillah had been impressed and mildly amused by Ahxenta's tactics to obtain sufficient authority over the *Velvet Emerald* to use her to repair *Arianrhod* and then to exploit her as a treatment centre for her injured crew. On the back of it, she had agreed to the bold proposal that the admiral use her ISP authority to requisition the *Velvet Emerald* for the war effort as a hospital ship and give full control to Ahxenta.

The next three days were spent in negotiating the sale of as many as were requested of the crystal comms array-sets created by Ahxenta's resident contact to the Freski group that dealt with military supplies. Turnover had been rapid and the captain felt that Zillah's people had a right to all the pieces they needed, but was unwilling to compromise on price as she had her various other costs to cover and was still in serious debt over *Arianrhod's* recent refit at Merkat.

Azular had in the interim been exercising his sharp brain over the relationship between the hostiles and Kelfennig and had come to the conclusion that the reactions of *Arianrhod's* landing team to the odd globe of energy and light, unlike those of Micklemouse, were part of the equation. The energy that enveloped the globe, he inferred, was similar to that bordering the anomaly within the Ginseng but was not identical. That the trader was drawn to the globe was either because he had been in close contact with aliens once native to Kelfennig and had been influenced by them or that he was at a subconscious level aware that, although alien and similar to his masters, the orb had no harmful intent towards him. He could after all detect the difference between hostiles and those altered by them. The landing team's reactions were understandable: there was some sensitivity present but it was negative, a result of the various depredations they had suffered as a direct consequence of alien action.

The results of his deliberations he brought to the captain once she had finished her business on Freskat. Ahxenta, fresh from a dialogue with Zillah, had called in her senior officers. The science officer had inferred that Micklemouse was probably correct in his belief that the energy form was part of an ancient technology still extant beneath the surface of Kelfennig. As the globe had provided the trader with light that had allowed him to explore the tunnel system in which he found himself and to lead him to the surface to search the craft close by for what he could lift, Azular surmised a form of intelligence, but how far its benignity stretched he was not prepared to estimate.

The captain was unusually silent during the report and the ensuing discussion, so much so that Apnis half-guessed the reason.

"What's up, Cap? Zillah's been upping the ante?"

"Admiral Zillah wants *Arianrhod* as back-up in the event a strategic withdrawal from the Ginseng goes belly-up. She's passed the data we gave her and Azular's best guess onto the ISP, so the Skyrtek system will mobilise for a possible attack. But unless she and her contact have been cautious, it may mean that the hostiles are aware that the Allies suspect their intent and are looking to stop them."

"Damn and hell and blast," Earbleat swore softly.

"But they *are* taking on board the notion that they might be next in line for a surprise," the first mate nodded. "But what's your take on it, Cap? I don't expect she passed on the news that she plans to mine the area around that energy field's perimeter, did she?"

"She hasn't confirmed that she will, so I don't expect she's made a final decision yet. But she *has* worked out that since we had additional data on the nature of the anomaly, we have a source of information that she doesn't and are holding back. She's okay with that, to some degree. Her take on it is that if we can find out more, it might help not only her people in the firing line but those preparing for a potential assault out at Skyrtek."

"The admiral has a point: more data on the nature of the anomaly would be an advantage," Azular concurred. "The amount of power needed to disrupt the light orb on Kelfennig suggests that punching a hole through the energy shell of the Ginseng anomaly is beyond the ability of one ship, and perhaps even the combined power of many."

"More data might be an advantage and Zillah was pushing for it," Ahxenta sighed. "But I just wonder about our pal Micklemouse and his pet energy globe: you wanted to know a while ago, Tallica, how he figured that traces of zukivianite would let us differentiate a hostile from an altered sentient, and Crizz, you thought he had help. If, as Azular suspects, there's sentience behind this energy sphere, it would explain not only a source of help but why Micklemouse freaked when Earbleat blasted it: he must have known."

"So we're heading back to Kelfennig to see Micklemouse?" Apnis scowled. "And how popular are we going to be there if some form of intelligence still exists, since we blew his last little pal to hell?"

"That remains to be seen," the captain replied shortly. "But in the absence of more business hereabouts, and the disposal of most of the crystals we picked up at Merkat to Zillah's people, we have the time. And I'd rather be out of the way of more hints to take up position for the defence of Freskat if push comes to shove. We're traders, not military. Lindell is trying to offload the last of the comms link stuff we do have in hand to Arrissia Five's defence department, as they're old customers and Arrissia is en route to Kelfennig."

"So we set for Arrissia Five?" asked the first mate.

"We set for Arrissia, amber alert, as I want the crew on its toes."

"I think most of them are already there," Earbleat commented as the team disbanded and the second mate set off, whistling chirpily.

"Why is she so damned cheerful?" Apnis asked.

"She managed to prise a few useful bits of kit out of Zillah's ops crew that'll help fit out *Loki III*."

"She could charm birds out of trees. You should assign her to help Lindell pick up a few more contracts: he's shorthanded as his trusty second's back on Merkat recuperating aboard *Velvet Emerald*."

"No way. I could well imagine the kind of cargo that would tickle her fancy."

Their departure was made with Admiral Zillah's go-ahead and the information that seeding the edges of nebular space with fusion mines had been agreed with the commanders of the Allied force. *Arianrhod's* nose was set for Arrissia and the crew bid farewell to any hope of shore leave on Freskat.

Once out of Lambda and in zone Epsilon the course was changed to that of the Starglass and Kelfennig. Dealings with Arrissia's defence department had been interrupted by news of a local disturbance there and Ahxenta was cautious of bringing *Arianrhod* into an area where agitators were on the loose. As it was, the days it took to reach the Kelfennig system were quiet, with little heard from any distant or local relays on the progress of current hostilities. As the ship drew close to her objective, the captain ordered red alert and cloaking, and all hands were summoned to stations. Although they could detect the signal being sent out by Micklemouse's ship and nothing else seemed to be nearby, two probes were sent down to scan whilst the ship maintained a safe orbital distance.

Suddenly, Gliss called out that a scanning beam had shot up from the surface and had locked onto one of their probes. The beam's source was the ruined surface structure under which was the tunnel system that led to Micklemouse's ship.

"If it's him, the little rat's been busy since last we saw him," Apnis snorted. "Life signs?"

"Neither probe is recording life signs, Commander," Azular said. "But if they're well below surface, that tracks. We're still receiving the signal we know is his ship from her last-known position and I have other energy readings from that location, some way down."

"Take us in closer, Ms Dox," directed Ahxenta. "Gliss, long-range scanners on maximum and every station maintain full alert. One peep from anywhere and I want to know. Status of probes, Azular?"

"Both probes are now being scanned and the energy readings are increasing but I detect no hostile intent, ma'am."

"Maintain surface surveillance. I'm not going to announce us but those two down there, if they're still there, will no doubt be aware that someone's showed up. They'll want to make sure we're friendly before they start waving their arms about and asking to be rescued."

"Still reading clear apart from the scanning beams, but they're doing sweeps now," Gliss confirmed. "No doubt they're looking for the source of the probes."

"Landing team…" began Apnis.

"We're not having that argument again," Ahxenta said firmly. "I'm going down, you're staying here. I'll take Azular and three security guards, two with me and one to guard the shuttle. Whisper will stay here with weapons at the ready and I want targeting of the surface to let anyone watching from down there know we mean business. And deploy linked probes to keep an eye on local space from all angles."

The first mate knew when she was beaten and insisted on adding another security guard and a medic, suggesting Dr Oak as an expert in cybernetics. She was also adamant that locating pins would be worn and that the team would be under surveillance at all times. The area was ominously quiet but the situation could change in an instant.

The shuttle descent was made without incident and the craft made a soft landfall next to the shell of the old cargo-carrier that had been found earlier. As Ahxenta climbed down from their vessel, she was aware of a subtle emanation of unease that she could see reflected in the faces of her companions, eerily lit within their protective helmets.

"Stick close," she told them as she activated her detector to find the source of the beams that were still scanning *Arianrhod's* probes. "Over there," she said after a moment, setting off to lead the way.

The half-roofed structure rose up to meet them and just within the overhang they found the source: a small hemispherical station.

"That device wasn't here before," Azular announced, examining it closely with his pet scanner. "I suspect its signal is being relayed to a station below us. Apart from the probe beams, I don't detect other external relays. I suggest we leave it intact as we don't want to give the impression that we're here to cause trouble."

"I agree," the captain concurred. "Marks and Goldwash, you stay with the shuttle. The rest of you, let's move."

Azular led the way into the rocky ruins and down into the dark tunnel beyond. The sensation of unease was palpable and increased as the five made their way down into the bowels of the earth.

"It was here that Dr Ma'Lappis first observed the energy globe, Captain," the science officer reported as they turned a corner. "It was up yonder but as far as I can see, there's… ah, that's interesting."

As the landing team raised their eyes to the roof, a small light grew in intensity to form a glowing orb that danced away from them and along the path. It stopped as they did, waiting, and Ahxenta could feel an insubstantial icy finger down her back as she looked.

"We have company," she said softly into the darkness.

25: ALIENS

Aboard *Arianrhod*, Apnis had requested a running commentary as the team advanced. The ship's scanners were picking them up clearly but she wanted audio confirmation of progress. As the tunnel gave onto the wide circular grotto with the two exits, the captain reported that the energy globe, which Azular had verified as matching the one the previous landing team had met, was suspended at one of the ways.

"Déjà vu," Ensign Hanx said cheerfully.

"Don't raise your weapons," Ahxenta told her people. "We don't want it to think we're unfriendly."

Continuing their descent, the party made its way by torchlight in the wake of the guiding orb.

"Light increasing, Captain, as it did before," noted Azular. "I read a shielded area ahead that equates to the site of Micklemouse's ship, exactly where it was before."

"So he's not moved it then. Life signs?"

"I read none; but if they're inside the ship they'll be shielded. There she is!"

Hanx and his fellow security officer had automatically raised their rifles but at a hand-signal from Ahxenta they lowered them quickly. The energy globe had skittered off but reappeared at the gesture.

"Interesting," noted Azular. "That suggests not only intelligence but knowledge of events last time."

"Maybe it's figured Lieutenant Commander Earbleat isn't here," Hanx suggested in an undertone to his security partner, Strawberry.

"Belay that, Ensign," the captain growled, tapping her external amplifier. "Anybody home?" she called, stepping into the full light of the Comet Six that she recognised as Micklemouse's small vessel.

The craft was festooned with extra pods that the man must have scavenged and two of the energy cells that she had left him when he and Doosbak were dropped onto the surface at their last visit.

"You come out, Micklemouse, or we come in," Ahxenta warned.

After a long pause the airlock slid aside and a short biped encased in a protective suit appeared. A second crouched furtively at its back.

"Yes?" the leading individual asked uncertainly.

"You know damn well who we are Micklemouse, so there's no point in pretending you don't," the captain barked.

"You've come to take us out!" the second apparition exclaimed.

"He should be so lucky," came the voice of Apnis over the comm.

"We've come to talk. We want some answers and they'd better be good ones," Ahxenta told the two.

"Mr Micklemouse, Mr Doosbak," verified Azular as he scanned.

"And in very good health," Dr Zaiklyn Oak added, examining his own readings.

The light enclosing the ship grew as the two stepped out and into full view. A strange bluish glow, increasing in strength, formed a large bubble around the craft and the seven on the ground. To the surprise of the other five, Micklemouse and his crony each checked a wrist-mounted device and then began to remove their helmets.

"A shell of thickened atmosphere, Captain; it approximates to an air mix of twenty percent oxygen, seventy nine percent nitrogen, with trace other gases. Source unknown, but the light globe's energy has decreased marginally," the science officer informed her.

"I see you have a new guardian, Micklemouse," Ahxenta noted, flicking a hand towards the orb. "How do you communicate with it?"

"You can take your helmet off, Captain, it's breathable," he said.

"That's not what I asked you. Answer the question. We're being scanned by my ship, by the way. One wrong move and you, your ship and this place will be reduced to rubble. Do I make myself clear?"

"Very clear, Captain," put in Doosbak, rubbing his hands together nervously. "It provides everything," he added, pointing to the globe.

"Nobody asked you, Doosbak. Well, Micklemouse?"

In fits and starts, the trader admitted that the strange light globe had appeared, as had the previous one, a day or two after he and his chum had been left on Kelfennig. It communicated with him, as far as he could tell, by some means akin to telepathy. In his opinion the orb was a manifestation of a lifeform comprised chiefly of energy and part of the planet itself. Doosbak could not to link to it. It somehow orchestrated the air bubble when necessary and had provided them with light and power. It was also the source of the information on the use of trace zukivianite as a means of differentiating hostiles from their dupes, and it had provided the means in terms of knowledge and transmitting power to contact the *Arianrhod*.

"That beggars the question why," Apnis put in from the bridge. "And where did all the hardware come from on a deserted world with nothing left worth scavenging apart from a few derelicts and those two comedians?"

Ahxenta had put the commander on speaker, partly to let the two know that the conversation was being monitored and partly for her own convenience. She had gone so far as to remove her helmet, as had Azular and Oak, but had instructed her guards to remain as they were. She could tell that the two castaways were eager to be removed from their isolation and pressed her advantage by instructing Azular to capture as much data on the still-floating energy globe as he could. Meanwhile she demanded that Micklemouse reveal all that he knew or suspected in relation to his guardian, its origins and its relationship to the hostiles and to the anomaly out at the Ginseng Nebula.

The trader's understanding was limited and amounted only to the deep but non-verifiable certainty that the entity, whatever it was, belonged to Kelfennig and was ancient. He was also convinced that the shattered structures across the planet were relics of a long-gone civilisation and the lifeform was what was left. It was as Ahxenta's questions were growing more searching that Azular called a warning: the globe had brightened and a second had appeared.

As Hanx automatically raised his rifle, Micklemouse yelled in fear and Doosbak interjected to maintain that they posed no threat. The captain again signalled lowering of weapons. Apnis' voice over the comm demanded to know what was happening and the landing team could hear the red alert being sounded aboard.

"Status quo, Commander," stated Ahxenta calmly. "Cancel the red alert but maintain amber. Well, Micklemouse? Reinforcements?"

"Another globe akin to the first, Captain; slightly different energy levels but otherwise unreadable, except for zukivianite traces," Azular reported dryly.

"Surprise. I felt the damn thing the second it popped up. Well?" Ahxenta demanded of the trader. "I'm assuming it's friendly or we wouldn't be standing here; and neither would you, come to that."

"I don't know, I'm not sure," he began.

"You'd better start making sense, Bick," Doosbak interrupted, his limited bravado evaporating. "It's here all the time," he elucidated. "Sometimes there's more than one."

"How many of the damn things are down there?" barked Apnis.

"I've only seen three at any one time," Doosbak put in uneasily but was quelled by a glance from Ahxenta, who then turned back to her quarry.

"I'm still waiting," she said ominously.

As the trader's pale face became paler, the second globe dropped towards him to surround him in a diffuse greenish glow.

"What the…" began Hanx as Azular and Zaiklyn Oak hauled up their scanners and began to sweep the twosome.

"I believe he's communicating with the entity, Captain," declared Azular. "He's capable of physical connection to an external source, as I suspected when first we met him. There's merging taking place."

"I concur," Oak said.

"It's done that before," Doosbak confirmed. "It tells him what to do and where to go."

"I'd be telling him where to go," muttered Apnis from the bridge. "Set up a locator probe with visual, Greffy and send it down there, homing in on the Cap's signal. I want to see what's going on."

"Aye, Commander," came the junior science officer's voice.

"There was a large population here once," Micklemouse said, his voice strained. "These things are all that're left. It was a war ages ago, interplanetary; most of the population cleared out. The ones left took shelter underground, in the tunnels that were part of their cities. They evolved over hundreds of centuries, became less substance and more energy. That's why they're almost bodiless now."

"Almost?" Ahxenta's tone was sharp.

"Some still have the ability to take shape, leftover technology from the past," Micklemouse mumbled through the haze. "There's only a couple of hundred or so left here now of the original population."

"Are you saying these are not the hostiles that are tearing up half the galaxy on their massive killing sprees?" the captain demanded.

"It says they're not," Micklemouse returned. "There are others out there; some were people from here that left long ago and settled the nearby star systems. The ancients here had the ability to adapt matter, including living matter, to suit their purposes. It says that after the last great war they sent out a genetically improved nucleus of their population to colonise other places, but I don't understand…" he trailed off miserably.

The trader's face changed as he was obviously trying to digest and relate the input he was receiving. "It's saying we viewed them as our successors, our children if you like, and we sent them out to colonise the empty spaces that the great war had left behind. It says, we were intent on teaching them our ways, passing on our knowledge and making them inheritors of a better galaxy than we had inherited from our ancestors… We endowed them with all we thought they would need, including bodies that could withstand the rigours of space travel in limited ships…"

"Anyone who thinks they can improve the universe by producing offspring and teaching them all they know is asking for a shit-load of trouble and deserve all they get," came the exasperated voice of Crizz Cottontail from the bridge of *Arianrhod*. "And these bodies that could tolerate the rigours of space travel were more mechanoid than meat, I bet; and were pissed when they found worse than they had at home. So they set up housekeeping for a few thousand years and then decided it was time to send out their own settlers, only they found a galaxy full of other people that had got there first and were weaker than they were, so they decided to take rather than ask nicely."

"Belay that, Chief," grunted Ahxenta. "What you're saying is that these hostiles operating out there originate close to here but not here. So why was *this* place seeded with traps to bring down ships to be scavenged – including, we suspect, their crews – by the hostiles?"

"A number of potentially habitable planets or those with resources around this area were targeted initially," the trader's voice continued. "To increase the chances of intercepting useful materials…"

"Nice way of putting it," the engineer was heard to remark.

"Here's the visual probe, Captain," Ensign Strawberry called. "It's made it through the atmospheric shell no trouble."

"Seeing you loud and clear," Apnis confirmed. "So that's an alien. Looks like the stuff around the Ginseng, only a different colour."

"There are still a lot of unanswered questions, but we don't have time," the captain said. "And I'm not sure I believe all this anyway. I don't like the company you're keeping, Micklemouse: you were an easy target for the hostiles that altered you for their own ends in the first place and here's this one that can use you as a mouthpiece. And it sends a shiver down my spine."

"It senses your reaction, Captain," the trader told her. "But it gave you the information about the zukivianite."

"And much use we've made of that so far," she retorted. "Apart from working out that Friskianx DNA has been incorporated into these hostiles, your people having such an affinity with them. What does this entity here, or you, know about the nature of the anomaly within the Ginseng Nebula in zone Lambda and what it's hiding?"

There was a pause before the man told her in anxious tones that the beings on Kelfennig tended to remain planet-bound and could pick up only on what they learnt from others using their world. Their information was thus limited but data derived from the few hostiles and their lackeys that had landed suggested that the locus around which the energy shield operated was likely to be a holding area for their ships coming in from sorties or from distant parts, or for ships being built in the local area.

"That doesn't help, Cap: ships built in the local area?" queried Apnis. "Where's local? Here? Arrissia? The Starglass? If that's the case and there's a massive hidden shipbuilding dock full of spanking new hostile warships in the vicinity, then we're in a heap of trouble."

"Well, mister? Where are these ships being built? They didn't just appear, they'd have to have been building for years even with stolen materials. And if hostiles keep coming back here, as we have reason to believe they do, your alien friend has to know why and when."

The man was cringing at the tone and muttering that he knew nothing about that, but slowly his features relaxed and he unbent.

"It's communicating through him again," Azular breathed.

"The ones you call hostiles return here to hunt for materials from our dead cities, but they visit many of the worlds close by and have several permanent bases," the trader stated evenly.

"Where?" Ahxenta demanded.

"They're showing me," he added nervously. "I don't know where, I can't figure the coordinates."

"Some navigator you must be," the captain growled irritably. "Gliss, can you set up the tactical holo, centre it at local space here and beam it down via the visual probe? Let's see if we can pinpoint what the hell he's trying to tell us."

"On it," came the voice of the tactical officer.

In moments the visual probe had collected the data and generated a holo of the immediate star systems. As the image spread to bring in more of the space in and beyond the border of zone Epsilon, a point of light lanced from the first light orb and circled one of the many nearby systems.

"It says there are other places they visit further out and established bases that that they know of," Micklemouse told them.

"This system is close to this side of the Starglass, Captain; not far from here, but in unmapped space," Azular noted, capturing the data. "The entity seems to understand what we need to know. If we can collapse the holo to show as much of the known galaxy as we can, we should be able to home in on the areas where it says these bases are."

"Got that, Gliss?" called Ahxenta.

"Reading you, Cap. Reconfiguring…"

As the holo became denser and denser as the stars came together, the captain was puzzling over a remark of the trader. "You said the beings here tended to remain planet-bound: does that mean they *can* leave this place if they want to?"

"They can," he responded. "But they don't like to. There aren't many of them left and I think they get afraid."

"What the hell for? They can't be hurt," Spendle Doosbak cut in.

"Want to bet?" Earbleat commented from the ship as Ahxenta asked Doosbak if he'd tried to hurt one.

"No, of course not," the man replied hurriedly but shiftily, eyeing his comrade for a fraction of a second.

Azular had been conning over the data that was being produced at a rate of knots as the holo before them expanded, the detail within shrinking further as the star mass became denser. "There seem to be five major planetary centres of hostile activity, Captain. That may be why they can strike at disparate targets with seeming ease. Four are in uncharted space: one is close to here at the edge of the Starglass, one is off zone Beta between Brown Amber and Mellifly, the third is in a system of the Outer Reaches Archipelago and the fourth is located at the edge of the Enigma Nebula off zone Mu, so again closer to here."

Ahxenta looked up sharply at his tone. "Where's the fifth?"

"Lartzeg Trine: an uninhabitable planet close to the boundary point where galactic zones Delta, Alpha and Epsilon meet."

"Bloody hell! And how long has that been there?"

"I've no information on that point, Captain."

"Lartzeg Trine!" Apnis repeated from the bridge. "Somebody had better warn the ISP at Skyrtek to be ready for one helluva big surprise if they launch from there as well as the Ginseng!"

"Zillah needs to know," Ahxenta declared. "If this is accurate, we owe your buddy here thanks, Micklemouse. If it isn't and we're on a fool's errand, we *will* be back to blow you and yours into very small pieces. But you haven't given us the lowdown on the field inside the Ginseng: its nature, its weaknesses and how we breach it; the number of ships it can hide; other similar places, and how we find them."

The man squirmed uncomfortably. "It's similar to the energy that the lifeforms here are made of but not sentient," he said diffidently. "If you fire on it, you'll disrupt the field momentarily but it'll absorb the impact and the energy. There may be weak spots but you'd have to get close enough to scan for them and then be able to send some disruptive power through. But it says there may be a lot of ships, it depends on how far it's expanded. They've been building ships for years. I don't think the ones here realised how far advanced the hostiles had become or how many other people had been affected by them. I think they're worried that this place might be on the hit list as the others keep coming back here, so…" he trailed off.

"So it would be good if we put a stop to them," Ahxenta finished. "How many of these hiding places are there?"

"There's only the one, as far as it and the others know – it uses vast amounts of energy that need to be generated."

"And what happens to all that energy when they do bust out?" Cottontail demanded from the bridge.

"One fizzing big bang, I expect," another voice interposed.

"It says the energy's used to power their ships," stated the trader. "They lose energy entering the space and pick it up on the way out."

"A form of energy exchange," Azular speculated. "When the field perimeter increases, it probably means that more ships have entered."

"We haven't time for a discussion on that now," the captain broke in. "We need to get back to the ship."

"You're taking us with you, I hope!" Doosbak cried out urgently.

"Like hell, I have enough to worry about," Ahxenta told him shortly. "But if we survive this, I *will* come back for you: you have my word on that."

As she spoke she was replacing her protective helmet. A hint had got through to the entity around Micklemouse, for the green haze coalesced into a globe as it drew upwards and away from him, to join in a frenzied overhead ballet with the original orb of light.

The trader let out a sigh but made no move to replace his own helmet. "We'll see you when you get back, Captain," he said.

She nodded brusquely and instructed her team to collect their gear. To their joint surprise, as the party made ready to leave by the way they had come, the first orb danced ahead of them, gradually brightening to the extent that they had no need of torches. There was a slight pop as the five from the *Arianrhod* breached the protective atmosphere and made for the tunnel and the way back to surface.

Their two security guards were expecting them and soon all were aboard and the shuttle prepped for departure. Ahxenta took the helm and in a short time the welcome form of *Arianrhod* was visible. The crew aboard her had also been busy and a top priority call had been put through to Admiral Zillah, who was out with the fleet that had by now pulled away from the Ginseng.

The captain lost no time in heading for her bridge office, where she was relieved to hear that the situations were status quo in zone Lambda and near Skyrtek. Conditions elsewhere had been ominously quiet. Ahxenta quickly brought the admiral up to date, advising her that although the information could not be verified and she had several reservations as to the reliability of the source, if it was accurate, then the lately-formed Alliance was heading for a meltdown of massive proportions.

"Ordering galactic defences on the basis of the word of a known felon and entities you're not actually sure are friendly? And dealing with allies whose upper ranks we know have been breached by the very hostiles we're up against? This is getting more like a lose-lose situation with every hour that passes," was Zillah's opinion. "All I can do is to pass on the information and hope enough of the various command staffs have things sufficiently under control to take action without being compromised. Our adversaries give the impression that they have a penchant for not caring what happens to them, given the losses they'll take without running for cover. It looks to me like they have some sort of hive mentality."

Ahxenta was nodding. "Interesting observation," she said. "If it's a hive, you take down the queen, but who and what and where?"

Zillah tapped her cheek, deliberating. "The hostiles originated from the neck of the galaxy you're in now," she began.

"No, Admiral, I will not," the captain stated before Zillah could go on. "My crew are not military, we're traders, and we sure as hell don't owe anyone service. We were drafted into this bloody war through the manoeuvrings of the Trades Alliance and so far it's cost me the lives and health of my crew, my livelihood and as near as dammit my ship."

"We lose this war and there won't be a galaxy for you to trade in," Zillah said bluntly.

"That kind of emotive blackmail doesn't work with me," Ahxenta declared. "If I were you I'd give more thought to what to do if a fleet of hostiles with chaos in mind does erupt out of Lartzeg Trine."

"What would you do?"

"I'd get in there first and check the place out: any suggestion of trouble and I'd blow it to bits before any fleet could get out of orbit or off the ground."

"You have a point. I need to get back to my duties. Good luck, Captain. I hope we meet again soon."

"Likewise. Ahxenta out."

Apnis looked shrewdly at the captain after hearing of her exchange with Zillah. "So what's our next step, Cinnabar? Oak's verified that the two down there haven't been technically or surgically interfered with since last we saw them, Azular's sure that the mouse believes he was telling us the truth and it looks like galactic war is imminent. And I don't have to remind you that we are damnably close to one of those permanent alien bases."

Ahxenta grimaced. "Probably the oldest one, if our information is accurate, since we've been told these hostiles originated there. And there's another one not too far away, off the Enigma."

"If our information's accurate," Crizz Cottontail grumbled from the engineering station. "Strikes me they or it told us what we wanted to hear. I'd head for Arrissia Five or Heligon and see if they have some big guns for sale. Even if we can't use them, you can bet your bottom credit there'll be a lot out there that are willing to pay over the odds for weapons at any price."

"Lartzeg Trine," Apnis frowned. "Deserted, zilch worth stealing and nobody goes there, no useful worlds in the local area and no bypass close enough to make it worth the bother. The closest big centres are Delta Iridium Colony and its outposts, the ISP stronghold in the Skyrtek system and the Friskianx system. No doubt the place made sense to somebody, especially the Friskianx bit; and it's pretty near central to the chartered galactic regions. It's a wonder the raiders didn't set up housekeeping there."

"Maybe they did and that's why the hostiles took it over: their ship designs are so damn near the raiders that many thought they were," Ahxenta posited. "If it *was* originally raider territory and a centre of raider shipbuilding, everything would be set up. Nobody ever figured where the raiders came from originally and they've terrorised the settled zones from time out of mind. Most thought they were based outside the mapped sectors, but right in the centre: now that's nerve. But the known galaxy's a mighty big place with plenty of unknown pockets. And there's a base by the Enigma Nebula, if Micklemouse's information is accurate. Ships could be built there using resources supplied by zone Mu independents, as well as meta-jurillium brought in from raids on the Dryssicon ore carriers as they expanded their ops. Isn't there a minor meta-jurillium ore source on Kirtish anyhow? It's the far side of Mu and well off the beaten spaceways."

"Yes there is and maybe there *could* be a shipbuilding yard off the Enigma," the first mate conceded. "Hell knows that area has been the source of rumours of strange goings on for forever and a day – as has the Starglass and most other nebulae come to that. And there *was* that huge yard over Mellifly and how the locals missed that is anyone's guess. But now our pet rodent's pals are telling us they're the good guys, really? I'll believe that when space turns pink. But that leaves us with another enigma, Cap: if these are the only places these hostiles are hanging out, what the hell's going on in sector sixteen of Beta? Why have we heard that things are going on there? You figured with Jurgall Three, Brown Amber and Mellifly on the doorstep and handy for gems for comms systems, meta-jurillium for ships and hell knows what else, that the empty spaces in sector sixteen would be a good bet for a base. Not to mention the never-ending local troubles among the smaller worlds, many of which are part of the Friskianx League, for resources and credit; and that damn space dock we took out around Mellifly sure was hostile. But now it looks like their actual base in that region is further out – maybe."

"Well, we have no contracts in hand at the moment as that trouble out at Arrissia Five prevented Lindell pushing for a trade for the last of the crystal comms materials we had modified at Freskat. We still don't know the nature of the problem at Arrissia so I'm loath to head in that direction and the local tactical relays have nothing other than an increased military presence out at Kellybar."

"They may need it, though they're not *that* close to the Enigma," reckoned Apnis. "One thing all this trouble *has* bought us and that's the way into ISP's tactical relay system, and the additional data that Zillah links through now and again. But without a next contract, we'd be best somewhere we're not sitting ducks if these hostiles do have a base down the road and decide to head out in this direction."

"I know. Box, set a heading for Aoria Six. There's a place there I know of that can supply scatter mines and a…"

The voice of Pollux Gliss cut across the bridge. "Picking up a change in local hyperspace! It's at distance but there's something."

Ahxenta shot to her feet. "Get ready to break orbit! Battlestations! Shields at maximum and weapons systems on line! Ready the cloak. Any more on the readings, Gliss?"

In answer, Gliss set the bridge holo to a full tactical readout. As the starfield expanded, a phalanx of small, bright dots appeared at the edge, slowly coalescing into tiny shapes that were the unmistakeable outlines of hostile warships.

"That's one helluva lot of ships, Cap!" breathed Apnis.

"Trying to get a bead, but they're too far!" Earbleat yelled.

"Cloak up! I want every gunnery station manned, fighters prepped for launch and every piece of kit we have trained on whatever's coming through. Drop a probe relay to monitor and get us to the other side of this planet, in its shadow. If they haven't spotted us yet, we may have a chance of keeping out of their range."

As the great ship manoeuvred and turned there was a gasp from Azular. "Something's heading this way from the planet, Captain! It seems to be an enormous shell of energy; it's almost off my scale! I don't understand... It's coming in..."

As he spoke the ship shuddered, straining against a mighty force.

"Cut engine power or we'll break up!" Ahxenta ordered, scanning her ops board closely.

"But Cap!" Cottontail croaked harshly.

"Do it! Station-keeping! Whatever this is, it's got a hold of us..."

As she spoke, the bridge holo-generator cut out and several bridge stations reported that they had lost all outside scanning, monitoring and comms signals. Her board flashed various warnings as Bellfish called out that reports were coming in from all decks that sudden power drains were being experienced.

"We're blind and deaf!" Tallica Apnis raged as she quickly called up various readings on her console.

Slowly the bridge holo expanded outwards again to show a pale blue-white glow, reflected against which were various shimmering, hazy shapes in shades of pink, silver and black.

26: BATTLES

The glinting mosaic of soft colour gradually coalesced into a discrete meshwork as the holo image sharpened to focus and the bridge crew almost simultaneously realised what it was seeing.

"It's our hull, a reflection of our hull!" Tallica Apnis exclaimed. "But we're cloaked! How in blazes can it read us?"

Ahxenta circled the holo like a predatory vulture. "Get a scan on what's surrounding us, Azular. Correlate it with the energy readings you took on the entities down there and on the Ginseng anomaly."

"On it," he said briefly. "You're right, ma'am: the readings, such as they are, are similar. It's a dense but ill-defined energy field and it's emanating from the planet below."

"Caught like a fly in a spider's web and we have a fleet of hostiles on approach!" the first mate said bitterly.

"I don't think so," Ahxenta countered as she tied herself back into her chair. "We can't see beyond the edge of this field and we're moving with planetary rotation, so we're caught in a tractor. But I'm guessing whatever is out there can't see us either."

"They're protecting us?" Apnis asked incredulously.

The captain shrugged. "I'm not sure, but why would they expend this amount of energy to hold us here for what's out there, when any hostiles in range could probably pick up our ion trail and home in? Even cloaked, we'd be a target if we made a run for it; and with *that* many ships, I doubt *Arianrhod* would get far or out in one piece."

"So why are those ships headed this way?" demanded Apnis.

"They could be skirting the Starglass on the way to where they're going, or crossing to the next bypass locus. Or they could have their own system of hyperspace beacons and bypasses: ways through that we don't know about. Let's see that last tactical of them, Gliss, and try to get a bead on their bearings," Ahxenta ordered.

"At this distance they could hardly pick us out, cloaked as we are," Cottontail objected. "One ship in orbit around a regular dead planet – we should be safe enough."

"This is hardly a regular dead planet, Chief; this is their place of origin," Azular interjected.

Gliss called up the tactical display and the holo enlarged to show the convoy. "They'll come pretty close, Cap, if they keep on that heading. But why cut through a planetary system at that angle? There can't be a local way onto a hyperspace bypass *this* close to the plane of the system."

"Habit," the science officer replied. "For all their advanced ways and their ability to learn from each encounter, there *is* some pattern in their attacks: they don't tend to back off even when outfought and outwitted, they sweep up all their leavings even when it costs to do so and they keep returning to Kelfennig and the local systems where they originated, even though they have bases elsewhere and have had for a very long time, eons possibly. And as we know, this particular planet is remarkably inhospitable."

"Hive mentality," Ahxenta broke in. "Zillah suggested it. Is there something that draws them back here, other than the search for what might have dropped in since last time?"

"Micklemouse said through his operator that they come back to hunt for materials from the dead cities," Azular reminded her.

"I don't suggest we go look," said Apnis. "So far we've nothing and every station is on full alert. We can't even see our probes. Even if this *is* an attempt by Micklemouse's pals to keep us hidden, I'm still sceptical that they have our welfare at heart – if they have hearts."

"You and me both," the captain told her. "But for now we work out what to do about what's surrounding us. I want every instrument we have capable of penetrating that energy field on the lookout."

"I wonder if this energy shell operates on the same principle as the anomaly," conjectured Azular. "It drains some of our energy to feed itself. But we've stabilised now and ship's systems appear to be running at near-normal, which suggests that the source of this field must itself be losing energy to maintain the projection."

"Your point?" Ahxenta demanded.

"Such a drain could be read by any ship coming close enough and with the technology to do so."

"Damn!" hissed the first mate. "But we couldn't penetrate the field in the Ginseng to see what was in it so how could another ship – unless it was one of theirs, I guess."

"I'm getting a signal through from our probe relay!" Gliss called. "There's a pinpoint hole opened in the field."

"They seem to know our thinking," Apnis noted dryly. "What have we got?"

"We've got the main fleet heading away from us on a track that takes it across uncharted space in the direction of zone Epsilon," the tactical officer reported after a moment, as he reconfigured the bridge holo. "But a couple of ships have broken off."

"This we don't need," muttered Apnis. "Are we on their menu?"

"We will be if they spy our probes," said the captain. "But we sure as hell don't recall them: we need them to keep sending us data."

"Hostiles approaching Kelfennig!" Earbleat called. "Two of them, big enough to eat us!"

"They're not targeting, as far as I can tell," said Gliss. "They can't have seen us or figured we're here. Why have they left the fleet?"

"Picking something up from here, perhaps," Azular predicted. "If they come close enough I could try to probe them, but they're likely to be able to detect my scanning beams."

"They come that close and they'll see us anyway," Earbleat told him. "What would they want to pick up? Lunch?"

"Maybe it's that zukivianite stuff," Greffy suggested. "This may be the nearest source and we know there are only a couple of places it can be got. Though why they would need it in a battle situation…"

"Repair of their crews," posited Azular. "But we don't know why they *have* diverted here, this is sheer speculation."

"That incoming warship isn't!" cut in Earbleat. "They've split up and one's heading our way!"

A huge black ship shot into the near field of view on a bearing that would take it within sight of the *Arianrhod*.

"It's maybe spotted one of our relay probes and is investigating," Apnis said to the captain.

"Dammit!" Ahxenta leaned forward, her eyes glued to the bridge holo as it shifted to show the massive warship, a shadow against the dark of space, alter course on approach vector. "They know a ship's here! Given our probes, they'll know it's not one of theirs and they'll know that damn energy field is planet-generated."

"They may figure we generated it as a cloak, Cap."

"Not if they work out we're cloaked within it. Cut our cloak, Dox, it's using too much power. Tactical, what's going on?"

"I think it's foxing them, ma'am," Gliss replied. "They're coming in for a closer look."

"All auxiliary weapons stations manned, secondary bridge on full alert," ordered the captain. "I don't know what will happen if they try to penetrate this field."

"That ship's turning," noted Apnis. "She's taking out our probes!"

"I don't recommend firing from within this field, Captain," Azular cautioned. "I could test what will happen using a tight energy beam."

"Do it. I don't want to run the risk of weapons fire bouncing back at us. Gliss, what are we getting through that hole in the field?"

"We've lost two of the probes in our relay and we can't see much from the other two, ma'am."

"We can't deploy weapons, they'll ricochet," warned Azular. "But hostiles must be able to leave such an area, so there must be a way."

"Control of what's generating the field," snapped Cottontail. "I suggest you aim a phase beam through that damn pinhole and blow the source to bits."

"We don't have to," Greffy announced as he scanned his display. "Hostile is doing just that: they've launched a massive spread!"

"You're right, she's targeting the source!" Gliss confirmed.

"We'll be next," the first mate predicted as she clamped her seat webbing tight. "Hell's teeth!"

"Chief, get the engines roaring, we'll need them!" barked Ahxenta. "Ready deflecting drones. All weapons stations prepare to fire on my mark. Dox, as soon as we're clear of this field get ready to break orbit and give us room to manoeuvre. Tactical, keep an eye on that second ship and let's hope they don't send for back-up. Earbleat, we may need *Loki III*."

"She's ready to run, Cap."

"Decoy, ma'am?" Azular demanded from his station.

"Not yet. Tallica, get the pilots to their fighters but I don't want to deploy unless I have to."

"Aye, Cap."

Seconds later the failure of the energy field caused the bridge-holo to collapse and reform as every external scanner flew into action. A mushrooming cloud from the surface of Kelfennig showed where the generation source had been blasted as Dox swung *Arianrhod* away from the planet at a tangent from the massive warship.

"They've launched missiles to the surface!" Gliss yelled. "They've spotted us now, they're turning!"

"Deflecting drones away!" Ahxenta roared. "Torpedoes, find your targets! Gunners, target their bays and comms. Gliss keep an eye on that second ship!"

"They're powering phase weapons!" the tactical officer bellowed. "They're trying to get close enough to deploy slicer beams!"

"Dox, evasive action... keep them guessing."

"They're not as fast as we've seen them; something's not right with them," Apnis grated.

"Confirmed! They're not running at full power and I detect only a handful of crew. They didn't expect to meet opposition here is my guess and they're unprepared," called Azular.

"Then we make this short. Take them down!"

"Aye, Cap!" Earbleat bawled. "Aft arrays, wide field, spray fire!"

"Tallica, take main weapons! Earbleat, get *Loki III* set to run. Dox, bring us round to optimum firing: that second ship's coming in."

The captain spun as the first mate reported the loss of several of *Arianrhod's* drones and the ship vibrated to multiple enemy weapons discharges. Dox strained at the helm as she manoeuvred the ship out of the firing line as Gliss called out that they had damage to their aft shielding and a cargo bay had been hit.

"Power spike from the surface, Captain!" Azular exclaimed in a ringing tone. "Energy beam directed at second enemy warship!"

"Pissed that their field was taken down," called out Apnis. "This bastard's making a fight of it; it's throwing everything at us!"

"Evasive!" yelled Ahxenta. "Respond in kind, all stations take down everything in your sights! Chief, how's our shielding holding?"

"Could be better, but still stable," the chief engineer returned.

"Second ship down!" Gliss cried. "It's being pulled to surface!"

"Micklemouse'll have a field day scavenging that beast," Earbleat observed in a carrying tone.

"Belay that and keep your hands on *Loki*," the captain ordered curtly as the ship shook to a sustained blast of enemy pulse cannon as the first hostile came on.

The bridge crew clung tightly to their stations and seat restraints tightened as *Arianrhod* slewed round to the deft manipulation of the helmswoman. Ahxenta gripped her command chair as the grind of ship's gravity systems strained to compensate.

"Ready to launch *Loki III*, Earbleat."

"On your mark, Cap," the second mate called.

"Belay!" Apnis yelled. "There's another energy spike from surface! It's targeting that hostile!"

Even as she spoke the bridge crew could see an intensifying green haze envelop their opponent. The black ship's weapons cut almost instantly and a blaze of bright light seared the watching eyeballs as what had been the enemy vessel imploded. The resultant ball of fire was pulled inexorably towards the planet's surface.

"All stations report," the captain commanded.

"Both enemy vessels destroyed," Gliss stated calmly.

"Did they get a message away?"

"Can't be sure, Cap, but there's no sign of incoming. What the blazes happened?"

"Friends in low places," Ahxenta responded dryly.

"And they're trying to make contact," Lynxi Bellfish announced from comms. "Incoming message: it's our old chum Micklemouse!"

"It would be," the first mate riposted, raising her eyes skyward.

"Stand down to amber alert; put him on visual," Ahxenta called over. "Let's see what he has to say."

"One word of truth in ten, I'll bet," Apnis grinned as she undid her tight seat webbing and stood up.

The round eyes and pinched expression told Ahxenta that the man was very scared indeed as he enquired after the wellbeing of *Arianrhod* and her crew. He and his crony had not been directly in the line of fire when the alien blast destroyed the surface locus that had been the source of the protective field, but they had been sufficiently close to feel the rumbles that signalled trouble. They had been aware of the alien intrusion into Kelfennig space and hence the likelihood of danger for *Arianrhod* and had thus alerted their minders and asked for help, he assured Ahxenta. The result was the protective bubble around the starship and the surface reactions to the subsequent hostile attack. The aliens would henceforth be disallowed landing on Kelfennig, now that they were no doubt aware that not only did ancient life exist there, it was quite capable of defending itself.

"So that's the kids cut off without a credit then," the first mate remarked wryly, raising one eyebrow in disbelief as she reclaimed her usual seat. "And as for those two, they were only worried they would lose their source of transport off-planet and back to civilisation."

"What about the main fleet?" the captain demanded, ignoring her second. "Their heading and purpose."

Micklemouse licked his lips. "I don't know. Neither do *they*."

"I expect you'll be lifting us off from here," Doosbak interrupted from the rear, peering hopefully over his mate's shoulder.

"You expect wrongly," Ahxenta replied shortly. "I said I'd come back for you and as you are aware, I haven't left yet. I *will* be seeing you both again. Ahxenta out."

"Not worth pushing for more information, then?" Apnis asked.

"It would take us too long to get it out of him. But I expect we should be grateful to his guardians. Let's get the hell out of here: Box, plot us an initial course for Heligon repair station. I'll get Lindell to sound them out for weapons resupply and minor repairs. Then we're for Aoria Six for major repairs to our weapons emplacements and a few additional munitions."

"Like scatter mines?" the commander suggested.

"Precisely. But I'd better let Zillah know she may have another fleet heading her way."

"That'll make her day for her."

"No doubt. Not much we can do, but we remain at amber alert. And get the crew onto as much ship's repair as you can. At least we have only a couple of bumps and bruises in medbay."

"This time," was the laconic rejoinder.

Heligon repair station was markedly quiet when *Arianrhod* hove to for resupply. The only heartening news they had had en route was that a mass exodus attempted by a flotilla of hostile ships from the anomaly within the Ginseng Nebula had run afoul of the perimeter mines that Zillah's fleet had planted. There had been fewer ships than expected but many had been destroyed before the rest were aware. Those that had made it out had forged on and were on a heading that implied a route across zone Delta that would take them into zone Epsilon and Skyrtek. In light of Ahxenta's news, it was likely that the fleet out of the Starglass was aware of the action at the Ginseng and was headed to investigate. Apnis considered it lucky for the *Arianrhod*, otherwise the hostile fleet may have turned back for them at Kelfennig.

Lindell had been busy and had managed to pick up a commission for the transport of small industrial modules from Heligon to Vellisa Colony, a route that would take them in their intended direction. The station itself was running short of necessary repair parts but as they were charging excessively for what they did have, Ahxenta was not inclined to help out by running supplies in from elsewhere. She felt the need for speed and as soon as basic repairs to *Arianrhod* had been completed, she gave the order for departure for Vellisa.

The trip to Vellisa took a couple of days standard and over that time the various comms relay systems to which *Arianrhod* was privy were disturbingly quiet. The ISP tactical relay was updated regularly and seemed to consist of lists of safe havens for ships trying to escape the skirmishes purported to be initiated by the hostiles in several pockets throughout the mapped galaxy. One puzzling feature was the number of alleged sightings of a band of hostile ships which did not engage with the vessels that reported it.

By the time the *Arianrhod* had dropped her cargo at the colony and was well on the way across the open reaches of Delta to Lambda and

Aoria Six, it was apparent that hostilities were intensifying. A number of mining stations in the Outer Reaches had been devastated by hit and run tactics and the miners were deserting in droves, leaving their intact ore carriers in orbit around their stations and booby-trapped in an effort to discourage boarders. The blockade at Jurgall Three was holding but attempts had been made to smash it by what looked like raiders pretending to be invaders and failing dismally. An issue more of interest to the *Arianrhod* was that the Trades Alliance had formally recognised all the Privates as vital to the war effort and was trying to revoke the flags of those who would not comply. Ahxenta, having been alerted by Bluejohn of the *Obsidian Sky*, was shrewdly remaining offline as far as contact with the TA was concerned. The *Obsidian* had been requisitioned to run refugees from the systems neighbouring Marridan to the safety of Selliden and her captain was mightily put out. Of the Merkat system and its vast Web there had been little word, but the situation there was held to be status quo. With that Ahxenta had to be content: her people there would have to do what they could if push came to shove, was all that she could say.

Admiral Zillah was holding her own at Freskat. She had refused to join the motley fleet of Alliance vessels heading to Skyrtek on the basis that there were known enemy bases as close to her neck of the woods as dammit and she was not about to leave her home world undefended. Ahxenta's news on the hostile exit from the area around the Starglass had increased her concerns and she was digging in.

It was three days later that the *Arianrhod* switched to the final beacon for Aoria Six. She was running silent, her long-range scanners set to maximum, when Bellfish picked up a distress call from a trading ship out of Freskat to Nyx, a small enclave close to the Aoria system. The trader had spotted the hostile fleet and had sent an alert to her home base of Freskat. The ship herself had been detected and a warship was closing in on her at speed. She had no chance of outrunning or outfighting the enemy and was calling for help.

"Damn! That's all we need and if we keep on this line, we'll meet it," Ahxenta declared. "Battlestations!"

"This is getting to be a habit," Apnis remarked, stepping onto the bridge to the wail of the red alert. "Does this mean all the artillery we picked up on Heligon is down the tubes before it even has a chance to lose its shine?"

"Probably. Earbleat, ready *Loki*. Maybe we can take it out in one fell swoop if we can come at it with surprise on our side."

"They'll have our spec locked into every damn ship of their fleet, I'll bet," the first mate responded irritably.

"Price of fame. Cloak up, Dox; Greffy, ready the decoy and get Azular up here. Medbay, set for casualties: by the time we get there we may have a few."

"By the time we get there, there may not be a ship left to rescue," Apnis said in a low tone.

"Do *not* respond to that distress, I don't want us picked up," Ahxenta ordered. "Chief, we need all speed. Helm…"

"On it," responded Dox. "Get us the most efficient and fastest way through," she directed the nav officer.

"You got it."

The great ship sped through hyperspace, the gravity wells causing her seams to creak. Box had plotted a course that would bring her out at the last known position of the distressed vessel. With every eye and ear alert, a large ship was spotted close to the edge of the Nyx system where the local bypass node would bring *Arianrhod* out almost on top of her. The captain was scanning the bridge holo keenly.

"We'll have to accelerate through to catch her. Azular, get all you can on that ship; make sure she *is* a hostile and not something else."

"Aye, Captain… status confirmed, she matches known hostile profiles. I get trace zukivianite with organic moieties, so she's crewed. She's armed with phase cannon, torpedoes, slicer beams and two novel external attachments that read as highly explosive."

"Might be their version of *Loki*," Apnis muttered. "I think she's aware that something's coming off the bypass."

"Earbleat, have the gunnery crews target and fire the second we're through and ready *Loki* for deployment. Target those external pods. We don't know what the hell they are but we don't want them in our face. Cloak down once we're through. Tie yourselves in people, this'll be a rough ride!"

As *Arianrhod* breached the exit to the bypass she banked swiftly to outwit incoming fire. Her weapons crews, well-used to these tactics, were ready and let loose with everything that would hit a target. Cursing volubly, Earbleat sent her precious *Loki III* into the firing line and followed her up with a spread of torpedoes.

"Weren't ready for that, were they?" the first mate bawled into the air as the enemy's flank burst open in a blaze of reddish light.

A second tight spread of torpedoes was sent through the rupture by the still seething Earbleat. The hostile vessel broke apart, great chunks of fiery metal spinning away into the night.

"Get us some distance, helm!" Ahxenta ordered loudly. "Any sign of that trading ship or its escape craft?"

Bellfish turned. "I'm picking up a standard distress, but it's not the ship."

"You won't pick up the ship," Gliss reported, his mouth tight. "The only thing left of her is flak. But there's one – no make that two – small escape craft, one damaged but intact; the other's okay, I think. They're both heading for Nyx."

"Let's pick 'em up, they'll be a long time getting anywhere. All stations, report in. Tallica, you take the reports and set us on course for Aoria once we're done here. Bellfish, let them know help's on the way and pass the details on to medbay: the doc'll want to be there when they come in. Crizz, get your teams to haul those two boats in using the tractors in aft cargo bay nine. I'm heading down there."

The nine dazed survivors of the small trader *Sunset Solo* out of Freskat were grateful for their rescue. They had been a crew of sixteen and had had no option but to run when they realised they were being targeted, the ship's second engineer told Ahxenta. Their missing crewmates had volunteered to man the ship and distract the hostiles while the two small escape craft made the run for safety. If *Arianrhod* had not shown when she did, he doubted they would have made it. All that the captain could offer by way of solace was that Freskat had already been warned of a fleet heading in their direction and were no doubt preparing to engage.

Ahxenta left the survivors with Flintlock in medbay and returned to the bridge. Azular had been sifting through the readings from the drifting wreckage to work out the nature of the external reservoirs of the hostile and had deduced that they were repositories for some sort of explosive devices such as mines. He could take no samples as once the ship had been made ready for departure the first mate had ordered the course set for Aoria Six.

"We have to assume that the rest of the fleet are carrying similar," the captain concluded. "I'd best pass that onto Zillah as well. If they do loose a spread of mines, her fleet won't get out of its own space. I hope Lindell's been able to source *us* more than scatter mines; we're down on torpedoes, energy cells and deflecting drones. These damn hostiles must have a pretty classy comms system: we only have to use a trick once and they're on it and have produced their own version before we can turn around."

"Crack their comms and you crack their fleet," Apnis groaned, yawning. "I could sleep for a week, I'm bone tired."

"Take a couple of hours; we have ten before we make port."

"Like hell, you've been on duty longer than I have. Once you've linked to Zillah, you take three hours sack time and then I'll take three. I'd best rotate the duty crews as well, they've all pulled double shifts. We really need to get our people back from Merkat."

"Done and done. See you on the flipside."

Aoria Six was quick to open her port to *Arianrhod*. She was known there and as the captain had called ahead to notify the authorities that she had shipwreck survivors and that she would require repair as a result of yet another run-in with the enemy, she was doubly welcome. Looking for the colour of their credit was the first mate's opinion when Lindell informed her and Ahxenta of the costs of bringing their weapons and arrays back to standard. The three had taken a shuttle down to their main suppliers to argue the toss but were tolerably realistic, realising that dealers were there to make a profit and when circumstances warranted it, they would push for maximum.

The threat that once the current conflict was resolved *Arianrhod* would take her custom elsewhere produced some concession but the price was a sore point, particularly for Lindell, who tended to regard the purse-strings of the ship as his own. Grist, the second engineer of the *Sunset Solo*, had taken a hand to persuade his Freskat employers to defray part of the cost as compensation for the recovery of himself and his mates but he was only partially successful.

"If you'd consider alternatives to the local titanium-alloy for our weapons emplacements, Captain," the supercargo had suggested over a schooner of ale in a local hostelry, "The cost would reduce."

"And so would the standard of my ship, Lindell. No go."

"At least we haven't had to pay for the beer," Apnis reminded her pacifically. "And this is as close as the crew will get to shore leave for the foreseeable future. We'll be here at least four days to get this lot fitted. And they will advance us credit; we're well-known enough to warrant that. Any news of more business for us?"

"I'm waiting confirmation from a local company that might take our remaining comms wafers. I've sent in the specs and they'll let me know," Lindell informed her. "They're pricy pieces but as they're in short supply, we probably have the upper hand."

"Do what you can," the captain told him. "They'll pay for the scatter mines at least. But we've got a visit to make, Tallica. We need a couple of new cargo pods."

"Hell, this isn't the start of *Loki IV* is it? Earbleat hasn't stopped bending my ears about it since she lost *Loki III*. She'd have a fleet of the damn things if you let her. She should patent the design and sell the rights: that would pay off all our debts and let us retire."

"You wish. This is a tip I got from Grist of the *Solo*: he has family here in the business and we'll get a good deal. And a few extras."

The first mate knew her captain well enough not to probe her on the last cryptic remark and swallowed the last of her beer quickly.

The following four days passed in a whirl of activity for *Arianrhod's* senior officers. The lesser ranks were given as much time on shore as could be spared as most of the exterior works were carried out by fitters from Aoria's orbital repair bays. The news from outside was limited as long-range jammers had blocked much of the output from numerous relay stations. The TA channel had remained clear and Ahxenta had little option but to connect when targeted calls came in. Her face dark with anger told her bridge crew that she was mightily unhappy with a message received two hours before the ship was due to depart on a long-haul trip to Merkat via Delta Iridium with a load of food supplies for the latter's small outpost world of Iris Three.

Apnis stepped in where most would baulk and faced the captain squarely. "What's to do, Cinnabar?"

"Freskat's under attack and it looks like Skyrtek Prime has trouble heading its way. We've been ordered to the defence of Freskat."

"Do we go?" the first mate asked softly as every breath on the bridge was caught for an instant.

"We go. There's another fleet of unknowns been sighted on a heading that'll take it straight to Alto Finglas…"

"Alto Finglas? The HQ of the TA Assembly and as close as dammit to one of the major ISP construction docks? But where's it come from?" demanded Apnis.

"Sector sixteen of zone Beta."

27: ARIANRHOD AT WAR

The bridge crew took a moment to steady its collective nerve as the captain ordered all hands to make ready for departure. The heading was Freskat Six and the order was silent running and red alert. The crew had been informed of the current mission, but Ahxenta refused to drop her cargo for Delta Iridium. As her engines fired up into life, *Arianrhod* released her docking traces and slid rearward from her bay, turning to face Aoria's yellow sun before making for the entry to the local bypass. The farewells of Port Control were muted as she picked up speed to align with the node that would take her through.

"Entry to bypass successful," Dox reported needlessly. "En route to Freskat. Estimate nine hours maximum."

"Now we wait for news?" Apnis asked quietly.

"Now we get the ship as ready as she'll ever be to protect herself," the captain said harshly. "Nobody gets *Arianrhod* without one helluva fight."

The hours to the Freskat system were spent by those teams not on watch in increasing and strengthening every defence mechanism the ship possessed. Her external weapons emplacements were legendary for their durability but Ahxenta had ordered reinforced hull shielding patches and intensified energy fields for her massive openwork cargo bays as well as sundry smaller sections. The captain had picked up the resources on Aoria, reckoning that if she had no need of them for *Arianrhod*, she could sell them on at a healthy profit elsewhere.

The local comms relay stations were being jammed, but after one mighty burst of static, Bellfish called that they were receiving garbled messages about various scattered firefights. *Arianrhod* was less than an hour from Freskat's nearest bypass intersection.

"Looks like somebody's taken out the jammers, Cap," remarked Apnis. "The good guys getting the upper hand?"

"Maybe. All stations, report status: I want continuous updates. I expected more fighting further out."

"We can't make out specifics until we're off the bypass," the first mate grumbled as the bridge holo-generator dropped down into full view and the two scanned the tactical readouts.

The ship moved ever closer to her endpoint. Ahxenta had decided to come out of hyperspace at speed to give her any advantage going. She expected some reception at the node but distorted comms gave no clues as to which way the fighting was going. As she erupted into the outer edges of the Freskat system, the great ship's seams creaked, pinning everyone in their seats as the helmswoman sent her into an explosive downward spiral to deflect incoming fire. The holo-readout expanded and swirled with the motion and as it slowed, a pinpoint of light off the edge of the display resolved into several discrete images that were moving inexorably towards the blip that was *Arianrhod.*

Through the wails of the alert and the flash of emergency lighting, the crew called out ship's status. Frequent blows from disruptive flak caused sparking on the holo and shuddering as *Arianrhod's* shielding strove to compensate.

"Catching the edge of a minefield!" Gliss yelled.

"Gunnery crews two and three take them out and cut us a path through!" Ahxenta ordered. "Dox, get us as close as you can without bringing us into sight range of Freskat Six. We'll try to come up in the shadow of her second moon. Most of the fighting seems to be on the far side of the planet. Gliss, make sure we can distinguish Alliance from hostile vessels. It looks like a full-scale assault's just begun."

"Planetary defence systems all but out, Cap," the tactical officer called. "There's a defensive wall of three Freski heavy cruisers this side of the orbital docking facility but they're up against a blockade of five hostiles, with probes and perimeter mines in several planes. The place is sewn up tight. Other firefights are ongoing further out, close to planet eight. Those blips headed our way are reading as hostile, though they're smaller than the usual warships."

"Akin to sweepers, Captain," Azular reported. "Several and well-armed. Set to take out anything that comes off the bypass is my best guess. They're showing minimal life signs."

"Target with phase cannons! And launch deflecting drones once that first ship gets in range!" Ahxenta roared. "Earbleat, ready your little surprises but do not launch."

The ship lurched to the onslaught of shockwaves against her hull but held her own as the senior science officer called out loudly that enemy fire was slow but steady.

"Their arsenals are running out. Punch us a hole through those ships! Get full tactical on them and take them down any way you can as we go in. They're trying to stop us getting through."

"There're too many for our guns, Cap!" boomed Earbleat.

"They're bunching for an all-out assault on our flanks! Permission to launch scatter mines! I can push them out of our side torpedo tubes and set for wide spread."

"Do so. Auxiliary gunners, take out any stragglers. Dox, get us into optimum position for firing forr'ad torpedoes."

A duo of incoming ships broke off to come up below *Arianrhod* as she banked to outmanoeuvre the pack. The remaining ships were fast and at the same instant the formation split in an attempt to avoid the highly explosive mines.

"Cap, something else coming through the bypass!" Gliss yelled.

"Ours or theirs?"

"Ours! It's a PSS! It's the *Tallulah*!"

"It would be," Apnis groaned. "I thought she'd be running for cover. What's she doing in this part of the galaxy? Wasn't she at Delta Iridium last we heard?"

Ahxenta was on her feet closely scanning the tactical display. "At least she's fielding some of the flak. Three hostiles have broken off to intercept. But look at the flight pattern: those two ships are following that larger one. As it moves, they repeat the manoeuvre."

"You're right. They're cutting off but reforming around her. That other three are doing the same. Central control?" guessed Apnis.

"Take out the queen," the captain reflected aloud as she pointed at the display. "Earbleat, launch cargo pod alpha at that larger ship off our port side. And make sure you hit her head on."

"Oh I will," the weapons officer promised. "My guidance systems are the best. Team three, you keep back-up fire going to distract her! And don't slack on those port and aft phase arrays!"

"Aye, ma'am!" echoed from the gunnery crews as *Arianrhod* shook again to another volley of incoming fire.

"They're certainly low on weapons and haven't launched fighters," the first mate muttered, puzzled. "Shit! Incoming! There's another two aiming to ram! Dox, evasive! Team two, get your torpedoes down those tubes!"

As the first of the two ramming vessels exploded, *Arianrhod* burst through the expanding shell of debris, pieces spattering her hull in a rain of hissing metal.

"There goes my paint!" Ahxenta spat as the ship slewed and she was almost thrown off-balance. "Get that other beast out of my sky!"

"Got you!" Earbleat hissed as the larger vessel of the closest trio exploded, its attendant craft continuing in decreasing spirals towards one another.

"They'll take each other out!" Apnis yelled.

"Advise *Tallulah* to target the largest of the attacking ships with all she's got!" Ahxenta bawled over to Bellfish. "How are they doing?"

"Not good, ma'am; they've taken quite a pasting."

"Breaching pod incoming!" one of Earbleat's seconds yelled out from his station. "Targeting… got it!"

Arianrhod shuddered to the rain of yet another volley of fire on her hull and Cottontail cursed fluently as one engine sustained a glancing blow. She yelled for increased internal shielding to compensate whilst striving to augment the power output of the others.

"Dammit! There goes another aft shield!" Gliss hollered over.

"The attack is definitely slowing, Captain," Azular affirmed loudly above the clamour of the battering. "But they'll not give up."

"Then we hit them with everything in our arsenal! All weapons stations, take out everything in your sights! Earbleat, ready *Loki IV*, we may need her. Helm, hard about!"

"Auto-repair active on hull plate," Cottontail broke in as the ship slewed around yet again and everyone held on. "But aft shielding is losing integrity."

The bridge holo was one mass of bursting stars and jets of flame as *Arianrhod's* firepower began to tell and the smaller hostile vessels were caught in the explosive backlash of their sister ships.

"Got you!" came the triumphant roar of the weapons officer as the PSS swept up and away from incoming fire. "That's the last of our hostiles accounted for, Cap."

"*Tallulah's* in trouble," Apnis gasped as she righted herself.

"She would be. Helm, set course to assist *Tallulah*. Let's see: we still have torpedoes and two full energy cells. Target the larger of those blips. It's almost done anyway, it's afire amidships."

As *Arianrhod* sped through the ever-increasing field of debris she loosed a pair of torpedoes and followed it up with phase cannon. The largest of the trio targeting the *Tallulah* broke apart in a bloom of red fire. Her two companion vessels were too close and as they shot through the wreckage of their leader they were caught in the energy wash of the explosion.

"Get us out of this damn flak field!" the captain yelled. "Bellfish, raise Fleetskup and get his status."

"Commander Goodsocks on the comm, Cap!" was the response.

"Hell, they're in a mess," the first mate noted as the dishevelled face of Melly Goodsocks materialised.

"Can you move out of the debris field?" Ahxenta asked.

"Barely," responded the first mate of the *Tallulah*. "But we'll make it. Thanks for the assist, Captain; that was close. We'll have to retreat, we've nothing left."

"So I see," was the dry reply. "You've got manoeuvring thrusters, can you make it back to the bypass and head for a safer place?"

"We'll have to. We've taken a beating and have a lot of casualties. You couldn't let us have Greenwing back could you?"

"I had to leave him on Merkat. He was injured in our bust-up at Kifferbuck," Ahxenta told her. "I can't spare a medic as we have our own casualties. And we're not finished yet. Where's your captain?"

"On sick leave at Delta Iridium Colony," she replied tartly. "With Tommy Buntle holding his hand."

"You got drafted," Ahxenta guessed. "And couldn't say no."

"We did. The captain *is* quite sick, though: a pesky stomach bug. I didn't want him infecting the rest of the crew and he wouldn't stay in the iso-bay. So I relieved him of command."

"Good for you. Sorry we can't provide more of an assist, but we're set for Freskat. Suggest you head for Aoria: it's close and was clear when we left."

"Thanks for your help. We wouldn't have made it without. See you on the flipside. Goodsocks out."

As the *Tallulah* limped slowly off towards the bypass and *Arianrhod* set for Freskat, Apnis turned to Ahxenta. "Think they'll do okay?"

"With Goodsocks at the helm, yes. Fleetskup may have his good points but he's no commander."

"His good points are well hidden. But we have a lot of casualties, Cinnabar; mostly minor, I know, but we're low on weapons and our hull is far from sound." Apnis pointed to the captain's console as she spoke in a low voice. "But we're still headed to Freskat? What gives? Something personal?"

Ahxenta responded with a slight nod. "The Alliance loses this war and we're unlikely to have a galaxy to do business in," she said. "But I've been looking at the configuration of the blockading ships. There are two heavy cruiser type battleships and four smaller warships and they're spread with the larger ships equidistant to each other and each with a pair of smaller escorts."

"You reckon the cruisers are directing the smaller ships? But there are relays of probes and mines as well and you can bet they're set to detect and take out any incoming ship or any escape craft."

"I agree. But according to Azular the ships are barely manned. And none of them are as large or as well-equipped as that first great beast that ambushed us in the Orriga Sector way back."

"Cinnabar, I hate to argue, but we're hardly in a condition to jump in all guns blazing against even one of those two big battle-buckets. And as your second…"

"I do something as rash as that and you relieve me of command?" Ahxenta grinned.

"Don't think I wouldn't."

"Appreciate it, but no, we're not about to jump in. This is where Earbleat and her protégées come in. According to the tactical display, the nearest enemy ships that can ride to the rescue of the blockading hostiles if they're in trouble are beyond the orbit of the eighth planet and they seem to be engaged."

"There might be others, shielded."

"True, but there would be signs and they would be here by now. My guess is they're overstretched and have met more opposition than they expected. So now is the time to strike. Lieutenant Commander Earbleat, what is the situation of your targeting heavy drones?"

"Ready when you are, Cap. Azular's fitted them with shielding as near as dammit to hostile specifics, so we hope they won't twig until too late that they're not friendly. They should be big enough to sting and my teams can control them accurately as long as they have clear target readouts. *Loki IV* also ready to go on your mark," she added.

"Bet she's got a sting in her tail as well," Apnis sniffed as the crew was ordered to standby action stations. "But if the drones are targeting the big ships, how do we take out the probes and mines?"

"Fighters," the captain said briefly, webbing in tightly. "They're far enough from the ships to be taken out with minimal damage."

"You hope. Our pilots are good but this isn't a simple search and destroy mission: they'll be targeted."

"A risk we have to take: all the relevant data's been uploaded to their onboard computers. And once we go in, Freskat should be able to mobilise more forces. Planetary defence shield's spitting still and those three heavy cruisers are maintaining tight orbits," the captain indicated the bridge holo as she spoke and circled the three Freski ships with her holo pointer. "And they haven't yet been destroyed so it looks like the hostiles are biding their time."

"Maybe they can afford to," warned the first mate.

"All hands, battle-ready! Earbleat, once we're in range, let go your first wave of drones and deploy *Loki IV* at the same time, targeting the engines of the closer of the two large ships. Helm, get us in under the shadow of the second moon and hold station unless fired upon.

That orbital defence platform should give us enough cover, though the hostiles know we're here. All fighters prepare to launch on my mark…"

As Dox announced final approach to their optimum deployment position, a flurry of commands volleyed across the bridge. The first wave of targeting drones was locked to target and held on course as *Loki IV* shot out of her hold like an arrow from a bow and *Arianrhod's* fighter squadron took to space in an expanding formation that ate up the distance to its goal. Ahxenta had ordered the launch of deflecting drones to draw enemy firepower away from her ship but had them sent in tight array to beyond the nearby defence platform before spreading, to confuse their opponents' tactical readouts.

Apnis had taken over the auxiliary weapons station to free other hands for action. She targeted long-range torpedo fire in rapid bursts alongside *Loki IV* to protect the small craft from retaliation by her objective, as the large battleship had not been idle and a small fleet of fighters was homing in on her.

"Directional torpedoes incoming!" Gliss yelled. "They've got our mark and are targeting!"

"Take them out! Helm, hold fast! Cottontail, augment forr'ad shielding!"

"*Loki* almost at target vessel…" Earbleat was hollering at the top of her powerful lungs. "Almost there… almost… go *Loki*! Choke on that, you big bastard!"

"Target vessel moving out of position," Gliss called. "Her engines have taken a direct hit and she's crippled. Her fighters are in disarray, but are attempting to protect her. She's still launching torpedoes."

"Those are manned fighters, Captain!" Azular was surprised. "Trying to get readings on the nearest but interference is high."

"Most of the nearby probes have been taken out," Apnis reported. "Our deflecting drones have set off the local mines and cleared the way in one sector at least."

"Detecting surface fire!" Gliss chimed in. "Freskat's sending up ballistics to bolster their defence grid! And one of their defending ships is taking on one of the two smaller hostiles."

"Breakup of target ship imminent," Apnis declared. "That was one good shot with *Loki*, Earbleat."

"Our fighters are reporting this area clear of probes; scattered mines remaining but they're on them," Bellfish put in.

The smaller warships were evidently under some sort of defensive coding or had received instructions from their control ship for they turned in unison on a course that set Ahxenta on her feet.

"Bastards! They're aiming to crash on Freskat! Break station and get us between the surface and those ships! Let loose with anything we've got left and take them down!"

As *Arianrhod* tilted sharply and swept towards the vast blue-green bulk of the planet, her forr'ad arrays spewing death, Gliss hollered that another vessel was approaching at full speed from the bypass. The captain had only a second to take in the silhouette of black against black before she was flung bodily across the bridge.

"Shit that was close!" one voice rang out.

"Massive warhead, just missed us," Apnis panted as she crawled over to assist her commanding officer. "Those warships pack some secret punches. Bastards must have been saving it for us. Dox, steady as she goes, the *Arianrhod's* not a bloody guided missile! Are you alright, Cap?"

"I'll live. What the hell happened?"

"Dox got us out of its path double quick and the *Obsidian's* taken it out," explained the first mate as she helped Ahxenta back to the command chair and strapped herself in alongside. "Bluejohn jumped in: *Obsidian's* up to spec, she's raining fire."

Assisted by ground cover, the two great trading ships made speed towards the hostiles and the planet's sky exploded in a display of light and flame as the enemy warships were sent to hell. Proximity alerts on *Arianrhod's* bridge gave warning of more trouble and the spinning holo-viewer brightened as the second threesome of enemy warships hove into sight, closely pursued by one of the Freski cruisers.

"If our fighters still have firepower left, instruct them to widen their sweep and destroy as many probes and mines as they can," Ahxenta ordered. "What have we got?"

"Pulse cannon are still operational but their energy cells read low, one high energy torpedo array, a bucketful of deflecting drones and that's it," Apnis read out. "Our surface arrays are capable of causing damage but only close up. The *Obsidian's* mopping up what the Freski Navy has left of that big battle-bucket and here comes the frigging cavalry at last: those are two more Freski ships, light destroyers by the look of them."

"Then we hold up for now. Helm, get us back on an even keel and away from the atmosphere, we're too close. Don't drop those shields. Reel our fighters back in," the captain directed, waving away a medic who was trying to repair a cut to her forehead. "Damage reports, all stations! Medbay, how are things your end?"

A harassed Flintlock sent through the casualty list. It was lengthy but the captain was relieved to note that there had been no fatalities. With extensive hull damage and one engine down, engineering was ordered to deploy repair drones immediately. Freskat had despatched hospital ships to pick up any escape pods that had made it out of vessels destroyed in the battle and reports were coming in of the extent of the devastation of parts of the planet by the first wave of blockading enemy ships.

"Stand down red alert," Ahxenta called, scanning her bridge crew, many of whom were cut and bruised. "Let's pick up the pieces."

The captain was assiduously checking the worst hit areas of planet six at the deserted comms station as news continued to pour in of the heavy losses sustained. Apnis looked over her shoulder.

"Most of the major outposts seem to be okay," Ahxenta said as she glanced up. "Looks like the hostiles were targeting large industrial works and they tend to be on the outskirts and well away from other structures or in mostly uninhabited areas."

The first mate looked closely at the area that she had homed in on. "Your buddy's place down there?" she asked quietly.

"Intact, no core losses reported. Just as well."

"If you don't mind me asking, Cinnabar, just who *is* your friend down there?" her second enquired in an undertone. "You've never as much as mentioned a name, you always go alone to do business and you're often in mufti when you do."

The captain tilted her head to one side and sighed. "My son."

"What!" Apnis was stunned. "Hell, Cinnabar, I never knew…"

"No; adopted son, I should say, he's not biologically mine. He was my brother's boy. He was badly hurt as a baby in that mining disaster at Limekiln years ago: my brother and his partner Jo were temporary-contract engineers there. They left Limekiln to bring him to Freskat for specialist care. They left him at the hospital here and made for their home on Lamella to sell their place and collect their gear for a permanent move to Freskat. Their ship was taken out by raiders on the way back."

"Bloody hell, Cinnabar, I'd no idea… But why you?"

"I've no other family; neither had Jo and the boy would have been sent hell knows where as an orphan. I'd little option but to adopt him officially even though I was so young: he's my only blood kin and the damn authorities wouldn't recognise the kinship otherwise. But I had to put him to guardianship as I was headed for my obligatory stint in military service and the bastards wouldn't rescind my warrant."

"Is that why you didn't go military as a career?" asked the first mate softly. "I always wondered why, you seemed cut out for it."

"One of many reasons. Anyway, his area at the edge of the main settlement's not been hit, so I have to assume that he's okay. And we have a ship to get to rights. This had better be where our military service ends, war or no war."

"My ear's here if you need to talk about it."

"Least said. With the rep *Arianrhod* has, he might be a target."

"Got you. Here's Bluejohn on the comm."

"Seems we meet again in similar circumstances, Cinnabar," the captain of the *Obsidian Sky* greeted her. "What's your status?"

"Not as bad as last time we ran into one another, Grey, but bad enough. What brought you to this side of the galaxy? I thought you were running refugees out Selliden way."

"TA," he said tersely. "Things are going badly and the Alliance doesn't want to lose Freskat as it's the major trade centre in this zone. Trade's practically non-existent but they say we'll get reparations after the end of the hostilities."

"*If* there's an end," Apnis put in. "But we're getting reports in that the Freskat Navy's got the advantage further out, so this place should be safer for a while."

"Yes, but there's something odd going on," Bluejohn stated, his brow creasing. "Once these aliens had started to get the upper hand, blowing up everything they came across and taking over places like Marridan and Brown Amber, we thought they'd got it wrapped up. But lately there's been a drop-off and the ships they're sending in now aren't as awesome as that beast that ambushed me at Orriga Two. And there are rumours of that new fleet from the far reaches of Beta headed into the central zones – though I heard it passed Alto Finglas with nary a look."

"Aiming big, then," Ahxenta guessed. "Out from sector sixteen, do you know?"

"So it's said. But the whole PSS fleet's been commandeered now, Cinnabar and the smaller systems and unions are running scared. But even if these hostiles *are* slowing, the terror they're spreading is not."

"That's one way to win a war. But passing a strategic place like Alto Finglas? That's not their style, surely?"

"Unless something really big's in the offing," he suggested.

The captain of the *Arianrhod* shook her head. "We've had dealings with these unknowns and we've got to know their tactics somewhat.

They've a hive mentality and they don't give up even when outfoxed. We figure they're chiefly mechanoid and that suggests robotic mental processes, though they have organic inclusions. They have a reliance on sheer numbers, and must have the capacity to produce more of their own kind. And we know they've altered others to suit their own purposes. But the ISP shipyard at Alto Finglas, where there will be ships ready to send out? No, I figure something else is at back of this fleet out of zone Beta."

"Good luck with figuring it out. Let me know of urgent needs that you can't get on Freskat, Cinnabar, and I'll see what I can do, though I don't want to leave myself short lest we meet more of this on the way to our next assignment."

"Which is?"

"Skyrtek. And I suspect you'll get the same, once the TA hears the outcome at Freskat."

"Thanks for the heads up. I'll get my supercargo on scouting for supplies and let you know before you leave. I see I've an incoming that I need to take. We'll speak later."

As Bluejohn broke contact, Ahxenta raised an eyebrow at her first mate. "Admiral Zillah. Good to know she's in one piece."

"Her ship's not," Apnis noted, pulling up the spec from tactical.

The admiral had linked in to thank *Arianrhod's* crew for their help and assure the captain that she would do all in her power to help them repair their damage and replace their armaments. Freskat's two naval dockyards had escaped with minimal losses and although they would have a major headache in refitting their fleet, those ships still capable of fighting were priorities.

In the event, despite Zillah's influence, all *Arianrhod* was offered was a free berth and minimal aid. The Freski had been seriously hurt and several settlements so badly hit that they were uninhabitable. Ahxenta would accept only the barest essentials from Bluejohn and Cottontail was left grumbling at the loss of an engine and the massive bother of trying to replace it. It took the persuasive powers of Lindell and the offer of part of their food cargo destined for Delta Iridium to obtain the most critical pieces and put a small smile on the engineer's face. The only completely cheerful soul aboard ship seemed to be Whisper Earbleat, who tore about blithely humming and setting her team to scouring the nearby debris fields for serviceable parts.

Tallica Apnis was suspicious. "What's Earbleat so chirpy about?" she enquired of the captain. "She lost a lot of her favourite toys. She gave up *Loki IV* far too readily for a start: I was expecting her to hold a wake for the damn thing. What's in her back pocket?"

"*Loki V*. She got most of the bits at our last stopover."

"You're right: sometimes I don't know what we pay her for."

The second mate's passion for the hunt produced benefits for the science officers, for they made a point of scanning every scrap that she and her team brought in. A few of their finds brought Azular to the captain's office with a serious look on his face. A scant hour later and the two set off in the *Gadfly* for an urgent meeting with Admiral Zillah that Ahxenta had no intention of putting out on any channel, however secure.

On the basis of what she heard and understood, the admiral called in her own team of medics to go over the data as a matter of extreme urgency, and once their findings had been confirmed and her own people and ISP Central informed, she was adamant the information be circulated as widely as possible. She believed that it would give added impetus to the case against any appeasement of the hostiles as one way out of their current situation.

The news soon percolated down to the rank and file: the samples that Azular had pulled up were, he believed, actual physical remains of one of the crew of a hostile ship. On further analysis he detected traces of humanoid tissue, the DNA of which suggested an origin on Silshoon or Berzic, two systems close to one another in zone Delta. Something triggered at the back of the science officer's mind and he did a little digging, the results of which had sent him to Ahxenta and ended in the foray to Freskat's Command and Control Centre, where Zillah had access to highly secure military records.

The admiral's medics were able to confirm Azular's findings: the traces were humanoid and the origin Silshoon. A trawl of ISP medical records identified the original owner of the tissue as a crew member of the *ISPS Nomad*, missing in action. Another piece of the puzzle had slotted into place, was the majority view, but not a very nice piece. The hostiles, needing organic material as part of their cyber systems, had been bringing down ships and exploiting their crews as spare parts.

"That must have been how they managed to recruit the first Friskies to be their dupes," Box surmised to his mate as they sat with their feet up in the crew's mess. "They would have had to look at least humanoid to carry that off, scare tactics notwithstanding."

"Maybe that's why they scavenged bodies from the ships they

drew in to Kelfennig and other places with keep-off reputations years ago: so they could use them to fabricate their own human-like shells," Romanna Dox responded in a sepulchral tone.

"That's gruesome! Imagine meeting an alien that was once your Auntie Marigold."

"Stranger things have happened."

"Not many," Box argued. "Pass the donuts; we have to keep our strength up, we're back on repair duty in half an hour."

28: ARIANRHOD AFLAME

Despite frequent updates from the ISP tactical relay system and other Alliance channels, bulletins on the situation at Skyrtek and its nearby systems were scarce. Most blamed the suspected infiltration of hostile spies in many central organisations and the reluctance of upper tiers there to facilitate them. A source of Admiral Zillah's hinted that the space around the alleged alien stronghold of Lartzeg Trine had been mined but the result was unknown. Ahxenta had heard through her private channels that a number of PSS vessels had been bidden to zone Epsilon for no specific reason, an issue that was raising concern among their captains.

"We can only hope they hold their own if they're pulled in for defensive or offensive action," was Tallica Apnis' opinion. "We're the best-equipped ship in the PSS fleet as far as weapons and shields go, but few others, apart from the *Obsidian*, come anywhere close."

"Equipped we might be but ready to fight we're not," the captain pointed out. "We're still low on armaments and energy cells, our outer hull looks like a battered biscuit tin and the plating's so scored you can see through it in places."

"Comms and most other stations are up to scratch though, thanks to your buddy and his stored supply of crystal components," the first mate said with only a twitch of her eyebrow. "Expensive wares: we'd have trouble sourcing them otherwise. You reckon we can exchange the food shipment for Delta Iridium for parts rather than credit when we get there?"

"Lindell's working on it. The shipment's critical, so they may be open to persuasion. At least that area of space seems to be free of alien influences at the moment."

"As far as we know – it's close to Elf One."

"Thanks for that ray of sunshine. But we can do little else here, so scratched paint or no, we're moving as soon as we're fit. Zillah's okayed it on behalf of the ISP and her local command. The TA has announced that all the Privates assist by any means necessary but they haven't revoked any flags to date so we still have our hands free."

"Could we operate without the TA flag over us?" Apnis asked.

Ahxenta released a sigh of frustration. "We're known well enough but in the long term the Trades Alliance could close gates against us. It has the advantages of antiquity and known form and it has other shipping lines tied to it. As part of the TA we get insurance and other benefits, and entry to ports that might be closed to us otherwise."

"Cleft stick, then."

"Looks like, unless things change in a big way. But ready her for departure now that our engines are all more or less back on line: we take the safest route to Delta Iridium Colony, drop our cargo there, pick up whatever we can by way of supplies and then see what the hell's next on our agenda."

The crew was well aware that the ride to Delta Iridium would take them closer to what seemed to be the main war arena. *Arianrhod* ran at amber alert but vigilance was intensified, with everyone on their toes. Despite her massive scarring and lack of external weaponry the ship was not far off her regular standards internally, engineering being the only seriously depleted area. Several of Cottontail's squad were in medbay and even with the engineering skills of *Arianrhod's* fighter pilots, the chief was short-handed and low on materials.

Arianrhod was ten hours from her destination when the news came in that a full-scale assault on the Skyrtek system had begun. The alert had originated from the main planetary affairs office of the ISP on Skyrtek Key, the third and only habitable planet, but the ISP's main concern was its shipbuilding dock around Skyrtek Prime, the sixth and largest planet of the system: that seemed to be the target of the first wave. The hostiles had come in on three fronts, their trajectories suggesting that their bases of Lartzeg Trine, the Starglass Nebula and the Enigma Nebula were the origins, boosted by the ragtag remains of those that had made it through from the Ginseng. The minefield deployed around Lartzeg had been partially successful but had not stopped the advance. An all-out call for help had been issued.

"Looks like their base beyond the Outer Reaches and the one near Mellifly are being held in reserve, unless they've despatched fleets that nobody's picked up," the first mate observed as the order for red alert and increased speed was given.

"How can they have so many fleets?" Box called up from the well of the bridge. "There seems to be no end of the damn things."

"You may be right that they took over raider operations," Apnis said to Ahxenta. "That would have given them a flying start in the shipbuilding business and we know they've no reservations about hijacking anything they need and no quarter given. They're far more destructive than any raiders ever were and hell knows we had trouble enough there. Any word on the ships that were headed in from sector sixteen of Beta? We'd better be careful we don't run into them on the way out of Delta Iridium: if they're on a direct line to Skyrtek, it would put them pretty close to us. Though I still don't get why they bypassed Alto Finglas."

"Keen to get where they're going," the captain surmised. "I'll be in engineering: we need to get our defences up to speed if we're ordered into Skyrtek."

"Shouting at Crizz won't help; it'll only put her back up."

"I can handle a phase-tuning wrench and I don't think I've lost my touch," was the grinning response. "You just keep us on course."

The authorities on Delta Iridium were grateful for the delivery of food: their Iris Three outpost was in sore need and local transports were standing by to transfer the load. The upshot was a rapid about-turn that hardly gave *Arianrhod* time to breathe, but did allow Lindell to call the shots to some extent on the exchange of their newly-won credit for additional hull shielding and weapons supplies and the use of a local orbital repair facility for the fitting of them. The readiness of the Port Authority to expedite the ship's refit was soon clear, as rumour of the unknown fleet en route from zone Beta to Skyrtek was sending shivers down spines: if Skyrtek fell, Delta Iridium Colony, as one of the largest and closest centres on the galactic map, was likely to be next on the menu.

Ahxenta had little time to digest all the information on hand. The expected call to arms came in on the third day of their stopover and the situation was critical. The Skyrtek Prime dockyard was all but out of commission, with practically every vessel within its web reduced to shards of metal. Attempts had been made to evacuate ISP Council members still at their HQ but an enemy blockade had put paid to that. Relief ships were on their way from almost every nearby sector, but there was little commitment to a concerted counter-attack in view of the unknown strength and purpose of the fast-approaching fleet that was already crossing zone Delta. Scattered relay stations had been plotting the route of the unknowns and they were heading directly in a line that would take them to the Skyrtek system.

"We go now and sure as hell we'll run slap bang into them," Apnis said, her forehead puckered as she stalked around the tactical holo.

"That seems to be the chosen place for the final showdown,"

Ahxenta admitted. "But something's still not adding up. They've now bypassed several worlds capable of sending out firepower that would have been prime targets, you would have thought. You don't want a taskforce outflanking you as you're coming in for a kill."

The captain crossed to the science stations, where both science officers were busy. "What's the status of our long-range scanners? We need to know the numbers and configuration of those ships and the nature of what's flying them, at the highest resolution possible."

"Do you suspect that these ships aren't what they seem, ma'am?" Azular asked. "I've analysed the data we have and it indicates they're on a par with what we've come to associate with hostile vessels."

"I'd imagine that we have more on these battle-buckets and their operators than most anyone else; hell knows we've had them in our sights often enough. But there's something. Do what you can. I'd like to know how many and what kind of ships they are, their weak points if any and the nature and number of the crew on board."

"You want to know what they had for lunch as well, Captain?" Greffy enquired cheerfully.

"If that information's available, yes, Lieutenant, I do."

"Cap wants the moon in a pail," the first mate told the two.

Meanwhile Cottontail had called from engineering with her latest report. She was happy with her new engine but still concerned over the state of the outer shielding that protected her drive systems and of her absent crewmen. Flintlock had refused to release the latter to duty from medbay and once *Arianrhod* was back in the space lanes, she would be understrength. The chief engineer was given little time to complain, however, as Ahxenta had other concerns.

"You'll have to make do, Crizz. I need you on the bridge right now, as we're breaking orbit in an hour. Leave Gem Ferry in charge down there and assign our pilots to engineering posts. I don't plan to deploy them in whatever we're heading into."

The first mate raised an eyebrow. "You don't?"

"No: there's precious little they can do against what's out there and they'll be more use aboard. Send the word round, Tallica. All crew at battle readiness. We're heading to Skyrtek."

Arianrhod was running silent and cloaked with every spare eye and ear manning external scanners and probes. She had not responded to the TA summons nor had she sent notice of their intentions to the ISP. The direct bypass route to their target would take them close to the Lartzeg system but Ahxenta had decided that speed was of the essence and refused to deviate. They passed the system, crossing into Epsilon without incident. A couple of distant signals suggested that others were on the beacon but nowhere near. It was as *Arianrhod* was slipping off the bypass at the node linking the hyperspace highways running close to Skyrtek that the first sign of trouble appeared.

"Multiple blips off our port side! Still distant, they're ahead of us!" Pollux Gliss announced.

"Must have just come off the main bypass across Beta," muttered Apnis as she strapped herself in. "Think it's them?"

"Let's find out. Azular, get me everything you can on those ships. Maintain cloak, helm, and keep our distance until we can figure what they are. Tactical, get the holo up. All crew, battlestations."

"Once they figure what we are, our number's likely to be up," Box said in a dismal aside to his fellow-officer.

"Stop griping and keep your eyes on your board," Dox snapped. "I'll need you to plot alternative jump lines if we run into trouble."

"We're already running into trouble: it seems to be our lot in life."

"Once we're through this, I swear I'll have your mouth sewn up," the helmswoman warned her partner.

"They must know we're behind them, but they're not turning," the first mate observed to the captain.

"Ready all weapons and prepare to target anything that looks as if it might spit in our eye! Azular, what are you getting?"

"At least fifteen ships, perhaps more; configuration definitely hostile, Captain and they're well-armed."

"Bring us up closer, helm, but keep us out of range. Try to get lifeform readings, Azular, I want to know what they have on board."

"You think they're unmanned, Cap, and set to take out whatever's left down there?"

"I'm not sure Tallica, but I have a peculiar feeling about all this."

"What in hell! Doc, do you read what I read?" Greffy demanded.

"I do, boy," Azular responded. "And good call. Captain, I read a number of lifeforms aboard the rearmost vessel in the convoy – but I do *not* read trace zukivianite in any form."

"You what!" exclaimed the first mate.

"Confirm!" Ahxenta ordered abruptly.

"Confirmed. No trace of zukivianite but I *am* reading organic physiologies and they're not all the same. I've relayed the data to Dr Flintlock but at this distance I can't get you specifics. That last ship is definitely crewed."

"Bellfish, hail the alien fleet."

"Cinnabar, are you out of your mind?" Apnis demanded.

"Maybe. Don't tell them who we are, just request their identity."

"If they're so alien, they won't be able to respond," the first mate hissed. "They won't have any of our languages."

"They used the Friskianx so they must have. Anything, comms?"

"A warning to keep out of their way, ma'am."

"You what? This is getting weirder by the minute. Who the hell are they?" Apnis snapped.

"Only one way to find out. Drop our cloak, helm, but keep shields up. Target that rear ship, Earbleat, and let loose if she so much as sneezes. Put me on speaker, comms... This is Captain Cinnabar Ahxenta of the private starship *Arianrhod*. Who are you and what is your purpose in ISP space?"

The seconds ticked by without response. The call was repeated with a demand for an answer.

"Something coming in, Cap! We have visual!" announced Bellfish.

"Put it up!"

The stark and sullen face in the holo was not pretty and probably never had been but it was humanoid. A series of scars and what looked like the remains of attached technology were clearly visible at the man's temples. His uniform, if such it was, was armoured. He declared himself as commander of the ship and repeated the warning that Ahxenta should keep out of their way.

"Why?"

The simple question caused the commander to pause. It was that as much as the flicker of uncertainty across his surly face that led Ahxenta to raise an interrogative eyebrow and smile grimly at him.

"That isn't your concern!" he spat out.

"It damn well is," she said levelly. "We're headed to Skyrtek at the request of the ISP. You're in our way. Your identity, your purpose."

Some message must have come in for him, for he paused again, touched his ear as if listening through an earpiece and dipped his head slightly. Meanwhile, Tallica Apnis, eyes ablaze, had widened the holo-field and cut out a part of the background. She enlarged the image and set it alongside the main figure.

"I'm authorised to tell you. We were unwilling conscripts of the aliens now attacking Skyrtek. We freed ourselves from their control and we're here to engage their fleet and take back what was ours."

"You're ex-raiders," Ahxenta rapped shortly, "With an assortment of Friskianx and others that you've recruited for your purposes."

"Your reputation precedes you, Captain Ahxenta, and I see it's not unfounded. You're smart," the commander observed coldly.

"So are you and flattery cuts no ice with me. Unless you want a taste of my artillery up your butts, you'd better cut to the point."

"Your ship's hardly in a fit state…"

"I've taken out better than you with a lot less than I'm carrying now. Get on with it, I don't have all day. And neither do you."

The commander tightened his lips in anger, but whatever message he was receiving evidently penetrated his brain and in short order he told her that a few altered humanoids had worked out how to disable their implanted trackers and remove much of their controlling cyber hardware and had banded together to recruit more of those used and abused by the hostiles. These included Friskianx and many ex-raiders that had fled encroaching alien influences. They had sought sanctuary in sector sixteen of Beta, drawn there by subtle organic sensitivities to one another that their alterations had caused in them. There over an undisclosed number of years they had amassed sufficient ships and hardware to form a sizeable offensive force against their late masters. Given the current situation and the final war that seemed imminent, they had chosen now to show their hand and stop the force before it became unstoppable.

"Yes and the band played believe it if you like," Tallica Apnis grunted in an undertone.

"So you're here to save the galaxy," Ahxenta snorted. "And you're headed for the fleet dockyard off Skyrtek Prime. Interesting heading when the main hostile fleet is heading the other way. But you'd better get on with it. And if I were you, Commander, I'd watch out for Len Lokterix, if that's what he's calling himself, at your back there. Have a profitable day. Ahxenta out."

As the link was cut and the captain ordered the helmswoman to keep pace and Earbleat to keep every forr'ad weapons emplacement targeted on the fleet ahead, the first mate looked over quizzically. "Hostiles heading the other way?"

"A gamble: there isn't much left of the shipyard so there's nothing left for them to destroy. Their next stop will be Skyrtek Key."

"Confirm that, Captain," Bellfish stated. "Skyrtek Key is reporting incoming and requesting assistance from any ships in the sector. The planetary defence grid is gearing up for major attack."

"Captain, I'm picking up a strange energy surge around the leading vessel of the sector sixteen fleet," Azular's voice rang out.

"It reads like that energy entity you met on Kelfennig, and similar to the field edge of the Ginseng anomaly," Greffy put in. "More like the Kelfennig entity, there were subtle differences."

"Are you saying that one of these Kelfennig energy forms is close to the leading ship?" Apnis asked.

"Micklemouse *did* say they could leave, although they preferred to stay planet-bound," Ahxenta mused. "Though how the blazes one would get way out here… But if that's the case, why?"

"The one that spoke through the mouse did seem to feel guilty for the trouble their successors were causing the galaxy, having gifted them with the means to do it."

"That was our take on what Micklemouse got from it, Tallica. But if one of them is guiding that ship, things might turn interesting."

"They're turning already," Bellfish announced dryly. "Call for you coming in, Cap: it's Captain Bluejohn of the *Obsidian*."

Bluejohn had identified *Arianrhod* by her call-sign and was linking in to coordinate a response to the all-out distress from Skyrtek Key. The *Quarkstorm* and the *Equinox* were also headed in.

"Better warn him that not all hostiles are allegedly hostile," Apnis advised. "Emphasis on allegedly."

As rapidly as possible, Ahxenta relayed their recent encounter and passed on the strategic data *Arianrhod* had garnered in relation to the fleet, but recommended that Bluejohn take no chances. Gliss was at that point coordinating the numbers they could count on as part of the defensive force and plotting them on his board. Many of the local systems had sent in one or more ships to the aid of Skyrtek, realising that they were likely to be one of the next targets. An ISP warship had been despatched to take command of the Allied forces and there were other ISP vessels on approach but no word had been received that the lead ship would be authorised to direct the Privates.

"That's one big enemy fleet," said Apnis, indicating the holo-grid. "They must have emptied Lartzeg and most of their other bases of everything they had, and then some."

"All their torpedoes in one tube, then: bad move," asserted the captain flatly. "Are you reading what we are, Grey?"

"Roger that, Cinnabar. We've got your alleged friendlies in our sights now. They've changed course and are on line for Skyrtek Key. I've just had word that the *Karillion* and the *Green Comet* are coming in but they're about an hour away."

As he spoke, calls from Captains Peakfrost of the *Quarkstorm* and Djassi of the *Equinox* announced their arrival, seconded by requests for situation updates.

Ahxenta scanned her bridge holo closely and expanded it to take in everything that Gliss could make out as Bluejohn acquainted the newcomers with the state of play.

"One helluva tactical operation to keep tabs on all that," she said. "Alliance vessels are being deployed around the northern perimeter as that's where the bulk of the hostiles are headed but they're way outnumbered. Who's in command? Better apprise them of the bunch of potentially friendly ex-raiders and assorted former victims on the way in from the other direction, just in case."

"Call coming in for the Privates, Cap, but the link's directed to us personally," Bellfish loudly announced. "*ISPS Repulse* by her call-sign and she's leading the attack. I have Colonel Ellin Myrtleberry on the comm, the Commander-in-Chief of the Allied forces."

"How the…" Apnis was cut off by a signal from the captain.

"Put her through! This is Captain Ahxenta of the *Arianrhod*. We are aware of your situation, Colonel. How can we assist?"

"You can aid the defence of the southern major land mass. I know of the approaching unknown fleet and I'm aware of their declared intentions. I want you and your ships at their backs. Do you copy?"

"I copy."

"Best of luck. Myrtleberry out."

"Well that was short and sour," Apnis commented.

"Copy that to the rest of our ships," Ahxenta ordered as Bluejohn linked in on another channel. "Keep us on the tail of those renegades ahead of us, helm. Did you get that, Grey?"

"I did. Looks like we've got our orders. You want to take point, Cinnabar? You've got more experience than the rest of us in dealing with the hostiles."

"Confirmed. Helm, take us in behind the raiders. *Obsidian*, you line up on our tail, *Quarkstorm* and *Equinox* come about and ride shotgun either side but keep your distance."

The four Privates formed a phalanx, their guidance systems linked to move as one. *Arianrhod's* tactical holo filled the well of her bridge and both her senior officers were on their feet directing operations.

"Hostiles are aware of us, Captain!" Gliss called out. "One of the two wings homing in on the southern continental region is breaking off – they're diverging, no discernible pattern!"

"They're trying to outflank us! *Obsidian*, get your guns trained on anything that gets past those raiders!" Ahxenta ordered.

"Raider fleet dispersing to attack incoming vessels!" Apnis yelled. "They're trying to engage them ship to ship!"

"Damn them, they're blocking our lines of fire! *Quarkstorm* and

Equinox, close up! Helm, evasive! Ninety degrees to starboard! Take us out of their targeting eyes. Earbleat, target forr'ad torpedoes on approaching enemy ships in our sky and punch us a hole through. All gunnery crews, fire at will, take out anything in your path."

"Missiles incoming!" came the warning from tactical. "Three ships have cut away from attacking hostile taskforce and are marking us!"

Arianrhod's forr'ad hull plates vibrated to the intensifying surge of enemy fire as the deadly discharge battered her already-scarred hide. Her sister ships rode the wave of torpedo fire and let loose with their own storm of destruction as the space around them lit up like the end of creation.

"All ships, concentrated fire on the engines of that leading hostile on my mark… Mark!"

As the order was given, a fusillade of firepower streaked towards the largest enemy vessel, bursting against her hull in wave after wave of light and power. Within a halo of fire she at last slowed and slewed sideways, her momentum carrying her clear of the attacking quartet. She blew apart amidships, a burst of red flame exploding into space.

The Privates had no time to draw breath for the two remaining ships banked to come in at steep angles either side.

"All batteries target weapons and launch bays!" Ahxenta roared as a tight spread of small blips, glistening like reflective flak, signalled the launch of fighters from one enemy vessel. "Gunners, get those fighters!"

"Peakfrost to Ahxenta! *Quarkstorm's* lost an engine: we'll have to haul back."

"Confirmed. *Equinox*, break off and protect *Quarkstorm*. *Obsidian*, you're with me. Reinforce our forr'ad shields, Crizz and power up for another push. Earbleat, target that nearest ship!"

"We're hardly stinging her, Cap! Permission to launch *Loki V*?"

"Negative, I want her for planetary defence. Azular, what in hell's protecting that ship?"

"Some type of resistant shielding. My probe beams can't penetrate it, but it's patchy. Target underside aft section, there's a gap."

"Helm, get us under her! Azular, relay coordinates to weapons and copy to *Obsidian*! Target torpedoes!"

"Targeting, aye!" Earbleat bawled. "Torpedoes away!"

"*Obsidian's* caught a side blast, Cap, she's lost shields!" called Gliss, as *Arianrhod's* target blew apart in a blaze of fire.

"Helm, move us into a position to protect her port side but keep us out of the sights of that second blip – she's heading in. Azular…"

"Similar pattern, Captain, patchy shielding and gap underside aft, rear section," he confirmed.

"Helm, get us into position below her. Earbleat…"

"On it, Cap."

"What the hell!" Apnis called out as she was caught off balance by a collision that shook the fabric of the ship.

"Fighter impacted on a damaged hull plate!" Gliss spat. "Our gunners got the rest of them. Major target down."

"Relay your information on apparent hostile weakness to the *ISPS Repulse*," Ahxenta ordered Azular as she hauled her first mate to her feet. "All stations, report status."

There was a momentary lull on the bridge as damage was assessed and the cost counted. In the glare of the holo-grid, a debris field that stretched into infinity lit the space, with drifting pieces of wreckage aflame as the last of the scattered ships' atmospheres burnt away. The space around *Arianrhod* and her sister ship was conspicuously free.

"Those raiders are holding their own against the hostiles," Apnis remarked, wiping a smear of blood from her cheek.

"We're still in one piece," Cottontail asserted from the engineering station. "Hull looks like a patchwork quilt and she's thin in places but no breaches. Shielding's down forty percent though, we don't want another beating like that one."

"Lost a lot of firepower, Cap, but we still have about thirty five percent of our capability, excluding *Loki*," declared Earbleat.

"Quite a few casualties in medbay," Apnis said, looking up from her console. "A couple serious but not life-threatening."

"*Equinox* and *Quarkstorm* report they're holding up; *Equinox* has taken a few hits but she's still afloat," Bellfish told them. "Captain Bluejohn for you, Cap: *Obsidian's* lost half her port shielding but sixty five percent of her arsenal's intact."

"Grey always did believe in being well-armed," Apnis grinned as the captain of the *Obsidian* linked in to confirm his status and his willingness to follow *Arianrhod* into the defence of Skyrtek Key.

Bluejohn had hardly finished when an alert from tactical rang out. "Last of hostile wing has almost completely taken out orbital defence grid over southern land mass! Surface missiles are getting through!"

"Damn! Increase speed and come about. Get me a visual. You copy, *Obsidian*? We're going in, you look after your own. Helm, direct line – take us right down their throats! Earbleat, ready *Loki*."

"Three hostiles turning about, approach vector!" Earbleat bawled across the bridge. "Targeting the largest of them."

"Helm, come up under them! Launch torpedoes, wide spread!"

As exploding charges blossomed outwards to herald the demise of one of the attacking vessels, Azular warned loudly that the remaining two were low on weapons but were assuming positions to ram. Dox hauled hard to starboard to evade the charge as Ahxenta warned the *Obsidian* of enemy intentions.

"Come between the two ramming ships!" Ahxenta ordered. "Pull out at maximum speed when you can see your face in their hulls!"

"Shit, Cinnabar, that's one helluva manoeuvre!" Apnis roared as she clung to her station.

The *Arianrhod* slid side-on through the narrowest of gaps to shoot up between the two approaching hostiles.

"Bloody hell, we were never designed for this!" the first mate yelled, swinging around like a rag doll as *Arianrhod* shot out above the ball of fire that was the colliding enemy craft.

"Auxiliary stations maintain fire! We have incoming!" Earbleat yelled. "*Loki* ready to go on your mark, Captain!"

"They don't give up, do they?" Apnis rasped painfully.

"Neither do we. Gliss, what's the biggest ship in our sights? Helm, get us in position to take her out. Gunners, get anything else that comes close! Earbleat, ready *Loki V* and launch when ready. I want that ship stardust!"

"Aye, ma'am!" resounded around the bridge as Bellfish called out the arrival of the *Green Comet* and the *Karillion* with all guns blazing.

Arianrhod burst through the dust of the massive enemy planet-killer with every weapons emplacement spewing lethal fire. As missile followed missile the weapons officer let out a yell of triumph.

"Got 'em!" she exulted. "Every last one! Sky over southern land mass now free of hostiles."

"Also free of planetary defence grid, but that's life," commented Apnis as she drew breath, wiping a streak of blood from her nose and across her face. "Those two here to mop up?"

"There may be work for them yet. Comms, link me through to *Green Comet* and *Karillion* and get me the *Obsidian*. Grey, how are you holding up?"

"Just about. Not much fire left and lost a heck of a lot of my shields but I can still manoeuvre."

"Good. You maintain stable orbit here to protect this area, as our friendly renegades seem to have left in quest of other employment. Captain Flintlock? Good to see you again. Request that you deploy the *Karillion* to assist *Obsidian* here. Captain Jikelleli, I'm heading to the northern planetary arena to ascertain the situation there."

"*Green Comet's* with you, Cinnabar, but you don't seem to have much left in your arsenal for a firefight."

"I know," Ahxenta conceded briefly. "But our reputation might do just as well."

The two trading ships turned slowly into a sky now aflame over the mass of the planet, the ever-widening field of debris spread like an enveloping cloud around them.

"This will take a lifetime to clear," Tallica Apnis commented in a sorrowful voice. "Bloody hell, Cinnabar, what was the point of it?"

"Maybe Myrtleberry can tell us. She's on the comm."

Colonel Myrtleberry had linked in to order the Privates to stand down. Thanks to the haphazard assistance of the ex-raider fleet, the invading ships had been repulsed and almost all destroyed. Those that were left in the immediate area were being systematically hunted down by Alliance vessels but there was little left of them to clear up.

"That's it? Thanks for your help and goodbye?" Apnis exploded as the colonel's face faded from view.

"Here's your hat, what's your hurry," Box piped up from the navi-helm console. "Just like my Auntie Ethellixa: you'd hardly get over the door when she'd want you gone, once she'd got whatever you'd brought as a present. Some people are just out for all they can get."

"Belay that Mr Box," Ahxenta said mildly. "I want to know where our friendly ex-raiders have gone. Apart from a few splinters that might be parts of their wrecked ships, there's not a one to be seen."

"Confirmed," Azular put in. "Detecting no remaining ships in the vicinity that read as renegade rather than hostile. There *is* one residual moiety that relates to them, however, and it's heading our way."

"What's that?" the captain demanded.

"An indeterminate mass of energy that scanners verify as identical to the phenomenon we observed in relation to the lead ship of the renegade fleet," the science officer replied, turning to face her.

"Seems we can expect a visitor," Apnis shrugged, her face twisting in pain as she eased into a more comfortable position in her chair.

29: ARIANRHOD AT REST

The captains of the *Equinox* and the *Quarkstorm* had announced their joint departure for Merkat Three for refit and made their farewells as soon as Myrtleberry's abrupt dismissal had been confirmed. As local tactical relays had kicked in again and the spaceways were reported clear of present danger as far as their route was concerned, they were expecting no trouble. The *Obsidian* had unfinished business at Delta Iridium and had called ahead to request repair but was hanging back lest *Arianrhod* required assistance: Bluejohn's science officer had also detected the mysterious energy globule heading towards Ahxenta's ship and had alerted the others. As the brightening and pulsating orb of light contacted *Arianrhod's* hull and began to expand around her main comms array, *Green Comet* and *Karillion* came about to train their forr'ad batteries on the spot where the emanation had halted.

The bridge crew of *Arianrhod* waited in something akin to unease as the bridge holo, augmented by information from the ships around her, coalesced into an image of their vessel. The captain had ordered armed security on deck and had broken out arms for herself and her officers. Azular was watching his board narrowly, as was Greffy at his side. Gliss at the tactical station was trying to estimate the spread of the phenomenon and how far *Arianrhod's* shields had been infiltrated. The three surrounding ships were watching a visual transmission.

"Something's broken from the main body and is penetrating our hull, Captain," Azular stated into the silence. "There's no damage as far as I can tell."

"Heading?" Ahxenta demanded.

"Directly for the main bridge. Overhead."

As they all instinctively looked up, a filament of green light slowly percolated through the plating above them. It spun there, collecting its semi-lucent threads around itself to blend into a greenish sphere, growing brighter as it rotated. Ahxenta recognised it only too well as a cold shiver crept down her spine. She could see by her first mate's face that Apnis was experiencing a similar reaction.

"A globe analogous to the ones we met on Kelfennig," Azular noted calmly. "Energy levels fluctuating, minimal zukivianite traces, otherwise virtually impenetrable."

"Figured," the captain murmured. "Felt the air shift as soon as the thing appeared."

"I'm reading energy shifts around the entity and pulses similar to the hyperlight waves that allow communication through hyperspace."

"Confirmed," echoed Greffy.

"Keep an eye on the external energy layer, I want to know if that so much as moves by a fraction," Ahxenta ordered.

"Maybe it wants few words," the first mate grimaced as she eased out of her chair and shuffled stiffly away from the advancing entity.

The globe approached the captain, but backed off when Earbleat raised her phase rifle warningly.

"Knows a gun when it sees one," Apnis commented raspingly.

"Remembers Lieutenant Commander Earbleat, more like," Box whispered from his station.

The orb moved sideways and over to the comms station. Bellfish slid out of its way, bending backwards to give it space.

"Get out of there slowly Lieutenant," Ahxenta directed. "I think it's trying to communicate. Evidently none of us have the innate ability to act as its conduit."

"It's learned to use the comm station? Now there's proficiency for you," the first mate said levelly, her breath coming in small gasps.

"Maybe it's trying to call Micklemouse," the navigator suggested.

"Shut up, Box," Apnis warned, elbowing him in the ear.

There was a concerted hiss, as of escaping air, and part of the substance of the entity seemed to melt into the comms console.

"Captain Ahxenta," a disembodied voice, vaguely reminiscent of Bick Micklemouse, crackled out of the speaker.

After a startled exchange of looks with her first mate, the captain responded with a frosty, "Yes."

"We are here to explain. We influenced fleet of those manipulated in the past by those you call hostiles to take retaliatory action to assist recovery of violated spaces. We cannot control outcomes but will continue to guide as we are able. Your response requested."

"Pinch of salt with that," Apnis snorted, wincing.

"Why me?" Ahxenta questioned.

"You are aware of us. You are part of violated spaces. You will not alert others who may destroy our place of being to our presence."

"My response is it's hardly my problem, but if you really want to help, you could try prising the aforementioned hostiles off Marridan and out of the systems where they've caused so much trouble," she returned harshly. "And persuade your newfound allies to take out any hostile bases that are still operating, though I suspect that saving the galaxy from invasion is hardly *their* modus operandi."

"Don't think it does sarcasm, Cap," Apnis observed huskily.

"Most hostile bases are known. Your response is valued. We will assist as we can. We cannot control results. We have limited power."

"Not what we've seen so far. I'd appreciate your leaving my ship as soon as possible."

"Agreed. We will go now."

The energy form slowly extracted itself from the comms station and reformed into the radiant green orb, rising upwards as it gathered its essence within. There was a ghost of a whisper as it melted into the overhead plating and disappeared.

Azular spoke into the silence. "Tracking: it's rejoining the energy mass outside the ship. No damage to *Arianrhod* detected."

The first mate breathed an audible sigh of relief, easing her tensed shoulders. "That's it gone then," she said roughly, easing herself back into her chair. "A blob with a conscience. Gives me the creeps."

"You and me both, Tallica," Ahxenta replied with a keen look as the comm came alive with Bluejohn requesting to know what the hell it was, where the hell it had come from and what the hell it wanted.

"I take it you saw all that," the captain of the *Arianrhod* nodded as Bluejohn's face materialised on the viewer. "It's a very long story and I'll tell it you one day over a very long beer. For now, we met it out at Kelfennig. It and its counterparts are all that's left of a long-defunct civilisation that was probably once the origin of the hostiles and they and their planet have been a target of the hostiles ever since their rise to power, allegedly. And according to that one or fragment of one, they're trying to make reparations, though I have trouble believing that. I suspect they're trying to make sure they're left in peace and can't do it on their own. If they want to expedite the take-down of leftover hostile bases or places of power then we can't stop them. My only concern is what will end up in place of it, given their choice of facilitators. Ex-victims, ex-raiders and their odd hangers-on aren't my idea of ideal instruments. But that's a topic for another day. I have a ship and crew to get fixed and so do you. *Green Comet* and *Karillion*, you got all that? Thanks for your assist. If you want to come over for a word with our chief medic, Captain Flintlock, you're more than welcome, but Dr Flintlock's ultra-busy in medbay."

"I'm headed for Merkat as I expect you are, Captain, so I'll forgo the pleasure of seeing my sister for now. I'm heading out directly, all speed. I'll catch up later. Flintlock out."

The *Karillion* slowly banked and turned, diminishing to a spot on the holo as she made for the bypass and the route out. The *Green Comet* also had business in the Web but Captain Jikelleli elected to escort the *Obsidian* to her next port of call lest she ran into difficulties en route. Ahxenta made her farewells, watching the two ships as they swept away. She then ordered *Arianrhod* to the bypass intersection.

"What's the agenda of this ex-raider and assorted ill-treated aliens Alliance?" Apnis asked as they moved off. "I can't believe they're doing it for the common good and a medal from Myrtleberry and a grateful ISP once it's all over."

"Taking back what they consider is theirs and then starting again with all the hostile hardware they've been able to lift," was Ahxenta's opinion. "Not to mention the bases, if they can commandeer those as well: the ones in the Outer Reaches and out by Mellifly that we were warned of that might still be operational, Xerophyte IV, Jurgall Three and everywhere else the hostiles seem to have left their claw-marks. And their own secret roost in sector sixteen where nobody knows what they've been doing for the past however many years they've operated there. And then there's Lartzeg Trine."

"Nothing left for them there but dust and ashes, I would think. The future will be fun, if that's the case," Apnis predicted with a sigh.

"Same old, same old," the captain groaned, rubbing the back of her neck to release the tension as she looked closely at her first mate. "It'll be nice to be back to normality of a sort."

"We still have our unfriendly little pals Micklemouse and Doosbak to pick up at Kelfennig. We did promise, so I guess we'll have to stick to it. It's our stock in trade after all, being the honest and honourable traders that we are."

"As I said, same old, same old," was the smiling rejoinder. "But first we get you looked over. Lieutenant Commander Earbleat, you have the conn; I'm escorting Commander Apnis to medbay."

"Cinnabar…"

"You walk or I carry you – your choice."

"I'll walk. What's next for us?" Apnis asked as she slid gingerly from her chair and stood up.

"Next we go find the rest of our crew at Merkat and get the old ship back up to some sort of scratch," the captain informed her as she placed a supportive arm across her first mate's back.

"I only hope our suppliers and fitters will advance us the credit, we must be over our heads in debt."

"Let me worry about that."

"How do you worry about something as significant as that?"

"I tell Lindell to worry about it," Ahxenta explained. "That's what he and his team are paid for."

"Or not, as the case may be," Box put in from the navi-helm.

"Just set us a course for Merkat, Mr Box; best speed, Ms Dox."

"Aye, Captain," came the joint response.

The immense Web was lit up by a thousand beacons and seemed like home to the majority of the *Arianrhod's* crew as the ship settled into her allotted docking bay within its outer lattice. Once the huge struts that held her impressive bulk secure were locked into place and helmswoman Dox had confirmed station-keeping, Ahxenta stretched and flexed rigid shoulders.

"I could sleep for a week," she confessed to the first mate. "But I'd best see the Docker's Guild reps to negotiate our refit. We won't be first in the queue but I'll see if we can be moved up a few places."

"They should be damn grateful: if we hadn't lent several hands at Skyrtek, this facility might have been next on the hostiles' agenda."

"I doubt it, Tallica: it's too valuable to all parties, even those as hive-brained as the hostiles."

"Well, don't tell the Guild reps that. Want me to come along to lend some pressure?"

"No, you're still technically under the doc's supervision. You stay here and start listing our priorities for repair; get Crizz to lend a hand. I'll take Lindell down with me. Flintlock's checking in with Merkat's medbay to see if she can transfer a couple of our worst cases down there. Thanks be most of the rest are on the way to recovery. I need to see our people aboard the *Velvet Emerald* as well; you can come with me then. Most of them must be fit for reassignment, so they can be put back to light duties here and that'll give some of the others time out on shore. Tell Flintlock she can use the *Gadfly* for patient transfer, I'm not paying out for medical transport. I'll shuttle down to the inner belts to speed things up."

"Noticed what ship's just arrived in the next berth but one?" Apnis grinned, checking the Web's listings as they updated.

"Given the smirk on your face, I'm not going to be enamoured. Go ahead, break my heart for me."

"The *PSS Tallulah*, Captain Murmur Fleetskup in command."

"Thanks for that. Melly Goodsocks picked him up from whatever rock he was hiding under then, him and Tommy Buntle? I've still got outstanding bills for the repairs we had done at Delta Iridium Six, despite his slimy promises it would be looked into. I'd have thought Goodsocks might have exerted a bit of insistence on our behalf."

"Tallulah Tommy's mouth is way bigger than Melly Goodsocks' is: means he wins every time," the commander reminded her.

It took three hours of hard negotiation to obtain a schedule of works and an assurance of credit from a clutch of Dockers' Guild, finance and marketing reps. By the time that the exhausted Ahxenta, having left Lindell in the marketing suite to sort out the details, was heading back to *Arianrhod*, her chief medic had organised the transport of the two most badly injured patients to Merkat's medbay, where she could count on excellent care, although she was less sanguine about the bill being paid on time.

All in all, the captain had had enough and was irritated when her first mate came in with the news that a shipment of replacement arms that had been pledged from the main dealership of Kanelian Juxta had been cancelled, as *Arianrhod* had been deemed a poor credit risk. That on top of the refusal of her insurers to pay up in respect of war damages topped off a day that she wanted to consign to the past.

"I am having a shower," she growled. "And then you and I will take a shuttle to the inner belts, where we will stop into the *Half Moon* for a jar. From there we'll head out to the *Velvet Emerald*. She's been moved to a smaller bay closer to central, for reasons best known to Helly Pinkhorn; but as she's Lindell's second, she knows how to save credit. Greenwing and Ma'Lappis are saying nothing, but Greenwing was looking smug."

"I bet they've been up to something between them. But what if Murmur Fleetskup wants Greenwing back and sues him over breach of contract if he won't come?"

"I'll have Axellina Flintlock certify Greenwing as medically unfit to practise and backdate it to the second he came aboard. Fleetskup won't have a leg to stand on. See you in ten."

The only bright spot on the short trip through the labyrinth of metalwork that led to one of the small landing bay complexes of the inner belts was the breaking news that Marridan had been liberated, or rather the remaining hostiles had left in a hurry in the direction of the Outer Reaches, leaving those in the know to speculate that the hostile base believed to exist beyond mapped space and on the edges of the Archipelago was in imminent danger.

Once safely on the ground in inner two, the two officers lost no time in locating their chosen anchorage. Ahxenta marched up to the *Half Moon's* substantial bar but before her order could be placed, two jars of Ally's finest ale were decorating the counter.

"Good to have you back, Captain," Ally beamed. "We've been hearing a lot about the war and the *Arianrhod's* exploits. You're just in from the defence of Skyrtek, I hear."

"How did you hear that?" Apnis asked curiously.

"A couple of crewmen from the *Karillion* were in here earlier and spread the word. So did a bunch from the *Ice Spar* – she's just in from a dust-up at Vrackin Twelve. They'd heard about it there as it's on a main route to Skyrtek. The Vrackin authorities had sent in two heavy cruisers as aid but they didn't get far: a pair of bandits jumped them, so the *Ice Spar* waded in. And you know how things get magnified around here. We've had a team from the *Tallulah* as well; they're not long back from Delta Iridium. They had to collect their captain. He was stuck there recovering from a major infection, was the story."

"Whose story?" Ahxenta asked dryly.

"Tommy Buntle's; he had the same plague, apparently, and they were both at Death's door, so he said."

"Pity Death didn't open the door and let the pair of them in," Tallica Apnis remarked, sipping her ale. "Busy in here tonight, Ally."

"It's been busy in here every night since you left the Web," the barman told her. "We've done good business over this war," he went on conversationally in a low voice. "There was a whole heap of ships out there when the conflict started to really hot up, mostly civilian or small transports of various kinds; and as Merkat seems to be one haven that everybody left well alone, a fair number made for here. Especially as there had been an increase in random attacks and nobody knew where these nasties would strike next. And especially as we have the best facilities this side of the known galaxy: berths, med facilities, hospitality, you name it."

"Second to none," Ahxenta agreed, with a slight lift of her lip.

"You angling for another free beer, Captain, ma'am?"

"Would I ever?" she responded jocularly.

"Well, as rumour also hath it that *Arianrhod's* strapped for credit and looks like a wash-bucket full of holes after all the fights she's seen, and that the insurers are not coughing up for war damage, it seemed a likely notion."

"How the hell did you get all that? And who says my ship's a wash-bucket?" Ahxenta demanded.

"Oh, just rumour, Captain," Ally assured her smoothly. "But we can see *Arianrhod* from here," he pointed out as he inclined his head towards a wall-mounted viewer, where a changing view of the mighty Web spun slowly in a hazy fashion. "You know a few of my regulars like to keep a weather eye on what's going on in the outer belts, see who's in and so on."

"See who's there to make a profit out of, you mean," Apnis said in a loud voice. "We know your regulars only too well, some of them."

She looked around the sizeable space. It was surprising how many of the occupants of the scattered tables and booths quickly looked at their drinks or at each other and swallowed nervously. Many of Ally's regulars also knew the captain and the first mate of the *Arianrhod* only too well.

As the second glasses of beer slid down, the two officers brought the proprietor of the *Half Moon in a Puddle* up to date on the latest doings of their ship, or as much as would be prudent to circulate in the likes of the *Half Moon*. Ally in turn asked after their current plans but was unsuccessful in eliciting much information beyond that they were off to see their crew still aboard the *Velvet Emerald*.

"A lot of changes there," Ally agreed sagaciously, nodding as he wiped his counter. He raised his eyebrows and smiled enigmatically.

"As you say, a lot is going on," Ahxenta countered calmly, looking him so straight in the eye that he shuffled and looked away. "So we'll have to love you and leave you, Ally. But we'll be back," she added forcefully, turning to scan the surrounding area.

The two replaced their glasses on the counter, thanked their host and turned to leave the way they had come. One toper in a corner booth turned to his companion.

"Ahxenta always looks taller when she's het up about something," he whispered to his mate.

"And how do you know she's het up, Jurry? She looks the same as always to me."

"She forgot to strap on her sidearm; and believe me, Malty, you're better off if she shoots you than if she raises her fist to your nose."

The other nodded in slow agreement. "You're right there, Jurry."

The first mate turned to the captain once the two had cleared the portholes of the *Half Moon* and were on their way to the docking bay.

"What's going on?" she asked quietly. "I got the feeling that Ally knows something about the *Velvet Emerald* that he thinks we don't. A lot of changes? Our people have been mighty quiet about changes."

"They didn't have an option: we couldn't contact them while we were out in the space lanes and I'd sure as hell no intention of letting anyone listening in realise we'd left a fair number of our crew back here, some in critical condition. And we've only been back half a day. But since we've come in, there have been a few enigmatic comments from Greenwing about bringing us up to date once we get over there. Maybe I shouldn't have left him in charge."

"Well, we're about to find out. You want to take her up, Cap, or will I take the hot seat?"

"Sure you're up to it? Your ribs are still strapped up."

"I need the practice."

"Then take it. Earbleat's just left a message about something."

"Bet you a jar of Ally's finest it's about her latest version of *Loki*," Apnis remarked as the two swung through the airlock and made for their shuttle.

Once fairly launched, the craft slid smoothly through the byways and out into the wider spaces beyond. The smaller bay assigned to the *Velvet Emerald* was on the far side from the *Arianrhod* and as the shuttle banked on approach, Apnis pulled her up for a closer look. Several small dinghies were anchored alongside the larger hulk and the ship herself blazed with light. Her hull glinted in the illumination of the network of restraining struts and she looked unusually dapper for a ship that had been stripped of her plating to provide *Arianrhod* with the means of refitting her own shell.

"What the hell!" Even the ordinarily level-headed Ahxenta was staggered. "I think our crewmates have a lot of explaining to do. I don't recall authorising a refit of that magnitude. They seem to have taken things into their own hands."

"They're experts at that," Apnis laughed in response. "I'm almost expecting them to shout *surprise* as we step aboard… This is shuttle *Arianrhod Six* to *Velvet Emerald*: permission to come aboard?"

"*Arianrhod Six*, welcome to the *Velvet Emerald*! Permission granted, Commander, slot her into our aft bay, there's a berth awaiting you."

"Ensign Jentle: since when's he been in command of arrivals?"

"He's an engineer," Ahxenta answered. "Knows one end of a boat from the other. But I'm reading way more people aboard that ship than should be there. What in blazes have they been up to?"

As the shuttle made berth safely and waited repressurisation, the two aboard had leisure to look at their boards and at the interior of the small docking bay. They disembarked, to be greeted by a smiling but apprehensive Ensign Pinkhorn, with Doctors Puzzle Greenwing and Flish Ma'Lappis alongside.

"The crew must be quite fit if you two could be spared from the medbay," Ahxenta observed matter-of-factly.

"Our crew are all fighting fit, Captain, as are most of our other patients," Greenwing assured her. "We've some refreshments set out in a side lounge, though we'd best keep the news until we get there."

"This had better be good," Ahxenta threatened. "Or all your butts will be in slings."

The news was more than good. As Ally had noted earlier, the war had brought a large number of displaced persons into Merkat seeking refuge. They came from civilian and other transports that had been trying to escape the fighting and the threat of random attacks. Some ships had carried refugees and other travellers who required medical assistance. As Merkat Web's medbay had been straining to cope and as Admiral Zillah had confirmed the *Velvet Emerald* as a hospital ship for the duration, with Ahxenta as designated commander, Lindell's second Helly Pinkhorn had had no qualms about opening a treatment and recuperative facility on board and charging high rates for the privilege. That had funded the hull repairs as and when parts became available and had allowed the refit of the *Emerald* to a sound spec. As the majority of *Arianrhod's* own crew that had been left behind were well on the way to recovery by the time the first paying clients came aboard, they were able to provide increasing assistance with running the vessel. A few medical staff had been recruited from the incoming ships and Merkat medbay to provide additional care and there were sufficient and luxurious berths for those preferring something more than the usual accommodations available around the Web.

"Kept our people out of trouble and out of the bars," Greenwing assured the two. "We *did* have to borrow a few extra security from among Merkat's finest but as we were taking a bit of pressure off, they weren't too upset. In fact there was a bit of wrangling as to who would be assigned, though as our people here got back up to full strength, they were more than able to cope. Any disorder and I set our own security on it. We didn't have too much trouble. Badges with *PSS Arianrhod* on them tend to engender respect."

"I'll bet," the captain observed sardonically. "I hope you've kept a close tally of the accounting, Ensign."

"Yes, ma'am, it's all accounted for. It was Lieutenant Bottle who suggested we get the ship back up to full fitness – his sister Erinna is a senior weapons engineer in the yards here and has a lot of contacts among the repair crews, so we managed to get first dibs on a lot of stuff that made it in."

"Bottle? One of Earbleat's acolytes," Apnis chuckled. "That fits: all her people are expert scroungers. But that would no way fund the coverage of new hull that we saw on the way in."

"No, Commander. We sold off some of the *Emerald's* more fancy fitments to civilian passenger ships that had been damaged. We didn't need them here and there were a few that could be persuaded to part with some credit for pieces of a ship that was under the flag of the *Arianrhod*," she added a little uncomfortably.

"You didn't stamp them 'Souvenir of *Arianrhod*' did you?" the captain asked dangerously.

"No ma'am, we wouldn't have dared."

"Very wise," Apnis declared, trying to keep a straight face. "Pass the coffee and let's have a look at the records."

The records so meticulously kept by Ensign Pinkhorn not only indicated that the *Emerald* was running at a fair profit, they showed that there were reserves that could be drawn upon. After a prolonged question and answer session, Ahxenta was satisfied that every part of the business was above board and that the precious reputation of the *Arianrhod* had not been tarnished in any way. As the two medical officers were obliged to return to their own domain, she suggested that the young ensign take them on a tour of the ship to see the alterations and catch up with the crew that had been left behind.

Some time later, as the shuttle slid out of *Velvet Emerald's* docking bay and set course for her home berth, Apnis glanced sideways at the captain. "You realise we'll have to promote Pinkhorn? She could certainly give Lindell a run for his credit."

"I'll consider it," Ahxenta declared.

The savvy ensign's final suggestion had been that they tell no-one outside those involved of the *Velvet Emerald's* recent refit, purchase the remaining shares from the absent shareholders and sell her on to the highest bidder when the time was ripe. There were various large conglomerations out there that were likely to have made a fortune in the aftermath of war and would be eager to invest in some serious hardware. A large cruiser of the *Crystal Mist* class, with meta-jurillium hull plating and the superior standard of weaponry that Lieutenant Bottle considered suitable, would be reckoned a prime asset.

"We seem to have one helluva crew, Captain Ahxenta," the first mate beamed, a grin creasing her face.

"Roger that, Commander Apnis," Ahxenta replied as she skilfully piloted the small craft through the busy lanes. "I know that I said authorise shore leave for all that can be spared and assign our crew here to their duties, but this lot certainly haven't been sitting on their butts for the duration. You'll have to reorganise your rota."

"Aye, ma'am. And I'll make sure we're near the top. Ally's going to fry in oil for this; he damn well knew the score."

Despite the commander's promises it was a good two weeks before she and the captain could take time out for shore leave. Ahxenta was adamant that *Arianrhod's* other senior officers be given furlough as soon as possible, as they had borne the brunt of the recent strife on their wide shoulders. Continuing to run under strength, *Arianrhod's* refit was developing into a lengthy process, as the *Velvet Emerald*, still operating under Ahxenta's authority, was also taking considerable time. In addition, although few but the command staff were aware, the situation beyond Merkat's sphere of influence was still grave and the war was by no means over.

The latest news suggested that remnant enclaves of hostiles were being targeted by unidentified fleets of similar ships and although holding their own to some extent, their numbers were being depleted. This had not stopped their sporadic forays into populated space and the ongoing systematic destruction of outposts and facilities. The ISP had considered investigating, but as it had plenty trouble of its own to deal with, the attempts were deemed futile; it could count upon no aid from its member systems or its allies, who were all bandaging their own wounds and in some cases counting on the fingers of one hand what was left to them of their possessions. The possibility also remained that many institutions were harbouring alien infiltrators and identifying them was a slow and painful process.

Admiral Zillah, whom Ahxenta had contacted over the situation out at Freskat, was of the firm opinion that apart from defending their own, the non-aggressive worlds were best leaving the hostiles and their adversaries to fight it out. Whilst they were hammering lumps out of each other, they were hardly likely to get in anyone else's way. The captain of the *Arianrhod* was less sure: the winner was liable to come out of the scrap stronger than ever, and if the victor happened to be the ex-raider Alliance, supplemented by a bunch of malcontents with massive cyber-chips on their shoulders, it boded ill for both trade and galactic peace.

"At least much of Freskat's still in one piece," Apnis consoled her after the conversation. "Very little fleet left, but that'll bolster the shipbuilding trade no end for the foreseeable future."

"If they can get materials for building, not to mention dockyards for the actual construction. The ISP still has Alto Finglas capable of churning out warships but there's only flak left of Skyrtek Prime and of many other Alliance shipbuilding sites. And we're still technically drafted: I've tried to get some sense out of the TA reps here but they're saying little. They've had several Privates on their tails and they're trying to keep out of sight. But being on the military payroll does get us access to supplies we might otherwise miss out on."

"How much does this military payroll actually direct our way?"

"I've had Lindell chase them but all we've seen so far is what Piskettle approved and what Zillah gave us," Ahxenta told her. "The Dockers' Guild demands a look at our cash flow before it'll authorise repairs, but thanks to Pinkhorn and Greenwing, we have a packet of credits over the odds, although we do have a backlog of unpaid bills. I tried to contact Piskettle as he did advance us the fees for our trip out to Kelfennig Four on the trail of the *Nomad*, but so far nothing."

"Given the outcome of that mission, I'd be wary of pushing him too far. But things are slowing; materials are getting scarce as most of the ships that would normally bring them in are unfit or still running scared. But the Dryssicon carriers are about again, so meta-jurillium production should start gearing up once the processing stations get back online. And as the repair yards here are running at full tilt, this place should soon have all the hull plating it needs. But some trade to bolster our budget that doesn't involve a fight would be handy."

"We have one slight advantage that might be useful to the ISP and others that have been infiltrated by hostiles," the captain said slowly.

"A way of identifying them at a distance," the first mate replied. "But there are several bodies that are going to be seriously pissed if we announce that we've known how to detect them for some time and haven't told anyone."

"Not our problem and they only need to be told the minimum. But we're officially on shore leave and we still have Ally's pate to crack. As well as Murmur Fleetskup's ear to bend. He's still refusing to cough up what he owes us for the repairs we needed after saving his hide a month or so back."

30: ARIANRHOD ARISING

The *Half Moon in a Puddle* was as busy as usual when the two officers of the *Arianrhod* reached it. As Ahxenta and Apnis slipped through the holo-door, most heads in the place turned to look. The eyes were openly appraising and a faint hum ran around the tables at the back.

"Haven't seen you for a while, Captain, or you, Commander," Ally greeted them. "Been ultra-busy aboard, I expect?"

"Is that all you expect?" Tallica Apnis asked him.

"Have a drink, Commander," the barman replied hurriedly. "I've seen a few of your crew in over the past few days. And I hear more of the Privates have shipped into the Web. *Green Comet*, *Firedrake* and *Opaline* all came in last night."

"What else have you heard, Ally?" Ahxenta asked, accepting the glass that was placed before her with a nod.

The man squirmed but held her eye. "I heard that your crew are still running the *Velvet Emerald* as a medical rest and rec facility. Some people are wondering how you did it. She looks pretty smart," he added as a sop which had absolutely no effect on his two customers.

"And what are you telling some people?" the captain demanded.

"To mind their own business," he said. "What would you like me to tell them?"

"To talk to me if they want answers."

Ally shrugged and looked sideways. "Many would be reluctant to do that," he admitted. "I heard from a couple of officers out of the *Tallulah* that Captain Fleetskup's figured that you must have a finger in some pie or other, as she's registered as a hospital ship under your command for the duration and you're taking advantage."

Ahxenta's eyes bored through him. "Oh yes?"

"I'm only telling you what I heard," Ally continued hastily. "You know me, Captain, I don't make stuff up; well not very often," he admitted. "But the ones who told me didn't reckon it was your style and that Mr Buntle had been whispering in Captain Fleetskup's ear."

"And how many other ears?" the *Arianrhod's* first mate enquired. "Where's Fleetskup anyway? He was supposed to meet us here and have a nice civilised conversation over what he owes us for refit at

"

Delta Iridium after we saved his butt off Elf One."

"I hadn't heard that story, Commander, Captain," Ally put in, perking up immediately. "Care to enlighten me?"

Ahxenta shrugged and began on an edited version of that incident, and the other out by Freskat, seemingly oblivious to the avid interest being shown by several lookers-on at nearby tables. One pair of eavesdroppers looked up as the light-veils of the holo-door rippled to allow the entry of two uniformed individuals.

"Oops! Look who've come in: Fleetskup and his sidekick Buntle. Buntle won't be welcome. I vote we move over to the back there out of harm's way and watch the fun," Jurry advised his mate.

"Seconded. Let's move it," Malty whispered.

Captain Murmur Fleetskup and his exec, Lieutenant Tommy Buntle, sailed up to the bar as if they owned the place.

Ally looked up with a welcoming smile on his face. "What'll it be, gentlemen?" he asked civilly, having no intention of providing them with free beer.

"Two schooners of your best ale," Buntle immediately responded. "Put it on a tab."

"Yours or Captain Fleetskup's?" the barman enquired.

The pause could be cut with a knife until Tallica Apnis announced that it wouldn't be hers.

"Mine," Buntle conceded at last. "Shall we take a seat over there, Captain?" he added to his commanding officer, indicating a board near the door that most customers had avoided as it was too close to the comfort cubicles to be pleasant.

"Too public. Let's take that one," Fleetskup announced, pointing to a circular table by the bar already occupied by a quartet of the *Tallulah's* crew. "They can move."

"Just stay where you are Captain Fleetskup and stop maundering," Ahxenta told him pointedly but irritably. "This won't take long. If you'd wanted privacy you could have asked for it. You know why we're here. You owe me for the repair of my ship at Delta Iridium, damaged rescuing yours from a pair of hostiles that attacked you out of Elf One. You gave me your word that the issue would be looked into. I expect it has been. When can I expect recompense?"

"We've already discussed this. My insurers assure me that they will not cover the incident as it has been classified as an act of war and as such is not covered. You *did* receive all the tactical and science data from the incident that I expect assisted you in your own endeavours," he added sanctimoniously.

"That is not the point, Captain Fleetskup. My ship answered your distress call, which incidentally you sent out before a shot was fired, and my insurers indicate that you are liable for the damages incurred as a result. I *am* prepared to sue."

Fleetskup was adamant. "You won't win. I repeat, you will not be compensated by me for your repairs at Delta Iridium; my insurers are clear that it was a war situation, you were obliged to give aid under the terms of your contract with the Trades Alliance and they will not cover it. And I can't afford to as I have an almost total refit to have carried out, thanks to the TA's insistence that we lend a hand at Freskat and Goodsocks' sloppy response to the alien attack there."

"And there's absolutely nothing you can do about it, Captain." Tommy Buntle's eyes gleamed in triumph as he looked up at her, casually wiping beer froth off his top lip with the back of a hand.

"Oh no?" Ahxenta responded calmly, standing away from the bar as she slipped her retractable hand shields into place.

The man failed to see her left arm move, but her fist sent him sideways to land among the feet of his crewmates at the nearby table. He lay stunned for a moment and no-one helped him up. Fleetskup began to bluster of reparations and reports to the Trades Alliance. A glance from his fellow captain quelled him and he subsided, just as Buntle struggled to his feet, fulminating.

"That was only a taster," Apnis comforted the deflated executive officer. "You're lucky Captain Ahxenta didn't deliver the full menu. But it was just as well Commander Goodsocks *did* have a response to the attack at Freskat, Murmur, else you wouldn't have had a ship or a crew to come back to, after your sojourn on Delta Iridium during the fighting," she added to Fleetskup. "You and your best friend here."

"Fleetskup's lost any chance he had with Tallica Apnis, then," Jurry whispered to his crony over a mug of Ally's bargain ale and the clamour of Captain Fleetskup's furious rejoinders.

"I don't think he ever had one," Malty responded equally quietly. "He just imagined he had. She wouldn't take on anyone who calls his ship after his mother and employs a scallywag like Tommy Buntle to think for him."

"Fleetskup's Ma put up the money for his ship, so I've heard."

"I'd heard that as well and more fool her," Malty stated. "Just as well her name isn't Floozy Dishmop then, I guess. That would look rum painted in large letters on the side."

"Give the other pirates a laugh, though," Jurry snickered.

"That they get already, with Fleetskup in command. He probably has trouble commanding the ducks in his bathtub."

The captain of the *Tallulah* was helpfully dusting down his tousled officer, who had turned red and was balling his hands rhythmically into fists.

"You won't get away with this, Ahxenta!" Buntle snapped angrily.

"Captain Ahxenta," Apnis corrected.

"You and your illicit tactics over the *Velvet Emerald*; we all know how you engineered the command of that one."

"Oh do tell," Ahxenta responded. "I'm sure everyone here would be delighted to be informed, as I'm sure they don't *all* know."

"Your secure cams are operating I take it, Ally?" *Arianrhod's* first mate enquired genially.

"As ever, Commander. You're welcome to the footage."

"We'll need it for our legal rep," Apnis informed Buntle. "Those are serious allegations. What illicit tactics are you referring to? We'd like the definitive list, in order to keep things straight. And we'll need the call-sign of *your* legal rep, Captain Fleetskup, for the record."

"Don't be ridiculous!" snorted the enraged Fleetskup, recovering his poise. "You've had your answer, Captain Ahxenta. You will not be recompensed and I have the backing of my insurers. Let's go, Tommy: we have other matters to attend to."

His exec paused, twittering in rage but unsure how to respond. Ally sorted the matter for him.

"Your tab," he announced. "You want me to hold it 'til later?"

"Won that round," Apnis said comfortably to the captain as the other two retreated to the snickering of the crowd in the bar, the *Tallulah's* own crewmen among them. "Won't win the war though, he won't cough up; and given our insurers are being sticky, his probably are as well. He's just seriously annoyed over the *Velvet Emerald*. He thinks we've stolen a march on him."

"We haven't – yet," Ahxenta replied, a quirky look on her face. "Drink up and let's get a bite to eat. Arguing the toss with Murmur Fleetskup always gives me an appetite."

"Tell me about the *Velvet Emerald*," Ally invited, propping his elbows on the bar.

"Go take a hike," Apnis told him. "And bring us another beer on the way back."

Over an excellent meal at one of Ally's tables, the privacy shield in operation but smiles lighting up their faces to deflect any notion that they were discussing business, Ahxenta and Apnis pondered an issue that might bring in some much-needed revenue without having to leave the Merkat system. If Azular, Flintlock and Cottontail between them could produce a prototype hand-held probe that could scan for trace zukivianite linked to cyber-organic bodies in proportions known to indicate hostile physiology, it could be exemplified as a rapid and reasonably covert means of detecting alien infiltrators that were more than likely to be loyal to their own. *Arianrhod's* science officer and chief medic had after all already produced the device that Azular had used successfully to ascertain that the man Lokterix was not alien in origin, despite having undoubtedly been altered and used by them. As the data collected by *Arianrhod* was extensive as far as it related to alien make-up and technology, potential moles of non-hostile origin but still under their influence might also be brought to light.

"I'm sure our three can do it as they're most of the way there already. But any device would have to be tried and tested, and show positive results, before I could promote it to the ISP or whoever as a tool. If we could pull that off, they'd be queuing up at Port Control to get in here, and I could use it as leverage to get our dues for our support at Freskat and at Skyrtek," the captain declared.

"Get engineering to produce a clutch of them and send the crew out on fishing expeditions to every bar in and around the Web," the first mate advised. "That'll bring a few creeps out of the woodwork I bet, and please our own people to boot, especially if you supply the beer money."

The captain grinned widely. "That's one way of filling up the cells in Merkat security's lock-up. And we have the technology to disable much of the hardware and software of said creeps into the bargain."

Ahxenta's officers were more than willing to enter into the spirit of the scheme as endless rounds of duty aboard a ship going nowhere was beginning to pall. Flintlock in particular was in need of an excuse to escape the well-meaning but tedious company of her brother, as the *Karillion* was also awaiting release from military obligations. It was a full two weeks, however, before the first handful of probes was run off a clandestine production line that had been set up in a small lab off main engineering, out of the way of the prying eyes of Merkat's inquisitive repair crews. Tinkering with tech was a pastime all ships' engineers seemed to enjoy and the team set to the task had done well. Positive results gathered by the devices could be relayed direct to a central station and any necessary responses put in process.

Over the time the project had been ongoing, other senior crew members had been set their own charges, mostly in relation to ship's business. Captain Ahxenta was known for a firm hand and tolerated no slackness during downtime. Relentless harassment of local Trades Alliance officials in the Web had resulted in the eventual release from direct secondment at the behest of the ISP and its allies and freed the Privates to take up long-distance contracts. That had triggered a rush for the business available among the ships able to operate normally.

Ahxenta had sent out feelers concerning the general need for arms supplies, and had borrowed a small but hardy and well-armed launch with the incongruous name of *Jessamine* to pick up the arms shipment she had ordered some time before from the Kanelian Juxta ordnance works. Having confirmed that she would pay up immediately upon inspection of the goods, she also shrewdly hinted that if the arms were up to the high spec promised and more were readily available, she would be back, credit on collection. She was hard-headed enough to realise that *Arianrhod's* supposed credit unworthiness would hardly stand up before that offer and the company would be grateful that it would not have to brave the current situation to ship the stuff out. Apnis, now fully-healed, was despatched in command of the mission and had been gone several days by the time the first testing of the new probes was underway.

Two days and several bars into the operation later, a happy Azular shuttled back aboard for a private word with the captain. As far as he was concerned, the new devices were an unqualified success: they had had one positive result. *Arianrhod's* security team had apprehended the suspect lest news of the testing leaked out; he was currently under sedation in an iso-lab in medbay. A bonus of the capture was that the probes could be refined with the new data collected. As the suspect was ostensibly listed as a minor member of one of the lesser known medical supply companies and as such had free access in and out of the Merkat facility, the captain widened her net and approached a couple of trusted members of Merkat's security to voice her concerns of alien infiltration and to apprise them of her potentially valuable means of combating it. She also hinted that longer-range scanning for large sources of the elusive zukivianite might also avert danger to the Web; and as her ship, in dock as it was, could perform such a task, she was open for business.

"We could've done that when we first came in," Flintlock pointed out at a meeting to discuss results.

"Hardly: scanning without authorisation is an offence at Merkat and we'd have needed a damn good excuse," the captain informed her. "And our long-range emplacements, good as they are, couldn't pick up the emanation from just one or two individuals in a place the size of the Web. But as the hostiles we met at our last little sortie to Kelfennig may have come back to the place for a supply of the stuff, it may be that they need it on a regular basis. We know they often return to their original planets to scavenge, so it makes sense that they'd need their own supplies to colonise elsewhere. And Merkat's Web's a handy port to stash anything, as we know."

"You have a point, Captain," the science officer agreed. "Let's hope the Merkat authorities bite over the long-range scans."

The authorities in charge of Web operations bit to the point that blood was almost drawn. Brought in after cooperation with Merkat security had yielded another two positive results, their upper ranks were so alarmed that Ahxenta had little option but to acquaint the Interstellar Systems Protectorate via Admiral Zillah at Freskat with the new device and the promise of passing on the evidence of its successful testing in due course. It was no part of her plan that ISP should find out from somewhere else. That brought its own problem in a comm from an irate Colonel Ellin Myrtleberry, demanding why the ISP had not been brought in at the initial production stage. The captain left Lindell to defuse the situation with his habitual smooth tact and Azular to attend to the long-range scanning for zukivianite. She and Ensign Helly Pinkhorn were engaged in another scheme that required a deal of diplomacy and even more discretion.

Commander Apnis returned successful, with the arms and the news that there was plenty more high quality goods to be had. Whilst *Arianrhod* remained in dock and under refit, the *Jessamine* could be usefully employed as a carrier to bring cargoes in and sell them on at profit to the smaller vessels that were still shipping into Merkat in the aftermath of the major hostilities. The first mate had much to hear and was as vexed as her captain when Lynxi Bellfish interrupted their debriefing with the information that Colonel Ellin Myrtleberry of the ISP Council was on line and requesting urgent communication.

The colonel had signed in on a highly secure channel to announce that in light of the latest evidence she had received from Admiral Zillah, she would be coming over from her HQ in person to assess the new devices, with a view not only of procuring all the existing pieces on behalf of the ISP, but of assuming control of production.

"Not on my ship you won't," she was summarily told.

"That I expected," the colonel rapped out sharply. "I'll bring my own team and my own facilities."

"*If* we can agree terms," Ahxenta returned frostily and then began to outline her claims in respect of *Arianrhod's* actions on ISP's behalf, the damage the ship had sustained and her outstanding repairs.

In the face of the colonel's increasing ire, the captain declared her intention of submitting a full statement of accounts, abruptly signed off and then turned to her first mate.

"Not flavour of the month at ISP HQ, but they now know where we stand and how much it's likely to cost them for a means of sifting out most of the bad apples from their various barrels. At least with Merkat security's help, such as it is, we've found a handful here and a small stockpile of zukivianite besides."

"And thanks be the moles are stuck in the cells down there and not in our brig or medbay," Apnis stated. "Including that medical rep guy we had. But what's Myrtleberry doing back in ISP HQ as part of the Council? Isn't she supposed to be Commander-in-Chief of the Allied Fleet and its offshoots?"

"That was last month; now she's on our backs again."

"You want me to stay here and help field the flak we'll get from her rather than head back to Kanelian, Cinnabar? You can bet she'll be over here as fast as her latest ride can fly now she knows we've got proven test results."

"Yes; we have plenty of pilots capable of flying the *Jessamine* and credit transfer can be left to Lindell's team. That job can run itself. As for Myrtleberry, she knows she has no option but to comply with our terms, though I guess she'll squeal a bit. But if ISP can deploy our technology sooner rather than later, it can carry out a clean sweep of all its major installations and get rid of most of the subversives that ongoing ops have missed and work out where stores of zukivianite might predict the presence of more. And given what *she* is, I expect that's the colonel's latest directive."

The first mate pursed her lips at the implications. "That would up her prestige no end, I guess. And it would more or less shorten the duration of this blasted war, what's left of it, and let us get back to our real trade. We have reports still coming in of scuffles across half the mapped sectors; and not one of the glorious galactic Alliance group members has officially stood down, as far as I know. Though I note we hear very little of what that renegade band of ex-raiders, Friskies and whoever else thinks they might make a quick credit or three is up to."

"I strongly suspect that once the charted galaxy's back to what passes as the usual peace, these ex-raiders will metamorphose into the usual raider rat-packs that we know and love so well."

"Only they'll be better equipped if they still have the ships they were riding in at Skyrtek; and if rumour is to be believed, at that base at the Outer Reaches that was attacked," Apnis speculated.

"You haven't heard the latest then," the captain told her. "They've been sighted out near Mellifly as well and it looks like their next stop will be Brown Amber, though there's little left of the hostile blockade there. Most of the baddies skipped when the assault on Freskat failed – though where the hell they skipped to is anybody's guess."

"So that leaves the hostile base off the Starglass by Kelfennig and the one supposed to be out by the Enigma Nebula, but we've heard nothing about those. Maybe we should give Micklemouse a call and enquire: he and Doosbak are in the vicinity after all."

"I'll assume you're joking, Commander. And as we've worked out, Kelfennig's resident population, excluding our two rodents, can take care of itself, so that base shouldn't give them too big a headache. But let's get back to the deal in hand. Once we've gone over the rest of ship's business, we are heading down to the *Half Moon*: we have a few rumours of our own to circulate."

The *ISPS Repulse*, erstwhile flagship of the Commander-in-Chief of the Allied forces but still under the command of Ellin Myrtleberry, made short work of the distance between its new base at Alto Finglas and the Merkat system. Despite uncharitable suggestions that the relocation left the ISP Council and its hangers-on with much better offices and less mess to clear up, as well as the dubious company of the Trades Alliance Board Assembly, Myrtleberry admitted that the move had allowed the Council to weed out many of those believed to have enemy sympathies and permit improved communications links. Any expectation that the attempts at bonhomie that the colonel had been refining would improve her rapport with the *Arianrhod* and her crew was sadly misplaced, however, and the quartet of negotiators that the captain had assembled as aides were both well-briefed and intransigent.

An office in Merkat's main marketing arena had been set aside for the meeting once the small lab in engineering had been viewed, the production line assessed and one of the new probes examined by a member of the colonel's team. Testing of the device was carried out in the detention facilities of the Web's inner belts, on two human-like hostiles that had been incarcerated there. Whilst the ISP officer's scientific advisors completed evaluations of the test probe, the terms of transfer into ISP hands were negotiated by the colonel and a pair of legal acolytes.

Talks continued over the two full days that Ahxenta had ruled as the limit of her availability, strongly suspecting that it would also be the limit of her patience. She had ensured that her supercargo had built plenty of room for manoeuvre into the details of any potential contract, but each concession was granted only after a good deal of tenacious bargaining. In the end, the captain thought that they had extracted as much as they could out of the situation and accord was reached. The contract had no sooner been drawn up, scrutinised and authorised when she announced closure and bid a heartfelt farewell to Myrtleberry and her associates.

Ahxenta stood, arms folded, watching the ISP trio depart down the long corridor outside the meeting room. As they turned a corner and disappeared from sight, she turned to her fellows.

"*Half Moon*," she said.

"*Half Moon*," Apnis, Lindell, Pinkhorn and Azular echoed as one.

The five straightened aching shoulders and navigated the series of highways and byways until the welcome portal of the bar greeted them through the gloom that passed as evening illumination in the inner belts public areas. Once safely around a table with large jars of beer in their hands, the captain surveyed her team.

"I reckon we got a good deal," she said. "Well done all."

Apnis raised her beaker in response. "One problem solved," she agreed. "We'd never have been able to produce enough to suit them and they'd not have given us the price we asked. And within a few weeks, they'd have worked the technology out for themselves, for all the mind-work that went into it."

"True," Lindell smiled cheerfully. "And with the fee we received and the reimbursement for our war work in the pipeline, we're almost back on an even keel."

"Let's hope it stays even," the first mate put in. "Even if just for a while. How long have we got until *Arianrhod* looks like herself again?"

"That's easier to estimate," the supercargo announced. "I reckon at the current rate of work – and if you can keep the Dockers' Guild reps up to speed and the repair teams sweet, Captain – we'll have hull and shield repairs done and all weapons and scanner emplacements in place in twenty days tops. A new paint job will take a further ten if you want her spanking and back to her usual trim. Internal repairs and reinforcements can run alongside as we can call on the facilities here and our own people will pitch in. In all, forty days should see us clear. That's a maximum estimate and it could be shortened."

"And we have the *Velvet Emerald* to deal with," Apnis reminded the table at large in a low voice.

"I've given my opinion," Pinkhorn put in brightly. "I think…"

"Not in a public place, Ensign," warned the captain. "Some things you do not discuss openly, even with a privacy shield in operation."

"Sorry, ma'am," was the abashed reply.

"Which reminds me," Ahxenta went on with a ghost of a twinkle in her eye. "Something I meant to give you some time ago."

She fished a small envelope from an inside pocket and passed it over. The young ensign opened it in some trepidation to find a note and a pair of stat bars. Her mouth dropped open in absolute surprise and she turned scarlet, staring at her captain.

"We'll have the party back aboard *Arianrhod* later and let everyone in on it," Ahxenta promised as Apnis, Lindell and Azular started to laugh. "Drink up, Lieutenant Pinkhorn, and we'll order some more."

Thirty eight days later the last inspection bot of the mighty *Arianrhod* logged the final sweep of the hull clear and slotted itself into its allotted bay. With her arsenal up to full strength, two new cargo pods of meta-jurillium plates destined for the docks at Freskat Six secured in her outer holds and consignments of crystal comms components and various engineering parts safely stowed in inner storage bays, she called in her departure intentions to Merkat's Port Control. As she awaited confirmation, her crew, every member now back in post, stood or sat smartly to attention as another freshly-painted private starship prepared to set out on her maiden trade voyage, and in the manner of traders everywhere, dipped her holo-flag in recognition of the *Arianrhod*, which was to precede her out.

The solution to the problem of the *Velvet Emerald* had in the end been agreeably though less economically settled, to the satisfaction of the *Arianrhod* and her crew, the mortification of the *Tallulah* and her captain and the unmitigated amusement of the entire Merkat facility. The remaining shares belonging to the absent shareholders of the *Velvet Emerald* had indeed been bought up at bargain prices as young Pinkhorn had suggested. Ahxenta had, however, agreed to lease the vessel out as a trader cum cruiser and the ship was ready to set out on her first voyage under her new name and her new colours.

The private starship *Emerald*, flying under the shell-pink flag of the

Trades Alliance and dazzling in new hull paint of dark metallic green, would follow the *Arianrhod* out under her new commander, Captain Melly Goodsocks. With Commander Primrose Toadflax as a capable first mate, the highly experienced Puzzle Greenwing as chief medic and the young but savvy Lieutenant Helly Pinkhorn as supercargo, Ahxenta considered that she would do well. Erinna Bottle, once part of Merkat's repair yards and as obsessive as Whisper Earbleat when in pursuit of spare parts for her precious guns, had been appointed weapons officer; Grinsard Yellowfork, immensely pleased with a hike in pay and promotion to first lieutenant, had accepted the position of senior science officer. A chief engineer had proved more difficult to recruit but Crizz Cottontail had routed out a gruff ex-spacer of recognised expertise, an old friend that she had known for years and swore could fix an engine on a lame paddle-boat. All in all, the *PSS Emerald* would no doubt make her mark.

Ahxenta had considered sending *Emerald* out to Kelfennig to pick up Bick Micklemouse and Spendle Doosbak as her first mission, but reckoning that the fewer people who knew about that disreputable duo the better, she had reserved that assignment for her own vessel.

The lattice-like structures that constituted Merkat's huge docking, storage, supply, repair, marketing and ancillary facilities stretched out like a sparkling three-dimensional net around the central body of Merkat Three itself, the docked ships looking like glorious metallic flies caught in the insubstantial, glistening web of some vast, ethereal spider. Permission to depart was at length conveyed to the waiting starship, the lights on her restraining struts glowing green in approval that they could be disengaged at her discretion.

Ahxenta was watching her command console closely. "All boards show ready. Cut our cords, helm, and get some space around us."

"Aye, Captain."

Fresh in her new hull plating and resplendent in her customary coating of deep pink rad-repelling paint, the massive starship rose like a phoenix from her repair lacuna, hanging suspended for a moment as her systems powered up. As *Arianrhod* smoothly slipped her last remaining docking struts and slid backwards out of her own part of the Web, a soft cheer swept her bridge.

"Let's cook those engines," Captain Ahxenta instructed as she inhaled a satisfying breath of fresh bridge air. "Lock us on course for Freskat, Mr Box and take us out, Lieutenant Dox, nice and easy: we need a bit of sunshine in our bones."

"Aye, aye, Cap," came the chorus of assent from the well of the bridge.

As the mighty *Arianrhod* turned on her axis and set her course forward for the beacon and the local bypass, the final farewells of Merkat Port Control crossed the gap between them, to be lost in the immensity of starlit space.

Far, far away, two pairs of eyes watched the departure from a floating viewscreen convenient for the bar of the *Half Moon in a Puddle*.

"There goes the *Arianrhod* then, Jurry my lad, fresh as a daisy and twice as dandy," Malty whispered to his companion, raising his mug in a toast. "Off to pastures old and troubles new, no doubt. Wonder who's next for a feel of Ahxenta's left hook?"

"You can speak out loud, she can't hear you from here," Jurry told his mate.

"I wouldn't be too sure," responded Malty.

FINIS

ABOUT THE AUTHOR

SANDI CAYLESS is the author of the Mars-based *Sub Martis* series of novels: *Dome Lowell; Dome Beagle;* and, *Starship* and other literary works. Find out more on her website www.submartis.com, where you can also find free stuff to download, street maps and guides to help you navigate your way around the Mars domes Lowell and Beagle and information on more strange places such as the *Half Moon in a Puddle* and Glow Worm Alpha.

www.submartis.com